THE

MASTER

OF THE

MILL

D1561396

Frederick Philip Grove

THE
MASTER
OF THE
MILL

Introduction : R. E. Watters

General Editor : Malcolm Ross

New Canadian Library No. 19

M&S

PR
9199.3
677
M3
1961

Copyright, Canada, 1944, by The Macmillan Company
of Canada Limited
Copyright, Canada, 1961, by McClelland and Stewart

Canadian Cataloguing in Publication Data

Grove, Frederick Philip, 1879–1948.
The master of the mill

(New Canadian library ; N19)
ISBN 0-7710-9119-2

I. Title. II. Series: New Canadian library ; no. 19.

PS8513.R68M38 1987   C813'.54   C87-095120-3
PR9199.2.G766M38 1987

Manufactured in Canada by Webcom Limited

McClelland and Stewart
The Canadian Publishers
481 University Avenue
Toronto, Ontario
M5G 2E9

CONTENTS

INTRODUCTION

Although *The Master of the Mill* was first published in 1944, it was like all of Grove's novels in having been conceived and even written many years before. Just when the initial ideas or characters occurred to Grove is unknown, but quite possibly they may owe their origin to the same late nineteenth-century phenomena which inspired Frank Norris and Theodore Dreiser in such books as *The Octopus, The Pit, The Financier, The Titan*. The practices of vast industrial trusts or combines which had made possible the characteristic careers of men of ruthless power and wealth like Rockefeller, Vanderbilt, Huntington, Carnegie, and Yerkes were under widespread public scrutiny around the turn of the century when Grove was an itinerant farm labourer already dedicated to becoming a novelist. Unquestionably the following years provided other usable events and concepts, including the emergence after the First World War of such social and economic patterns as Russian communism and Italian fascism. Grove's autobiography, *In Search of Myself*, tells us that it was in 1928 that he made an "exhaustive" study of the flour-milling business which forms the background of the novel. The dates 1930-1944 are appended at the end of the novel, presumably to indicate the time-span of the actual writing. By June of 1934, however, the autobiography tells us, he had completed a draft "much too long for publication." On the urging of a publisher he rewrote the book but was unable to shape a final structure which satisfied him, and when the manuscript was returned from the publisher it was shelved for several years. When he again tackled the manuscript, Grove says, he "at once succeeded in finding the inevitable form—the only form in which the book can convey its message." From the date of the "Author's Note" prefacing the book we can assume that this successful revision was completed in 1939—five years before the novel finally appeared.

Successful though this "inevitable form" appeared to the author, it is this very narrative structure that has often been criticized as being at best a brave experiment that failed. Grove's narrative machinery creaks, it is said, and the frequent changes in time sequence and point of view are bewildering and irksome. In all his other novels, Grove pursues a straightforward chronological line, unfolding his narrative in objectively presented episodes, analysing his developing characters in the conventional manner of the "omniscient" author. In *The Master of the Mill*, however, he rejects his former methods completely. Here the time sequences are discontinuous, even apparently erratic, and the general technique is a mixture of recollection, reminiscence, association of ideas, and historical sketch.

The narrative opens in 1938 when the principal character, Senator Samuel Clark, is an old man in his eighties with obviously little time left to him, and the Clark mill as seen through the large windows of his home is a great towering pyramid bathed in light that casts everything around it into mere shadowy existence. In the second chapter, a few days later, the huge structure is blurred by gusty rain, and in the Senator's mind the scene shifts to an April day in 1888 when the vast mill of the future was no more than his own veiled dream. The third chapter again returns to 1938 when an elderly Captain Stevens calls to report to the Senator just before the latter leaves on his regular drive around the private park. This visit by Stevens starts a train of thought in the old man's mind which takes him back in time to about 1896, when Stevens was an ambitious young chief clerk in his twenties and Samuel himself was only forty.

In subsequent chapters we oscillate between 1938 and earlier years, the backward swings gradually becoming less remote in time but not consistently so. What determines the years revisited in memory is some association of ideas, persons, or objects suggesting a new aspect of events past. The Senator is consciously preparing himself to die and is, in a sense, remembering and even reliving the past in a final effort to discover the meaning and justification of his life and actions. Other characters in the book, alive in 1938, are influenced by his example and his needs into similar reminiscence and questioning, for they have all been closely involved with the Clark family and the mill. In their own way they too seek a sense of significance, and this fact makes necessary and credible their inquiries and broodings over the past, even the diary kept by Odette Charlebois and the historical manuscript written by the aging Captain Stevens.

The narrative method may well seem unduly complicated to a hasty reader, yet it is essentially true to real life. The *process* of summoning up the past is, for anyone, a discontinuous recall of fragments to be worked into a meaningful sequence, and Grove was neither the first nor the last story-teller to be interested as much in the realism of the process as in that of the result. Such novels as Conrad's *Chance* and *Lord Jim*, and a motion picture such as Orson Welles' *Citizen Kane*, attempt to portray a final comprehension achieved through the piecing together of fragmentary glimpses of the past. In his last days Samuel Clark was not calmly reviewing the history of the mill and his life under its shadow—and Grove by his narrative method sought to prevent the reader from receiving any such impression. Instead, the old man was groping desperately to find the significant moments, the possible turning points from whence his life had taken its direction, in order to assess his conduct and possibly find self-justification. Not the events themselves interested him, nor their precise chronological sequence, but solely their ultimate significance to his life. Irony is present, of course, in the fact that his knowledge is incomplete. Others know fragments he never learns, just as some things he knows continue as mysteries to them. Imperfect knowledge of what concerns our fate is part of the human tragedy. Similarly, to Lady Clark, Samuel's daughter-in-law, and to the other living members of the household, it is the meanings of events, not their orderliness, that is crucial. To them, too, as well as to Grove as author, the "inevitable form" of their experience would be exactly the one Grove finally found.

Consider the first and most obvious departure from chronology, the impressive description of the overwhelming, completely mechanized mill towering seventeen stories high in 1938. To have begun the novel with a description of the original tiny mill founded by Douglas Clark and to have followed this with an account of the successive expansions under Rudyard and Samuel would have thrown the emphasis upon the building of the eventual colossus rather than upon where the emphasis belongs, the effect of that huge pyramid as first a dream and then a reality upon three generations of the Clark family. The meaning of the mill, not the manner of its construction, is all important.

By way of contrast Grove's novel *Fruits of the Earth* may be cited. This book appeared in 1933 at the very time he was working on the unsatisfactory first draft of *The Master of the Mill*. It opens at the chronological beginning of Abe Spalding's career, his arrival on the bare prairie on which he is eventually to build a vast farmhouse and barns. Spalding's career is followed step by step to his peak of economic success accompanied by domestic and spiritual failure. The eventual collapse also of his material dreams is not shown in the novel proper, but it is not merely left implicit, for in a prefatory author's note Grove tells us that one of the imaginative sources of the story was his coming one day during a prairie drive upon the woefully dilapidated remains of a magnificent farmhouse and barn and hearing the history from his companion. Failure to incorporate the ultimate end as an integral part of the narrative structure weakens this novel very considerably. Grove evidently wanted to convey to the reader from the beginning a sense of time's ravages and the futility of Abe Spalding's herculean efforts, but had either not discovered how to achieve his purpose or was not yet ready to depart from his customary chronological line into reminiscence, flashbacks, and other narrative devices which such a departure would demand. He contented himself with a makeshift both clumsy and ineffective.

The mill is, of course, the most dominant and unforgettable symbol in *The Master of the Mill*, but there are other symbols not less significant for being more subtle. Human characters are sometimes invested with symbolic overtones. Like the mill itself, all the chief characters are seen first not in the process of becoming but as what they finally became. Structurally, such presentation is admirably consistent, and it is dramatically effective also, for there is contrast between the undiminished because renewable mechanical power of the mill and the death and decrepitude enveloping its human "masters."

The three women most closely associated with the Clark family are all named Maud, a fact which may confuse or irritate some readers but which is a deliberate part of Grove's design. Samuel Clark in his thirties marries Maud Carter, attracted to her in part by shared aesthetic interests, in part because he then wished escape from the mill and the dominance of his father and she was a person who never took seriously the mill or his involvement in it. In his forties Samuel hired as a secretary the brilliant and dynamic Maud Dolittle, then little more than a schoolgirl. This second Maud was one of few who fully appreciated his role as engineering genius planning developments in the mill for which he was never given public credit. She epitomized and shared one aspect of his nature completely foreign to his wife. He admired his wife rather than loved her and she in turn underestimated him. His secretary admired him to the point of love. Looking back from 1938 Samuel could see that his wife Maud, in her relation to him, was "primarily mind," whereas his secretary Maud was "primarily heart and instinct." The third Maud was Maud Fanshawe, who became his daughter-in-law (and eventually Lady Clark) when she married his son Edmund in a cool arrangement of mutual need and convenience. She later became the centre of Samuel's home and old age after the son's death. In different ways Samuel loved all three women and they him. In his life they tended to fuse into a composite image. Between him and the third Maud there developed a greater spiritual affinity than existed with either of the first two, so that in the end the three women represented something encompassing the trinity of mind, heart, and spirit, with varying degrees of the physical intermingled.

Two of the women became in succession the pivot of his home life, as symbolized in two portraits. One of these was a painting of his wife showing her in all her magnificent beauty; the other, mysteriously evocative of his daughter-in-law as he first knew her in her youth, was actually a fine copy of a life-sized painting representing Stella, Dean Swift's lifelong friend, "at the moment of receiving the letter which seemed to prove the Dean's unfaithfulness." This painting, which Samuel treasured because of its "uncanny resemblance" to the third Maud, was by 1938 hanging in the place once occupied by his wife's portrait.

Not only the women but also the three principal men of the family intermingle in a kind of unity. The men are named individually, to be sure, and their differences are readily apparent, for they are in constant conflict. These differences are perhaps exaggerated by the fact that we enter the mind only of Samuel; of his father and son we know only what he or others saw, heard, or inferred. Yet more than mere blood unites them. Each of the three in his own way is a visionary, dominated by the possibilities of the future, eager for power. Rudyard, the most colourful and vividly realized as well as the least complex, ruthlessly grasps after power for its own sake; Samuel dreams of humanitarian benefactions that can be achieved through power; Edmund schemes to bring about an efficient social and economic structure to replace the present unplanned society and is ready to disregard the human dislocations that would ensue. Rudyard and Samuel equally built the mill, the former acquiring the capital, the latter supplying the intelligence. Rudyard and Edmund are both ruthless and clear-headed. Samuel and Edmund both value the mill less for itself than for the social consequences it could produce, though they differ radically on those consequences. Moreover, both of them become involved in the same trinity of women named Maud. For Samuel the three became wife, secretary and potential wife, and beloved and trusted daughter-in-law; for Edmund they were mother, mistress and mentor, and marriage partner.

In these intricate interrelationships Grove risks credibility and avoids the absurd only by lightness of touch—as in the subtle overtones of Samuel's attitude towards his daughter-in-law which are finally revealed in chapter XIX. Yet in the overall design Grove had to assume the risk, for in his view of mankind cyclic repetition is central, as the final conversations in the novel suggest. Moreover, every man is caught in a tangled web of relationships not all of his own choice.

The Master of the Mill can be considered in several ways as being a culmination of Grove's previous novels. In his earlier books he had dealt with pioneers breaking the prairie sod, with farmers struggling to increase their harvests and acquire some of the amenities of rural civilization. To move on to the subsequent processing of the harvested grain would seem as inevitable as the growth of rural villages into industrial towns. Conflict between human beings and their industrial and financial organizations simply replaces the earlier conflict between man and untamed nature. Grove's characteristic ideas also reappear in this novel. In *Our Daily Bread* (1928), *Fruits of the Earth* (1933), and *Two Generations* (1939), if not also in other books, conflict between generations, especially between father and son, is central to the action—possibly stemming in part from Grove's relation to his own father. In *The Master of the Mill* there are two such conflicts. Another characteristic theme is the human cost of the ownership of property : in the rural books possession of land dominates the owner; now it is possession of an industry. Owners or masters are equally enslaved by what they nominally control. Related to this theme is Grove's constant concern with the threat to mankind inherent in increased mechanization of processes, whether in agriculture or industry. In the present age of what we call automation, the reader is apt to detect overtones hardly as perceptible to Grove's original readers.

The erosion of time, the inevitable crumbling away of humanity and its works—possibly a consequence of Grove's early and continuing interest in archaeology—is implicit throughout the novel and becomes explicit at the end. Above all, Grove's acceptance of a kind of determinism in human life— that men are pawns with an illusion of freedom while gripped fast by forces larger and stronger than their conscious will—is everywhere apparent. The individual is only a pulse in the rhythm of the generations. Edmund considers himself a tool of destiny: "We are sitting at a table and playing a game of chance the laws of which we don't understand; and somewhere around the board sits an invisible player whom nobody knows who takes all the tricks; that player is destiny—or God if you like, or the future. . . . I am humbly content to be a tool of evolution." Rudyard and Samuel feel equally impelled by forces or circumstances, but their helplessness disheartens rather than exalts them.

Some features of *The Master of the Mill* cannot be found elsewhere in Grove's fiction. This novel is the only one in which Grove deals at large with the political and social scene in Canada, or with the relations between capital and labour. It is the only one in which we find any trace of the life of wealth and fashion he knew in Europe as a young man. The elaborate and formal social life attributed to the Clark family is not, indeed, very convincing as a picture of wealth in a small Ontario or Manitoba town either in 1938 or in the 1890's, however true it may have been of European capitals when Grove reputedly knew them. Finally, *The Master of the Mill* is his only novel in which his narrative technique can be described as in any degree contemporary or experimental. Though many deny that this technique is wholly successful, nevertheless Grove here demonstrated that even as he approached the end of a long life of griefs and frustrations in his career as novelist he was still young enough in spirit and flexible enough in talent to adventure into a new world.

R. E. WATTERS

University of British Columbia
August 1960

Ideas expressed by the characters in this book, especially in its second part, must be read as their private opinions. Since none of these characters is purely imaginary, the author merely records, without endorsing or refuting, what they think. The problem presented is, of course, anything but imaginary.

F. P. G.

Simcoe, Ont.,
August 1939

PART ONE

Death of the Master

Give me a spirit that on this life's rough sea
Lives t'have his sails fill'd with a lusty wind
Even till his sail-yards tremble, his masts crack,
And his rapt ship run on her side so low
That she drinks water, and her keel ploughs air.

CHAPMAN

CHAPTER

I

THE two women looked at each other with a smile of comprehension as the old, old man who, considering his years, was still so amazingly active, rose restlessly from his arm-chair to go to the northernmost window of the enormous hall in which they were sitting and to look, over the west end of the dark lake, at the mill. He did this night after night now; but there had been years when he had carefully avoided that view.

All three were in evening clothes; it was the custom to dress for dinner, at the great house on the shelf of the hillside overlooking the two arms of the lake. The women were busy with embroidery; it was rare that either of them spoke on these long evenings after they had risen from table; and if there was occasion for an exchange of words, they were uttered under their breath.

The younger of the two, Lady Clark or Maud, as she was called by her intimates was the old man's daughter-in-law. Though she was still in her early forties, she had, to all appearance, at least for an outsider, only one aim left in life, namely to ease the old man's lapse into that senility which had to come at last, long as it had been staved off by her husband's unexpected death more than a decade ago. The older woman, Miss Charlebois, had once been the 'companion' of Mrs Samuel Clark, the long-dead wife of the old man, a senator of Canada, who had gone to the window whence he looked at the mill as if he must watch that nobody walked off with it.

Life in the house, as was natural in a place which stood aside from the main stream of life, followed a strict routine; and even Lady Clark lived largely in the past, perhaps for the very reason that, as far as the mill went, the future was hers; she was its largest shareholder; and there was now only one other, the old man who had certainly long since made her his heir.

Yet it was doubtful whether either of the women realized what went on in the old man as he looked at that mill which towered up, seventeen stories high, at the foot of the lake, like a huge pyramid whose truncated apex was in line with the summits of the surrounding hills. The mill which, in a physical sense, he had largely created had been his love before he had owned it; it had become the object of his hatred after it had become his; it had always ruled his destiny; it had been, it still was, the central fact in his life; it had never permitted him to be entirely himself; it had determined his every action. The history of the mill had been his history, beginning with the time when his father had started to build it; and again beyond the time when his son, having done something to it of which he himself disapproved, was killed by the stray shot of a striker. Whatever had happened to him, in his inner as well as his outer life, had been contingent upon its existence. His father had forced it on him; his son had thrown it back on his shoulders. It had led a life of its own, more potent, more decisive than the life of any mere human being. The individual destinies connected with it had merely woven arabesques around it. But, perhaps naturally, it was these living arabesques which held the old man's thought.

There it stood, two miles away, seen across the west basin of the artificial lake which the great power-dam had created by flooding back the river over its bottom lands which it had drowned.

Its image lay on the mirror-smooth water like a fairy palace inverted, bathed in light; and beyond the line where the base of that image touched the white line of the dam, its real counterpart rose steeply. It was flooded by the light from two score huge reflectors which converged their beams upon it, from the dizzy height of its narrow topmost storey to the wide ground floor with its eight cave-like openings through which led the tracks of the trains that carried the wheat in and the flour out, day and night, never ceasing, year after year. This vision of light, snow-white—for the whole tremendous structure was dusted over with flour, inside and out—closed the valley through which the turbulent North River had once run, though it was now tamed into the pleasant lake which, in its bosom, mirrored the stars.

The very perfection of the picture owed something of its beauty to the fact that the night was inky-black. Nothing of what lay between the house and the mill had a more than shadowy existence: the park sloping down, terraced, to the water's edge where huge retaining walls of concrete overlaid with marble checked the wash of rains and waves; and, beyond, the shoulder of the hill which had become a peninsula, screening the so-called Terrace from view. The spot-lights picked the mill out of the darkness, nothing else. The trees and slopes which intervened were mere silhouettes against the double vision of light.

To many people, as the old man was aware, that mill stood as a symbol and monument of the world-order which, by-and-large, was still dominant; of a ruthless capitalism which had once been an exploiter of human labour but had gradually learned, no less ruthlessly, to dispense with that labour, making itself independent, ruling the country by its sheer power of producing wealth.

To others, fewer these, it stood as a monument of a first endeavour to liberate mankind from the curse of toil; for it produced the thing man needed most, bread, by harnessing the forces of nature. The amazing thing—incomprehensible to one who had seen different methods of production—was that that monstrous edifice was filled with machines only which had come to be by a logic of their own and which did man's bidding without man's help, supervised by a handful of skilled workers who watched them, listened to them, oiled them, adjusted a screw here and there, and wiped accumulating flour dust from their swift and shining limbs. The machines worked silently, or at the worst with no more than a hum to which the human ear became habituated till it was no longer perceived. The few men needed to keep them running were engineers, electricians, chemists and . . . sweepers.

To still others, fewer again, the old man among them, it was the abode of gnomes and hobgoblins, malevolent like Alberich, the dwarf of the Rhinegold, but forced, by a curse more potent than their own, to do man's work. The uncanny thing about it was that these gnomes and hobgoblins—or were they jinn?—had the power of binding man to their service in turn, or to the service of the machines, as he, the old man, had been bound; and whenever, in his hoary old age, he fell under the spell of these dwarfish beings, he visualized them with two faces: one that of his father, one that of his son. In many ways these two had been alike.

Night after night the same thing repeated itself. He was sitting with these two women, in utter silence, essentially alone; for even with his daughter-in-law he communed only when they were by themselves; and then only about the trivialities of the day; never when a third person was present. Night after night he rose at last and went to the window, here in the hall, or upstairs in the gallery, to stare at the mill, at first puzzled, but gradually working out in his mind certain things which, the clearer they became, the more amazed him. Till at last, in order to explain them to himself, he began to review his whole life; or at least such parts of that life as stood out with sufficient decisiveness.

He could never get away from the feeling that, whatever he had done, he had done under some compulsion. Yet it was he who had determined the development of the mill; but it was, first his father, then his son who had chosen the time for every change proposed, thereby twisting his own purpose. The peculiar thing about it all was that neither his father nor his son had ever acknowledged him as the moving spirit. Even the world had not acknowledged him. His father as well as his son had ben called 'great men'; he, who had always tried to temper necessity with a humane purpose, was called the 'octopus'!

It was true, his father, Rudyard Clark, had himself been a man 'of the people', a workman who had run the mill as it had been for the greater part of his lifetime by his own labour, aided by a few helpers and a single foreman; while he had been seeking his place in the sun, he had been a democrat; but when he had won success, he had become an autocratic ruler. His son, Edmund Clark, had done what he had done with the ultimate purpose of giving the people what they needed as a gift from above; if he had lived, he might have revealed himself as a public benefactor; but he had died. Between them, the two had forced *him*, Samuel Clark, to assume all the odium attaching to a task which he had not been allowed to fulfil in his own way.

Somewhat sadly, yet not without a feeling of relief, the old man at the window, staring at that mill which had come into being like a fact of nature, helping and harming the good and the bad alike, with that indifference which is nature's most striking attribute, realized that what he was doing in thus analysing and finally reviewing his life was preparing himself for death. He was setting his mental and spiritual house in order; not till he had done so could he rest, could he lie in peace. . . .

When, one night, after an hour or so at the window, he turned back into the great room with its bright, cheerful light, shed by the hundreds of bulbs in the central chandelier, and broken by the cascade of prismatic crystals surrounding them, the older of the two women, Odette Charlebois, stopping her needlework, glanced up at him with the benignant smile of the spinster to whom her employer is perfect. The younger, Lady Clark, Sir Edmund's widow, without laying down her embroidery, became conscious of the fact that in his sunken eyes hung two tears.

In the things of the daily life he had become like a child; and Lady Clark looked after him in a quiet, unobtrusive way which, to an outsider, would perhaps not have betrayed the profound affection which she harboured for him. The historic bearings of his life escaped her as they escaped the other woman. She saw in him simply a human being that had lived beyond his time, lovable, frail, and tragic because he who had once been young was old; because he who had lived and no doubt was still wishing to live was about to take leave of this world which to her, in spite of all, was a beautiful and desirable world, for leaves were green, and the stars were twinkling. She had married the son of this man without love; she had lost him without any shattering shock to the foundations of her being; but she would have thought it a suggestion of treason to her inner nature if anyone had advised her to snatch at the moment and let old age take care of itself. That she must acknowledge the claim which the father of her dead husband had on her went without saying.

He, almost tripped by the edge of the deep-napped and enormous rug, made for a door without stopping: the wrong door as it happened more and more frequently of late. She knew where he wanted to go.

But she waited till he was past the chesterfield on which she was sitting before she dropped her embroidery-frame and quickly rose to take his arm. He wished to sleep in the library instead of going upstairs to his bedroom; he often did; and by a slight pressure of her hand she directed him, pushing at the same time a button to summon his valet who was his junior by only fifteen years.

CHAPTER

II

Reliving a past life is a different thing from merely reflecting upon it. So, when, a few days later, things began to crystallize in his mind, the senator rose again from his arm-chair to go to the window and to stare at the mill; his deeply-cut features had been working for some time, even during dinner, which was taken late in this house, with three maids, two footmen, and a butler ministering to the needs of the three members of the household. For no reason whatever the old man had led the way to the smallest of the four drawing-rooms—the 'blue room'—where they had then been sitting for an hour.

As he rose, his eyes had a faraway look in them, as if, mentally, he were in another world—as indeed he was. He was in the world of 1888 when he, though in his thirties, had still been held down by his father in a quite subordinate position in the old, wooden mill.

As always, when he reached the window, he stared out through the glass. But the mill was blurred; it was raining outside; and a gusty wind blew over the lake, so that the reflection of the structure on the water was shattered and broken into a million luminous shards, all blurred by the rain. The mill itself seemed to stand behind a veil; which was appropriate enough; for on April 14, 1888, it had been no more than a dream, suggested by him to his father and eagerly taken up by Rudyard Clark.

At the site of the old portage between two landings where canoes and scow-boats had once had to unload in order to carry their trade goods around the rapids of the North River, there had grown up, by 1888, a small village, the village of Langholm, the sole reason for the existence of which consisted in the rambling, wooden mill at the foot of the rapids.

At the time, the village was formed of one long street, Main Street, which sloped steeply from east to west, lined with two or three stores, butcher shop, drugstore, and a so-called general store which carried everything from shoe-laces to furniture and plough-shares; with a blacksmith shop, a lumber yard, a small real-estate and insurance office thrown in. At its extreme lower end, on its north side, stood a diminutive, one-roomed building, painted white: the office of the mill. At the upper end of Main Street, three or four short side-streets ran at right angles, formed by the houses of the merchants and that of the owner of the mill, Rudyard Clark.

Since, at the foot of the rapids, the river made a swing to the north, the mill lay northwest of the village: a ramshackle compound of structures, all of them low: warehouses filled with flour; granaries filled with wheat; and, of course, the two mill-units properly speaking which roared with the rickety machinery driven by undershot wheels, for the varying volume of water pouring down the rapids forbade the use of the more efficient overshot wheel.

Across the river, near its north bank, and still farther west, stood the station, only a little over ten years old; for it was not till 1875 that the railway had come in; and it had only been three years ago, in 1885, that it had linked the Atlantic and Pacific seaboards. Below the mill, between it and the station, a narrow steel bridge connected the banks.

Over that bridge a messenger came that morning, making for the little office of the mill and bearing a telegram. He delivered it to the single occupant of the office, a man in his thirties named Samuel Clark, son of Rudyard Clark—the same who now, as a senator of Canada, stood there in his extreme old age, looking at the pyramid of the mill blurred by the driving rain and the wind-tossed darkness.

This Samuel Clark, overawed by his father, had, in his early days, attended college at Winnipeg where he had taken a degree in engineering. But his gruff, autocratic father, though secretly proud of his son's academic accomplishments, had promptly set him to work, under Rogers, his foreman, who had successively put him through his paces in every department of the mill, as a common workman, till he had learned the small-scale milling business from the ground up,—though occupied most of the time with dreams and often fuming in revolt against his father. After several years of such labour he had been put in charge of the office where, in addition to him, a man by name of William Swann was employed as a part-time book-keeper. There, his father told him to 'go to it' and, according to his dreams, solicit orders by mail. In this he had been amazingly successful, for, with the opening of the west for settlement, the east had prospered and expanded.

As, standing in the window of the great hall, he saw himself in that office, he felt strangely moved. He had been young then; and now he was old. He had been ardent, ambitious, and callow; he had been rebellious; for, till he had proved himself to be an efficient salesman, drawing modest emoluments in the form of commissions, his father had used his labour, his ability, his inventiveness as if they had been his own; he had paid him no salary but had handed him an occasional five-dollar bill, perhaps twice a month. When the young man had protested, he had been told that he was being fed and lodged, and that his fourteen-dollar suits were being paid for. These suits, too large, for the Clarks were small men, had formed an additional item in his indictment of the father, for he had hated them.

He had been a dreamer.

The eyes of the old man narrowed, losing their focus, thereby blurring still further the picture of what had come of those dreams: that colossal mill at the foot of the lake.

His efforts at selling the output of the mill by mail had, at first, been slow and up-hill work; but at last they had borne fruit. Here was that telegram: an order from an Ontario firm of bakers—so large that he did not dare to hand the waiting messenger his acceptance without having asked his father whether he could fill it. He rose and reached for his hat to cross over to the mill.

That mill was no longer what his grandfather Douglas had made it. In his day it had been a purely local affair, buying wheat from the straggling and struggling farmers in the bush, grinding it, and selling it at a slight advance to the people of the town; its main income, however, had come from chopping feed and cleaning seed. But when the great Interoceanic Railway had been built, touching the little village as a tangent touches a curve, for it had remained north of the river, it had brought a change, first in outlook, then in fact. A year later, Rudyard Clark, Sam's father, had built the first addition; and from 1880 on warehouses and granaries had gone up in a planless, haphazard way, makeshift after makeshift, every one designed to enlarge capacity for the moment, without plan or thought of a greater future.

The first vision had been Sam's; just as the vision of the dam had been his; and slowly he had imposed it upon his father: the vision of a mill capable of being enlarged as needed without destroying the architectural and technical unity of the whole. When, in the course of time, Rudyard Clark had carried it out, however, he had never given his son the slightest acknowledgement; in fact, he had kept him jealously away from any participation in his counsels.

That morning, as Sam approached the central part of the wooden compound, the original mill which his grandfather had built, he saw, with impatience and irritation, that a farm wagon piled with bags was drawn up along the loading platform. His father was standing in the open slide-door, small, spare, naturally grey and, like the mill and everything near it, dusted white with flour. His right hand was raised to the door-post; his left, resting on his hip. In dealing with farmers, Rudyard Clark had a quick, testy, absent-minded way which, people said, did not help his trade. Yet Sam slowed down; if he intruded, the old man, fifty-odd, might flare up and treat him like a child.

But when Rudyard saw his son, he dropped his hand from the door-post and flung it out sideways, with a decisive gesture. "No," he said in the tone of finality without raising his grating voice. "Not at that price. I don't care to buy retail anyway."

Sam concluded that his approach at this precise moment was not unwelcome. The farmer had apparently had a few bags of grain ground into meal, at five cents a hundredweight, a sort of business for which Rudyard no longer made any bid; and incidentally he had offered the miller last year's wheat crop, at 'the market'. But Rudyard never bought wheat locally at 'the market'. If the farmer sold through the regular channels, brokerage and transportation had to come out of the market price; and the farmer had to wait for his money. Under the pretext that he disliked to interfere with those regular channels, Rudyard made it a point to exact a profitable discount.

But there was something else. It was quite true that Sam's father did not care to buy retail. Farms in this country of rock and forest were small; their crops ran to two or three hundred bushels; since he had found a market in the east, Rudyard had begun to buy by the carload. Sam had seen him watching the great grain trains go by, from the prairies where wheat was beginning to be grown on the large scale: trains of a hundred cars each, every one of them filled with wheat. The West was revealing itself as the last great wheat area of the world; millions of acres awaited the settler. These trains would multiply till there was a steady stream of them: another idea which Sam had implanted in his father. All this grain, this potential wealth, would pour past the little Langholm mill: Langholm might become a sort of gateway between East and West. Behind the father's restless, flickering eyes a new dream had germinated: stop that wheat at Langholm; buy all the West could produce; grind it; sell it to the East, to Europe even; levy a toll on every bushel. What, in comparison, did the local trade amount to? Not that *Sam* cared about the profits. It was a dream.

In the way of the realization of that dream stood one obstacle: could the mill ever grow to handle that wheat? Could it grow to handle even an appreciable fraction of it?

"Well," the farmer said, frustrated and resentful, "getting high and mighty around this shebang, are you? Might feel the pinch one day if we farmers cease to bring in our chopping."

"I'll risk that," Rudyard said to the upper air with a sneer. "That sort of trade costs more in bookkeeping than it's worth."

"I guess you know your own business," the farmer said, clicking his tongue to his horses.

"I ought to," said Rudyard, unmoved, and turned to his son.

When Sam handed him the telegram, the old man, having glanced at it, said with a sudden alacrity, "Wait. I'll see." And with quick strides he entered the vast white dimness of the mill.

Sam, one elbow propped on the loading platform, stood looking into the wide valley to the east the whole bottom of which, the flood plain, was russet with the stems of dwarf red willows and dusted over with the yellow pollen of the catkins; for it was April.

A minute later his father reappeared out of the cavelike structure. "All right," he said. "Wire your acceptance. We'll work double shift till June."

The vision faded, a thought remained. It was his father who had seized the opportunity; but it was his grandfather Douglas who had created it. Had he known what he was doing? Or was it mere chance that, coming from a little Ontario town, coming, in the last resort, from Devonshire, he had set up his business in this wilderness?

It was only at the time into which the old senator had glanced just now that the supreme wisdom of the choice had become apparent. Douglas himself had prospered in a modest way only by dint of hard work and an unlimited capacity for going without.

Of the few score settlers of his day not half a dozen were left. Most of them, having wasted substance and effort, had 'pulled out' after two or three years. Those that remained in 1888 did so because they lacked even the means of moving their chattels.

But Rudyard, Douglas's only son, had reaped where his father had sown. The supreme wisdom of that choice rested on the fact that the railway, originally surveyed along a line twenty miles north, had, by the pencil stroke of a chief engineer, changed its route so as to utilize the valley of the North River which, apart from the Langholm rapids, had a singularly level course.

Had Douglas foreseen that? Or would he, had he lived, have been as much surprised as Rudyard had been when his son pointed out those stupendous calculations which were to change the old wooden mill with all its additions into that colossal industrial enterprise which had its ramifications throughout a continent and its markets overseas?

For, so the old senator at the window pursued his thought with a sinking of the heart, the acceptance of that order of Friday, April 14, 1888, had had to be cancelled on Monday, April 24.

Most opportunely, the whole mill, with all its additions, grain-bins, warehouses, repair shops, and milling units, had, during the night from Sunday to Monday, been burned to the ground.

And that had cleared the way for the building of the first four and of all the subsequent units of the new mill; for the building of the great dam, repeatedly raised; for the erection of the grain elevators holding hundreds of thousands of bushels of wheat; for the construction of the great office pile, the 'Flour Building' on Main Street and of the equally towering Palace Hotel opposite; as well as for the mushroom growth of the village of Langholm into a city.

Incomprehensibly, on the day after the fire, Rudyard Clark had done what he had never done before: he had handed his son a cheque for $200 and told him to take a month's holiday. At the time of this retrospect the senator knew, of course, that this had been a stratagem to get him out of the way.

CHAPTER

III

THE whole house was upset. The senator was in a vile temper and found fault with everything. He was a poor sleeper; and at night he often looked at his watch to see how far it was from daylight. For that purpose he insisted on using a flashlight which was supposed to stand upright in a certain spot on the floor by his bed; but when he was in a given mental state, neither the maid that looked after his rooms nor his old valet who had been with him for forty years could place it in the right position. Only Lady Clark could do that; and it so happened that, last night, he had gone up before her. It was a week after the evening when he had seen himself and his father at the loading platform of the old mill; and in the interval another grand conspectus of a phase of his life had prepared itself in his subconscious mind, only trifles, so far, emerging into full view. The fact that things seemed to elude his grasp made him impatient and unappreciative of the efforts which his servants put forth to do things in a way to please him. The few who had known his father, like the valet, saw in him, on such occasions, a reincarnation of the founder of the mill; but, since, throughout their long term of service, he had almost invariably been the personification of kindness, they overlooked, and forgave him his occasional lapses into testiness and dissatisfaction.

On the morning in question, having grumblingly told the old valet that, during the night, he had groped and groped for the flashlight; having next scowled at the maid whose special duty it was to make him comfortable in his bedroom, he betrayed the same temper at the breakfast table, in spite of the fact that his daughter-in-law, who, in his view, could do no wrong, presided and greeted him cheerfully. He frowned at Miss Charlebois who was late. And when he reached for his cup which the footman had filled, it was only just in time that Lady Clark read the signs.

Quickly she reached for that cup, forestalling her father-in-law, and lifted it to her lips. "The hot water," she said to the footman; "and let me see the toast before you serve it." Having added a few drops from the silver jug and glanced at the toast which she approved, she handed the cup back; and the old man drained it without comment and began to nibble at the single slice of toast, unbuttered, which Dr Sherwood allowed him for his morning meal.

After breakfast, an hour or two went by during which the senator went hither and thither, without plan or purpose. For a while he sat at a small desk in the library where he rummaged about in the almost empty drawers as if in search of what he could not find. Nobody interfered. Lady Clark was dressing for their daily drive. On the days of his 'moods' it was always doubtful whether her father-in-law would accompany her. Yet it would have been a mistake to count on his refusal. One could never be sure.

Having opened every drawer, the old man sat at the desk in evident perplexity. Shaking his head, with its remnant of carefully brushed snow-white hair, he rose and resumed the restless wanderings characteristic of extreme old age. Snatches of thought flitted through his mind, mirrored in the sunken features of his face. Sometimes he stopped and stood perfectly still as if to give them a chance to define themselves without letting muscular sensations interfere.

At ten o'clock a footman came and stood deferentially, waiting for the senator to notice him. It was in the large room-like recess of the gallery upstairs which separated the two apartments once used as the masters' suites—the one formerly occupied by the senator's wife, now by Lady Clark, to the left; the other, once occupied by himself, and later by Sir Edmund, now vacant. The far wall of this recess, which was furnished like a sitting-room, was taken up by a fireplace; and above it hung a large, life-sized painting. Whoever saw that painting for the first time, mistook it for a portrait of Lady Clark in her twenties; it was the brilliantly executed copy of a painting in the Manchester Art Gallery in England, representing Stella, the famous Dean's lifelong friend, at the moment of receiving the letter which seemed to prove the Dean's unfaithfulness. The uncanny resemblance had something mysterious about it; and it still puzzled the senator.

Suddenly, becoming conscious of the footman's presence, he asked irritably, without stirring, "What is it?"

"Captain Stevens is waiting in the library, sir."

"What does he want?"

Which, considering that Captain Stevens called daily at that hour, to report on the business of the mill, was an irrational question. Once, hearing it, a young footman had smiled to himself; and he had instantly been dismissed. This morning, the valet had tipped the butler off; and the butler had warned every member of the household staff to be careful. To this butler, himself a newcomer in the house, the vagaries of the old master were not pathetic but comic; but since Lady Clark punished any lapse in the respect shown to her father-in-law by discharging the offender, he humoured the old man.

"He didn't tell me, sir," replied the young footman.

"Ask him to wait. I'll be down."

As the mill stood, all its executives were old men, none less than seventy; but, as they knew very well, they had no longer any real power. The senator was president, Captain Stevens general manager only in name. The latter had once been general manager in fact; he had even held that position in fact before he had held it in name. He had never had any great respect for the senator, had never thought him 'any great shakes' as he expressed it. Himself had been a 'find' of old Mr Rudyard Clark's. After the latter's death, he had been eclipsed; but when young Sir Edmund had ousted the senator from the position of supreme power, he had come into his own, though not for many years; for, with Sir Edmund's death, the 'logic of circumstance' had deprived him as well as everybody else of the substance of power, leaving him only the empty shell. Now it was the enginers who did what they judged should be done. If new invention or accumulating experience demanded a change, they made it, letting Captain Stevens know *ex post facto*; and he invariably gave his approval to the accomplished fact. He was wise in the ways of the world and liked to go on drawing his comfortable salary of fifty thousand a year. He knew that, had he chosen to assert his nominal power against the engineers, the consequences would have been appalling, to say the least. If only in the interests of the Canadian export trade in flour, the federal government would have had to step in; it might have taken over the mill and all its subsidiaries.

Of course, Sam—Captain Stevens still called the senator by that name, to himself—had never approved, would never approve, of him, Captain Stevens; just as he, Captain Stevens, did not approve of Sam. To Captain Stevens nothing counted except that abstract being, the mill. No personal consideration, for administration or men, had ever mattered; just as it had not mattered to old Mr Rudyard or young Sir Edmund. The mill was supreme. If, at this time, he accepted what the engineers did without consulting him, he acted not from mere worldly wisdom alone, but from a fanatical devotion to something beyond him.

In spite of his seventy years, the captain was still a dapper little man; he still wore loud-checked suits, brilliantly flame-coloured neckties, smart, heavy-soled English shoes of brown leather, a gold-headed cane. He still bore himself very erect; he still gesticulated sparingly with his free hand which clasped a pair of new and immaculate lemon-coloured dog-skin gloves.

When the senator entered the library, the caller was sitting on the forward edge of a leather-bottomed chair, both hands on the knob of his cane, his chin resting on the knuckles of his upper hand.

"Good morning, good morning, senator," he said without rising. "I hope you slept well, sir?"

"I didn't sleep a wink," the old man said.

"Sorry to hear it. No fun, I suppose, lying awake at night. Never happens to me, I'm glad to say. Sleep like a log."

"You're lucky," said the senator. "Anything new?"

"Not a thing. I've got the production sheets here. Want me to read them?"

"What's the use?"

"That's what I say. No news is good news." And the little man rose to take his leave. "Till tomorrow."

"Till tomorrow."

And they issued into the enormous hall which reached through two stories, surrounded, on the second floor, by the gallery.

As the captain made for the vestibule which separated the hall from the *porte cochère* under which his high-powered car was waiting, the same footman who had announced him stepped forward, holding his light silk-faced topcoat.

A moment later, the senator still standing in the hall, the car, driven by a liveried chauffeur, slipped smoothly away; and instantly its place was taken by another, a Lincoln limousine, olive-green.

The senator turned to glance at the grand stairway; and indeed, Lady Clark was descending, dressed for the drive.

The sight softened the old man's mood. He remembered how, decades ago, in 1919 or 1920, he had first heard of her through his lawyer who had met her at Toronto where he had gone to argue a case. Already there had been rumours of an impending match between Miss Maud Fanshawe, daughter of Sir Alphonso Fanshawe, the late chancellor of Eastern University and the then Mr Edmund Clark. Asked to describe her, the lawyer had pondered for a moment as if at a loss. "She's a great beauty," he had said at last. "There's only one word in the English language which fittingly describes her . . ." — "That word?" Mr Samuel Clark had asked. Slowly and impressively the lawyer had rolled the word on his tongue. "That word is 'regal'." Regal she looked today, her beauty matured but unimpaired.

A minute later, a footman holding the door, they entered the car.

Whether it was that something in Captain Stevens's manner had touched a spring in the senator's memory; or that the interval since his last excursion into the past had simply become ripe, the senator's face, the moment he reclined in his corner of the tonneau, assumed a closed expression which warned Maud that he must not be disturbed. She was not certain what his mood signified; but she knew its effect on him and respected it; and thus it was that the whole drive of two hours was made in silence.

Between these two there was a relation which caused them to observe, with regard to each other, a considerate and affectionate politeness, poised between, on his part, the attitude of fatherly love and the homage he still rendered to beauty and elevation of character; on hers, of reverence and motherly indulgence. When they spoke, it was often what stood between the words which counted. He had tones which vibrated with unspoken things; her voice, a soprano, deepened into a contralto. Neither had ever let the other witness tears; but it was easy to see that, in the contemplation, by each, of the other's fate, there was a comprehension which, under circumstances of lessened restraint, might have caused them to join in an effusion over the tragedies hidden below the smooth aspect of the days.

The drive took them up the south hill, through the park, and, by way of the columnar gate of basalt and wrought iron, out on Hill Road which led down to the town, past the Terrace. This Terrace lay to the right, between lake and road, but at a lower level. The vast agglomeration of the charred ruins of workmen's cottages, burned in the second great fire of Langholm, was nearly vacant; for most of the mill-hands had left when automatic operation had been introduced; in fact, only those who, by reason of old age or infirmity, or because the workmen's compensation act had made them pensioners of the mill, found it to their advantage to remain still occupied their old quarters; and there were less than fifty of them. The senator, sole owner of the Terrace, had long since ceased to collect rents. When the mill, assuming the town as a private property, had become the sole owner of its institutions, paying off its debentures, the Terrace, once valued at two millions, had become a total loss.

In the descent of Hill Road, below which the Terrace lay spread like a map, with only here and there a few garments fluttering from clothes-lines in the breeze, they were bound to reach a point whence the mill came into view. But before that point was reached, the chauffeur turned left or south. Instead of entering the once populous Main Street, they passed, in two or three successive turns, through what had been the best residential quarter, spread over the hill that reached down from the wooded plateau in the south. Through Clark Street, where the Clark House of forty years ago was still standing, boarded up now, they swung out on the highway which led straight south, cleared, graded, and paved by the senator for the express purpose of providing the ladies of his household with a driveway of one hundred miles; for, by means of three more turns, it led through the woods back to the park-gate of the present Clark House.

CHAPTER

IV

DURING the drive, swift and smooth, the senator relaxed till he sat as if his body were unsupported by a skeleton. Maud never looked at him; she knew it might break the train of his thought.

This is what passed through his mind.

After Captain Stevens had been taken into the concern as chief clerk, by the senator's father, he had soon held a high and responsible position for one so young. Simultaneously, the senator, then universally called Mr Sam, had engaged a young lady, younger even than Mr Stevens, as his private secretary. That had been two years before Mr Rudyard Clark's sudden death.

These two, Mr Stevens and Miss Dolittle, were destined to play opposite if complementary parts in the history of the mill; whenever either rose, the other sank; for, as Mr Stevens had loyally aligned himself with all the policies of the founder of the mill, so Miss Dolittle had, from no calculation of future advantage, but rather from temperament and inclination, championed the cause of his son.

Had Mr Rudyard Clark lived, Mr Stevens would most likely have moved up into the inner circle of those who, in that interval between Edmund's birth and death, determined the development of the mill. For, while Mr Rudyard Clark kept his son in entire ignorance of the financial and administrative structure of the concern, Mr Stevens had rapidly risen to all sorts of confidential posts—that of the head of the employment bureau, for instance, which enabled him to engage and dismiss, with few exceptions, the whole personnel of the office staff as well as the superintendents, foremen, bosses, and hands employed at the mill as such—till he had finally become the secretary-treasurer, a paid, not an elected functionary, of the vast concern and all its subsidiary enterprises. Had Mr Rudyard Clark lived, he would undoubtedly have made him one of the three chief executives.

But Mr Rudyard Clark had died, and his son had taken his place; and so it was Miss Dolittle who, backed by the son, assumed the title and the somewhat empty function of the vice-presidency. At the time, during the last years of the century, it was an extraordinary thing for a woman to rise, by sheer ability, to such a height in the business world. In any enterprise like that of the mill there are two fundamental and opposite activities: producing and selling; and production depended on sales. From the start Mr Clark junior had been in charge of the sales-organization; but as, with the growth of the mill, brought about by his very success in selling, the ramifications became ever more complex, till there was an organization, international in scope, with offices at New York, London, and half a dozen capitals of European countries, Miss Dolittle had come into her own; and since this growth had coincided with the partial assumption, by Mr Clark junior, of the functions of a general manager, due to Mr Clark senior's accident—he had been caught up by a belt and hurled against the wall—Miss Dolittle, nominally private secretary to the vice-president, had imperceptibly assumed all his duties as sales-manager, till, feeling that he was losing touch with things, he had turned the sales-office over to her entirely, engaging Miss Albright as her successor in his own office. For two reasons, however, he had retained the nominal sales-managership: in the first place, his father would have asked awkward and sarcastic questions if he had openly resigned, for, coming from an era when he had held every executive office 'under his hat' as he expressed it, that father would have said his son was trying to shirk. While he, the father, had organized the mill and had provided for the channels and methods of its growth; while he had, with a grasp and cunning amazing in a 'man of the people', so split up the manifold functions of the vast enterprise that no outsider and few shareholders ever could unravel the structure as a whole, he had entirely failed to realize the complication and the multiplication of details taken care of by subordinates, whether they were his son, Mr Stevens, Mr Brook, 'superintendent of works', or Miss Dolittle. He had never realized, as had his son, that, if any one of these left, there would have been serious disturbances. He would indignantly have denied that he depended on them; to the very end he considered himself as the all-sufficient source of power. In the second place, the sales-crews, consisting now of several hundred men all over the country, and in foreign countries as well, would, at the time, still have resented being directed by a woman; and so all letters leaving the general sales-office, even those of which Mr Clark junior remained in ignorance, were signed with a rubber-stamp of his signature so cunningly made that only a graphological expert could have said that the signature was not written by hand and in ink.

After Mr Rudyard Clark's death, Mr Clark junior assuming the presidency, the vice-presidency had become vacant; and the choice for that office stood between Mr Stevens and Miss Dolittle; to the vast surprise of outsiders, it had promptly fallen to the lady.

Mr Stevens and Miss Dolittle, both still in their twenties, had, each in his own sphere, been geniuses. But for Mr Clark junior there had never been any hesitation.

He was in his forties at the time; and for years he had been a dreamer. He had never spoken of his dreams; but by a sort of divination, he had felt that Miss Dolittle understood and applauded. Like himself, and unlike Mr Stevens, she belonged to that younger generation—spiritually younger—which was more sensitive, more vulnerable, less sure of itself, and certainly more interesting than the older generation of the fathers had been. Those fathers, for instance, had bluntly spoken out to convey their meaning; to the younger people, a glance, or a motion, sufficed: such as lifting a finger or drawing up an eyebrow, both gestures familiar to the new president. They were more complex, more difficult, perhaps cleverer, too; and certainly less confident; they did not have so robust a conscience.

Nobody knew, of course, that, had he not been married before he came to know her, Miss Dolittle might in many ways have been an inspiration to him; he would more openly have allowed her to fight his battles. He had never admitted this even to himself; but thus it had been. The time was to come, and to the senator reclining in the car as it shot through the woods it was already present, when another woman, trying to break down his resistance to her own attack on him, boldly asserted that Miss Dolittle was in love with him and that, behind her loyalty, stood the plain, sexual fact. He was to feel then that he might have succumbed had it not been for that allusion to Miss Dolittle. Yes, as he sat there in the car, reviewing those facts, a still later time was present to him, a time at which, after the death of his wife, many years later, he would gladly have taken her to himself had it not suddenly been too late. Why had it been too late? An idle question. All questions beginning with 'why' were idle. Nothing counted but fact.

Theoretically he would, in his old age, say that he and Miss Dolittle had been socialists; and socialists are dreamers.

What had that dream of his been? One day, so he had said to himself before his father's death, *he* would be the master; *he* would direct the fortunes of the mill for the good of mankind. To do so, he would have to buy out the other shareholders till the mill was his property. Whether that would be possible, he did not know; for, beyond the fact that there were outside shareholders, he knew nothing of the mill; his father, with his secretive ways, had never allowed him a glimpse into anything that was not a matter of public record; and public record was fragmentary. It was characteristic that, when he had been promoted to the vice-presidency formerly held by a 'dummy', and when, therefore, it had become necessary for him to be a shareholder, his father had given him one 'qualifying share', making him sign a paper which appointed him, the father, his son's proxy in matters requiring a vote.

He had dreamt of many things; above all of the Terrace, that vast flat covered with cottages in which the mill-hands lived. They were all exactly alike, four-roomed, closely packed, distinguished from each other by their numbers only, in six parallel streets. All had diminutive front and back yards with lanes between them; all had running water, tiny bathrooms, and a fireplace each. Any single one might have been called convenient, compact, sanitary. In their agglomeration they were a horror. Unfortunately he had been down there, had seen how cramped they were, had breathed the disheartening atmosphere of worry and trouble which filled these little abodes of men who worked and slept and at best knew one recreation : to get drunk at intervals.

All that he would change. He would begin by building a huge hall with a gymnasium, with rooms for games and reading, with a swimming-pool and a lecture hall. He would raise wages and give the men a voice in the administration.

He had dreamt of the farmers whose wheat was bought by the mill. His father, of course, had always bought in the cheapest market, depressing that market by every device known to human cunning; never, for instance, letting it be known that the best-milling wheat was not the coveted grade Number One Northern, but a mixture into which a lower grade, Number Three, entered largely. That same father had raised the price of his product to the consumer by every means in his power : by price-agreements with other producers; by price-wars eliminating competitors; by refusing to let dealers handle his flour unless they agreed to handle no other.

It was true, that father had never made any personal use of

the resulting wealth; he had used his son and his daughter-in-law, spending vicariously.

All that he, Sam, was going to change. He was going to pay the farmer a price for his wheat commensurate with the price the milled flour fetched in the market; he would sell flour at a price which would just ensure the prosperity of the mill and yield a modest income for himself.

Producers, mill-hands, and consumers, all were to profit. That had been his dream.

When his father had died, he had suddenly become the master of the mill. Had he? On the very threshold of this new era he had encountered the sinister figure of William Swann.

CHAPTER

V

AT various stages of his career prior to his assuming power he had met Swann under puzzling circumstances; and as the car ran swiftly along the road between the walls of primeval forest. he reviewed those circumstances to himself, in brief glimpses.

The first time had been on the day when the first four units of the mill had been inaugurated by letting the water from behind the dam into the great turbines which set the dynamos spinning.

It was on that day, too, that he had met Miss Maud Carter, realizing with a shock that he was not, after all, to be entirely master of his fate. He had just now been thinking of Miss Dolittle and of what she might have been to him; but she would never have upset him in all his notions as Miss Carter had done precisely because she had taken the mill, had taken him as one of the millers, ironically only. But there had been something else. At first sight he had felt that Miss Maud Carter concerned him with a fearful immediacy. In this retrospect he could even say that the region of his own self, and probably the region of her self, which were in some mysterious fashion stirred by their mutual sight were not within their consciousness at all, certainly not within those parts of their being that were under their control or directed by thought and reflection.

At the time there had not yet been any thought of Miss Dolittle who was no more than a school-girl. But, so the old man reflected, the one had gripped him by the things which were beyond, whether above or below, all reason; whereas the other, the younger and later, had left all that the former had stirred as if it did not exist. It was tragic that the older woman, who became his wife, should have turned out to be primarily mind; whereas the younger who, in him, called forth the mind, was, in her relation to him, primarily heart and instinct. He could not explain it; but, with the clairvoyance of old age looking back on youth, he saw that it had been so.

Having seen Miss Carter, having led her through the mill, he had felt that he must, must see her again before she went to join her mother on her way to the Pacific coast; and when, timidly, he had suggested that he drop around to the little hotel where she was to spend the early half of the night with her brother, before boarding the midnight train, he had been amazed at the laughing frankness with which she had encouraged him.

So, the ceremony of the inauguration over, he had gone home to what for the first time in his life appeared to him as his father's miserable little house on Fourth Street. But his father had not yet arrived. It being a great occasion for that father, he, the son, had been reluctant to sit down at the table. Yet, impatient at being delayed, he had paced the floor in dining-room and adjacent parlour. Every now and then Mrs Leffler, the slatternly housekeeper, had peered in from the kitchen.

At last, after an unconsciously long half hour, he went impulsively to the curtained bay-window of the parlour; and, drawing one curtain aside, he saw, to his vast surprise, his father standing on the wooden sidewalk, engaged in an angry exchange of words with his former part time bookkeeper, Bill Swann, dismissed after the fire. What in the world could the two have to say to each other?

Both moved. The old man did not dismiss the man at the gate. Swann followed him to the door of the house and into it.

To see what this meant, Sam stepped into the hall.

"Had yer supper?" his father asked grimly.

"I was waiting for you."

"I don't want to eat. I want the house to myself. Have a bite and get out."

Sam saw his father was dangerously excited: the Clarks had high blood pressure and were subject to strokes. But without a word he turned back into the dining-room, calling for his tea, taking with him the picture of Swann, of a man under stress, the bald dome of his head beaded with sweat; but also of a man who stood like a rock over which an angry sea was breaking. Like doom he stood: broad, high-chested, flesh-padded: powerful, flabby and shabby; silent, ominous, evil.

The father entered. "Finished?"

His appetite gone, Sam rose, wiping his mouth. "I'm going."

The old man who had not meant his single word as a question but as a command paid no attention, proceeded to the kitchen door, and spoke to the housekeeper who stood in the passage, dressed in a skirt that hung unevenly about her shanks, her none-too-clean apron tucked up diagonally by a corner. "I want ye to go home," he said.

"I've got to wash up," she objected shrilly.

"Ye'll wash up tomorrow." His tone forestalled contradiction.

Without a word she untied her apron strings.

"Are ye going?" the old man asked, turning to Sam.

Sam risked a question. "What does he want?"

"None of yer business. Don't come back inside the hour."

Sam, taking his hat, passed out through the door; and his father shot the bolt home.

Sam was profoundly disturbed. He suffered from a bad conscience. Decades ago, when he was a child, his father had never allowed him to forget that he had been the cause of his mother's death. Any encounter with his father renewed that memory; and in this unsettled state he went to stare at the girl who had stirred in him he knew not what.

For years Sam had not seen Swann again, for he himself had gone east as a salesman for the mill. He had made a success of his work; he had married and continued to live in the east; even when he had taken a holiday, he had not felt the urge to go home to Langholm, in spite of the fact that the mill had grown without a break. Unexpectedly a summons had come through Mr Stevens whom he did not yet know.

The accident which had laid his father low had dislocated certain vertebrae of the spine; Sam had to act as his father's deputy at the mill. At first he had gone alone, leaving Maud in the east; but, seeing that his father's disability would be slow to remedy, and having become moderately well-to-do himself meanwhile, by means of an overriding commission of one half per cent on all sales effected by his staff, he had built the house on Clark Street, a palace compared with any other house so far erected at Langholm.

He had returned into a town transformed. Langholm had become a city.

The first thing which, on alighting from the train, he had seen was the mill which, being in process of enlargement, made a lopsided, truncated impression. It consisted of eleven completed units instead of the four he had known, arranged in three tiers of six, three, and two units, the latter squatting at the north end like a hood. He calculated the present aim as being one of twenty units.

The second thing that struck him as, on foot, he made for the old Queen's Hotel on Main Street, before going to see his father, had been the new track vaulting the river: a curving viaduct standing on tapering steel trestles as on stilts. He knew it had been built : he had suggested its construction seven years ago; had made the drawing for it, but he had never seen it. Always, as an engineer, he had suggested; others had carried out.

And the third thing to amaze him had been the sight of Main Street itself, crowded with stores and office buildings, all of stone quarried nearby, grey, fossiliferous limestone which underlay the whole district. This change in the aspect of Main Street was due to the activities of a new firm called Langholm Real Estate of which Mat Tindal was president, the insurance agent who had handled the insurance of the old wooden mill. Dick Carter, Maud's brother, too, had had his hand in it all, having designed almost every one of these new buildings. Uncannily, Sam recognized in them his own influence; for the whole town had assumed a façade of steel-framed fenestration between pillars of concrete; only the chief bank was a Greek temple.

Among the buildings on Main Street, still uncompleted, were two which promised to rival the mill in impressiveness : one whose hoardings, on the south side of the street, proclaimed it to be the future Palace Hotel; the other, opposite, on the site of the old little wooden office, though occupying two lots in addition, was the 'Flour Building' in which all the administrative departments of the mill were to be housed. In passing, Sam noticed that the lower floor, still screened by the hoardings, was already in use and bore, in huge gold letters, above its plateglass windows, the legend, 'Langholm Light and Power'. That, he said to himself, was of course part of the mill, for the power was produced in the vaults at the foot of the dam.

He had, that night, seen his father who was in a cast but perfectly clear in his mind; and he had received his instructions. It was only a week since the accident; but already there were hundreds of letters to be answered. Casually his father mentioned that a telegraph office had been installed on the ground floor of the Flour Building, behind the show-rooms of Langholm Light and Power.

Next morning, he was awakened in the dingy hotel room by the fearful din of pneumatic riveting machines which made the valley resound with their abomination of noise.

All which had been bewildering; but the most bewildering thing came when, around nine o'clock, going over to the Flour Building, he met, in the entrance between the hoardings, Bill Swann who stood there with a proprietorial air, hands in his pockets, a cigar hanging from his mouth.

Seeing him, Swann removed the cigar, smiled, and bowed obsequiously. "Mr Sam!" he said. "I've often wished to show you over the place." His voice was clear and distinct above the enveloping clangour.

Sam's eyes narrowed. "Are you employed here?" he asked.

"I am the manager of this concern"—with a wave of his hand towards the two small signs on the inward-slanting windows of the entrance. "Won't you come in?"

Mistrustfully Sam followed the man as he led the way into the display rooms crowded with such electrical appliances as were in use at the time. Behind, spacious offices were arranged like the cages in a bank: 'New Subscribers', 'Pay Clerk', 'Complaints and Adjustments'. Everything glittered with brass and plate-glass.

"So this is where you hang out?" Sam said.

"I am in charge here."

"Did you leave Ticknor's store?"

"Years ago."

"You bettered yourself?"

"Very much so," Swann replied with a jerky bow of his loose, heavy body—a motion which detached a bead of sweat from his shiny forehead.

Involuntarily Sam's eye followed that bead until it formed a star-shaped splash on the tiled floor of the place.

But even that Sam had come to accept without serious question. He had always disliked the man; but his necessities had been notorious. His wife was paralysed; he had a daughter ambitious to be a teacher but forced to stay at home because Mrs Swann could not be left alone; the expense of keeping a nurse had been prohibitive for a man earning less than fifty dollars a month even though he held down three part time jobs at once. One of these he had lost with the burning of the mill for which he used to post the ledger, once a week, besides making out the weekly stock-sheet required by the insurance company.

All this had been a matter of public knowledge; for the little two-roomed shack where the Swanns had lived had had to be exempted from taxation, so that his financial affairs had once a year to be raked over by the town council. Sam, with his humanitarian views and socialist leanings, had theoretically pitied the man; but his personal dislike had neutralized that feeling. Still, being himself at last a highly paid official of the mill, he tried to convince himself, without quite succeeding, that he was glad to see the man provided for. He heard that Swann had built a house of his own, on Argyle Street, next to the manorial town hall; that he kept a maid as well as a nurse; that his daughter attended high school.

Daily, henceforth, he passed the man's 'hangout'; often he met him in the great hall of the office building on the second floor of which he had his own temporary quarters. Ultimately all the executives of the mill were to be moved to the sixth floor now under construction.

A year went by. Maud had moved to Langholm, into the house on Clark Street which Sam had built for her. Strangely, Maud, the aristocrat, formed a close friendship with his father, the *parvenu* who, from obscure origins, had risen to a position of wealth and power. influencing legislation in Dominion and province.

Then, one night, his father lying in the parlour of his house, a strange thing happened. Two trim nurses were in charge there, though Mrs Leffler still looked after kitchen and dining-room, dressed in clean clothes now, forced to be so by an ulti-matum from Maud.

It was Maud who, when Sam had come home for dinner, had given him a message from his father, to the effect that the old man wanted to see him. Dick Carter, her brother, was in England at the time, evolving plans for Clark House. Maud had already two saddle horses and a fine carriage-and-pair, gifts of the 'old gentleman' as he was now called. Sam and Maud had both urged him to let them take care of him in their house; he had refused.

When, after dinner, Sam, already the quiet, reserved, well-dressed man of his later years, had gone over to his father's, he had found him in a state of strange disquiet. While the night nurse remained in the room, nothing was said of the purpose of the summons. When she left, Sam, ascribing his father's con-dition to physical causes, followed her into the hall.

"No," the nurse said in reply to his question. "Dr Cruik-shank was in this afternoon and said things were going famously at last; he promised to have Mr Clark on his feet inside two months, though he might never walk without crutches; and again he might. The cause of Mr Clark's condi-tion is mental. He's been restless since Mr Swann's call."

"Mr Swann's call?" Sam echoed sharply.

"Every time he comes we have to use sleeping powders."

"Does he come frequently?"

"Every now and then."

Sam nodded and returned to the parlour where the bed had

been set up by his own instruction. After a glance at his father he asked, much as his father had used to speak to him about the past, "What's Swann been bothering you about?"

His father gave him a mistrustful look and said, nagging, "Don't stand there. Sit down. I can't talk to you while ye're standing . . ." Then, Sam having obeyed, "Ye'll find my cheque-book in the upper right-hand drawer over there. I want ye to make out a cheque. Make it payable to yerself. I want ye to bring me the cash in hundred-dollar bills, before eleven tomorrow morning."

Sam did as he was bidden. "What sum?" he asked.

"Two thousand."

"What's that for?"

"None of yer business," the old man replied with his favourite phrase, signing the cheque and promptly turning to the wall.

AND then, the senator reflected, as the car in which he sat with his daughter-in-law turned the last but one corner on the way home, there had followed that brief but shattering series of events which centered around his father's death in 1898.

As if to defy Dr Cruikshank, Rudyard Clark had recovered till he was able once more to walk without crutch or cane.

Clark House had been built; and, little Edmund having been born, it had been made over to Maud, together with a sum running into six figures, to be held in trust, the interest to be used for the upkeep of the place which was to go to the wife of every future eldest son.

The mill, its symmetry restored, consisted of twenty units, resting on a base of six, with one unit less for every storey, ending with a fifth storey of two units only; there was talk of further expansion to come shortly. The Flour Building was completed, the sixth or uppermost floor now holding the private offices of the president and the vice-president, their secretarial staffs, and the huge boardroom in the centre, lighted by a sky-light of enormous dimensions. Opposite the Flour Building stood the great Palace Hotel, erected by an international syndicate, and holding such dining- and ball-rooms as would serve the rising plutocracy of Langholm for their social needs.

One evening, late in the year, Sam, his wife, just recovered from her difficult confinement, Mrs Carter, Maud's mother, Dick Carter, her brother, and Dr Cruikshank were sitting around the fireplace of the big hall at Clark House, humouring Maud who, in her newly recovered consciousness of health was reluctant to go to bed.

With a somewhat grim setting of his lips the senator remembered how he, in his former self, had still felt uncomfortable amid the luxuries of his surroundings which were so new to him. It seemed unnatural to step on that gold-coloured, hand-made Chinese rug sixty feet long by forty broad which covered the centre of the floor of the hall; it seemed wrong that, upstairs, in the sitting-room recess opposite the grand stairway abutting on the gallery, a portrait of Maud was hanging, painted, on his father's order, by Langereau, a Montreal artist who had charged two thousand dollars for it; it seemed incongruous that he, the son of a working miller, received, when he left the house, hat and cane from the hands of a liveried footman.

It had just struck eleven when Perkins, the butler, huge in girth and carefully balanced, entered the hall and, bending by his side, whispered to him.

"What's that?" Sam asked. "Swann? What's he want?" But he had already risen and was following the butler to the vestibule.

There, on the wide step leading down into the *porte cochère*, Swann, the ominous manager of Langholm Light and Power, stood broad, flesh-padded, the shining dome of his bald skull beaded with sweat, in spite of the cold wind blowing from the west and striking Sam in his evening clothes through the plate-glass door which a footman held open.

"Come on in, Swann," Sam said testily. "Come in and close the door."

Swann having entered, Sam started sharply at his first word. "What's that? My father? Wait. I'm coming." And, returning to the archway of the hall, "Cruikshank, come on. Something's happened to my father."

The little doctor promptly joined him in the cloak-room where a footman held his coat for him; he liked being waited on.

"Had I better come, too?" Dick Carter asked.

"Sam," Maud's voice rang out, "what is it?"

"I don't know. Nothing serious, I hope. Swann found my father lying on the ground, on Hill Road. Sounds like a stroke. Yes, better come, Dick. Lie down, Maud. Please do. Don't wait up for me. I'll ring for your maid."

Swann leading, a lantern swinging from his hand, the four men hurried up the winding driveway which rose south and southwest between two hills, close to the crest of the declivity which fell away to the Terrace. From the mill, two miles away, came a diffused radiance.

A few minutes later, having turned east on the road and jumped the ditch to its south, where he searched the ground by the light of his lantern, Swann said, "There he is."

The others followed him.

And there lay the old man in his worn but carefully brushed black suit, without an overcoat, staring with open eyes at the four men.

"Come on, dad," Sam said, bending down. "It seems you fell. Could you walk if we helped you to your feet?"

The old man did not answer, did not stir.

"Here, Dick, help me lift him."

He stood. But when they withdrew their support, he would have pitched forward.

They carried him down to the gardener's lodge just inside the park-gate which was never closed when the family was at home. Having wakened the inmates by a knock and a shout, they deposited the old man on a couch in the dining-room, the gardener and his wife helping to arrange things, both having hurriedly, if partially, dressed. From the kitchen wide-eyed children in their nightwear stared at the formidable little man, terrified and excited.

Sam ordered all doors closed, and he and Dr Cruikshank stripped the old man to the waist. By a black shoelace a key was hanging from his neck. The doctor, drawing up a chair, began his examination with stethoscope and thermometer, the only instruments he carried in the pockets of his overcoat. In their evening clothes, the three men formed a weird contrast to their surroundings.

The doctor looked up. "A cerebral haemorrhage is the only explanation."

An intensification of the stricken man's stare betrayed that his ears still heard, his mind understood. Sam touched the doctor on the shoulder, summoning him outside by a nod.

They ran into Swann whom Sam despatched to the stables of Clark House to fetch a carriage.

In the chill of the night, under the still, faintly rustling cotton-woods, there followed a brief exchange of words.

"Any idea of what may have caused it?"

"Overexertion or overexcitement; or both."

"Would the climb uphill explain it?"

"If it was hurried."

But why should the old man have climbed the hill? Since he had gone past the gate, Clarke House had not been his destination.

"Any sign of foul play?"

"Not the slightest. One thing is suspicious. There is sand on his clothes; he was lying on grass; that's not where he fell."

"I had noticed that," Sam said.

Shivering with the cold, they returned inside.

A few minutes later the wheels of a carriage were heard

crunching over the gravel of the driveway. The doctor turned to Sam.

"Before we move him, I'd like to run down to the hospital to get a hypodermic and a bit of camphor. Wait for me here, will you?"

Sam nodded. "Take Dick and Swann along. No use keeping them here. You and I can handle him."

Left alone with his father, Sam turned back to the couch, with a sudden misgiving of something catastrophic taking place there. The eyes of the old man were straining, as if trying to convey a message.

At that moment Sam's eyes fell on the key hanging from the corrugated neck; and there recurred to him certain instructions which his father had given him years ago. Should sudden death overtake him, he had said in his gruff and at best forbidding manner, Sam was at once to possess himself of that key which would open the small private safe in his office. Thence, at the earliest possible moment, he was to remove a certain account book which, having studied its contents, he was to destroy. Money he found there he might consider as a gift.

Sam picked the key up and untied it.

At once the old man relaxed. Within ten minutes, before the doctor returned, he had quietly died on his couch.

The car was on the home stretch now, on the last of the four sides of a square described by the paved road through the woods south of Langholm which, in the household, was called 'The Loop'.

The old man who, in his revisualization of the nocturnal scene on the hill, had become tense, relaxed in his corner. The memory excited him more deeply than the reality had done in the past; a future having supervened, every trifle had revealed its hidden significance.

Thus, had he, on the morning after the funeral, not gone down to the Flour Building to obey the instructions of the dead man to the letter; had he ignored them and never opened the safe; had he, instead, walled it up, for with the old man's death it had become useless, then his whole life, and with it that of everybody connected with him, yes, the development of the mill would have taken a different course. The old man, being buried, would not have re-arisen; he would never have made him, his son, the slave of the mill. The will, which was read a day later, in the presence of the family, could not have done that, for the few relevant clauses would have remained meaningless.

He, Sam, having taken certain measures, would have left the administration of the vast concern, the vastness of which was still hidden from him, to others. Being a very rich man now, he would have done what his wife had wished him to do; he would have gone to Europe and become a *dilettante* in music, a collector of paintings and articles of *virtu*, a patron, perhaps, of the arts; and he would have been happy. Perhaps his wife would have ceased seeing in him a plodding mediocrity, well-meaning, faithful to a trust, but without imagination or creative force.

They were rapidly approaching the gate to the park; and only a few flashes of vision intervened before they turned in.

He saw himself sitting in his swift open landau, dressed in a black morning coat and stiff bowler hat, with his striped trousers hidden by the camel-hair rug thrown over his knees. He remembered how, turning into Main Street, he had reflected that, fifteen years ago, Langholm had been a village of wood; whereas now it was a city of limestone, new, showy, crude in its newness, but full of a surging life.

There had been no grief, no sense of bereavement; on the contrary, the feeling had been of relief. At last he would do what he had dreamt of. But first of all he must familiarize himself with the thousand-and-one details of administration. As soon as he had done so . . .

Within a night, within half a night, sitting by his father's body, he had matured by years. A sense of responsibility had settled on him; he was no longer the rebel; he was the master now, at forty-three; his turn had come; no longer was he going to allow himself to be used. . . .

To be used!

With that word, his carriage turning into Main Street, a sort of synopsis and condensation of an earlier scene had arisen in his mind, gone almost as soon as it had come.

The occasion was this. The mill was to be enlarged on a scale unheard-of even for this fast-growing concern: seven units were to be added; and in addition three grain-elevators were to be erected, with a storage capacity of 600,000 bushels. His father had called a special shareholders' meeting to discuss ways and means. It had been a year or two before his death; and he had tipped his son off in advance: certain statements would be needed, estimates of the growth of the market, especially overseas. He relied on Sam who would be present on that occasion by special invitation.

The scene was set in the huge boardroom of the Flour Building, around the long walnut table. Under the blinding light of many clusters of unshaded electric bulbs sat a strange assembly of men.

Next to Rudyard Clark who was in the chair sat Mat Tindal, the former insurance agent, now president of a million-dollar concern called Langholm Real Estate; then Rodney Ticknor, general merchant, whose one-roomed store had become a five-storey department store of imposing proportions; then Gaylord, once a blacksmith, now owner and editor of the local paper, the Langholm Lynx. Art Selby was there, manager of the leading bank in town, huge, square, slow to move; above all, there was Mr Cole from Winnipeg, a short, thick-set, choleric man without a neck who held proxies for a score of small shareholders. Besides, of course, there had been Charles Beatty, Q.C., solicitor for the mill, a medium-sized, slender man with a face resembling a death's head.

At the upper end of the table sat a whole staff of stenographers, lorded over by Mr McNally, the former secretary-treasurer recently replaced by Mr Stevens.

Sam, who had been told to be there at nine sharp, was at once called upon by his father to give his report.

"That'll convince ye," his father said when his son sat down. "The question is how best to finance. We can increase capital and sell stock; or we can borrow. If we needed less than a hundred thousand, the directors would have gone ahead on their own responsibility, according to by-law. But we need three-quarters of a million. If we borrow we shall have to repay; that means no dividends for a year."

"You've sold your stock on the understanding that there will be no break in dividends," Mr Cole objected.

"After a while dividends will rise to twice the old rate. The market value of the stock will double. That should be satisfactory."

"You can't borrow," Mr Cole insisted. "Who'd loan you that much?"

This question Rudyard Clark treated as negligible. "It's all arranged," he said. "Mr Selby's here. His bank has agreed."

"Gentlemen," Art Selby said, rolling his bulk around in his chair to face Mr Cole at his right. "Our Bank has a great faith in the future of the west. We are prepared to commit ourselves heavily. I am instructed to take any reasonable risk. If it were a question of an ordinary accommodation, we'd grant it unconditionally. But the demand is for a very large and indeterminate sum, for an undefined time. So the directorate has seen fit to tie a string to its consent. They will grant the loan if the present shareholders endorse all notes personally, pro rata of their holdings."

"Out of the question!" Mr Cole exploded. "Even if I were willing to agree for myself, which I am not, I could not commit those for whom I am acting."

Rudyard Clark did not reply. There was a long pause.

Then empty-headed Mat Tindal tried to pour oil on troubled waters. "Mr Clark, I'd be inclined to favour the issue of new stock. Any Langholm offer is readily snapped up by the investing public. Langholm Real Estate issued half a million three months ago. It was oversubscribed in a week. We could sell above par."

Rudyard Clark had nothing to say.

"That's sense," said Mr Cole. "Why in the world borrow when the capital is there, begging to be used?"

"Because I won't give my consent."

"Why not?"

"I owe no man a reason."

"Ah, ah!" cried Mr Cole, getting red in the face. "I'll tell you, Mr Clark. You hold a precarious control. If we issue new stock, that control might be in danger."

Rudyard Clark gave a grim laugh. "That's so. It's my perfect right to oppose any measure for any reason. You know that I can."

"Unfortunately," Mr Cole sighed. "On the other hand, no power on earth can force us to put our signatures on those notes. That's the one thing in which control doesn't help you. Even if those present agreed, you'd have to get the consent of the absent ones."

"The bank would waive the endorsement of minor shareholders—say those who own no more than ten shares," Art Selby said impartially.

Everybody realized that this placed the issue squarely between the two chief opponents. Mr Cole was the only western shareholder whose holdings ran into six figures.

Rudyard Clark gave another grim laugh. "Ye reproach me with scheming to retain control," he said. "I'll tell ye what's behind it all. Ye want to get that control out of my hands. Ye can't have any doubt, from what my son's told ye, that the loan will be repaid. But let me tell ye; this mill is going to run with me in control; or not at all."

This was a bombshell. Everybody in the room, except Charles Beatty, sat up. Sam divined that Mr Beatty had advised that procedure.

Mr Cole became very quiet. "How is that?" he asked.

"I'd cut the power off."

"I knew it!" Mr Cole cried, thumping the table. But he also knew, as did everybody else, that he was beaten.

This scene rose before the senator as it had arisen before Sam, forty years ago, not in any detail, but, as it were, in the form of a single fact.

And just as they were turning into the gate of the park, the senator closed his eyes in his corner.

He saw himself alighting in front of the Flour Building. A huge Negro in olive-green livery, with yellow trimmings, jumped forward to offer his arm; another, behind him, held the door to the hall. Opposite the Flour Buildings, of equal height, no less supercilious, stood the Palace Hotel, its face closed.

"Don't wait," Sam said curtly to the driver who saluted.

Then he entered the hall of the building, constructed, outside, of concrete over steel, inside, of coloured and highly polished marbles.

In this hall, crowded with comings and going, two Negroid attendants sprang up from a black-marble bench in the centre of the right-hand wall which was of plate glass, permitting a survey of the premises where Swann had his 'hangout'. Both, at Sam's sight, dived rearward where one of them entered the third elevator cage, while the other, saluting, stood ready to close its grilled slide-door the moment Sam had taken his stand inside. Both of them wore the same olive-green livery trimmed with yellow as the two at the outer door. This third elevator was the 'express', never used by those whose business was below the sixth floor.

Sam paid no attention to the commotion about him. Even to the saluting attendants he gave only the briefest nod in reply. But he took note of the proud, disdainful bearing they observed with regard to all but the highest executives; it was the bearing which Rudyard Clark had demanded from menials serving the business. *He* would change all that . . . .

His father, on the other hand, had never hesitated to talk to these men about their private and intimate affairs; or to correct them if their manner did not meet with his entire approval. How strange, the senator thought, that his father, the autocrat, the never-to-be-contradicted master, should have shown himself more affable, ready even to jest and to laugh with his subordinates; and that he should have commanded an all the more unquestioning obedience, yes, an affectionate anticipation of his desires. Did these men know that he, the son, sympathized with everyone in servitude? That he planned, and spent sleepless nights in planning, how to better their lot?

From the vantage point of his great age, the senator pitied the man he had been. For, though the magnificent Negroids of that day lay in their graves or nursed a decrepit old age as pensioners of the mill, they had been replaced by others: he had become used to them when his own great purpose had been broken as he might break a match.

CHAPTER

VII

THE car came to a stop under the *porte cochère*.

Leaning on the extended arm of a footman, Lady Clark alighted.

It took the old man longer to follow her; but he, too, at last took the single step to the floor of the vestibule, the young butler holding the door for him.

This young butler, engaged a few years ago by Lady Clark, the senator still regarded as an intruder; for thirty years old Perkins had held his place: huge, Falstaffian Perkins, between whom and his master there had been a tacit understanding that the social distinctions were mere pretence; could not a duke and lord, in a play, consent to take the part of an underling? Perkins had been the lord; he, the senator, barely his equal. Maud, of course, his long-dead wife, had never known that; or she would have laughed and laughed. . . .

It did not matter. But the senator could not yet, when he met him, refrain from staring for a moment at this new butler, as if to make sure he was real; or as if he expected him to say something, to betray at least by a gesture what, in his heart, he thought of this world of his masters. No such gesture ever came; it was disconcerting.

This time the senator found it so disturbing that *he* stopped as if to say something; and the butler bent forward as if to catch a command like a ball which he expected the other to pitch to him. It was this attitude of submissive readiness which struck the senator dumb; for he had actually intended to say something.

As if on second thought, he did speak. "Make my excuses to the ladies. I want another drive."

"Very good, sir," said the butler. "Had I better call McAllister to take the wheel, sir?"

"McAllister?" the senator repeated. "Wasn't it McAllister. . . ."

"No, sir. Excuse me, sir. It was Waugh who was driving her ladyship."

This correction, in spite of its impeccable form, irritated

the senator who seemed to scent in it the insolence of the young to the old. "Well," he said testily. "Call him. I'm waiting."

The young butler, letting go of the door, strode over to the telephone connecting house and drive-sheds. "McAllister wanted," he said. "To drive the senator." Then, half-turning, "Same car, sir?"

"Any car."

Since the matter was thus left to himself, the young butler, thinking of the fact that the Lincoln was dusty, said briefly into the transmitter, "The Rolls-Royce."

Which again the senator chose to take as an impertinence, for the Rolls-Royce was the oldest of the big cars available. But it was not worth while to object. Let it be the Rolls-Royce.

The reason for this scene which remained unnoticed by Lady Clark—for, out of consideration for the old man's mood, she had at once withdrawn—was simply the reluctance of the senator to return abruptly to the world of the living. He wanted to remain with his thoughts.

The car having been brought around, and the senator having taken his seat, he was in the past again.

But the butler had followed him. "We won't hold lunch, sir?"

The senator, disturbed, almost barked. "Didn't I tell you to make my excuses?" And, McAllister having pushed back the glass-slide between cab and tonneau, he added, still irately, "Around the loop."

The car shot forward; the senator was in the hall of the Flour Building on Main Street.

It was the morning after the funeral. The three days that had elapsed since the death had served to confirm him in all his old plans. *He* was the master now; he never doubted that, apart from minor bequests, the bulk of his father's estate, ensuring control, would fall into his hands as if the old man had died intestate. Now he must promptly carry out the dead man's instructions with regard to the safe, thereby winning his freedom, cutting himself loose from the past, breaking with a system which he hated.

While entering the elevator, he was conscious of a girl in a niche opposite the cage reaching for a telephone. No doubt she was signalizing his arrival to his subordinates upstairs; and so, reaching the top floor, he was not surprised to see Miss Albright coming out to meet him in the boardroom.

It had puzzled him how he was going to get into his father's office. Miss Albright solved that problem for him.

"Mr Clark," she said, sweeping towards him, "I have taken the liberty of moving you into the president's suite. Have I done right? The late Mr Clark had left nothing in his desk. The drawers were open."

"Quite," Sam replied without surprise at the last statement; the old man had always believed in working from memory.

"There wasn't time to move myself and the stenographers," Miss Albright went on, following him as he entered, through the anteroom, into his father's office to the left. "The telephone in the drawer connects with the one on my desk. I am within call. Pending arrangements, the late Mr Clark's staff and ours are doubling up for the day."

Sam had turned and was hanging overcoat and hat on the cloak-rack behind the door; so he stood revealed in morning coat and striped trousers. With a familiar gesture he raised one eyebrow and said, "Let's get through with the routine. I want to be undisturbed."

"There is only Miss Dolittle," Miss Albright said.

"Let her come." And he sat down at the desk in the centre of the room. A leather-covered armchair stood by its side, a straight-backed chair facing it. The floor was covered with a Persian rug.

Miss Albright withdrew; and he noticed her flowing dress of black satin; she was a large girl, too florid for his taste.

On the glass-topped mahogany desk stood two wire trays, one filled with opened letters; the other with daily papers from east and west.

Without touching either, he rose again when he was alone, going to the wide windows, four of them in a row. They gave on the lower end of the lake, with the wooded hills beyond, mill and dam in the foreground. Though only five stories high, the mill towered above the Flour Building, for each of its stories rose twenty-five feet. To the left or west he had a glimpse of the elevators, past a shoulder of the mill. Everything visible, even the dam, was dusted white with flour.

All which he knew. During his father's illness he had often gone here for that view. Somewhere he had read a phrase in the story of a medieval mystic which had stuck in his memory: *Ecce animula tua!*—"There stands your little soul!" He had been in the habit of repeating it to himself whenever he saw the mill. Through his father's death, his aesthetic appreciation of the buildings before him had, at a blow, become a moral one; the responsibility was his now—the responsibility for making the mill a blessing or a curse to mankind. And another thing became clear: the mill was not a man-made thing: it was an outgrowth of the soil, the rock, the earth, subject to laws of growth of its own, independently of himself. All the more....

He turned back into the room with a feeling familiar to him, a feeling of the futility of human effort. What, in a moral sense, was this mill, this whole enterprise which the old man had called into being during the last short years of his life? What was this town which, for its very existence and subsistence, depended on the mill? His confidence, his far-reaching plans paled. Mill, dam, and town were the work of the man who was dead—who had supplied the driving power to call them into actual being. He, Sam, was nothing. He planned, he did not carry out. He was the engineer; his father had been the 'entrepreneur'.

That feeling he must overcome; it was still part of the effect which his father had had on him.

Idly turning to the desk, he opened one or two of the papers and folded and dropped them again. He had not thought of the publicity which would attach to the event of his father's death. Here it was: flaring headlines reported the end of the 'Flour King'. Inconspicuous little man he had been, his father was mourned as a 'national figure'. One obituary called him a 'Titan of Finance'.

Sam sat down again and stared at the pages. He was not reading; he was thinking. Who are we? What is the reality in us? That which we feel ourselves to be? Or that which others conceive us to be? The things that surround us are known to us by the way they affect us. Their inner reality is as mysterious to us as the universe itself, or as life and death. What was the reality? Was there a reality? The man whom he, his son, had known by that sympathy of the blood which, in spite of all their antagonisms, had united them: a man of fears, of doubts, of hesitations, scruples, forebodings? Or the bold buccaneering adventurer who had been successful; whom the world saw expressed in his work, in that dam out there, in this vast organization which he had created and held together? Nothing but the latter lived in the reports of the death at which Sam stared with unseeing eyes: *he* only would live on in his work and in legend. For the moment his father became even to Sam an august stranger.

Nobody ever knocked at a door on this sixth floor of the

Flour Building; the theory was that nobody could enter un-announced.

Sam became conscious of the fact that Miss Dolittle was in the room. He rose and faced her from the windows.

As always, her mere presence cheered him; after all, he was not absolutely alone. It was to be the first-fruit of his power to give her a position nominally next in authority to his own.

The girl, medium-sized, extraordinarily good-looking—though, no doubt, she would get stout in later life—above all vital to her fingertips, greeted her chief with a half confidential smile and handed him a large sheet of stiff, squared paper exhibiting graphs in three colours.

Sam scanned it. "How," he asked after a while, "are we going to meet that demand?" With a pointing finger he traced a red line which soared over the blue line indicating production.

Miss Dolittle, still as if discussing personal rather than business matters, gave a shrug.

"How about Western Flour Mills?" Sam asked.

"Full up. Running to capacity, day and night. We have reserves for a month or two. Shall I send Mr Eckel up?"

"Not this morning. I am busy."

"Of course."

Western Flour Mills was a subsidiary concern operating four comparatively small mills in western centres. Mr Eckel was Chief Chemist, in charge of buying.

"But perhaps Mr Eckel will be able to advise. Consult him. Meanwhile draw on reserves. We shall have to build again."

"Very well."

"Sit down a moment," Sam said, his tone changing.

She obeyed.

"There is the problem of my signature," Sam went on, still standing.

"Of course." Again Miss Dolittle understood at a word.

"Suppose Mr Stevens' rubber stamp takes the place of mine?"

Miss Dolittle gave a slight laugh. "Mr Stevens!"

Sam also understood. Bob Stevens, very efficient in his sphere, was unpopular. "Too bad you were not born a man," he said, smiling.

"Is it? . . . Well, I don't like the idea of reporting to him."

"I didn't say you were to report to him. Suppose you were put entirely on your own feet?"

She looked up at him, anticipation suffusing her cheeks.

"As a mere formality . . . If it is not presumption . . . Is Mr Stevens going to take your place?"

"No. Matters will, of course, have to be ratified by a directors' meeting. But since, most likely, I shall hold control. . . ."

Miss Dolittle squirmed a little, her fine mouth half open.

And Sam betrayed, as he rarely did, that he was human. "Mr Stevens is indispensable as secretary-treasurer," he said tantalizingly. Which could only mean that he was to rise no higher. "Of course, we shall need a new vice-president. The former arrangement worked well?"

"You mean the vice-president being nominally sales-manager also?"

"Exactly."

"Yes. But I don't see. . . ."

It was rare for Sam to play on a woman's feelings; but he enjoyed the experience. "Well," he said, "I can't be my own employee. How would it be if we made the real sales-manager the nominal vice-president?"

Miss Dolittle looked up sideways. Her smile would have given most men a thrill. "I am not a shareholder. . . ."

"Neither is Mr Stevens."

"You mean. . . ."

"You need one qualifying share. It is true, the stock stands at eight forty-five."

"Oh," Miss Dolittle cried. "If the ban is lifted. . . ."

"The ban will be lifted in the rarest cases. It is all predicated, of course, on my being my father's heir."

"There can't be a doubt about that, can there?"

"I don't think so; but I don't know. I am presuming on the fact. Such an arrangement would convince Mr Stevens, would it not, that his stamp under your letters is the merest formality?"

"It would settle all possible objections."

"Very well, then," Sam said in the tone of finality.

Miss Dolittle rose as if in confusion. "There is nothing else?"

"Nothing, thanks."

That, the senator reflected, had been the last time for many years that he had stood face to face with a woman unselfconscious.

But instantly he was back in the past.

He stood in that office, absent-mindedly fingering a key in his vest-pocket. Before him stood Miss Albright. "Take this correspondence away," he said. "I shall want it again. Just now I want to be undisturbed till noon."

"Very well, Mr Clark." And the secretary vanished.

Unreasonably, Sam felt annoyed with the girl as if she pursued him.

But the click of the door brought him face to face with his task. He took the key from his pocket; for the first time, in the execution of his father's instructions, he felt hesitation. In the light of the sudden death, those instructions had taken on the nature of the expression of a last will which must be obeyed. He was to open the private safe, to take what it contained in cash, as a gift *inter vivos*, to make himself familiar with the contents of an account book, and to destroy it. The task went against his inclination. Evasively he asked himself whether it was wise to undertake it in daytime, during office hours, with the vast hive of the building humming. But would it not cause even more damaging comment if he returned to the building after hours? What with three watchmen circling through it at night, he was as good as certain to be seen. He needed a light which would be exposed to full view from the mill. He would be suspected of trying to discover assets which he ought not to touch till the will was known.

As for surprise, he felt safe. The operator downstairs had by this time been told not to let anyone pass; a sign 'Private' was hung to the grilled and closed door of the express elevator below; its cage was on the top floor, the Negro drowsing on his stool. The whole staff, Miss Albright at its head, was on the lookout.

With a shrug he looked at the celluloid tag attached to the key and read the combination. Squatting down before the low door of the safe, in the wall faced by the desk, he twirled the button.

A moment later, the door of the safe gaped open.

To the right, two open compartments; to the left, two deep drawers.

Sam turned his attention to the latter. One held three bankbooks, a small envelope with a key in it, marked 'Safety Deposit Box', and a large number-ten manilla envelope marked 'Swann'; the other, a not inconsiderable sum of specie in small linen bags: gold of English coinage, silver dollars of historic dates. Apparently his father had collected numismatic rarities. The balances of the bankbooks totalled close to a hundred thousand. He returned them to their drawer and transferred the cash, including the manilla envelope, to the desk.

Then he examined the upright compartments. One contained three sheaves of papers dated 1899, 1905, 1920 respectively. Examination showed them to be plans and specifications for the expansion of the mill. That expansion his father had mapped out for over twenty years! Was he, Sam, after all, not going to be the undisputed master?

The other compartment held a single book of the type which, in small business houses, is used as a journal. It must be the account book referred to in his father's instructions. He took it to the desk and sat down.

A dull sort of excitement invaded him. What could this book contain which demanded its immediate destruction?

As far as a preliminary scrutiny revealed, it contained a record of the dead man's personal earnings and expenditures, beginning with October 1867 when Sam's grandfather Douglas had died of stroke.

The senator, in his corner of the tonneau of the car which was swiftly travelling over the road of 'The Loop', meeting a town car now and then, for the driveway was open to the public, felt reinvaded by that excitement of forty years ago. In pursuing his evocation of the past, he closed his eyes, one hand grasping the other.

Many things came back to the man at the desk as he turned the pages. For the nineteen years following the opening date the entries showed a multitude of small, often negligible sums drawn from the business for the most various purposes: household expenses, telegraph fees, postage, equipment for the mill. Up to 1880 the yearly totals were insignificant, now rising above, now falling below $400. Then they increased; there was a building account. All equipment for the expansion of the mill was apparently bought second-hand; there was one item, "Lower Grindstone, $75.00". There came another, a sum spent on the acquisition, from the Crown, of a large tract of land, several square miles of it: the land now covered by, and bordering on, the lake: it was bought at a nominal price.

In spite of the fact that business expenditure ceased to be entered, larger and larger sums appeared. There were increasing entries on the credit side, too, running into thousands of dollars; and each was balanced by a corresponding outgo. Many referred to safe investments; others were harder to understand. Till, with the effect of a sudden enlightenment, the fact stood revealed that the ageing man had been speculating in wheat, first on a small, then an ever larger scale. As he began to grind for the eastern market, he had used his growing knowledge and taken advantage of seasonal fluctuations; and he had done so shrewdly and successfully. There were entries of wheat purchased by "Rudyard Clark, Private", resold to "Rudyard Clark, Miller". This manoeuvre made Sam smile: it foreshadowed the Napoleonic skill with which the old man must have marshalled his assets in 1888 when, on the basis of his slender private holdings, he had launched a three-million-dollar concern in such a way as to retain control. Though, come to think, were his private holdings so small? Even the total of the profits made on wheat deals between "Rudyard Clark, Private" and "Rudyard Clark, Miller" ran into six figures.

Sam knew that the land covered by the lake stood on the books at a valuation of $100 an acre; whereas he could now verify that it had cost his father precisely ten cents. Without the land, the dam could not have been built; without the dam, the river could not have turned the turbines; without the turbines, the mill could not have been run.

Sam's admiration was mingled with a peculiar misgiving. The thing was magnificent; but in some indefinable way it was ruthless.

Besides, it was "Finance". Was that panegyrist right who had called his father a Titan of Finance? In practical things, in the working-out of the plan, the old man had relied on others: on engineers, on architects, on chemists: on Mr Eckel, Dick Carter, and, yes, on him, Sam, who, after all, had furnished every fruitful idea, often in a round about way, working through Dick Carter or the engineers. To what extent had his father known of the part his son had played in determining the structure of the mill? The pyramidal outline, for instance; the layout in units; the flood-lighting: ideas actually put forward by Dick Carter, though originated by Sam.

A line in red ink across the last page of this chapter of the record brought it to an abrupt close:

"Mill destroyed by fire, April 23-24, 1888."

As Sam went through the remainder of the record, he found ever larger items, culminating in an entry of $250,000, without comment, balanced by another, recording the sale of 1000 shares in Langholm Real Estate, yielding slightly more than that sum. That was the money spent on Clark House. Another entry, balanced by another sale of stock in the same concern, recorded, at the very end, that $200,000 had been placed to the credit of "Maud Clark, née Carter, wife of my beloved son Samuel, in trust, for the upkeep of said property".

In this part of the record there was one puzzling thing.

Seven entries, each of $2,000 or over, all on the credit or expenditure side, were made without comment, totalling $15,000. Nothing explained what they stood for; but each of them was marked, in pencil, with a figure enclosed in a circle:

(267) . Sam wondered.

He could not see a single reason why this account book should be destroyed; on the contrary, it was a valuable document throwing light on the genesis of the mill. Since the mill bade fair to become a great institution of national and even international importance, the document should be preserved in the archives at Ottawa.

At this moment the unexpected, the unheard-of happened: a caller slipped past the watchers and burst into the presidential room.

This was Dick Carter, Sam's brother-in-law, designer of mill, Flour Building, Clark House, Palace Hotel, and many other edifices in town.

Sam looked up, startled. Behind the intruder he saw three women, Miss Albright leading, trying to restrain him; but Dick, irrepressible, waved a happy hand at them, laughing a gold-flashing laugh, and closed the door behind his back.

Sam frowned. Behind the caller gaped the open safe; on the desk lay account book, money, and manilla envelope. The book he closed quickly.

"Hello," Dick sang out cheerfully. He was a medium-sized, gay-looking man of Sam's age; somehow, in spite of signs of dissipation in his face, he looked younger. "I've a hurry-call to Vancouver. I'm leaving by the noon train. May go on to Seattle." At this point the fact that he had to name the man whom they had buried but yesterday recalled the mournful occasion to him; and he subdued his exuberance which, Sam suspected, was partly due to his having had a bottle of wine. "You know," he went on, "the old gentleman"—had he been living, he would have called him 'the old codger'—"had asked for additional plans and an elevation. Any hurry about that? I'm off on the biggest job yet."

"Elevation?" Sam asked, puzzled.

"Hadn't he discussed the thing with you?"

"Not a word."

"Well, well . . . It's this way." And he reached for the pad on which Sam had been figuring. "This of any account?" And, Sam shaking his head, he tore the top sheet off and let it flutter to the desk. Then, with a gold pencil from his pocket, he sketched the outline of an elevation comprising thirty-five units, with an illegible legend running from side to side along the fifth tier. "Here," Dick added, "he wanted two lines of twenty-foot letters in black marble. See what I mean? That's what he was playing with in his mind."

Appalled, Sam asked, "And what was the legend?"

"Clark Flour Mills. The Home of Canada's Flour."

Sam fairly jumped in his seat. "No," he cried in distress. "No!"

"Well," Dick said doubtfully. "You're the boss now."

"The Home of . . ." Sam said with ineffable scorn in his voice.

Dick made a *volte-face*. "Ridiculous, isn't it? He probably knew you'd object . . ." He was on the point of adding, 'The sly old dog!' but changed it into "He was secretive, wasn't he?"

"Of course," Sam said, "we have to enlarge. You may be needed for the floor plans. But I don't think there's any immediate hurry."

"You won't want blue-prints within a week?"

"Not within a week. I shall let you know. Usual address?"

"Usual address. If I leave there, I shall give instructions to forward. So long, then." And, with a thrust of his arm, he threw the pad back on the desk.

Now, in this movement of his, a button of his cuff caught behind the stiff cover of the account book which had refused to lie flat; the book was brushed to the floor.

"Sorry," Dick said, bending down; but Sam had forestalled him.

Sam was alone again. Dick did not matter. Most likely he had not even noticed the open safe; if he had, he had given it no thought.

There was no reason to destroy the book. He would return it to its resting place in the safe.

But, having risen to do so, a peculiar circumstance struck

him as he reached for the book. In being tossed back on the desk, it had fallen on its spine and opened at a point where a brief series of entries had so far escaped him. That series stood on a page near the end of the book; and the page bore the number 267.

Sam dropped back to his seat. He felt weak-kneed with foreboding; a new wave of excitement ran through him. A glance showed the page contained every entry from the front part of the book which had been marked with the encircled number. In his father's fine, flowing hand it bore the heading:

"Account of William Swann."

Beyond that, it made no disclosure. Sam compared the entries with those he had jotted down on the slip of paper. They tallied.

That the book had opened at this page was readily explained: it had been carefully flattened.

Sam was startled.

The senator, in recalling it, felt his hands tremble; for this had been the most decisive moment in his life; all else had flowed from it: Swann was raising his head again. What was his connection with his father? In his mind he saw him as he had seen him in the narrow hall of his father's house; broad-shouldered, heavy, middle-aged; as if he were built for manual labour, not for clerical work. Even as a bookkeeper Sam had disliked him: he was too oilily subservient, too much given to obsequious bowing.

He felt more profoundly disturbed than ever before in his life; vague misgivings flooded his mind. He turned back to the book.

The first payment had been made in the fall of 1888, shortly after the first units of the mill had been put into operation: $2,000; the last less than half a year ago; and in addition there was that manilla envelope. It being unsealed, he examined its contents which consisted of twenty one-hundred-dollar bills.

Worriedly he picked the account book up again and turned the pages, coming, almost at once, upon a list of receipts written in the dead man's hand and signed by Swann in a bold, calligraphic script:

"Received, from Mr Rudyard Clark, the sum of ....
     in payment of blackmail."

Sam's first impulse was to press the button under his desk and to have the man summoned. But on second thought he refrained. He must ponder the matter. He would go home, to return after luncheon.

He trembled as he rose; but, controlling himself, he replaced all but the cash in the safe which he relocked. Sitting down once more, he made out a deposit slip for the money which he counted, stowed gold and silver in his pockets, and put on his coat.

In the boardroom, Miss Albright met him, flushed. "Shall I ring for the carriage, Mr Clark?"

He shook his head. "I'll walk."

"About Mr Carter, Mr Clark. He happened to be on the fifth floor and used the stairs. That's why we could not stop him."

Sam, with a nod, made for the waiting elevator cage.

On the way home he dropped in at the bank with the Grecian front, to deposit the cash he carried. It was the noon hour; and he had to tip his hat to a score of people. But the bank was deserted.

Art Selby, the manager, who, like the Clarks, had his lunch at a later hour, saw Sam through the open door of his office, and, pushing his glasses up on his capacious forehead, came to meet him.

"Anything I can do for you, Sam?"

"I have a certain amount of cash in my pockets; from my father's safe."

The manager chuckled. "Succession duties are the devil," he said.

Sam felt acutely that he was in a false position and resented the fact. His voice was icy when he said, "Let's go to your office."

Which acted as a sufficient check on the other's facetiousness to make him do what had to be done in silence and with despatch.

Within a few minutes Sam was back in the street, half wishing he had sent for the carriage after all. He was not used to moving in crowds; it interfered with his effort to clear his thought.

CHAPTER

VIII

IT so happened that, on that very morning Odette Charlebois and Lady Clark had met in the upstairs living-room which served as an ante-chamber to the senator's bedroom suite. Both, for a moment, glanced at the portrait of the senator's late wife painted by Langereau.

As if talking to herself, Odette said, "That picture gives her to the life."

"Does it?" Lady Clark asked. "It's a fine painting. But it tells me nothing of her real being. I look and I look. I cannot but admire. I think I'd have adored her; and suddenly I am repelled."

"She and I were classmates at college. She ruled us all by sheer force of personality and an indomitable will. She was fascinating."

"Did she have charm?"

The older woman pondered. "I don't think you'd call it charm. She was a great beauty. She was an aristocrat, like yourself."

"Myself!"

"Yes," Miss Charlebois insisted. "But she lacked something you have. She was always ironic. I wish I could put her before you in action. . . ."

"Try to think of some little incident."

"I will," Miss Charlebois said.

A few hours later, the senator being on his second turn around the loop, the two women met again, half an hour before luncheon. Being both at leisure, and Odette betraying the desire to continue their conversation, they sat down, close to each other, in the hall.

"I think I have it," said Odette Charlebois.

"It was a few weeks after the birth of your late husband. But it is not self-explanatory. I must reach back in time.

"You know how they had met? Miss Carter was the sister of Dick Carter, the young architect who was in charge of the building operations when the new mill replaced the old. He built the dam, too, of course; and later the endless additions to the mill; and the office building; and the hotel; the elevators; and numberless houses in town; and this house; in fact, he built Langholm; and Langholm built him.

"In his way he was a remarkable man, I believe; his sister always gave him credit for it all. But during his early years, up to his disastrous marriage, he invariably called the senator the genius; he made no secret of it that it was the senator who had evolved the plan whereby the mill could go on growing and growing, so that you never could say, This is old; this is new. At the time of the meeting there were only the four lower north units; but the senator had already visualized the present structure with its one hundred and seventy. Yet the lower part of the present north wall is still the original one. It had been placed where it is because of what the engineers said; they could not go further north because the river-bed consists of shale and quicksand, down to a depth to which no struts could be set. The mill had to stand on the bed-rock with which it forms a monolith. All growth had to be to the south where the so-called vaults which hold the turbines and the dynamos were blasted out of the living rock.

"I mention all this because it was that north wall with its concave, buttressed sweep from bed-rock up to the first floor of the mill which brought Mr and Mrs Clark together in a common enthusiasm. There was an old foreman employed in the mill, a Mr Rogers who, having worked in the wooden mill, had privileges, especially after he had been retired. He used to come up here and walk in the park; and so he told me one day that the senator used to go out there, both before and after his marriage, through the huge, copper-studded door which leads from the vaults into the old river-bed; and thence he looked up at that sweep of concrete wall with a strange, rapt expression on his face; not once but many times.

"Now it so happened that Miss Maud Carter, being in the west, with her mother, came down to Langholm to be with her brother on the day on which the dam was inaugurated; it was not yet of its present height, of course; and in the course of the day it fell to Mr Clark junior to show her over the mill as far as it was completed. As was natural, Mr Clark wished to show her the wall which he so much admired. He took her through that copper-studded door into the dry river-bed, floored, as it is today, with huge limestone slabs. What she said when she saw that tremendous curved and upward sweep she has told me herself. Like Mr Clark she experienced a thrill. 'Magnificent!' she cried. 'I shouldn't have thought that Dick had it in him!' Dick being her brother's first name. And she added, 'It's the most impressive thing I have seen made by man.'

"You can see one side of her in that; she looked at everything from an aesthetic point of view. As you know, the senator, too, has that aesthetic sense. I believe this common feature attracted them to each other. Aesthetic sensibility is, of course, only one side of the senator's composition. Her, I believe, it summed up pretty well. I know that, if I had not had my share of good looks, she would never have thought of engaging me for her companion after her marriage.

"That marriage did not come about till a year or two later. Mr Clark went east almost immediately, to take charge of the sales-organization of the new mill. They met again at Toronto where her parents lived, her father being the senior partner in the firm of engineering architects of which Dick Carter was the junior. After the marriage they lived for a number of years at Montreal where Mr Clark made his headquarters. It was there I met Mrs Clark again.

"Then old Mr Clark, Mr Rudyard, had an accident which, for the time being, crippled him. The young people had to come home; and I came with them; Mr Sam, as we called him, had to relieve his father of the routine work at the office. They moved into that house on the southern hillside, on Clark Street, which Mr Sam had built, a fine enough place, though, of course, not to be compared with this.

"Strange to say, Mrs Clark, Maud as I still called her from our college days, and old Mr Rudyard took to each other in a most extraordinary way. 'Strange' because Mr Clark senior was 'a man of the people', rough in his ways, outspoken when he had something to say, and lacking in the social graces to which Maud had been accustomed. Old Mr Clark lavished on her all the affection of which he was capable, indulging her in everything. He never went to office or mill except afoot; but he not only gave *her* saddle and driving horses but even connived at Mr Sam driving to the office and back because she insisted on it.

"And then, I believe it was in 1896, he built her this house. By that time he was reputed to be enormously wealthy. The mill grew from year to year; on its south side there was always a new tier of units under construction; and it had already the outline of a pyramid. The business was expanding at a fabulous rate, now of its own momentum. But old Mr Clark was still living in his little frame house on Fourth Street where a slatternly woman, a Mrs Leffler, kept house for him.

"I don't know whether the old gentleman knew what he was letting himself in for when he undertook the building of this house. But Maud persuaded him to send her brother Dick to England to study the layout of great country estates and to work out the most lavish plans. These plans were predicated upon a household conducted on a scale unheard-of even among the wealthy in Canada. A butler would be needed; three footmen, coachmen, grooms, gardeners, maids by the dozen; all which was quite against Mr Sam's inclination. But old Mr Clark not only did not object; he openly approved. One day he said to Maud, in my presence, 'I'm building that place. If, before I die, you present me with a grandson, it's yours; and I'll settle funds enough on you for its upkeep. Not Sam's, mind you, but yours.'

"Mr Sam was at that time very keen about the mill; he was always poring over plans for its improvement. You see he was the last of the Clarks to be a miller."

Lady Clark looked up at the older woman who was smiling as if she had expected this movement of surprise.

"Well," Miss Charlebois explained, "your husband was only a mill-owner. Mr Sam could have taken charge of any machine, any operation in the mill. Sir Edmund's interests were too scattered; he directed things; I doubt whether he could have originated a new process; for that a practical knowledge was needed which Mr Sam was the last of the Clarks to have. Am I right?"

"Very likely. I had not thought of it in that way."

"Few people have. That's why I lay stress on it. The senator has never received his due. His father treated him like a cog in the machine; his wife never abandoned her superior attitude; his son ascribed growth and success of the mill to his grandfather only. Yet, as it stands, it is the senator's creation; though I have an idea that there was a time when it assumed a life of its own and took charge; when it was directing Mr Sam rather than being directed by him. But the power of assuming that life of its own had been imparted to it by Mr Sam himself who was always too modest to claim any credit. There were never more than three people who saw that. Dick Carter was one, though only in his early days, before his marriage; and I was another."

"Who was the third?" Lady Clark asked when Miss Charlebois stopped.

The older woman looked strangely at the younger; and it

was half a minute before she replied. "It was the second Maud in his life."

"Maud Dolittle!" Lady Clark exclaimed. "But . . ."

"I know. I know. But don't you see . . ."

"I don't."

"In certain ways the three Clarks were so exactly alike."

"You mean . . ."

"When Mr Edmund returned from the war, he was, physically, Mr Sam resurrected."

"But that is not what the senator says. According to him my husband was a reincarnation of his grandfather."

"In his methods. But physically they were all three alike."

"I have often wished to know more of Maud Dolittle. I saw her once, in the railway station at Montreal, when Sir Edmund and I were engaged to be married. It's of no use, of course, to try to hide anything from you who have seen it all. Suspecting that there was something between the two, I could not very well ask my future husband for enlightenment; with my father-in-law I have never dared to touch on the subject. It was the briefest of glimpses I had of her; but I thought then, and I still think that, if I could have become acquainted with her, I should have admired, perhaps I should have loved her."

"She is still living, you know. She has a house in the Gatineau Valley. I have no reason to be grateful to her; perhaps I'll tell you about it one day; there was a time when I had my own dreams. I will say this. She was the most dynamic woman I had ever met. But at the time of which we are speaking she was a star newly risen in the mill. Hers was the most spectacular career; she came as a clerk; within three years she was vice-president of the whole concern. She had only two passions. One was the mill; the other she shared with all the women who lived in contact with Mr Sam."

"Is it possible?" Lady Clark cried.

"Granted that she was a genius, Mr Sam inspired her."

Lady Clark sat pensive.

"But we are digressing," the older woman went on. "I must come to the point. This house was built at last; and Mr Sam and Maud Clark were living in it with a retinue of two score servants and retainers like myself. After six or seven years of married life little Edmund was born; and a few weeks later Mr Rudyard had a stroke and died. No doubt you have heard of Mr Swann . . ."

"I haven't. But go on."

"He was an employee in one of the concerns connected

74

with the mill. It was an open secret that, in some mysterious way—I've never succeeded in clearing it up for myself—this Mr Swann and old Mr Rudyard had been connected. At any rate, one night late in the fall, it was Mr Swann who brought the news of the old man's stroke to this house. I'll tell you the details another time.

"That death had national reverberations. From coast to coast the newspapers were full of it, calling the dead man a Titan of Finance. Nobody mentioned Mr Sam, except to say that likely he would be the new president. The mill, as you know, was owned at the time by a stock company, not, as now, by the family. Many expected that the end of its growth had come.

"The old gentleman was buried at last; and the day after the funeral Mr Sam drove down to the Flour Building to take over. For some reason or other he came home afoot, at noon; and I had hardly set eyes on him when I knew that he had gone through some shattering experience. I remember thinking that it must have had something to do with his having passed the Terrace, walking."

"You mean the workmen's town."

"Yes. That long, flat stretch of 'back-to-backs' as Mr Sam called them. He hated them as a flaw in the scheme of things; they always moved him; he preferred not to look at them. But, this house standing where it did, he had to pass the abomination whenever he went to office or mill. I remember his mentioning, one day, over the dinner table, very briefly, as he always spoke when he spoke of himself, that he had had to go down there because a mill-hand had been injured. 'When one comes to think about it,' he added, 'the contrast of that sort of life and . . .' His glance embraced the dining-room where we were sitting, the 'small' dining-room, four times the size of a whole cottage down there.

"Well, when he arrived in the park, we were all outside, on the lawn at the foot of the southern hill. It was a marvellous fall day, mild and clear; and it was the first time that old Dr Cruikshank—he died before you came—had permitted Mrs Clark to go out. She was slowly and imperiously walking about with the help of a tall cane which she never discarded again. I was with her, of course; and so was the nurse who was carrying little Edmund, about a month old.

"I wish I could give you the atmosphere of the scene. Across the lake, the hillsides were golden-yellow, for the leaves of the aspens had just turned colour; the lake lay smooth as a mirror; the air had that bronzed appearance which it never takes except in the fall. Perhaps it was the fact that, at that time of year, every phase of the seasons is so transient, so brief; one hardly expects to see the same sight twice. You look; and you look again; and the aspect has changed. When I think of that setting, my impression is of something that partook of the nature of a miracle and seemed only half real.

"Yet Mrs Clark was real enough. She had had a hard time of it in her confinement and for the three or four weeks that had followed; and so she was enjoying herself, taking long steps, energetically, planting her cane which she grasped at the height of her shoulder. Mistrusting her newly-recovered vigour, I kept close by her side without letting her see my solicitude. The nurse trailed behind, crooning to the child. Up and down we walked, up and down, parallel to the front of the house, and every now and then we were conscious of Perkins, the portly, middle-aged English butler, peering out from the veranda, as though he, too, was watching over Mrs Clark or anxiously waiting for the arrival of the master of the house.

"We were facing the south hill with its dense plantation of young maples, crimson in their fall garb, backed by oaks, choco-late-coloured, with the sunlight streaming down over them, when we suddenly saw Mr Clark descending the winding drive-way.

"Perhaps I should add that old Mrs Carter, Maud's mother, was still with us; but she was in the house; she would have left us a few days before; but the death and the funeral had delayed her.

"The moment Mrs Clark saw her husband, she sang out, 'At last, at last! I've been watching Perkins. He's rung the stables a dozen times to find out whether the carriage had been sum-moned. We are to have a *soufflé*; it might fall together. We're famished. Did you walk?'

"Mr Clark did not reply till he had joined the group; but his smile betrayed the effort it cost him. Then, 'I walked,' he said; and, having kissed his wife's cheek which she tilted down to him, for she was taller than he, he went to the nurse who was presenting the child. 'I had to make up my mind,' he added. 'So I started early.'

"'And did you make up that mind of yours?' She touched his chin with a playful finger, her other hand resting on the cane.

"'I believe it's made itself up of its own accord.'

"'Good!' she cried. 'I was afraid we'd have the mill for lunch.'

"I, wishing to take the edge off that remark, laughed. 'Since Mr Clark is on time after all, we'll have the *soufflé* instead.'

"It had not escaped me that Mr Clark had winced. His wife never took him seriously, in connection with the mill. He, or it, remained the target of her jests even now.

"But Maud, as usual, was merciless. I have mentioned that this was the first time since his father's death that Mr Clark had been down to the office. So she, with a sort of played-up affectation of tom-boy gaiety, sang out, '*En avant!* Let's have that *soufflé*, Mr President.'

"I could see that the sarcasm she put into that last word touched him to the quick. In order not to betray himself, he turned back to the nurse. 'Just a moment. I want to have another look at the mite.'

"But as they turned to the veranda, Maud, as if to make up for a moment ago, though I've often wondered how far she was conscious of how she wounded him, took his arm and said teasingly, 'Well, old boy, are we getting big and strong again? Walking like this on the lawn? Never been ill at all, have we? How does it like him?'

"'It likes him well enough,' Mr Clark said, entering into her whimsicality though his smile remained strained. 'But the old girl wants to be careful.'

"'She is!'—with the intonation of a male bass.

"At the steps she released her husband's arm to let him hold the door for her.

"As I said, Maud's mother was at the house; she had come up from Toronto for the confinement; and there was a brief passage-at-arms between her and Mr Clark in the hall.

"Whatever you might think of Mrs Clark, she was a lady. Her mother was not. She considered her son-in-law a mere appendage to her daughter. I had known the family in Toronto where they were cutting a wide swath. The father was no doubt making a considerable income; but it was common talk that they were living beyond their means. Even fifty thousand a year is poverty when you spend seventy-five. So the mother worshipped money. But nearly all the money there was among the Clarks, even though it already ran into millions, had been the old gentleman's. Mr Clark junior, therefore, had counted for nothing; and while he was too modest to assert himself, it must have been hard even for him to put up with her snubs.

"As I entered behind Mrs Clark who had been directing the nurse to put the child to sleep on the veranda, I just heard the towering old lady say to him, 'I should like to see you before you go out again.'

" 'Very well,' he said; and, to his wife, 'Shall we go in?'

"At luncheon, after a few minutes of casual conversation, Mr Clark asked, 'Has the doctor been in this morning?'

" 'He has,' Maud said as if refuting an aspersion. 'And he gave me an almost clean bill of health.'

"As though, by that remark, reminded of something, Mrs Carter asked, 'Did you see Mr Beatty today, Sam?'

" 'I didn't. I saw nobody but Miss Dolittle and Miss Albright.'

" 'Miss Domuch!' Mrs Clark mocked. 'Was she in black?'

" 'I didn't notice. I did see Miss Albright's flowing weeds.'

" 'Sam!' Mrs Carter reproved as if he had hinted at some impropriety. Momentarily she forgot that he was the president now. Sententiously she added, 'When a man doesn't notice a woman's clothes, he notices her.'

" 'According to that,' Mrs Clark said, 'Sam didn't notice Miss Albright at any rate.'

"Again, to come to Mr Clark's relief, I spoke. 'Not every converse of a valid proposition is valid itself.'

" 'Pedagogue!' Maud cried. 'Does Euclid apply to psychology?'

"Mr Clark glanced at his mother-in-law. 'Any reason for asking?'

" 'About Mr Beatty? . . . I'll see you later.'

"You knew Mr Beatty, Lady Clark, didn't you? For decades he was solicitor for the mill, and Mr Rudyard's private adviser."

Lady Clark nodded. "He became my husband's later on."

Miss Charlebois smiled in confirmation. "But Mrs Clark," she went on, "who knew her mother's mind, mischievously turned to her husband. 'Mother would like to hear the will read befores he leaves.'

" 'Oh, the will . . .'

" 'Naturally,' Mrs Carter defended herself. 'I have a right to be interested, have I not?'

" 'Of course,' Mr Clark said. 'I'll try to arrange it. We might have Charles for tea tomorrow. I'm sorry I shall be busy today.'

" 'Tomorrow will do,' the old lady said tartly. 'Unless you're in a hurry to be rid of me . . . Who is going to step into your shoes now?' she asked after a while. So far, Mr Clark had been vice-president and sales-manager only; and those were just then nominal titles. The real sales-manager was Miss Dolittle; and so long as Mr Rudyard had been alive, the vice-presidency had carried no serious responsibilities.

" 'Nothing can be decided till the shareholders meet,' Mr Clark said evasively. 'For the moment I have moved into the president's office.'

"Now that has always puzzled me. It is for that reason, no doubt, that it has remained in my memory. Honours always had to be forced on him; he did the work; but as a rule he remained behind the scenes. You know that twenty years later it was he to whom the knighthood was offered; it went to his son only when he had declined. I mean I have never been able to understand why, the day after the funeral, he should have promoted himself as it were without the usual shareholders' or directors' sanction. There were other puzzling things. Perhaps they were connected with Mr Rudyard's will which was read the next day when, of course, I was not present. But we are not discussing Mr Clark. We are concerned with Maud."

"You must have a marvellous memory," Lady Clark said. "All this was forty years ago."

Miss Charlebois smiled. "It isn't memory only," she said. "I kept a diary. You must know there was a time when I had the ambition of writing a history of the mill. It is the gaps in my knowledge, and they are considerable, which prevented my doing so . . . . Now you may have the impression that I criticize Mrs Clark. I don't mean to. In many ways she was a marvellous woman. I'll give you an example of her admirable qualities right now; perhaps it illustrates what you called charm.

"Luncheon over, it was decided that coffee was to be served in this hall. Mrs Clark rose, standing at the head of the table while a footman drew her chair away and handed her the cane. She curled her lip. 'So we did have the mill for lunch after all,' she said. But simultaneously she raised her free hand with a smile at her husband, as a summons for him to offer his arm.

"At the door, she stopped to let me and her mother precede, holding him back. When we hesitated, she called out, in her quasi-theatrical way, 'Out with you, mother! Out, Odette! Don't you see I want this boy of mine to myself for a moment?'

"We laughed and passed on. Maud, for whom servants simply did not exist, lowered her lips to Mr Sam's before we were out of earshot and whispered, 'Must you go?'

" 'I'm afraid I must,' he replied, tilting his head to meet her lips.

" 'Very well, Mr President,' she said in a caressing voice as they followed us, thereby taking the edge off her previous taunts.

"When the footman served the coffee, Mr Clark said briefly,

'The carriage, please'; and five minutes later—Mr Clark having reminded his mother-in-law that she had wished to see him and received the answer that her question at the dinner table had served her purpose—he rose, bent down to his wife who remained sitting, and passed out to where the carriage was waiting in front of the open door.

" 'The office,' we heard him say; and then he was gone.

"I was looking at Mrs Clark who was sitting erect in her arm-chair, the cane leaning by her side. I was startled to see her expression; it was not that of a happy woman."

Sitting in the car, swiftly gliding along over 'The Loop', the senator suddenly realized that they were already on the home stretch. He looked at his watch. McAllister must be a faster driver than Waugh. Of course, when Lady Clark was in the car, none of the chauffeurs drove her over fifty miles an hour. The senator felt he could not yet face the familiar surroundings of the house. He bent forward, opened the slide in the partition, and said sharply, "Around the loop once more. Slowly."

"Very good, sir," the chauffeur said, slowing down.

The senator felt a twinge of emptiness; it was not yet hunger; but it was the beginning of it. It did not matter.

After lunch, that day, he had returned to the office. And with that thought, as with a click, his mind switched back into the past which, to him, was living with a sudden harassing intensity.

As always, Miss Albright met him in the boardroom. "The correspondence, Mr Clark?"

"Not today. Mr Beatty in his office? I want to see him. After that I shall be busy again. Have a table placed over there, with a girl mounting guard. It is imperative that I be not disturbed. When you see me coming back from Mr Beatty's, ring Mr Swann and ask him to be good enough to come up. Let him enter without announcing; but no one else."

He spoke without emphasis; but Miss Albright felt that he considered her responsible for Mr Carter's intrusion. "Very well, Mr Clark."

Sam entered a suite which was the only one in the whole building to bear a name-plate instead of a title : 'Charles Beatty, Q.C.'

Passing through the anteroom where Mr Beatty's secretary rose from her desk while two stenographers bent more closely over their work, he opened the inner door marked 'Private'.

"Hello, Sam," said the medium-sized, delicate-looking occupant of the room. His movements as he crooked his elbows and planted his hands flat on the desk to raise himself, his middle fingers touching each other, were strikingly angular. His face, surmounted by a bald skull, resembled, when he smiled, a death's-head, with his lips drawn back as in a snarl. This was the man who for ten years had been Rudyard Clark's legal adviser and largely responsible for the financial structure of the concern.

"Hello, Charlie," Sam said unsmilingly. "You have Father's will?"

"In the vault, Sam." Which referred to a steel-and-stone chamber on the ground floor, behind the offices of Langholm Light and Power.

"My mother-in-law," Sam went on, "has outstayed her time on account of the death. She leaves for the east at midnight tomorrow. Could you come over for tea, tomorrow, and bring that will?"

"I could do that, Sam. Anything to oblige the mentor."

"Say four o'clock. I'll send a carriage."

"Very good of you. Thanks."

And, turning, Sam passed out.

In the boardroom his instructions had been obeyed. As, still in his coat, hat in hand, he crossed over, he spoke to the girl. "Let Mr Swann enter; but nobody else unless I myself change the order."

Half turning to open his private door, he saw Miss Albright in the opposite room reaching for the telephone on her desk.

In his office, he deposited coat and hat and sat down. The trembling of his fingers betrayed his excitement. With an effort, taking the manilla envelope from its drawer, he focused his mind on the task ahead.

He had certain facts which raised certain presumptions. The problem was so to use facts known as to compel a surrender of those unknown....

Within a few minutes Swann entered briskly. "You were asking for me, Mr Clark?"

Without a word Sam waved his hand to the straight-backed chair facing him. He gave a shrewd glance to the man's clothes. Swann never looked well dressed; his figure prevented that; but his double-breasted blue-serge suit was of excellent cloth and made by a good tailor.

Swann obeyed the gesture. As always, his shining skull was beaded with sweat; but his broad, ordinarily loose body was tense; his step was poised like that of a sword-dancer or tight-rope walker; his face, commonly red, was pale. He would have instilled pity had it not been for the fact that he tried to carry the situation off jauntily.

Leaning back, Sam took a violent grip on himself. His task was that of a surgeon faced with an unpleasant, perhaps dangerous operation.

"I want you to explain two things, Swann," he said. "Firstly, how you came to be with my father when he had his stroke. Secondly, why he paid you blackmail."

Swann's thin lips straightened. Then he gave a nod. "As for the first question, I have explained. I needed exercise. I came on him . . ."

"It's no use, Swann," Sam interrupted. "I advise you to speak the truth. I have asked Dr Cruikshank and Mr Carter to observe a strict silence with regard to the circumstances under which my father was found. Like myself, they observed things which were puzzling. Unless you speak the truth—and when I hear it, I shall know it—I must ask the police to investigate."

Swann pulled himself up and spoke in a new, scoffing tone. "You wouldn't do that, Mr Clark." His eyes, so far glued to the desk, met Sam's for a moment squarely.

"I shouldn't?" In spite of his icy tone Sam's heart beat wildly.

"I don't think so."

"Why not?"

"You are bound to protect your father's good name."

There was a pause, Sam casting about in his mind as in a dark chamber. "Well," he said at last, "that is something. And it is quite true. I am not anxious to have things divulged which might be liable to misinterpretation. But I must see clear in the matter myself."

"I'll tell you the literal truth, Mr Clark. I had called at your father's house. I had private business to discuss. As a matter of fact, he owed me money; and I wanted a larger amount than he was prepared to pay. He grew angry; he felt in need of what, if you don't mind, I'll call a quarrel. It was he who proposed that we go out; he didn't want his housekeeper to overhear us. It was he who led the way up the hill; and he talked himself into that excitement which brought on the stroke. He threatened me; he shouted at me; and then he fell down."

"On the grass?"

"No. On the road."

"I noticed sand on his clothes," Sam nodded. "What next?"

"I carried him to the side of the road."

"Did you reflect that that might give your story away?"

"I couldn't help it. If he'd been dead, I'd have left him. But he might have been run over by buggy or wagon."

"Why did you not tell this part of your story at once?"

"I was excited. I didn't think. I hoped your father would recover."

"You hoped it? Why?"

Swann raised a trembling hand. "I am human," he said.

Sam shook his head. "Doesn't go down, Swann." And, after a moment, "You were in a devil of a fix and wanted my father to pull you out."

Swann drooped. Beads of sweat rolled down from his skull, "You know?" he asked.

Sam knew nothing of what he wanted to know; yet his had not entirely been a random shot. If this man had hoped for the old man's recovery, there had been a cogent reason for doing so. Otherwise he would have left him and never breathed word of the fact that he had been with him. Sam's mind was clearing. It would be as well to leave the man under the impression that he knew more than he did.

"I know how much he was willing to pay you that night. I know the date when these transactions began and the amount of every payment he made you. I know you had a hold on my father. I am acting this minute at the wish of my father, expressed to me years ago. There is only one thing I don't know. The nature of your hold on him. Now, Swann, what was that nature?"

Again Swann looked squarely at the man who was now his employer. More than a minute went by while he was weighing his chances. Then he pulled himself together again. "Will you promise me impunity if I tell you?"

"So you admit your crime?"

"*My* crime!" Swann exclaimed.

"Naturally. You were exacting blackmail."

"I merely asked for my small share of the loot," Swann said with unexpected brutality. "If there had been any justice, I'd have had hundreds of thousands instead of a paltry fifteen."

"Good," Sam said, growing cool on one plane of his being, while on another he felt as if his substance were melting away. "Now you'll have to tell me; or we'll have to have this out in a court of law."

"Very well, sir. But don't blame me if it hurts."

"I'll take care of myself."

Again there was a pause. Swann wiped his bulging forehead with a silk handkerchief. In extreme agitation he prepared to speak.

"Up to the time the old mill burned down, I was, as you know, your father's bookkeeper. I came once a week, on Saturdays, to post the ledger and to make out the statement for the insurance company. The premiums were adjusted on the basis of the stock on hand that day; and so, of course, was the amount for which it was insured.

"On Saturday, April 22, 1888, I was prevented by domestic circumstances from coming. I saw your father at night and proposed to go early on Monday so as to have the statement ready by ten when Mat Tindal was in the habit of calling for it. For reasons which I leave to you to guess when you've heard the story, your father insisted on my coming on Sunday. When, during the night from Sunday to Monday, the mill burned down, the books were posted, the statement ready, lying on the table in the office which you know.

"Now your father had recently bought thirty carloads of wheat which were shipped from some point in Assiniboia where arrangements had been made to issue payment against the bill of lading. I, of course, knew nothing of these details except what I could infer from the documents to hand. You know how secretive your father was.

"When it came to making out that statement, I found a copy of that bill of lading; and when I scanned it, I was doubtful whether its date was April 4 or 14; the '1' in front of the '4' was a mere smudge. Since, however, the bill was placed there for me, I decided that the date must have been April 4; and I entered the shipment as received at the mill and unloaded on April 21. If it had been April 14, it might not have reached Langholm; but then your father would have held the bill of lading back. I happened to know that a shipment had been unloaded on April 21; and I inferred that it had been this wheat. Then I became doubtful again; for there was a second bill of lading, for 3,000 odd bushels, shipped from Winnipeg, bought on the track. It might have been this wheat which was unloaded on April 21.

"I was in a hurry; this Sunday work threatened to interfere with my attendance at church. It was utterly unnecessary to have the statement completed before ten o'clock Monday morning. Yet I could not risk incurring your father's displeasure by disobeying orders. I made up my mind to see him on Monday morning and ask him. If the shipment had not been received, I could rewrite the statement with this entry corrected. It wouldn't have taken more than half an hour to do so. The correction would have meant a saving on the week's premium.

"But by some perverse impulse, just before leaving, I picked that bill of lading up once more; and I became so doubtful that I took it to the window to scan it closely. I convinced myself that the date was April 14; the bill had found its way to the table by mistake.

"It was nearly eleven. You know I've always been a churchman. At the time I was people's warden. I hated to miss the service. As I said, there was no necessity to straighten this out before Monday.

"Now it so happened that, in going to the window, I was, without being aware of it, holding an eraser in my hand. With no intention whatever, out of sheer perplexity, I gave the slip of paper a flick with that hand. It was the idlest gesture in the world. But to my amazement the smudge of a '1' disappeared under the chance touch of the rubber. It didn't matter. Your father knew whether that wheat was in his bins or not. If not, he wouldn't want to pay the extra premium. He carried every smallest detail of his business under his hat.

"At this moment I caught sight of another slip of paper on the floor. It was the warehouse voucher which shouldn't have been at the office; it belonged at the mill. On Saturday or Monday no doubt could have arisen; you'd have been at the office; Rogers would have been at the mill. But here was something just as good. This voucher was signed by Rogers. I was angry at myself for having picked it up; for it answered my doubt. On April 21 three thousand bushels only had been unloaded. My statement was wrong. But I wasn't going to correct it. Yet, right or wrong, it had to be consistent with the papers at my disposal.

"It was fully eleven. The rector was waiting; he did not like to begin the service without the wardens. But he could not wait long.

"And suddenly it struck me like a huge joke that the statement would be consistent enough if, on the warehouse voucher, there was another three in front of the 3,000-odd. It showed only approximate weights, arrived at by measurement, not by reweighing; they were meant merely to confirm roughly those on the bills of lading.

"All that was needed, then, was to look up the market value of wheat on Monday morning. Mat Tindal did that. It never struck me to pocket the voucher. If it could stray to the office, it could stray anywhere; nobody would have suspected me. But it was such a joke for Rogers, of all men, to be caught out that I reached for a pencil and, imitating Rogers' hand put a '3' in front of the 3,000-odd.

"Straightening the papers, I hurried to the church. I laughed to myself. The thing did not matter. It would be corrected; it even occurred to me that the bins would most likely not have been able to hold that additional 30,000; your father kept them filled. But I didn't know and cared less. I'd go into the thing on Monday morning.

"And then, that night, the mill burned down."

There was a long pause. Swann wiped the dome of his skull.

As for Sam, the solid earth had moved under his feet. His father, grim, gruff, but incapable, so he would have thought, of anything that was questionable in a moral sense! He stirred; and then he became conscious that he dared not ask Swann whether he meant to insinuate that his father had set fire to the mill. "And nobody had any suspicion?" he muttered feebly.

"Apparently not. The statement had always been made out on Saturday. Even when made out on Monday morning, they were dated Saturday; they were Saturday statements, no matter when they were made out."

"Go on," Sam said.

"There is nothing to add. The claim was settled on that basis."

"As though the grain in transit had been at the mill?"

"Exactly."

"How do you know?"

"I ask you," Swann argued. "I had, on occasion, made out other statements; for the bank, for instance. I knew pretty accurately how your father stood. I figured it all over, later on. It was that thirty-odd thousand which enabled him, not exactly to build—he could have sold additional stock for that—but to gain control."

Sam's hand trembled. Control! That had been his father's chief aim and purpose.

"It was I," Swann went on, "who, by a joke, gave him control."

"You are very sure of your facts," Sam said slowly.

No less excited than Sam, Swann hung his head.

It was this excitement of the other man which enabled Sam to say with some measure of firmness, "Come on, Swann, what next?"

Once more the beads of sweat on Swann's skull began to run. Then, for the third time, he pulled himself together. "I spoke to him one night in the street. I had been earning fifty dollars a month, most of it coming from Ticknor's store; and Mr Ticknor had always given me the Saturday afternoon off for the work at the mill. But, from overwork and worry, I had made an annoying mistake; and Mr Ticknor had discharged me. I had a crippled wife; she's dead now; I had a daughter who wanted to train for a teacher. I asked your father to make provision for me; the mill was being built; jobs went begging. He refused. . . . And then I dropped him a hint. He flew off the handle. Getting angry, I told him that it was I who had changed the figure on the voucher; and I claimed my share of the loot— I used that word. He asked me to come to his house. It was the night of the inauguration."

"I know," Sam said.

"He put me in charge of Langholm Light and Power at a hundred and fifty a month."

"Which sum has since been raised two or three times?"

"Twice."

"To how much?"

"Three thousand a year. I had made good at the job."

"Then how about these sums?"

"I had to have a nurse for my wife; and a housekeeper; the place I lived in was too small; it had only two rooms."

"I see," Sam said. "I see."

"Besides," Swann went on, agitatedly, "I considered myself entitled to half the loot. As I said, I could have asked for much more."

"You had fifteen thousand before my father's death. That was half."

Again there was a long pause. Swann did not answer.

Sam picked up the manilla envelope. He had to lash himself into a display of decision. "You said my father owed you money. What was the occasion of this latest demand of yours?"

For the third time Swann betrayed extreme distress; for the third time he wiped his capacious skull. "Will you promise me impunity?"

"Not till I have all the facts."

Swann fought a silent battle. Then he threw himself on Sam's mercy. "I'd been playing the stock-market with Light-and-Power funds."

Sam whistled through his teeth. With a quick, mental glance he gauged his father's predicament. If that had happened once, it might, it would happen again. His father had been in this man's clutches. Giving him money was like pouring it into a bottomless pit. It was this realization which had caused his death; that death had handed the problem on to him, Sam; it was he who must act. One point remained unresolved. Did Swann mean to insinuate that his father had not only taken advantage of the situation by keeping silent; that, in addition, he had deliberately seized an opportunity by letting the mill burn down? Swann knew. But he, Sam, did not dare to ask the question; it simply would not out. Yet he despised himself for keeping silent on that point. He rose and said in a changed voice, "I can't go on employing you, Swann. You see that yourself. You'll have to clear out. This envelope was marked for you by my father; you see his hand. It proves that it was not the first time, that night, that the question had been raised. What sum did you ask for?"

"Three thousand five hundred."

"Is that the amount of the defalcation?"

"That's the exact amount."

"Very well. I shall clean that mess up out of my private pocket. I shall protect my father's memory for the sake of my son. You have your house. I advise you to sell it at once. What did it cost you?"

"Four thousand five hundred, including the lot."

"You've lived in it for how long?"

"Eight years."

"You can't expect to get full value. I'll drop Mr Tindal a hint to let you have three thousand five hundred. Is that satisfactory?"

"It'll have to be."

"You'll have that plus these two thousand to start life over with. Your daughter, I take it, is provided for; she has her job as a teacher. This is a payment made by my father; I want to make it clear that I am not paying blackmail. I'll give you a week before I'll have the books of Langholm Light and Power audited. You had better cross the sea and go back where you came from. The shareholders might get wind of the matter. I shall protect them from loss; but once they start on your trail, I can't do a thing. If, a week from today, you are still about, matters will take their course. I repeat, I shall pay no blackmail. Whatever my father has done, I haven't done it. I shall indemnify the insurance company; but I won't shoulder an incubus; I'd rather let it come to a full exposure. You can start life over elsewhere. You aren't penniless. . . . And now you'd better go. No. Take that money. My father marked the envelope for you."

It had cost him an effort to speak with some show of assurance; but he felt far from assured. If this man chose, he held even him in his power. The thing had to grow in his mind till all its implication stood revealed; so far, they were by no means apparent.

Swann stood for a moment, swallowing. Sam had the uncomfortable suspicion that he was going to do something melodramatic, throw himself at his feet or at least thank him. So he looked forbidding.

At last, wiping the bulging dome of his skull, Swann turned and went to the door without a word.

That night, having made arrangements with Mat Tindal, the pompous president of Langholm Real Estate, Sam could neither sleep nor think. This mental paralysis continued through the next day, even while, in the afternoon, the will was being read in the library—an occasion on which Charles Beatty, for once, remained serious throughout.

Figures and names of minor legatees went past Sam's ears; even when his wife was remembered with three separate bequests, he barely listened. Only when his own name occurred as that of the residuary legatee did he give a momentary heed to what was being read; and even in that part of the document only one thing struck him, namely that he was now the owner of, or in control of, not one but half a dozen concerns.

When, the reading over, the ladies rose to join Miss Charlebois in the hall, he detained the lawyer by a glance.

"I don't understand," he said when they were alone. "Are all these things, the dam, the elevators, The Terrace, the Flour Building, and the power plant, held by separate companies?"

"Didn't you know, Sam?"

"I know nothing; except that the will throws responsibilities on me for which I am not prepared."

The lawyer gave him a curious glance. Sam did not look like a well man and knew it. He was greenish in his pallor.

"Listen," Charles Beatty said. "I happen to be aware of the fact that Bob"—Mr Stevens—"is trying to acquire merit in the heaven of your favour by preparing statements for you. He holds office in all the companies. I could explain the structure; but I haven't the figures; I'd have to ask him myself or look them up."

"All right," Sam said. "Let us join the ladies."

At midnight Mrs Carter left for the east, with high praise for the will which had made her daughter a wealthy woman. Sam spent another sleepless night. Twenty millions in shares, at market value!

Next morning, he felt that he should show himself at the mill. But his relation to that mill was changed: he could not do it. He went to the office. Miss Albright, with her staff, had moved over to his side.

On his desk lay a sheaf of statements prepared by Mr Stevens. He spent an hour in studying them. But, though they confirmed Charles Beatty's hint as to the complexity of the structure, he was as much puzzled as ever. Pressing the button under his desk, he asked Miss Albright to summon Mr Stevens.

Within a few minutes the young man entered, smiling, debonair, arrogant. Like most of the executives of the mill he was small and slender, but athletic and wiry. He was dressed with an exaggeration of what was fashionable which provoked furtive glances and smiles among his subordinates. He worked as indefatigably in the interests of the mill as Miss Dolittle; and he knew the value of his services. Often he spent half the night in the building, analysing figures and interpreting facts. What had recommended him to the late Mr Clark for rapid promotion would, by many, have been considered a defect: he did not possess a trace of imagination. Whatever was he accepted; he studied and defended it. Nobody could outdo him in the strict logic and tenacity with which he reasoned from, and held to, a given basis of fact; the conclusions arrived at he followed up in an unhesitating, ruthless way which commanded respect and even admiration. But it never occurred to him to examine that basis or to challenge a fact. Nobody, at the present moment, was so well fitted to ensure continuity. Brief as the life of the mill had been, Bob Stevens represented its tradition; and that tradition had resumed itself in one aim: profit. Profit was his god; not *his* profit; not anyone's; profit in the abstract.

Sam nodded to him, distantly, coolly, as was his way. "Sit down," he said. "I've been going over these statements. There are some points on which I'd like additional information. There's that statement of Light and Power. I'd never seen one. It was a sort of pocket enterprise of my father's, was it? He owned all the stock?"

"He did. No statement was ever published."

"I see. But there are files which throw light on the thing? Surely no five millions were ever invested in the concern?"

"The original capitalization was of a hundred thousand, of

which twenty stood in the names of Messrs. Ticknor and Tindal. They were transferred to the late Mr Clark in 1894. The capitalization was twice increased."

"By an issue of stock?"

"No. The first time your father sold the company the area covered by the lake which it had held under a lease. That added eight hundred thousand to the capital; for Mr Clark took payment in shares. When the dam was raised, out of earnings, the capitalization was raised to its present amount by issuing a bonus."

"And Light and Power owns that dam?"

"It does."

Sam pondered. At last he understood that Light and Power, a 'pocket enterprise' of his father's, could hold the mill as such to ransom. It could cut off the power indeed.

"What about this lease mentioned here?"

Mr Stevens laughed. "It *is* a bit involved. Light and Power owns dams, turbines, and dynamos. It doesn't own the vaults."

"Naturally. They are part of the mill."

"Architecturally," Mr Stevens agreed. "They are leased to Light and Power under a ninety-nine-year lease, against a rental of thirty thousand a year."

"I don't find that thirty thousand in the statement of the mill."

"Not in the operating statement; in the balance sheet; under the heading of Real Estate."

"I see." Sam dropped the statement to pick up another. "Here is the operating statement of the mill for the first eight months of the year. What constitutes the enormous cost of the power used?"

"The mill pays for the current it needs."

"At what rate?"

"At the rate at which Light and Power sells current."

"Do you mean to say, at the rate at which a householder buys current for lighting purposes?"

"At half that rate. Current used for power is cheaper than current used for light."

"And the rate for lighting is ten cents a kilowatt hour?"

"Exactly."

"The mill, then, with its consumption of hundreds of thousands of kilowatt hours a month pays at the rate of five cents?"

"Precisely." Bob Stevens held his steel-grey, arrogant eyes steadily fixed on those of the new president.

"It's staggering," Sam said at last.

"It's where the profits of Light and Power come from."

"Last year it paid dividends . . ." Sam searched in his papers.

"Of eleven point two five per cent a quarter," Bob Stevens prompted.

"And all that passed through Swann's hands?"

"Oh no. Swann had nothing to do with it. He handled local business only."

"All right," Sam said. "Can you offhandedly give me the figure for the cost of that power per kilowatt hour?"

"I can. Point eight nine four cents."

Sam sat and stared.

"That," Stevens went on, "is the cost of current supplied at the mill. For private consumption, the cost of transmission must be added."

"But it takes account of the cost of the lease?"

"It does."

Sam sat silent for fully a minute. Then, "Where is the statement of the elevator company? The capital is two million dollars; of which my father held . . ."

"Sixty per cent. The balance is held by Winnipeg shareholders."

"Dividends on that stock have been comparatively modest?"

"Four and a half per cent a quarter."

"Deriving from two sources: speculation and storage. Who pays storage?"

"The mill; for its requirements until used."

"I see," Sam said again. "That explains why Western Flour Mills, each owning its own equipment, paid a higher rate of profit than the Langholm mill. Who owns Western Flour Mills?"

"The Langholm mill owns sixty per cent of the stock."

"Whoever controls Langholm, therefore, controls Western Flour Mills?"

"Exactly."

"I see," Sam said for the last time. "Thank you, Stevens. I think that will make matters clear."

Stevens rose. "Any further information . . . I shall be happy."

Sam had listened without moving a muscle in his face. Now he paced the floor for half an hour.

The mill had been the mill to him, comprising its necessary adjuncts, dam, elevators, turbines, as parts of the whole. In reality . . .

There was the Flour Building, another independent concern. The little white frame office with its two vacant lots in which he had been sitting ten years ago and which, at the time, could not have been valued at more than $800 stood on the books as sold to Flour Building Limited for one hundred thousand.

In the building, all the various concerns had their offices. All paid rent for floor space used; the total amounting to $175,000 a year. Yet these concerns were held in one hand, his own. . . .

What was the meaning of it all? There was only one meaning, that of disguising and dividing the profits of the huge concern, profits which in a single aggregate would have been monstrous. Only one concern yielded monstrous profits undisguised: Langholm Light and Power; and it was a pocket concern of the owners which published no statements.

Given a certain purpose, the thing was a marvel of organization. It testified to the dead man's powers as a financier in a manner which was a revelation to Sam. In spite of his inferiority complex and his rebellion against his father, he had felt superior to the old man. In sheer self-defence he had fostered that feeling. He had an appreciation of great literature; he had a keenly developed sense, developed by his marriage, for serious music; he took an interest in world affairs. But, while he would never have wished to do so, he was honest enough to admit that he would have lacked the ability to devise that financial structure which his father had built.

His father's ability to create half a dozen enterprises at once, all interlocking, yet all separate, each preying on the others and yet contributing its share to the welfare of the whole, testified to a power verging on genius.

Sam thought of the old man in the chair at the shareholders' meeting: bullying, threatening, cajoling in turns, juggling one thing against the other till he got what he wanted. In spite of passionate opposition he had passed his resolutions without resorting to the power of his control. His control had remained in reserve.

"Control!" What would the loss of control have meant?

It would have meant the probability of exposure . . .

Yet he had driven even mill-stock to a fabulous figure. . .

Admiration? For the driving power, the shrewdness of the old man—yes. Admiration even for the secretiveness with which he had screened his machinations from the eyes of others, even his son. Even that son must not know all while the old man lived . . .

Sam had often said to himself that his father, in doing what he had done, had done a great thing for the country. There had been doubts, though. He had thought of the mills driven out of operation by this colossus; he had thought of the mill-hands who lived in poverty; he had thought of the farmers who sold their wheat at a figure below its ultimate value; he had thought of the millions who were paying more for their bread than, on a reasonable calculation of costs, it was worth; he had thought of the secret agreements with the few remaining independent mills; and now he was thinking of the complexity of the structure, devised for the purpose of veiling the aggregate of the profits.

As for an outside enquiry, a Royal Commission, say, probing into the earnings of the milling industry, his father would have been safe. The balance sheets of the mill told a simple, straightforward story. They showed a high rate of profit; but a rate not incommensurate, by accepted standards, with the amount of enterprise and investment that had gone into its making. But—there was the rub—essentially, the picture presented was untrue!

"The Terrace Limited!" Having walked about for half an hour, he took up the statement of this second 'pocket enterprise'. To his relief it showed a low rate of profit: about ten per cent per annum.

Again he paced about. He simply could not fathom it. His father had been the pioneer, hard, ruthless, grasping. He himself was of the second generation: critical, soft, full of doubts and hesitations; and he realized that this was in part because that first generation in this industrial revolution had been able to give its successors that education which it had lacked itself.

But those were problems to be thought out later. For the moment, there was a definite task. He would build a public library; he would make provision that gifted children of mill-hands could attend high school and college. He would found that recreation hall; he would endow a maternity ward in the hospital; he would do no end of things. Beatty had estimated his inheritance at twenty million dollars . . .

But, and he stopped in his walk, there was one thing he could no longer do. He could not leave the mill to run itself. His father's crime had made him, the son, the slave of the mill. . .

Suddenly he became conscious that Miss Albright was in the room. "The carriage is at the door, Mr Clark. And, Mr Clark, there is a man staying at the Palace who says he came from Germany in response to a cablegram from the late Mr Clark.

He is a partner in the largest firm producing milling machinery over there."

"Have you a record of that cablegram?"

"No. The late Mr Clark often did such things in secret."

"All right," Sam said. "Tomorrow morning at ten. Put these" —pointing to Mr Stevens's statements—"into my private file."

CHAPTER

IX

He went home for his lunch. To his relief he found Dr Fry who had known Maud at Vienna where he had been a medical student while she attended the famous conservatory of music. Sam knew that rumour explained his settling at Langholm by the desire to meet her again.

Dr Fry was a young man sixteen or eighteen years Sam's junior, with independent means and artistic leanings. He was an accomplished violinist and a connoisseur in the pictorial arts. He was tall and slender, with drooping eyelids and a pale complexion. To Sam's annoyance, Dr Cruikshank had called him in as a consultant in Maud's confinement. Between them, the two physicians had decided on having Dr McIntosh down from Winnipeg. Sam had not uttered his objections to Dr Fry; they rested solely on the fact that this young man who was supposed to have an extraordinary flair as a diagnostician called Maud by her first name, being called Victor by her. From the beginning the two had played together, she the piano, he the violin.

But on this particular day he was glad to see somebody in the house who would shoulder the burden of conversation.

Now, in spite of the fact that this was Thursday, four days after the funeral, he became, during the luncheon, conscious with a shock that the account book was still reposing in the safe of his office, undestroyed; and that he had not yet looked at the plans for the enlargement of the mill which his father had left behind, mentioning them in his will, thereby taking matters out of Sam's hands.

He was living in a private chaos of his own; and as he watched the two others, Maud and Dr Fry, he wondered how far their intimacy went. Suppose a domestic tragedy were to be superimposed on his troubles? What of it? Would it be a thing to be wondered at in a state of the world where such other things were possible? Moral standards were shattered. Why should not he seek consolation himself? He shuddered.

Then he thought of the fact that the German engineer was waiting his pleasure. That made it imperative that he should familiarize himself with his father's intentions as expressed in those plans. He would return to the office to fetch them. But deep down there was another motive for leaving the house; he would give these two their opportunity if they were waiting for it. He wouldn't stand in their way.

Yet it was after three when he left the house in his carriage. Maud and Dr Fry were in the music room.

In front of the Flour Building he told his driver to wait; and again, deep down, there was that motive : he would return furtively to spy on those two. . . .

Within fifteen minutes he was back in his carriage, account book and plans under his arm.

The senator sat up, opening his eyes; the car was going down a steep slope; that had caused his sudden motion. A glance through the windows showed him that they were in the park of Clark House and that, in a moment, they would emerge on the shelf bearing the buildings. Precipitously he bent forward, opened the slide, and spoke.

"Stop at the fork,"—meaning the point where the driveway to the house parted from that to stables and car-sheds.

By this time he was so keyed up that he was no longer remembering the past, he was reliving it. That the rapidly-moving vehicle was a motor car and not his landau remained unnoticed; so, when he alighted at the fork, remained the fact that he was over eighty, not the swift, alert man he had been forty years ago. For the moment, in his externals, the situations were the same. Past and present fused; by a simple coincidence they were to go on fusing for hours.

McAllister stared after him as he moved to the house walking briskly, as he had walked in his prime, the left arm pressing his side, to prevent account book and plans which were not there from slipping. In spite of his hurry, there was something furtive in his movements; for, living in the past, he did not want to be seen.

Stealthily he entered by way of the *porte cochère* and, having made sure that no footman acted as doorkeeper, he hung up coat and hat and proceeded to the hall to slip into the library unobserved.

At the door to the library, however, he almost ran into a footman coming from the service door behind the near ramp of the great stairway.

The footman looked startled.

"Dr Fry still here?" the senator asked, more to cover the secrecy of his return than to elicit information.

The footman looked still more startled. How could the old man know that Dr Fry had called and stayed for luncheon; he had not been in himself. But the senator, in his intense pre-occupation, noticed nothing of the menial's stare; and when the latter replied, "Dr Fry is with the ladies in the music room," he merely nodded. The 'ladies', to him, were Maud and young Odette Charlebois. The presence of the Frenchwoman relieved him, for the moment, of the task of spying.

"There's a fire in the library?" he asked.

"The fire is laid but not lighted, sir. Shall I light it?"

"No. I want to be undisturbed till dinner."

"Very good, sir." And the footman went on his way.

All which had been a repetition, almost literal, of what had happened and been said on that October day of 1898.

The senator, now Sam of forty years ago, felt feverish and in need of a hot bath, of stewing in hot water. Heat had always helped him in times of stress.

But first he must dispose of the account book under his arm.

He turned to his right, entering the library, switching on the light, and putting a match from the mantelpiece to the paper under the wood in the fireplace. It was warm enough without that fire which was needed only for his purpose.

The large, lofty room occupied the southwest corner of the house; it had two tall French windows, close together, in its far angle whence they gave a view into a narrow lane planted on both sides with spruces over thirty feet high. North of that lane, behind the house, stood the old Gymnasium; to the south, a greenhouse. At its far end, invisible on account of the wind-ings of the pathway, lay a circular open-air swimming-pool of white marble, reserved for the ladies. All which the senator knew; and it formed part of the memory-complex released when he thought of his library. The swimming-pool had not been finished forty years ago; he had laid it out as a surprise for Maud, his wife; but she had died before its completion. It had been finished twenty years later, for his daughter-in-law. The spruces, too, had, forty years ago, been only a few inches high and the senator was half conscious of these contradictions; but somehow the past and the present remained blended. He went the length and the breadth of the room, to make sure he was alone, his left arm still pressing the imaginary account book tightly against his ribs.

Returning to the fireplace, he stood for a moment, contemplating the blaze. Then he reached for the account-book, disconcerted because it was not there. But, half wilfully, half instinctively he explained its absence to himself. He had put it down on the desk which stood between the jutting wing-shelves of his books; and when, on looking for it there, he did not find it, he drew the central drawer open, catching sight of the three sheaves of plans which had laid there these forty years. He was perplexed and on the point of awaking to the reality—that this was 1938, not 1898. For the fraction of a second there was a trace of make-believe in his action, as of a child pretending in play that a thing is what it is not. He seized a book containing an alphabetically-ordered catalogue of his library and rose.

Behind him, the fire was burning brightly; and he turned to balance the book on top of the wood where it would speedily be consumed. He dared not leave the room; he watched the process; and as the curling pages charred, he crushed another block of birch-wood down on their remains, from the huge brass container by the side of the fireplace.

Then, having placed a spark-screen in front of the fire, he returned to the desk, picked up the plans, and, pressing them under his arm, slipped back into the hall, first opening the door slightly only, to spy out the lie of the land. Seeing the coast clear, he hurried upstairs, using the near ramp of the stairway. He tried to run trippingly up to the landing where the two ramps joined, which dominated the hall; but he stumbled and came near falling. Half a dozen steps brought him thence to the gallery.

Whenever, in the past, he had reached that point, he had seen, in front, the life-sized portrait of Maud, his wife, over the fireplace in the far wall of this intimate sitting-room. Instead of that portrait he saw the painting of Stella by Millais which everybody mistook for a portrait of his daughter-in-law. The fact made him pause; and once more he was on the point of awaking to reality. He had to change his direction; if he had gone on, following his original impulse, he would have entered the suite which he had ceded to his son in 1921.

But again he overcame his momentary uncertainty by a piece of deliberate play-acting, substituting, in his mind, his present suite, in the north wing of the house, for the one which had been his in the past. The fact that it was laid out on an identical plan helped him to re-establish his illusion; and at last he was aided by the sight of the portrait by Langereau above the mantelpiece there. Once more the time was that of the October day of 1898; once more the faint sounds of music reaching him from below were those of Maud and Dr Fry practising a sonata by Beethoven. He stood and listened. Yes, it was the ninth, for violin and piano. What he heard was the fourth variation of the second movement.

He nodded, entering his dressing-room. He started; for the door slammed shut behind him: something wrong with that pneumatic silencer. Passing through, he entered his bedroom and threw the papers on his bed, emptying his pockets on the night table at its head.

But the slamming of the door had warned James, his valet, who entered noiselessly to gather up his clothes as he dropped them. Intentionally the senator did not look at the man who, in 1898, had been in his twenties and was in his sixties now.

"Lay out a dress suit," he said. "Run some hot water into the tub; and put these away. I won't need you after that."

His desire to be alone was overpowering. Not in order to think—what was there to think about? In order to gather himself together; as though, being of a brittle material, he had been shattered. He knew himself to be capable of courage in the face of physical or spiritual danger; but against this blow out of the dark and from behind his back he was defenceless. He would have to face the world and his tasks with a new sense of disillusionment. Compared to the present—October 1898—he had so far lived the life of a child, reckless, carefree, innocent. He had rebelled against his sense of subordination; but the air he breathed had never been one in which life could not be sustained.

He had had worries: Maud was his wife; she would remain a problem; but that problem could be coped with by being he. . . .

The present problem was that he would have to live a life from which the bloom was gone, in which he would constantly have to be on his guard; spontaneity was a thing of the past. The world was changed; and he did not know where to turn for guidance. He had been searching for himself; everything had seemed hostile. But he had never doubted that one day he would live his own life; that his father's death would give him his final freedom. The world consisted of the same constituent parts; but they had rearranged themselves in a new, puzzling pattern.

What a figure his father had been! Gruff, sarcastic, impatient of all but technical innovation, looked upon as commercially the soul of honour. If he had taken advantage of a political contingency to advance his interests by making a bargain with a candidate willing to promise him the sale, on the part of the crown, of such lands as he coveted, he had done what everyone in his place would have done; the device was time-honoured, unquestioned, legitimate in the eyes of his contemporaries. If he had sold these same lands at a thousand times their cost because he had manoeuvred a buyer—himself, in the form of Langholm Light and Power—into a position where he was willing to pay the price; he had done what his contemporaries admired. In matters of ethics, custom had been his god. But any proceeding, on the part of another, not sanctioned by custom, would have found him firmly planted on the bed-rock of precedent. Even in his cunning disguise of the profits derived from the operation of the mill he had not only remained within the law, but within the limits of what every merchant would have pronounced right, if rather clever. It was the American game to 'put one over on the other fellow'.

Yet, what a colour this very proceeding took on in the light of the one transgression! And that transgression had been made possible by the unflawed reputation of honesty which removed a statement of assets issued by him from all scrutiny. Sam knew that the bins of the old wooden mill could never have held that additional 30,000 bushels of wheat; but, ten years ago, nobody had dreamt of challenging the fact. No doubt this knowledge had been the motive that had induced the old man to send his son away on a holiday. The wheat, on arrival, had been shipped on, as it had been meant to be, and resold at a profit. It was to that fact that the old man had owed his precarious control; it was to that fact that he, Sam, owed his present control which, knowing what he knew, he dared no longer either use or surrender.

As, under the impact of this thought, he stopped for a moment and then, James being still present, gathering up the clothes which his master strewed over the floor and bed, stripped to get into his hot bath, he felt alien to himself: he had been, he was, this man's son!

As he stepped into the scalding water, he peered into the misted mirrors of the white-tiled room; it was incomprehensible that, though he was pale, there was no essential change in his features.

By a twist of sympathetic insight he suddenly realized the havoc his father's conscience had made of his composure. During the first years, till he had become habituated to the thought that he was the victim of a blackmailer—hearing a step in his house at night; seeing in daytime an unknown person entering his office—he must have blanched, his heart missing a beat: had someone come for him? Had someone found out how he had created his opportunity? How he must have hated the idea that he, Rudyard Clark, depended on the discretion of Bill Swann.

In him, Sam, his father was uncannily coming to life as he sat there in his bath, breathless with the heat of the water. He remembered his father's look, absent-mindedly staring, realizing, no doubt, that in his dreams his son was plotting against him, planning to undo at least part of what the father had done, waiting for his death to do so. It had been the fact. Suddenly a grim smile had drawn the father's lips into a twisted curve; he must have thought, then, of how and by what bonds he held that son's whole future on this globe in an inescapable grasp. On occasion, this relation between father and son had impressed Sam like a game of chess: whenever there was an argument in which he, the son, had advocated modifications in his father's plan—modifications ultimately to favour his own intentions, to be carried out when he would be the master. . . .

By this discovery of his father's crime his own dreams had been blown into non-existence.

Yet, for the first time, Sam thought of the old man with sympathy. Like Swann, like every transgressor, he had yielded to temptation—to an irresistible lure of temptation to which who would not have yielded? For, by this time, even Sam did not feel sure of himself.

In spite of the early hour—it was only half-past four; and the gong would not ring for dressing till seven—Sam, or the senator, caught himself hurrying in all he did. It took a conscious effort to force himself to lie down and relax. But the moment he did relax, his mind was off again, on independent paths of its own. He saw his father before him in various circumstances; saw the way he had behaved on this or that occasion, his flat eyes assuming a faraway look. Only now did he understand; the man's mentality had become his own.

He thought of a day, a year after the accident, when his father had discussed with him his plan of making over a not inconsiderable property to Maud, Sam's wife. He had talked as if he were going to take his son fully into his confidence. Forgetting himself, he had gone so far as to ask, "Ye think that'll stand in law?" "In law?" Sam had asked. And, checking himself, as if stopping on the brink of an abyss, his father had said impatiently, "Yes. I might die a bankrupt, mightn't I?"—Sam had laughed; and then he had said, puzzled, "But if there's any doubt, why not ask Beatty?" "Beatty!" his father had exploded as if Sam were talking utter nonsense; and, bethinking himself, he had turned his face to the wall.

The extraordinary care he had taken not to let anyone see the inner workings of the administration of the mill and its subsidiaries had stood in strange contrast to his liberality to Maud; there had been a time when Maud was richer than her husband. It was all clear now. Always fearing exposure, for Swann must always have been threatening, the old man had tried to save at least part of his property from being involved in the ruin that might come any time; as if, in advance, he wished to screen Sam, through Maud, against sharing in the general condemnation with which the world would view him. Suppose Swann had asked, not for half the proceeds of that wheat, but for half the mill stock? A wrong shared with an accomplice was like a seed which, planted, grew into the poison-herb blackmail. In his perplexities which, unlike his crime, he shared with no one, his father had tried to transfer as much as possible of his wealth, except mill stock, to his son, through his wife. For wealth acquired by crooked ways had to be protected by ways that were winding. Mill stock, of course, would have given Sam the opportunity to enquire into origins.

Mill stock! It had now been thrust on him in a block; but his free use of it had been restricted by the knowledge of what had taken place on April 23, 1888.

For ten years he had resented it that he had not had the right to sit in the shareholders' meetings except by special invitation. This resentment had been one of the reasons for the peculiar relations between father and son. The whole layout of the mill, the smoothness with which it worked had been due to his planning, to his imaginative grasp of the business of grinding wheat into flour; to his cleverness in finding ways and means of accomplishing a given purpose with a minimum of friction and lost motion—quite apart from the stroke of genius, as Dick Carter had called it, by means of which he had seen a way for the mill to grow step by step without interfering with those parts that had already been built. That idea of the pyramidal outline to which layer after layer could be added on the south side had, from his father, never received the slightest acknowledgment.

And how he had suffered from the only interpretation which, in the bitterness of his spirit, he had been able to find for his father's attitude, namely that his father mistrusted his abilities.

'A stroke of genius'—perhaps, but born out of an aesthetic need. With his modesty, his feeling of inferiority, he had accepted it when his father, one day, had said to him, "In business I don't think ye're exactly a genius." It was true. He had never felt a Titan. He was an ordinary, honest, well-intentioned man, ready to be the first to doubt his own powers. Yet he had suffered from the fact that his father did not think him able to assist in holding the giant concern together.

That apparent mistrust of his father's had done something to him. Uncannily, his father had, by means of it, put himself in the right. His father had used him, had used his mechanical genius, his appearance, his way of dressing, his ability to inspire confidence, even his inclination to spend; but Sam had never been allowed to do things on his own responsibility; and so he had lost the power to do anything but follow a lead.

From his insight supreme knowledge sprang. His father, whether actuated by that mistrust or not, had made himself his master. If he, Sam, lived to be a thousand years old, he would remain the slave of the man who was dead. Others would call *him* the master of the mill; they might even call him a Titan. He would be nothing of the kind. Though the real master of the mill lay in his grave, he would remain the master even thence. That, the old man had, by means of his crime, most cunningly devised. So far, Sam had lived for a future; now he would have to live for a past. Never could he, in any way or degree, dissociate himself from that mill which, as an architectural monument and an industrial organism, he had loved; and which, as a taskmaster, he would no doubt come to hate. A taskmaster: for he would have to cover up his father's devious ways; he would have to stand in the breach to defend it. Let anyone else step into his place, and would not that somebody else at once delve into the past, lured by a mystery, just as he, Sam, was delving into it right now? Well, he would carry on as one carries on with what one cannot shake off. He had seen himself a prophet; he would have to be the defender of that which is.

He was hurrying again as he rose out of his bath and rubbed himself dry. And suddenly he stood still, ceasing all activity under the impact of a vision of his father as he had been in the last weeks of his life. He saw him walking about in odd places, about town or in the mill, bent over, talking to himself, flinging out a long, bony hand, sideways, as if dismissing an argument—or was it a threat?

A quarter of an hour later, the senator, in evening clothes, still impersonating the man he had been, was in the library, poring over the old plans under the light of an electric floor-lamp. He was not conscious of any impersonation; he was reliving, living the past.

As a matter of fact, certain details in those plans struck him only now; in the interval he had never looked at them; and nobody but servants had ever opened the drawers of his desk.

Dinner was at half-past seven; it was five when he sat down. But it was fully seven when he finished with those plans. He rose from his seat in response to the dressing gong.

On the way to the library he had once more met the footman and said briefly, "Should Mrs Clark enquire, I'm in the library. I'm not at home for anyone else." Irately he had returned the startled stare of the man, due to his use of the word 'Mrs' instead of 'Lady'.

Each sheet which he unfolded bore, in one corner, a label with the name of the German machine company whose representative was waiting for an interview, initialled by Mr Hermann and Rudyard Clark.

Briefly, the plans showed that the mill was to be brought to its full stature of seventeen stories or a hundred and seventy units in three stages: by adding, in 1898, 35 units; in 1905, 35 units; in 1920, 80 units. From then on it would be capable of supplying the needs of a continent: a Titan's enterprise indeed. For each step there were detailed floor-plans and vertical sections.

While the senator scanned them, he was, for the third time, half slipping out of his impersonation, for he was fully aware that he had seen these plans before; they released in him the same feelings of consternation and awe which had invaded him forty years ago. On the other hand, even while he relived those hours of 1898, he became aware that certain trifles had, at that time, remained unnoticed.

Thus, in front of the dates, there was, in his father's writing, the word 'by'. In other words, the expansions were planned, not *for*, but *by* 1905 and 1920. Had he noticed this little word in 1898, it would have afforded him a certain latitude which, as a matter of fact, he had arrogated to himself on his own initiative but with a bad conscience.

There were sheets with endless calculations which, forty years ago, he had impatiently put aside; among them was one which, today, aroused his intense curiosity; it dealt with rates of profit. But for the moment he put it aside once more.

He reached for the third plan which embodied the idea of automatic operation. That idea he had himself put forward in 1895, playing with it, never advocating it, but working it out in his mind like a geometric puzzle. His father, seizing upon the idea, had apparently set a whole staff of engineers to work, utilizing his son's ingenuity but debarring him from any share in the working-out of the details. As these details unfolded themselves, on that October afternoon in 1898, Sam felt dizzy. For every hundred men employed in the former process of milling only one would be required; and that one not a miller or a mill-hand but a mechanic or an engineer. The mere fact that his father had adopted that idea had raised it to the dignity of a definite plan; and not a mere plan which one might follow, modify, or reject, but a goal to be striven for and ultimately to be reached. The total number of men employed in the mill was, by 1920, to be reduced to one hundred.

But the 1905 plan, which raised the number of units from 55 to 90, nearly doubling the capacity of the mill, remained predicated upon hand operation. This had puzzled Sam, for it involved an expansion in more than one sense. It involved increasing the number of mill-hands from two to nine thousand; or the number of the population of the Terrace from ten to forty-five thousand; and that meant, not a mere expansion of the Terrace which was already crowded, but the addition or erection of another mill-town with space for thirty-five thousand people. This creation of a new mill-town Rudyard Clark had coolly contemplated; yet, by 1920, when the mill was to run automatically, he had planned to cut this whole population of forty-five thousand adrift. The provisional increase in the number of mill-hands would, however, involve a corresponding growth of the town to take care of them, to cater to them, in food, clothing, school facilities, and a thousand other things. And all those employed in these secondary functions, at the least an additional thirty thousand, would also be cut adrift in 1920; to that Sam's father had seen no objection.

It meant something tremendous, cruel, soulless.

Absent-mindedly, the senator reached for that other sheet which had newly aroused his curiosity. As he did so, he was suddenly the senator only, not the Samuel Clark of 1898.

Accustomed to reading graphs and argument presented in a mathematical form, he saw the drift of this one at a glance. Two points stood out.

Firstly, the whole plan of the expansion was predicated upon paying for building and equipment out of earnings, leaving comparatively little to be distributed in the form of dividends; but . . . the earnings were largely those of Langholm Light and Power which was a 'pocket enterprise'. Langholm Light and Power would, after that, be the largest shareholder of the mill, itself owned by the Clarks.

Secondly, calculations being based, pro rata, on present earnings, that is, on earnings in 1897, it was shown that hand operation as heretofore practised would, in view of the lack of perpendicular height needed from gravity to become the chief motive power, be more profitable than automatic operation.

That, then, was the reason why the installation of automatic machinery was to be deferred to a point in time posterior to 1905. A consideration of profits explained the reckless procedure of first assembling the population of a city and then cutting it adrift, involving the ruin of tens of thousands of artisans and tradesmen who were meant to lose their investments in plants and dwellings at a blow. Technically, it was entirely possible to introduce automatic operation in 1898; financially, it would be unprofitable to do so.

The technical part of the reasoning in that sheet was again based on arguments put forward by Sam; and this recognition led the senator back to not merely thinking of but being the man he had been.

What was it that had led him into such speculations? It was this. Any given development, once started, leads on by a logic of its own. It has not reached maturity, it has not come of age, till that logic has been pursued to its ultimate conclusion. When it has done that, it ceases to move, balanced in a state of perfection. Nothing remains but decay, brought about by a new development, from a new point of departure, contained, perhaps, in some phase of the old development, or furnished by some new and startling invention. Thus, if a source of power other and cheaper than electricity were discovered, it would make the whole mill obsolete at a blow.

As Sam had done, the senator switched off the light, returning the papers to their drawer.

What was it that stood at the end of the development of the machine? It was the at least partial liberation of mankind from the ancient curse of labour. That was what had led him on in his dreams till he himself had furnished his father with the ways and means of ever more rapidly enriching himself. The liberation of mankind had not figured among the aims of his father's generation; what had actuated it was the size of its profits.

Yet, was this fair? It was not. Rudyard Clark also had been driven by a blind urge. He had created something superhuman; something which made the universe—a universe he did not understand—subservient to man. Even for Rudyard Clark the profits were, ultimately, incidental. It was true, his income had risen, first into hundreds of thousands, then into millions; but, personally, he had not known what to do with it. Even at the last his personal expenditure had remained below three thousand dollars a year. If it had not been for his son and that son's wife, he would have had no outlet for his wealth whatever.

The senator, now in darkness, rose and went to that niche between the book-shelves whence the tall, narrow windows looked out into the semi-obscurity of the sombre lane between the spruces. He was moved to his depths; his very body felt as if it were not his own. Was the dead man himself merely a link in a chain—a slave handing his slavery on? If so, what was the Titanic thing to which he had been enslaved?

It was the logic of a chain of events, that chain which had started millennia ago, with the invention of the first wheel, the first lever; with the impulse that had prompted the caveman to take a stone in his hand when levelling a blow at the head of his enemy; the logic of man's desire to lighten and at last to shake off the burden of labour without which he might have lived the life of the gods.

If only . . .

For these steps which his father proposed, yes, imposed out of his grave—what did they imply? They implied, indeed, the elimination of physical toil; but at the expense of the present distress of a majority of mankind. The industrial revolution had not only made possible, it had postulated the multiplication of numbers till cities had grown where there had been hamlets, till whole populations had been withdrawn from the green of the fields and reassembled in factories; and now, by drawing, from its own premises, the final conclusion, it drove those numbers out again; it handed them over to that ogre called unemployment. Was man, once started on that road, going to go the way of the mastodon and the dinosaur?

As the senator stood in the window niche, screened by the projecting book-shelves and staring into the dark, he seemed to hear the tramp of revolution marching through the night. Was there salvation in revolution? Or did revolution—proletarian revolution—necessarily mean the destruction of what the past had built?

Shivers were running down his spine. He did not know what was happening to him.

At that moment the lights of the chandelier flashed on above the centre of the room.

The senator knew he could not be seen from the door. But in the half-light which penetrated into his niche, he was conscious of the incongruity of the fact that he who had been wrestling with phantoms from the grave stood there, attired in evening dress.

He turned. The lights were switched off. He cleared his throat. They came on again.

"So you are here after all?" said a gay voice which he seemed to recognize as his wife's.

He stepped forward into the light and saw its owner.

"Somers said you were here and had been here since five o'clock. I could not believe him. So I came to investigate."

He stared at the woman. She, too, was dressed for dinner, in a long sweeping dress of heavy white silk, with diamonds in her dark-brown hair and about her neck; a magnificent figure, regal, redolent of wealth, power, and feminine charm. Who was she?

Still under the influence of his experience, the senator was blinking apologetically. "I'm sorry," he stammered. "I had important things to think over. When I came in, I was told Dr Fry was still here." He felt puzzled. Had Dr Fry been here for the last forty years?

"And so you hid away by yourself?" the magnificent woman said in a bantering voice. "Dr Fry? Yes, he's back again; for I sent him home to dress. We were practising the Kreutzer Sonata to play to you . . ."

Behind her, in the door, appeared a tall, slender man with drooping eyelids and long, snow-white hair: the aging Dr Fry.

Painfully, the senator awoke to reality. He was not Sam; this was not Maud. It was that Maud who was Lady Clark; and he was a man over eighty years old.

It was too much of a shock; he sat down; and the tears were running down his hollow cheeks.

CHAPTER

X

DURING the next few days the senator remained more than usually restless. Repeatedly a plan had been touched upon over the dinner table: a party was to be given shortly to the higher executives of the mill, some twenty in all, an annual affair. It disquieted the old man; he did not quite know who he was. Was it he who had lived through those things that had come back to him in the library? His memory played him strange tricks. He feared to reveal his weakness to others.

Being conscious of his great age and his many infirmities, he even dreaded those excursions into the past. Yet they would come, of their own accord. And then he wandered about, listening to snatches of that sonata which Maud had played forty years ago, and circling about the hall and the drawing-rooms. He avoided any approach to that window whence the mill could be seen.

Yet his thoughts were with the mill. What else was there to think about? The mill had been his life. Yet, had it?

Guarding against an actual lapse into the past, he tried to think of it in the abstract.

Yes, the crisis of the change from his father's administration to his own had been telescoped together into the five or six days after the old man's death. He had come to the conclusion that he must carry on. He could not run the risk of letting others delve into the mystery surrounding the origin of the mill.

On the other hand, he had made up his mind with regard to two things.

His father, obsessed by his dream, had not been responsible for his actions. All considerations of honesty, fairness, integrity had counted for nothing compared with the realization of that dream.

And he had made up his mind to defy that father in his grave and, instead of obeying his instructions to the letter, to begin the process of conversion to automatic operation at once.

His reason for this change in the programme of expansion had been that he could not countenance a proceeding which would draw tens of thousands of people into the town, to invest their all in the venture, merely to enrich such predatory enterprises as Langholm Real Estate, with its two chief 'realtors', Messrs Tindal and Ferguson; and then to let them lose their all after a short tale of years.

To his surprise, he had found that Mr Hermann, senior partner in *Die Magdeburger Maschinenwerke*, instead of being a blind acolyte of his father's, shared his own view and offered to co-operate.

This fact had necessitated the visit to the mill which had been overdue and from which Sam had shrunk. Critically, without surrendering to the past, he reviewed certain features of that visit.

His father had never, except during the interval following his accident, allowed a day to go by without visiting every department, from the 'screen-house' where the wheat was cleaned and graded down to the bagging and loading rooms on the ground floor. While the dead man had not exactly been popular with the 'hands'—he had been too hard a taskmaster for that—they had looked upon him as a man of their own kind to whom, if the occasion arose, they could talk. As he had bullied and cajoled them, so they had challenged and derided him—as when in November 1894 they had threatened to strike unless he conceded the ten-hour day.

Sam remembered an occasion when, towards the end of his father's life, he had had to enter that bagging-floor in company with his father. In one sense this was the busiest floor of the mill, for all work there had, so far, been carried on by hand.

The flour came down from the floor above in chutes; and bags had to be held under them, resting on scales. Whenever the bag showed the proper weight, a man lifted it away to the stitching machine operated by a girl. Another man lifted it thence, to place it on the trundle which stood waiting. Whenever a trundle held three of these bags, it was rolled away to the loading platform whence the bags were carried into the waiting box-cars. All these operations went on in a feverish hurry, for the flour came down inexorably in an unceasing stream.

His father, noticing that one of the trundlers invariably caused an ever so slight delay, by reason of his inability to raise the trundle in a single lift, looked at Mr Brook, the superintendent of works who, notified of the presence of the boss, had hurried over; and the consequence was that the man did not reappear; between turns he had been discharged; and his place had been taken by a huge, burly man—one of those who were always waiting for just such a chance.

Sam was a stranger to these men. With a weird sort of lucidity he saw that they considered him as a being of a different class; that they thought *he* considered himself as a being of a different class. And were they wrong? Yet he was more sparing of their feelings than his father had been. Never, for instance, had he driven up to the mill in his luxurious landau. When, from Clark House, he had gone to the mill, he had stopped at the office and proceeded afoot.

But, up to his father's death, he had never hesitated about entering the mill. Now he had a bad conscience; as if his father's transgression had placed him in the position of one who was taking an undue advantage of the men.

Why, he had asked himself, could he not run the mill without profit to himself? Miss Dolittle had smilingly supplied the answer. Because, to lower the price of flour would mean final ruin to the independent mills; such a step would have been interpreted as designed for that very purpose, the purpose of ridding himself, by means of a price war in which he was bound to be victorious, of all competition. If he had raised the wages of the men, he would have unchained an endless series of strikes in the other mills. He had meant to do these things; he still meant to do them; but Miss Dolittle, by a sort of passive resistance, converted him to the doctrine of gradualness. Yet, sudden or gradual, the result of the change must essentially be the same.

Through his father's death and the disclosure following it, the mill had changed its entire character. It looked at him out of an ironic, Mephistophelean face. Like himself, the mill held the dead man's blood: the blood of one going forward on his path under the compulsion of his own nature unmodified by humanitarian thought. Not as an individual had the old man faced the world; he had faced it as a cog in a machine.

When Sam did go to the mill, to meet Mr Hermann there, he went blindly.

The north side of Main Street still ended abruptly with the Flour Building; and though, on its south side, a few private houses still perched on the hillside beyond the Palace Hotel, these were mere outposts of the new west end of the city which overlooked the rock-strewn plain to the west where, fifty miles beyond, it merged into the prairie. To the north, opposite these houses, a bay of the lake bathed the rear of the Flour Building and part of its west wall.

Beyond this bay Sam turned north, crossing the successive railway tracks which led into the mill, and entered the former first unit via the laboratories. The men frantically wheeling flour across the loading platforms north and south of the tracks where they worked as in enormous caves, hurrying their trundles along, never gave him a glance; nor did they call to, or nudge each other as they had done when his father had appeared.

But, as he passed through the laboratories where the product of the mill was tested in all the stages of the milling process, the white-smocked chemists greeted him; and he replied by nod after nod. At the door which led to the bagging-floor, he collided with a tall, good-looking young man of thirty-five who gave him a bright smile, saying, "Not a moment to spare just now. Sorry." This was Max Eckel, chief chemist whose long white smock floated out behind him as he moved.

Sam used the stairs to reach the next floor; and there he passed old Rogers who had been his father's foreman in the old wooden mill. Rogers, a tall, cavernous man with the lean, narrow face of an intellectual, turned to speak to him. Sam stopped, listened with averted eyes.

"I wish to express my appreciation of being remembered in the old gentleman's will. You are his representative now. So I thought I'd mention it." He spoke with a catch in his voice, towering above Sam.

Sam nodded sympathetically. He knew the reason for that catch in the voice. Rogers had spent his whole life in the Clark mills; but there were those in the management, Mr Stevens among them, who considered him to be due, overdue, for retirement. The man could afford to retire, for his old employer had left him a pension; but, if he ceased work, there would be nothing for him to do but to lie down and die. That had been the rule with men like him of the older generation.

"That's all right, Rogers," Sam said; and after a moment he added, "I'm glad my father remembered you. I hope to have you with us for a good many more years."

And then he went on, again using the stairs. His appointment with Mr Hermann was on the fifth floor, below the roof; but he found him on the fourth where Bruce Rogers, old Rogers' son, operated a crushing machine.

When Sam joined the German engineer, the latter, turning and raising his voice above the din of the machines, speaking with the clear enunciation of the educated foreigner, said as if his words were meant for the operator, "These crushers should long ago have been linked up with those machines over there; you would save half a dozen men."

Bruce, an extraordinarily handsome, quiet young man of twenty-odd, gave Sam a half-sullen, half-challenging look which Sam took as a reminder of the fact that Bruce himself had one day made that very remark. Bruce had ideas. He had first spoken to his foreman; then to Mr Brook, the superintendent, who had gruffly told him to mind his own business. But Bruce who, like Sam, suffered from the consciousness that a machine was not yet doing all it could be made to do, as if it were a reproach to himself and a flaw in the organization of the mill, had boldly gone over Mr Brook's head, speaking to Mr Stevens; and, having been put in his place by that gentleman, he had stopped Sam in the street. Sam had listened patiently; but he had promptly forgotten all about it. Mr Hermann's remark consti-tuted a major triumph for the young man even though it placed his job at stake. Mentally, Sam marked the young fellow down for early promotion.

The German and the new president had gone on to the roof where Mr Hermann had talked and talked, speaking of em-placements, strains, and shearing thrusts. Sam had barely listened. He had the queer feeling that the dead man was bodily with them. Only once had he, Sam, been able to persuade his father to accompany him up here; and though, at this point, they had been surrounded by the perfectly level roof, asphalted and gravelled, the old man had, weak-kneed, held on to the pipe railing surrounding the pit of the stairs, almost screaming when Sam went to the very edge of the roof whence he had wished to point out something or other to his father.

He had lost the thread of what Mr Hermann was saying. Noticing it, the engineer concluded, "My business is with your architect rather than with you, Mr Clark."

"All right," Sam said. "He's in the west. I'll send him a wire."

One evening the senator, restlessly wandering about and stop-ping here and there, reflected on the strange way in which, in life, one thing leads to another. For, on receipt of his wire, Dick Carter had returned a married man; and his wife, appropriately for a man who had had multifarious affairs with women, had been Sibyl, of the Seattle Lanes, the Pacific-coast lumber men : Sibyl who, in the long run, might have ruined his own domestic peace and who had turned the little city of Langholm inside out and topside down.

"Won't you sit down, Father?" Lady Clark said when, in his wandering, he passed the chesterfield in the hall on which the ladies were sitting. "We were discussing the annual dinner for the executives of the mill. We were making a tentative list of the guests. Have you any suggestions?"

"No," said the senator. "Arrange it between yourselves."

"Well, there's no difficulty about members of the staff. The doubt comes in when we think of others. You wouldn't like it to be a big affair, would you? With guests from Winnipeg and Toronto?"

"No. I shouldn't like that."

"Well, the Tindals, then."

"Yes."

"Dr Fry?"

"I suppose so."

"Captain Stevens, of course. Dr Sherwood. Mr Inkster?"

"All right."

"The trouble is, nearly all of them are single men; most of them are old. There are no women left in this town."

"Not many."

"How about young people?"

"Young and old don't mix," Miss Charlebois said.

"That's true."

"The engineers and chemists are young. All but Max Eckel."

"And single," Miss Charlebois said.

"And they talk shop and nothing else," Lady Clark added, laughing.

And thus the discussion went on inconclusively; and shortly the senator betrayed by his absent-minded look that he was no longer listening. He was far away in his mind, a fact which he suddenly revealed by a question addressed to Miss Charlebois. "I've been trying to get something clear in my mind. You remember Mrs Carter, Dick's wife?"

Miss Charlebois stared and then burst into a laugh. "Do I remember her? I should say I do."

"Well," said the senator testily, "when she came to town, Maud and I . . ." His glance went to his daughter-in-law as if to make sure that it was not she to whom he referred. "We called on her, with Dick, at the Palace Hotel. What I can't remember is whether you were present."

"I was," Miss Charlebois replied. "I had gone downtown with Mrs Clark to the Flour Building, in the dogcart. When Dick, as we called him between us, came down with you, we crossed the street afoot and went up together."

"Then I was right," said the senator and rose to resume his walk.

He was sitting in the presidential office, bent over calculations. It was a week or so after he had sent the wire to summon Dick home. As usual, having arrived by the midnight train from the west, Dick burst in unannounced; he prided himself on his ability to get past the underlings guarding the president's privacy.

"Hello," he said as he entered. "Before we talk business, Sam, is your old house on Clark Street vacant?"

"It is vacant . . ."

"Is it to let?"

"It would depend on the tenant."

"I am the tenant."

"You?" Sam asked, surprised.

"I. I'm in for a job here, it seems. The wire reached me in the nick of time. I was off with Sibyl."

"Who is Sibyl?"

"Sibyl Lane that was, of Seattle, Washington. The Timber-Lease Lanes as they're called. You've heard of them. She's Sibyl Carter now."

In the quick way of the small man Sam looked up. "Do you mean to say you're married?"

Dick laughed. "I told you I was off on the biggest job yet."

"Well," Sam said unsmilingly, "I'd never have thought it. I can't think of you as a married man."

"Neither can I. But there it is. We were off on our honeymoon. When your wire arrived, we decided to take it here."

"Do you mean to say she is with you?"

"She is. We've taken a suite on the top floor of the Palace."

"The Palace? Why didn't you come to the house?"

"Impossible. Quite impossible. You'll see for yourself."

This made Sam hesitate. "Surely, she must meet Maud?"

"I suppose so," said Dick without enthusiasm. "What I'm doubtful about is whether she ought to meet you."

"Me?"

"You. She's a mere kid. That is, she's twenty-two; and I'm forty-four. She's advanced, outspoken, fin-de-siècle. I don't see it."

"You talk," Sam said with acid facetiousness, "as if you were your own grandfather."

"You'll see," was all Dick replied.

116

"I'll go over with you . . . No, wait, I'll ring Maud and tell her."

And Maud expressed the desire to join them.

"As for the house," Sam said while they were waiting, "you can have it, of course. Your business here, by the way, is with a German engineer, not with me."

And with that the senator's memories faded.

But meanwhile, his question having aroused Lady Clark's curiosity, she dismissed, when her father-in-law had left them, the dinner-party from her mind and turned to Miss Charlebois. "What about Sibyl Carter? Who was she?"

"Well," Miss Charlebois replied with an indescribable expression on her wrinkled face, half of scorn, half of an old-maidish itch to say more than was perhaps wise. "She was a phenomenon, physically and morally. She fell in love with Mr Clark at first sight. Perhaps she had already reasoned herself into some such thing. He was the multi-millionaire, you see. She came near wrecking Mr Clark's marriage; she upset the town; she was at least instrumental in bringing about a strike."

"Was she a socialist?"

Miss Charlebois laughed. "It wasn't as simple as that. Of course, I know only what I saw and what became matter of public knowledge; but that was plenty. To mention one thing, she drove, one night, through the town naked; though I will say it wasn't by choice. Her being naked, I mean."

Lady Maud stared at her companion, doubtful whether to encourage her to proceed. Curiosity conquered. "Tell me," she said at last.

Miss Charlebois remained silent for a minute or two. Then, with a peculiar smile, she began, "Perhaps it is best, in order to give you an idea of her, to tell you about that first meeting to which the senator referred just now.

"I remember the occasion very well. Maud had summoned me to go to town with her, in the dogcart. She was driving herself, tandem, with two calico ponies in front and a diminutive groom behind. She had completely recovered from her confinement and was as lithe and athletic as ever. But for the moment she affected the matron; and she retained her tall cane which she used like a sceptre. She felt neglected, you know; and she was at a dangerous age, thirty or a little over.

"However, when we arrived in front of the Flour Building, Maud had her husband and her brother summoned; and with much laughter and teasing of the newly-wed man who had the reputation of being a rake, we walked across the street to the hotel.

"When, a few minutes later, we entered the sitting-room of a suite on the top floor, a tall young woman rose animatedly out of an armchair at one of the windows, dropping a book to the floor. Her face, at first sight, seemed sharp and thin; but it was tremendously alive and attractive; it was dominated by her large, turquoise eyes and a bold nose as well as by a halo of fine, loose, straw-yellow hair. . . ."

"I fairly see her," Lady Clark said.

"Her features were flushed with pleasure. For some reason or other she had not expected this call on the part of her sister-in-law. The most striking feature of her narrow, boyish figure which had no curves, was its extreme flexibility. She wore a very plain dress of thin, dark purple chiffon-velvet which, from a certain angle, looked greenish; it fitted her like a glove. Over a flat breast she wore a nile-green fichu so light in texture that it floated up against her face at every movement.

"Compared to her, Maud, one gloved hand on her tall cane, and clad in a navy-blue suit with *écru* cuffs and collar, looked very mature; and she was the older of the two, of course.

"Both on their guard, both acting a part, they met in the centre of the large room, one running, the other striding with that air of affable condescension which she commanded to perfection. They embraced, kissing each other on both cheeks; each, by every movement, seemed to proclaim her ascendancy. Mr Dick laughed.

" 'You're Maud,' Sibyl said, stepping back. 'I'd have picked you out of a crowd, you look so like Dick; though much better, of course. And this,' she added, turning, 'is the flour king.' She dropped a court bow to Mr Clark who always felt uncomfortable in the limelight. 'Aren't you going to kiss me too?' she asked archly. 'I'm used to being kissed by the men I meet. It means nothing. Children are kissed by everyone. We are relatives now, are we not, if only by marriage?'

"Like the *enfant terrible* she was she presented her cheek. It would have been outright rude for Mr Clark not to touch it with his lips; but she, by the slightest twist of her head, observed by Maud as well as myself, contrived to receive the kiss on her lips.

"Maud stood by, smiling sardonically, but with a half-frown on her brow; she looked very straight, very superb, her one arm stretched to her cane at the height of her shoulder.

"Sibyl pushed chairs about, arranging them so that she

would face her callers in exactly the light she wanted. When she, too, sat down, the searching, shadowless brightness of the northern exposure failed to reveal the slightest flaw in the bloom of her complexion, though Maud did not suffer from the comparison. In moving about, Sibyl exaggerated her angularity. It was highly provocative. Provocation was the breath of her life.

"Maud, sitting down, wore a sympathetic, patronizing, but waiting smile; in some inexplicable way she conveyed the impression that she was inwardly laughing, not at the girl, but at her husband.

"I, of course, was a mere background figure; and as such I could devote myself to observation. I had my eye on Mr Clark; he did not show to advantage; he was trying hard to stand on his dignity.

"No doubt he had never seen a woman so self-conscious in a physical sense. Every motion of hers was studied and purposeful; she marshalled herself with the genius of a stage *ingénue*. One saw at a glance that she acknowledged no bond, no approach even, between the sexes but the physical one. Aware of the fact that her figure, theoretically, was the one least capable of arousing awareness in the opposite sex, she accepted her handicap, determined to find the ultimate triumph of her art in her ability to turn a weakness into a strength. Anticipating the wiliness of the present day, she sought a reinforcement of her very great powers in a studied slanginess of speech.

" 'Believe it or not,' she said; 'ever since Dick whispered into this pink ear of mine that he was gone on my charms, I've been thinking of this town, of the mill and its owners. It must have been years ago. I hadn't put my hair up yet.' She shook her head, so that her fluffy locks flamed about it. 'Dick is famous, of course, for taking to the kid kind. Innocence and all that. Purity is what every rake is after. I'm afraid he got sold. But he's told me so often that he wanted me just as I was that I said to myself, He must be a paragon of a lover to be fond of me as I am. Don't you agree, Maud? As far as you can judge on fifteen minutes' acquaintance?'

"Maud was queenly. 'Dick has known you so much longer, of course. But we are all prepared to like and love you.'

"Sibyl could not leave so easy a victory to Maud. She rose and threw herself at her knees. 'Darling!' she cried. 'Don't love me on Dick's account; love me on my own. Dick's so much more mine than I am his . . . Look at him!' Like a score of silver bells her laughter rang out. 'I've let the cat out of the bag!' In one lithe, effortless, leisurely twist of her limbs she raised herself and sat down on Dick's knees, ruffling his hair.

"Everybody laughed; though there was constraint in that laughter.

"Maud rose. 'I've asked the Beattys and Dr Fry to join us at luncheon. Would you care to look about? We'll leave the men to their business. I am sure they have business. The men I know all have. The dogcart is waiting.'

"Sibyl accepted with sudden demureness. 'I'd love to,' she said, comically hanging her head. One could see she did not relish being alone with women. That was the introduction of Sibyl Carter to what was then Langholm society."

"You have painted her graphically," Lady Clark said. "Even Mrs Clark becomes clearer to me. I expect to see her grow jealous."

"Oh, but you are hardly fair to Maud!" Miss Charlebois cried. "If you had lived in the house at the time, you'd have understood her. Jealous, you say. She was certainly not jealous in the beginning; though it may have come to that. The whole atmosphere of this house was oppressive. Mr Clark had forgotten how to laugh. If there is one thing for which Maud can be blamed, it is the fact that she was absolutely and utterly indifferent to the mill."

"To the social problems involved?"

"To them, too. She had married Mr Clark, partly at least, because he was—how shall I say it?—physically attractive to her; partly because he was aesthetically sensitive; she appreciated it, for instance, that, out of a thing so commonplace as a flour mill, the Clarks had made a thing of beauty. But partly she had married him because he offered her an escape."

Lady Clark looked up. "An escape from what?"

"Mediocrity in every sense. Financial mediocrity, for instance. Her father had made a good income; but it had never been good enough. Her home atmosphere had been one of making both ends meet."

"Is that so?" Lady Clark asked and remained pensive.

"I spoke of the atmosphere of this house, Mr Clark was going through some sort of crisis. What it consisted in, nobody knew. He was very reserved, very reticent. The many responsibilities which his father's death had placed on his shoulders absorbed him. An impartial observer like myself could not but wonder. He left Maud to herself. Often, when there were no guests, he withdrew at once when a meal was finished. With guests present, he remained, remotely polite.

"Now Maud was exceedingly vital; she was a woman who opened up in a crowd. She loved company, gaiety, splendour. Mr Clark—may I use the word that comes to my lips? Mr Clark was grey, down to his clothes. And he made the impression as if he were drifting away.

"As for Sibyl, Maud said to me—I believe it was on the day we had met her, 'She'll be an acquisition; she's just the sort of person needed to stir the town up.' Don't think for a moment she did not see through her. She did. But they had at least one thing in common: both were athletic; both had, in their early years, taken training in acrobatics. Maud had just built the gymnasium; they worked together in equipping it; soon the two were inseparable; they were riding, swimming, walking the tight-rope, swinging on the flying trapeze. Physically, it did Maud a world of good."

Lady Clark nodded, laying down her embroidery. "I think," she said, "I should see to it that the senator lies down. It is getting late. We'll talk more of this another time."

When she found him, she took his arm to lead him upstairs. He was barely conscious of her. He was in another world.

Leaving him in his dressing-room, she entered the bedroom of his suite and placed the flashlight on the spot marked on the floor. She knew it did not really matter except inasmuch as, when she attended to it, he professed to be satisfied. When she returned to the other room, she saw that he was paying no heed to her; and so she went out into the sitting-room niche that gave access to his rooms. The valet was coming along the gallery; but she gave him a sign not to enter; and when he had withdrawn, she stood for a moment, looking at that magnificent portrait of Maud's which represented her in the flower of her youth. She had never been able to make up her mind whether she pitied or despised her; for she, too, had fallen under the spell of this man who was now lapsing into decay.

Miss Charlebois was passing along the gallery, going to her rooms; her own maid came running from the opposite direction. Downstairs, lights were being turned off, all except those which remained burning all night. The house was sinking into its slumber. She, too, turned to go to her suite.

Inside his door, the senator stood listening. He was in the past. Outside, first on the stairs, then on the floor of the gallery surrounding the pit of the central hall, a step could be heard, muffled by the carpet.

The man in the dressing-gown stood and listened, his heart missing a beat. He hardly knew who he was, whether Samuel Clark of 1898, or Senator Clark, of 1938; or the man who had been his father.

Was someone coming to enquire about the fire in the wooden mill? About Swann's sudden disappearance from the town? About something which Swann might, after all, have revealed?

He stirred; and then he raised a trembling hand to his brow.

Thus had he imagined his father to have been disturbed . . .

Slowly and stealthily he opened the door the least little bit. No. It was only the young butler whose name he could not remember, making his last round before locking up.

One day, towards the end of October, he had written, with his own hand, a letter addressed to a detective agency in Winnipeg, asking that a reliable, confidential man be sent down to Langholm. He was, at the Flour Building, to give his name as Mr Walters who had private business with Mr Clark.

When, a few days later, Miss Albright had announced Mr Walters, he had assigned him the task of finding out where Bill Swann had gone.

CHAPTER

XI

DURING the days that followed, the senator felt exceedingly puzzled. He tried to visualize such matters as had led to his leaving the mill to itself; to the slowly developing tension between the men and the management; to his sudden flight, with Maud, to Europe. He could not get the chronology straight till he remembered that at the outbreak of the Boer War he had been in Italy; then he looked up the date of the war in an encyclopedia.

The most puzzling thing was his relation to Maud. Had there been a sort of reconciliation? But a reconciliation presupposed an estrangement . . . .

Slowly he began to refocalize a few facts. One scene became startlingly clear: between him and Sibyl. Sibyl had been at the root of all the changes that took place at this time. Her appearance and stay at Langholm had been in the nature of a catastrophe. Even to himself. For morally he had lived in chaos; the very foundations of his life had been rocked out of position. It took him even now considerable time before he could face that scene squarely; he averted his eyes. He had come through unscathed; but for days he had hung over an abyss. His thought beat about that scene; he fastened on to inessentials; he dared not look himself in the eye.

He had led a furtive sort of life; he had had secrets from everybody; he had known that Maud suspected and misinterpreted his secretiveness. He had been unable to help himself. Necessities had held him in their grip. What, in this cataclysmic upheaval, did his own moral integrity matter? Let catastrophe come if it must.

As for Sibyl, it was Maud who had taken her up, against his wish, in defiance of his wish. The time had come when Maud and Sibyl were inseparable; and he had been powerless to interfere.

From the mill as such he had withdrawn. Without appealing for the sanction of a shareholders' meeting, he had committed the company to an expenditure of millions in new machinery, delivery to begin in 1900. He would do what the old man had prescribed; but he would do it in his own time and way. It would take two years to install the machines. It would take two years to build the necessary additions.

Meanwhile mill-hands and townspeople looked on aghast at the scale on which the expansion was obviously planned.

Sam observed the most absolute silence with regard to his plans. The only two men who knew of them: Mr Hermann, the German engineer, and Dick Carter, the architect, took their cues from him. Mr Hermann, of course, was shortly thousands of miles away; Dick Carter had never been intimate with men of the town. Besides, he had his own worries. Keeping Sibyl in funds kept him, as he expressed it, 'hopping'. He was careful not to displease Sam.

Mat Tindal, of Langholm Real Estate, tried to get him to talk. Dick told Sam who said, "None of his business". Mat Tindal next approached Sam himself. Sam told him there was only one reason why no announcement had been made, that reason consisting in the fact that no decision was final till a shareholders' meeting had ratified it.

This was, of course, the merest evasion. For Sam had by this time agents on every stock-exchange, buying up every share that found its way to the market, at no matter what price. Soon his control was so overwhelming that no minor share-holder would have cared to oppose him. The cost of the new expansion would ultimately be covered by an issue of stock which he intended to take over *in toto* to reimburse himself for the advances he personally made to the mill. If his father had held auxiliary enterprises in absolute ownership, Sam made it his aim to own the mill as such. It would take many years to realize that aim; but only when it was realized could he feel safe from enquiry; for only then could he dispense with pub-lished statements. Thus his father forced him into the very paths he himself had followed.

Yet Sam could not hide the fact that the mill was expand-ing. Building operations cannot be kept secret. Hundreds of workmen, thousands shortly, were swarming over the site and over the roofs of the older units. So when Mat Tindal cornered him in the street, he put his question in a form which admitted of no prevarication.

The question was, "You'll double the capacity, won't you?"

"No doubt," Sam said after a moment's hesitation, satisfy-ing his desire for secrecy by the grotesqueness of the under-statement. 'Double it!' he said to himself. 'Multiply it by eight or nine!'

Mat Tindal promptly saw his partner and told him Sam Clark had allowed himself to be understood as admitting that the capacity of the mill and, therefore, the number of mill-hands employed would be doubled.

Henceforth, Sam had sat in his office on the top floor of the Flour Building, watching, with a sardonic irony not unmixed with dismay, the consequences of this prevarication of his. He knew on what sort of reasoning the revived activities of Langholm Real Estate were based. An expansion of the mill was expected to bring another boom.

In the course of the first boom, of 1888 and 1889, Langholm Real Estate had acquired ten square miles of territory, subdividing it into 36,000 building lots which, assuming 5 persons to the household, would have accommodated a population of 180,000. A few of these lots remained unsold. The resident population of Langholm was less than 15,000, of which the mill-hands, including their families, furnished 10,000. It was reasonable, then, to infer that a ratio of one to six or seven, between mill-hands and population, was a natural one, established in conformity to laws inherent in the situation. If the number of mill-hands was doubled, the population would double.

But by far the greater number of lots sold in the first boom were never built upon; they were held for purposes of speculation; and the number sold for speculation again bore a definite relation to the number of mill-hands, say 10 or 15 to 1.

In the case of a doubling of the mill's capacity, it would be entirely reasonable to assume that the coming boom would equal the first boom in extent.

Originally, Langholm Real Estate had owned little more land than Rudyard Clark had sold, in 1888, to a holding company, at $60,000. The holding company, formed for that sole purpose, had promptly resold it to Langholm Real Estate at a figure of $150,000, paid for by stock certificates which, from below par, had rapidly risen to 250 and over. Whereupon Langholm Real Estate had gone on buying and subdividing. Since, by that time, the first units of the mill had been in operation, a wave of speculative buying had broken over the town, coming from east and west. That procedure the company meant to repeat at last.

But for the first time in the history of the real-estate firm it was swamped with a local demand. In the former boom it had had to employ high-priced, high-pressure salesmen who had invaded every town and village in east and west, selling lots, buying them back, through 'dummies', at an advance on the price paid, thereby stimulating the demand until it had assumed the proportions of a national boom. Since the small investor does not learn from experience, it was to be expected that a similar proceeding would bring similar results. But this time, it seemed, even such a proceeding would prove unnecessary.

A few of the more provident or better-paid foremen of the mill started the run by coming into the offices of the company and pre-empting the corner lots. That set a local avalanche going.

Sam was told that it had been a revelation even to Mr Ferguson, the huge vice-president and manager of Langholm Real Estate. "It's a cinch," he was reported to have said. "We'll sell at a fixed price, on the instalment plan. $30 down, $10 a month for a year. There's more money in that than there ever was in the first boom. Five dollars' worth of advertising will sell more lots than a thousand dollars' worth of commissions did ten years ago."

Next, Sam was told, through Mr Beatty, the humour of the thing struck Mr Ferguson. He emitted a sound which came as near to being a laugh as any sound this single-minded man had ever given vent to. "Know what we're doing?" he asked. "We're emptying that Terrace. The mill-hands are going to move out to a man. We'll get even with that old devil in his grave for refusing to let us handle that pocket concern of his."

Which filled Sam with a sense of distaste rather than foreboding.

Early in December, his father's will having been probated, he gave orders to his Toronto brokers to sell the forty one-thousand dollar shares in Langholm Real Estate which remained to him; and ten days later he read the letter covering their cheque with an up-curled lip.

"Owing to the renewed activity in Langholm Real Estate we are glad to report that we have placed your holdings at the highly satisfactory figure of 275. We take pleasure in enclosing our cheque for the amount minus our commission of ¼%, namely $109,725.00, which, we trust, you will find correct."

So far, then, the process of transformation through which the town went had been entirely the result of Sam's own actions. What followed was in part traceable to the operation of natural law; in part it sprang from Sibyl Carter's residence in town.

As for the operation of natural law, that which is bound to happen where 'easy money' is made happened here. Some easy

money was made; more was expected; savings lost their sacro-
sanct character; wherever the 'easy-come, easy-go' applies, that
also will go easily which has come hardly; and the spending is
injudiciously done, on useless trifles, knick-knacks, gewgaws.
Some of the mill-hands were of sturdy immigrant stock; others
were mere transients who did not look on their jobs as a provision for life; it was the latter who were swept off their feet.

The mere change in the presidency had had its effect. Sam
was what his father had not been, a gentleman. He never wore
a suit of clothes two days in succession; his shoes had a high
polish; in the presence of the men he was silent; when he did
speak, his words were reserved, objective, decisive. He was not
'of the people'. He did not, like his father, live in what had
become the slum-district of the town; he lived in a mansion
said to hold fifty rooms. As he knew, it was remarked upon
that a footman held his coat for him when he donned it; that
a valet laid out the clothes he was to wear. Coarse, jocular
details were added which made the hearers laugh; but even
that laugh left a note of aversion.

And now there was Sibyl.

First at Clark House; for whatever happened there soon
found its repercussions in the town, if only through the servants. The newly-finished gymnasium was a huge, barn-like
structure of steel and glass in which the most varied equipment,
athletic and acrobatic, was being installed. At the height of ten
feet from the concrete floor a net was stretched; from steel
girders flying trapezes were being suspended. In addition, there
were horizontal bars, double bars, spring-boards, rowing-
machines, jumping-horses of steel, all arranged within the
spaces between net and walls. Soon Sibyl and Maud, in shorts
and tunics—popular report said 'as good as naked'—were exer-
cising there, visible to anyone from the windows of the house
as well as from the hillsides of the park. Servants said it was
as good as a circus, Sibyl, having had advanced training in these
things, took the lead; Maud, exulting in her new health after
the confinement, soon surpassed her instructor in daring, if
not in skill.

As the senator pondered these things, his memories every
now and then assumed that uncanny quality of presentness
which was charged with his old emotions. He could not have
said on what grounds he had felt so profoundly shocked; they
were neither moral nor social grounds. But Maud was his wife;
she was the mother of his son. Then . . . why?

He asked her that question.

She laughed. "I'm hard as nails. Why grudge me a pleasure?"

"I can't look on without feeling weak."

"Don't look on, then." And, sharply, "What would you say if I wanted to perform in a circus?"

Sam made a helpless gesture.

Again Maud laughed. "Because I'm the great miller's wife?'

"Why should you wish to do such things?"

"Because, from day to day, I need something to live for."

On occasion, Bob Stevens found time to join the women Sibyl called him 'the only real sport in town'.

If only one could live from day to day! If there were no memories, no foreshadowings of things to come!

Maud's social activities, interrupted by her pregnancy, were resumed. Again there were dances; at first the big affairs for which guests came from east and west; then local gatherings. When Sibyl first talked of 'livening up the town', Maud had raised the standard objections: there were no people at Langholm socially their equals; people were not used to 'going the pace'. With some show of justice Sibyl replied that they must make the best of what material was to hand. She enumerated a score of professional men with their wives; a score of well-to-do business men; a score of executives of the mill. "We live in a democratic country. I want to dance; you ought to. Let's train our partners."

The ambitions of many in the second and third ranks of society were realized. Mrs Tindal who, so far, had seen the inside of Clark House only on vast, formal occasions was, with her husband, invited to informal dinner parties and improvised dances. The younger set modelled their manners on what they saw, especially in Sibyl Carter.

Soon Maud found herself trailing in Sibyl's wake. It was Sibyl who wrote out the lists of invitations. Maud had had an irresistible aversion to Bob Stevens; he became a frequent caller wherever Sibyl was to be found. The fact that Maud kept open house placed her under an obligation to accept invitations from others; the ballroom at the Palace Hotel came into demand.

Sam was bewildered. He wanted time, time, time to disentangle the chaos in his mind and soul. Yet he felt that, if he could plunge into iniquity himself, if he could break every moral and social law and convention, he might dull his inward pains. Occasionally he wished for such a thing.

Early in the new year came one relief. The detective agency

which he had employed reported that William Swann had gone to England and secured a position in a company supplying gas to a section of London.

Gradually, irresistibly, Sibyl's influence spread through the strata of Langholm society. A young woman left much alone by her husband transformed the manners and morals of the town. In spite of this unifying factor, social gaps widened. A shop girl might dress like a lady; the lady could put her in her place by ignoring her finery. One significant change was widely observed. Adolescent sons and daughters of professional and semi-professional men—bankers, brokers, wholesale merchants —had never hesitated about acting as auxiliary salesmen and salesgirls in the stores: on Saturdays; in the holiday rush. They were supplanted by the offspring of mill-hands. Young people in the high school divided into two groups: those who left off giving such services, and those who replaced them. Those who left off declared that, in the past, they had served only 'for the fun of it'; and, carried away by the flood of frivolity and extravagance, they now made exorbitant demands on the pocket-books of their fathers.

Few even of the well-to-do matrons refrained from imitating Sibyl in conversation, conduct, dress. She showed them how, in a wider world, a woman could think, speak, act, and not only 'get away with it', but harvest admiration. Admiration, especially when won by novel and startling means, seemed the only thing worth living for.

What this was bound to lead to was revealed one night in the second year, the winter of 1899 to 1900, on the occasion of a great ball at Clark House. Dick Carter happened to be at Vancouver where, by imitating himself, he was repeating his sensational success at Langholm on a larger scale. Sibyl had gone to New York to buy a frock for the occasion; she wanted to outshine herself in boldness of *décolletage*. Any man who came within the magnetic field of her physical attraction she provoked and challenged; and when she succeeded in driving him to the point where he forgot himself, she stopped him coldly, cruelly, cynically, showing him by her contempt that he was merely an experimental victim. She barely concealed the fact any longer that her aim was to seduce the master of the mill; and that her attacks on others were only oblique attacks on him.

This time she selected Bob Stevens as her decoy.

Clark House, with its thirty guest rooms, as well as the Palace Hotel was filled to overflowing; some fifty local guests, a hundred from distant centres, were invited, with their wives. Even in the large ballroom of Clark House, in the four drawing-rooms, and in the great hall, there was a crush. There had been a scene between Maud and Sam because he had tried to beg off, partly, he remembered, for the very reason that he was tempted.

By one or two o'clock even Sam had been struck by the fact that Sibyl had danced exclusively with Bob Stevens. She had led him on till he was barely responsible for his actions.

It so happened that, at a given moment, there was a crowd of breathless, excited young people who had stopped dancing, in the recess formed in the hall by the eastern ramp of the grand stairway. In a sudden hush, the music broke off; then, with a clash of cymbals and a flourish of brasses, it struck up a rapid waltz. Sam, who happened to be coming across the hall, realizing that a crush must follow the musical challenge, slipped into that crowd where, unexpectedly, he found himself next to Maud. To their right, as they faced the hall, were the doors leading to the dining-rooms; behind them, a narrow passage stood open which led to the service quarters. All about, couples were re-forming; others, breathless, took their places; the wild, rousing tune filled them as with new blood. Maud, without her cane, marvellously dressed in snow-white, diamonds sparkling in her ears, her hair, around her neck, looked down on Sam with a curious expression, as if challenging him; and he, accepting the challenge, was on the point of asking her for the dance when, from the wide-winged doors of the ballroom opposite them, the crush bore down, led by Sibyl and Bob Stevens. Ever faster they turned, frantically, followed by a dense, bacchantic crowd of other couples.

Maud and Sam both watched, forgetting to dance; for simultaneously they were seized with the feeling that something was going to happen. Since, like a tide, the dancers flowed into every corner available in the hall, they retreated laughing, to the very door which stood open to the service quarters, finding themselves, as the wave broke into the recess, on opposite sides of it.

Bob Stevens and Sibyl were still leading. Bob's face was a study: tense, confident, arrogant even; he was an apt pupil of his partner. Suddenly his eyes flickered. He saw neither Maud nor Sam; but he had seen the door open behind them.

As they whirled past Sam, Bob, by a dextrous manoeuvre, forced his partner into that door, as if he wished to lengthen the dance by that much; the rest, seeing the narrowness of the passage, swept on.

In the semi-darkness behind, neither Maud nor Sam could avoid hearing what went on. With a grip around his partner's waist, Bob brought her to a stop and tried to embrace her; he felt his hands slapped; and he heard an angry cry: "Stand off!"

"No," he answered.

"Stand off," she repeated. "You are not my game."

He, sobered, stared at her, mockingly. In cold-blooded insolence he was her only match. "Not yet, you mean?"

She tried to outstare him; but before the cynical, level, physical challenge of his grey eyes she compromised. A smile broke over her features. "Perhaps!" she said and, seeing Sam and Maud, she slipped away, knowing every passage in that house.

It was a revelation! even Sam knew that *he* was her game; that it was he to whom she displayed herself.

Maud's reaction stood in flagrant contrast to her usual attitude to her husband. A frown spread over her brow. Walking quickly, she crossed the hall and entered the library.

Sam followed her; but he went slowly; and she was no longer in the room she had entered. There was only one way out, through the French windows in the far corner which led into the lane.

He stopped. Those windows reminded him of what had recently taken place there. "What is to be, will be," he said to himself.

In the morning, the dance having ended only with the break of dawn, mischief began to work. Sam saw everything in its bearing on the mill.

The first day shift of the 'hands', summoned by the piercing call of the siren, was on its way to work: hundreds of men trotting sullenly along on the north side of Main Street which formed the only route from Terrace to mill. There they were overtaken, first by a string of carriages proceeding to the Palace Hotel, crowded with guests from Clark House; then by a crowd of pedestrians who, as if to emphasize the division of classes, at sight of the workmen, noisily ran to the south side of the street. These were young people, barely out of their teens. In the exuberance of their spirits they were playing tag, hunting each other, calling, waking the echo. All were in evening clothes, the women wrapped in costly furs, the men in silk-lined cloaks, wearing high hats.

It did look as if they were of a different race from the toilers who, in their white-dusted jeans, were trudging along to their toil while the sons and daughters of the gods were returning to sleep off the effects of their revels. Catcalls and provoking remarks sounded across the street; it was by reason of these that Sam heard about it.

Among the men was Bruce Rogers who had joined the procession at the corner of Argyle Street, for he lived with his aging parents on Clark Street. Though he had gone to high school and had recently been promoted in the mill, on Sam's personal intervention, he remained one of the men. When Sam heard of his offence, he knew at once that, though the young fellow's father was content to look on at the doings of 'his betters' with a feeling half of incomprehending respect, half of indulgent amusement, young Rogers was differently constituted.

A complaint was lodged against him by Sibyl herself; and Sam had to take notice and summoned him to the office.

The story which the young fellow revealed, reluctantly and under pressure, was, pieced together and interpreted by Sam, as follows.

One afternoon, half a year ago, in going home from the day shift ending at four o'clock, Bruce had met Sibyl Carter on the narrow board walk leading from her house, at the east end of Clark Street, to Argyle Street which, in turn, led down to Main Street. He had stepped aside to let her pass. In acknowledgment, she had given him an upward smile and a seductive glance. In listening to the younger man, Sam became increasingly aware that he was extraordinarily handsome, resembling his father who, even in his old age, had more than his share of striking good looks. His shyness bespoke his innocence in matters where women were concerned. Strange to say, from that day on, he had for some considerable time met her daily at the same spot. Invariably she had given him that brilliant smile which, however, had become more and more intimate. He, almost worshipping her, had taken to walking past her house which stood isolated at the very end of the street. He had seen her at the windows; and she had given him encouraging smiles and nods. One day, coming in sight of her door which was only half screened by young aspens, she had stepped out and, as if unaware of his presence, she had there, facing the hills across the lake, raised her long skirts to adjust her garters.

All which Bruce, under pressure, revealed to explain his offence. But what had happened thereafter—what had made

132

him hate her, Bruce refused to divulge; though he did not deny that things had gone farther.

On the morning after the ball, a last carriage had come down Main Street, bearing no less than seven guests. Among them was Sibyl who sat on the folded-back top, her feet on the seat. In one hand she held a bottle of champagne; in the other, a half-filled glass. The other six, all men, crowded on the seats of the landau, were toasting her. She, looking superciliously down at the stream of mill-hands hurrying west, had caught sight of Bruce who had turned at the clatter of the horses' hoofs on the pavement. Tipsily she had raised her glass to him, drained it, flung it over her shoulder, and thrown him a kiss.

He, boiling with rage, reddening to the roots of his hair, had hurled a single word at her, that word being "Bitch!"

The incident, witnessed by scores of mill-hands, caused excited talk at the mill which Bob Stevens reported to Sam. Strangely, the talk was quite irrelevant. It was said that this woman, living alone in her house, employed six servants, including groom and coachman. Six people to wait on a woman who had no children and whose husband was rarely at home! There was talk of Dick Carter looking for a divorce.

Well, so the talk went on, what about Clark House? Its retinue consisted of twoscore menials all needed to keep the place in order: gardeners, stable-hands, coachmen, maids, footmen, fat butler.

A middle-aged gang-boss, Watson by name, round as a football, a bachelor, struck up a friendship with Olmquist, the head gardener who lived in the lodge just inside the gate of the park. He supplied definite figures. Perkins, the butler, drew $100 a month; footmen, coachmen, chief groom, $75 each; the gardener had $90 and house, milk, fuel free.

By complex calculations Watson arrived at the conclusion that it cost $100,000 a year to run Clark House. "A hundred foremen don't get that much together; and you think a foreman's on Easy Street."

A week later the same Watson expounded at the bar of the Occidental Hotel, near the station, further calculations. So-and-so many bags of flour a day; at so-and-so much a bag wholesale; those who produced it got so-and-so much; the price of wheat was such-and-such; by far the largest item was 'overhead' as these beggars called it: dividends, interest, salaries, replacements; all profit, profit, profit to someone.

"Money makes money," a mill-hand said.

"*We* make it, you blockhead!" Watson cried. "Without us the whole show stops."

Rumour had it that Dick Carter, the absentee architect, got a fee of $1,020 for every unit added to the mill. The addition in course of construction numbered over a hundred units. If the total had been $100,000, nobody would have believed it. But $102,000? Who would invent such a sum?

This whole seething discontent was unleashed by a single word which an exasperated gang-boss had flung at the head of a woman. Sam was appalled; he was newly sobered; but he did not dismiss Bruce Rogers. How Sibyl took his refusal was hard to say.

The work of construction went on undisturbed. The cement masons were not employed by the mill but by a contractor in Winnipeg. When the mill-hands tried to rouse them, they laughed at the numbskulls. Trade unions were the solution. . . .

It did not come to an explanation between Sam and Maud. She dropped everything and went to Toronto and Montreal to shop. Sam only withdrew still further into his shell.

The house which, for a day, had resembled a hotel now resembled a dead-house. The child, of course, was being taken care of; but it was kept out of sight by its attendants. The whole vast establishment housed and fed a single man.

This Sibyl thought the moment to strike. She knew Sam's routine and laid her plan.

One day, early in the afternoon, as he drove down to his office in the cutter, for the snow lay deep, he saw her walking on Hill Road above the Terrace, with every appearance of being tired out. He did the charitable thing and bade his driver stop and pick her up.

"Where were you going?" he asked.

It was February; and Sibyl was wearing an excessively smart fur coat of mink; but the coat was hanging open, for she was hot from her walk. There was not a breath of wind; and the sun shone dazzlingly on the snowy landscape. Under her coat, she showed a dress of heavy, pearl-grey tussore silk. Her feet were shod in fur-trimmed goloshes.

She did not answer at once; she did not answer at all. Instead, she asked him to show her the mill.

"All is in confusion," he said. "We are building. Everything is covered with cement and flour dust."

"I don't care. I want to see it."

Nothing was left of the perverse attraction which she had exercised over him. "All right," he said grimly, "I'll show you."

"I've walked five miles," she said, still seemingly sullen. "It's made me tired. It was a godsend when you came along."

As always, Sam told the driver to stop at the Flour Building; and they walked over, entering via the laboratories. The chemists, most of whom knew her, greeted her. In the door to the bagging-floor she stopped and drew some pins out of her dress. A train fell to the dusty floor; she laughed at Sam who was impatiently waiting, laughed as if they had conspired for a given effect. She folded her fur coat back and bent to gather the train over her arm.

So far, the senator had looked at the scene from the outside. Suddenly he was in it; a feeling of distaste had sent him back into the past.

Ready for the trip through the mill, Sibyl, in full sight of two score hurrying men, rested her free hand in the crook of Sam's elbow, with a charming gesture of intimacy between relatives.

Too late Sam realized that he had made a grievous mistake in not refusing to comply with her demand. The men stared. His entrance, with this woman on his arm, caused a cessation of work. The mill-hands exuded hatred. But he could no longer retrieve the step.

Somehow they got through the first two floors; but on the third floor the first person they faced as they stepped out of the elevator was Bruce Rogers who, to make matters worse, blushed furiously when Sibyl, who had so recently lodged a complaint against him, gave him a demure and penitent smile, as if imploring forgiveness. Abruptly, without disguising his contempt, he turned on his heels and walked off.

Sibyl laughed and said in the most casual way, "That young man shows to advantage in working clothes. He changes for the walk home. I used to meet him near the corner of Clark Street. He did not look as well as he does here." Blushes came and went over her features.

She insisted on going through the whole of the mill, even out on the roof; but, if she had counted on being alone with Sam there, she was disappointed. Hundreds of masons were all about.

"And that's the last of it?" she asked, laughing.

"That's the last."

She stopped, dropping his arm. "Now," she said conspiratorially, "I want you to show me the spot from which you showed Maud the mill on the day when you met her."

This was a shock to Sam. Sibyl had spoken with the breathless intimacy and mischievous allusiveness with which one child playing truant speaks to another. How did she know? If Maud had told her, what reason had he to refuse the request? They returned to the top floor and re-entered the elevator which took them down into the vaults.

Grease-blackened men, long-spouted oilcans in hand, white wisps of cotton-waste hanging from the hip-pockets of their one-piece overalls, were tending turbines and dynamos, crawling on all-fours over the machines like spiders. The walls of these underground chambers were of the living rock: granite below a layer of limestone. Where, in summer, the rock had been dripping with trickles of water, icicles were hanging now, met from below by stalagmitic growths which here and there, meeting the hanging masses, formed glittering columns of fantastic shapes. On Sam, the men who were slowly, steadily moving about, in utter silence, had an uncanny effect; were they super or infra-human?

Sibyl was slowly picking her way over the icy floor with her toes carefully pointed.

Having turned to his right, Sam climbed the short narrow steel stairway to the gallery connecting the vaults with the power-houses downstream. The turbines hissed with the rush of unseen water. From the gallery opened the huge, copper-studded door which was hard to set in motion and equally hard to arrest when moving.

They stepped over the sill, into the river-bed now floored with snow. The limestone slab from which, a dozen years ago, he had shown Maud the buttressed sweep of the shoring wall was invisible; but he picked the spot with unerring instinct.

Then, as he turned, with an upward glance, his heart sank in him. At every window above he saw faces appearing and vanishing after a downward look: he and Sibyl were being watched.

What a vista that fact opened up! Only now did the feeling which had invaded him on entering the mill define itself: it was shame at being seen with this woman who had been the talk of the men.

Yet, as his wavering glance fell on her, in her fur-trimmed goloshes, her coquettish hat, her magnificent coat, still open and showing her close-fitting dress, she might have been to one less burdened with cares a captivating sight. Her cheeks were flushed with triumph.

She tripped over to him where he stood, ankle-deep in snow. She might well assume that they were in a spot the most hidden from spying eyes. Behind her hummed the mill, a hive of activity where nobody was presumed to have a second to spare. In front, beyond the old river-bed, now empty, rose the steep hillside with its cascades of leafless aspens. To the east stood the concave wall of the dam, sixty feet high, rising in an overpowering sweep. To the west, on spider-web trestles tapering upward, the viaducts swung north in a vast quadrant. Beyond, the squat arches of the new concrete bridge closed the view, flanked, to the south, by the towering elevators: each a sheaf of thick-set columns.

Sibyl, too, glanced up and about; and she burst into a fountain of laughter, a high, silvery chime which, in the exuberance of her spirit, she cadenced in *coloratura*. "Sam!" she cried, still laughing, with a shrug at the furtive, fleeting faces at the windows, "if you don't want me to kiss you here, you will have to promise me something."

He tried to pass it off as a jest. "Which is?"

"To have dinner with me tonight, *tête-à-tête*, at my house."

He frowned. "No," he said. "I've let Maud go alone because I need every hour. I should be at the office this minute."

"Take me along," she cried. "I've never seen where you work."

"I work anywhere. Always. Day and night."

"Always the mill?" she mocked. "Then I understand Maud."

This was another shock. But again, as the easiest way out, he made light of her request. "I'll show you the office." But even as he said it, he knew he was making another mistake.

They returned by way of the ground floor of the mill where old Rogers was looking for him. With an apologetic bow he came to speak to the master, standing deferentially above him, cavernous, pale, handsome, his glance on the woman who was tapping the floor with a toe.

At the office, Sibyl's entrance in Sam's company caused no less of a sensation than at the mill. Miss Albright, in a flowered, flowing gown, met them in the boardroom. Catching sight of Sibyl, she stopped, her face flushing. With an awkward bow she turned back into the ante-room as if hurt.

Ostentatiously, as they entered his office, Sam left the door open.

"So this," Sibyl mocked, " is where the tremendous plans are hatched?"

Sam did not answer. "Sit down," he said.

"Just a mo!" And, shedding her coat, she tiptoed back to the door and, with a derisive, yet confidential wink at the half-dozen typists visible thence, she closed it. Hitching her arms as if to embrace him, she returned to Sam at the desk. "Sam," she said, "why do you act as if we were at the end of a liaison instead of at its beginning?"

He was conscious of the interpretation the situation would bear. Yet, when he spoke, it was his own distaste which dictated his words: the distaste for the lighter side of life. "Just what is your game, Sibyl?" he asked, "You seem to consider me legitimate prey."

"Bird-catcher and bird?" she scoffed. "Nice little mouthful you'd make for someone to crunch, Sam, bones and all." Then she added, "I want to talk to you."

Sam sat down. The irony of his, "I am all ear," fell flat.

Her smile was vaguely intimate as if to say that they both knew where they stood with regard to each other. She came close, so she almost touched his shoulder, bent over and rested one elbow on the desk. Her chin she placed in her hand, turning her face back to him. "My own case is clear," she said in a whisper. "I make no secret of it. How about yours? Are you a child that you don't know? As our grandparents used the word, I'm not in love with you. Yet you give me no rest. I want something; and I'm honest about it."

He was balancing himself mentally. "And what is it you want?"

She laughed softly. "Do you know that all the women around here feel as I do? Down to, or up to, that precious Miss Dolittle. Did you watch the girl in the outer room?"

"No. I didn't."

"She all but told me I was poaching on her preserve."

"Don't forget Dick, Sybil."

She waved a hand. "Dick it gone. I'm whistling him down the wind. What you mean is, 'Don't forget Maud!'"

"Perhaps. What do you mean by saying, Dick is gone?"

"I won't discuss Dick. He's a different story. You'll know soon enough." As if she were marshalling all her powers, she struck a new note. "Listen, Sam. A month ago I saw a French frock in New York; I bought it to wear for you. But I couldn't wear it at that ball. In this town I can only try it on in my bedroom. Don't you want to see it?"

"Look here, Sibyl," Sam said, leaning back. "Is this fair? Deliberately to put me in a position where I must play the part of a cad."

"Nonsense. I know all about Maud. I'm not taking anything from her. She has Dr Fry in soul communion. I'm an animal and unashamed of the fact. Will you come and have dinner with me tonight?"

"After what you've said, especially about Maud, I can't."

"Nonsense," she repeated, bringing her flushed face close to his and reaching out with her free hand to ruffle his auburn hair. "Sam!" she whispered with moist breath. "I'll tell you. You think, She is thin. I am. But I'm not only thin. I have pretty breasts. Won't you see me in that frock tonight? Or, for that matter, without it?" And, failing to realize his mood, trusting in the power of physical contact, she slipped down on his knees, with a sinuous motion, twining her arms about his neck and pressing his head to her bosom.

Sam rose. For a moment, she clinging to him, they were in danger of falling.

Like a fury she recovered herself and faced him. "That's final?"

He did not answer at once. Sadness invaded him; he felt sorry for her. "Too bad it should have come to this," he said.

"You've fish-blood!" she hissed, turned, picked up her coat, faced him once more, "Joseph!", and was gone.

THE dinner-party at Clark House was an old people's party. Twenty guests sat around the board in the 'small' dining-room; with the one exception of Lady Clark there was no one less than sixty years old. Apart from her, there were only three women: Mrs Tindal, Mrs Beatty and Miss Charlebois.

The meal was excellent; the wines a marvel of selection; the service, under the young butler's direction, flawless.

This butler was perhaps the person who enjoyed himself most in the feeling of his youth and strength. The others, in their immaculate shirt-fronts and black evening coats, set off by white ties, white vests, and the white hair above, so he reflected, had one foot in the grave, even though, between them, they owned hundreds of millions. What did wealth count for in comparison with youth and vitality? It never struck him that old age would soon creep on him as well.

He could have laughed at them as they sipped their wine, careful not to take a mouthful more than their doctors allowed them.

That Mr Tindal, for instance, who, still pompous in the middle or toward the end of his eighties, still magnificent in figure and carriage, wealthy beyond the dream of princes, yet looking at his wife across the table before he dared to touch this dish or to taste that wine; for it was she who, by imperceptible motions of her hand, gave or withheld permission.

Or that little 'shrimp', Captain Stevens! Or Dr Fry, bachelors both, and both among the younger guests. Captain Stevens, formal, a stickler for etiquette, with his everlasting bows to the hostess. Dr Fry with his long hair and the drooping eyelids, affecting the flowing tie of the artist, black instead of white. All playing parts: the parts of men younger than they were.

Or Dr Sherwood who had replaced Dr Cruikshank as the family physician, a veritable tower of a man, like Mr Inkster, the lawyer, another man-mountain with the neck of a bull, though, in spite of his great age, he had not yet learned to eat sparingly; he visibly enjoyed food and drink; yet, visibly too, he ate and drank with a bad conscience. He dreaded the morrow.

It struck the young butler as strange that all directly connected with the mill were spare and small. Was there, to explain the fact, some principle of selection at work? No doubt. The Clarks, being small, had chosen small men as their lieutenants.

But their women had been tall and full-figured. Of any but Lady Clark he had, of course, had no personal knowledge; but one could judge from the picture of the senator's wife upstairs. Her daughter Ruth, of course, being a Clark, was reported to be small, too. She was a *Marquise*, he reflected, by her marriage, living in Paris, a widow....

Around the board, the conversation suddenly flared up and became general.

"Did you hear that over the radio?" Captain Stevens asked. "About our precious Mr Ferguson of blessed memory?"

"My former associate," Mr Tindal said. "It went without saying that he had to come to a bad end." But under the reproving glance of his wife, still fine-looking, though much wrinkled, he went silent.

However, such a topic could not be allowed to die. Even the senator raised an eyebrow. "No. What about him?"

"Sentenced to ten years in Sing-Sing for fraudulent real-estate operations. It was the 'real-estate' which put me wise to his identity even before Langholm was mentioned. He had a string of aliases to his name. Ferguson wasn't his last name by a long way."

"And who was Mr Ferguson?" Mr Inkster asked with his air of remote superiority.

As a general thing it struck the butler that everybody around the board spoke as if he despised everyone else. No doubt old age accounted for that. Since everybody, having run his life, had arrived at a point different from that anyone else had arrived at, he felt the need of justifying himself by an attitude of aloofness.

"Didn't you know him?" the captain asked.

"Must have been before my time."

"Perhaps. He vanished in some mysterious way from this town. Must have been in 1898."

"99," Mat Tindal corrected before his wife's warning look took effect.

"That is," Captain Stevens went on, "there was nothing mysterious about the *way*. What was mysterious was the *why*.

He left behind what looked like a flourishing business and went into the unknown. It all came out in the wash, of course. He didn't even leave a forwarding address, and he was wise. His mail must have consisted largely of letters protesting against sharp practice. He must have taken half a million out of this burgh...."

"Three-quarters," Mat Tindal could not refrain from cor-recting.

"Was it that much? Well, you should know."

"I do."

It was comedy for the young butler to watch the exchange of looks between husband and wife.

"I had to make up his accounts," Mr Tindal added.

A smile flitted over the captain's thin lips. "Couldn't trust any employee with the task?" he asked slowly.

Old Mrs Tindal's glance became eloquent. "There you see," it seemed to say, "what comes of talking when silence is golden."

Lady Clark looked from one to the other, an amused expres-sion on her even features. She was plainly curious to hear more of Mr Ferguson. The captain, always a ladies' man, gratified her.

"Mr Ferguson," he said, "was a character; in his way he was a genius. You say," he went on, turning to Mr Inkster, "he was before your time. But you've seen the shrinking of this town. It was spectacular enough; but its growth, from a population of 561 to one of 20,000, was much more so; and it was directed by Mr Ferguson, the great realtor."

"Ah," said the huge lawyer, his triple chin, balanced by a triple neck behind, shaking as with an earthquake. "I'm locat-ing him in my mind. I never knew him. But I had something to do with cleaning up the mess he had left behind. He must have been a character indeed. What build was he?"

"Bottle-shaped," the captain replied promptly. "Reminded one of Baobab trees in North Australia. Remember the Realty Building on Main Street? It was broken down some ten years ago, by a speculator in used brick. If you do, you'll also remember the plate-glass front on the ground floor. In Mr Ferguson's time, one could see, through that glass front, half a hundred typists hammering away at their keys, busy as bees. Over them floated a dense cloud of cigar-smoke; and over the cigar-smoke floated Mr Ferguson."

There was a titter around the board.

"I called him bottle-shaped. Pear-shaped would have been

more graphic perhaps. Most of his weight was contained in his paunch. From the rear of this office a spiral stairway led up to the second floor, the Olympus where our good friend Mat Tindal throned." The captain had his eye on Mrs Tindal to guard against a flank attack. Everybody watched this with secret amusement. But since nothing happened except that withered, if once beautiful lips were straightened, betraying that she heard, he ventured further. "He was the Zeus who ... well, not exactly directed but watched the activities of the lower gods. The secretary-treasurer, by the way, was the cashier in his cage. I wish I could show you the figure of Mr Ferguson ... You knew Charles Beatty, God rest his soul, didn't you?"

Mr Inkster nodded as he raised his glass of champagne.

"Well, then, you know what a story-teller he was." And again the captain held his eye on Mrs Tindal as he proceeded, feeling his way, uncertain how far he might go. "I once heard him describe that scene on the lower floor of the Realty Building. It was a scream. He'd been talking of our good friend Mat; and he had said, 'Commercially speaking, that whole concern of Langholm Real Estate was a hoax; though the millions it made were real enough.'" The captain laughed and turned to Mr Tindal. "You don't mind, Mat, if I repeat what he said, do you? Nobody ever minded what Charlie said."

"I don't mind," Mr Tindal replied with an air of detachment, though he had just begun to stand a little on his dignity.

"I knew you wouldn't. Well, what he said was this. 'If ever the attorney-general becomes interested in that concern. . . .'"

This beginning, however, filled Mr Tindal with vague misgivings. He straightened. "Nothing was ever done there that the law could object to. At least not to my knowledge."

"Exactly," the captain hastened to agree with the final phrase. "It was all Mr Ferguson's doing. That's what Charlie Beatty said. But, being Charlie Beatty, he could not have expressed it so badly. In his metaphorical way he used a figure of speech. 'In scheming ability,' he said, 'Mat compared with Mr Ferguson, is a dwarf. Mr Ferguson is a giant. Mat ...'" And Captain Stevens hesitated. Even to him who despised Mat Tindal, what he was going to say seemed a bit strong to be said in the presence of ladies; but he could not resist. "'Mat,'" he went on, with Charles Beatty's words, "'is a dwarf who could walk upright under Ferguson's bed ... on stilts.'"

A shout of laughter went around the board, though five

people were frowning instead of laughing: Lady Clark, the senator, Mrs Tindal, Mrs Beatty, and the young butler. The rest were carried away by their senile mirth, Mat Tindal included.

The captain, noting the signs, hurried on. "I am going to give you Charlie's description. 'It beat me,' Charlie said, 'how this fellow Ferguson, with his six foot three and his rotund bulk and his always freshly-pressed and expensive clothes and his linen which he never wears twice, manages to look like a youngster who's been out in his Sunday suit playing in mud. Of course, that black cigar which he keeps hanging from his pendulous lips is always scattering ashes over his lapels, his vest, and everything, while his booming voice drones forth an incessant dictation of sales-talks and circular letters. He lives at the Palace Hotel where every convenience known to civilization is available; but I don't think he has a bath from one end of the year to the other. Whenever I have to go to his office, I nearly choke in that malodorous atmosphere made up of the reek of his sweating body and the stale smoke of his cigar. How the typists bear it I don't understand. Of course, they use gallons of cheap scent with which they impregnate their clothes and the handkerchiefs they keep handy when he approaches them. No matter how early it is in the day, no matter how late at night, Mr Ferguson is always on deck. I wonder whether he sleeps there, too? I know he has his lunch brought over from the City Café across the street. He hasn't even a private office; he claims the whole lower floor. To cap it all, he is subject to terrific colds, always taking a fresh one before the old one subsides; and invariably he sneezes a wet cloud into the dry one before, absent-mindedly, he searches his pockets for a handkerchief.' "That," Captain Stevens concluded, "was the way Charlie described him; it may not be delicate; I apologize to the ladies; but it is graphic."

"Why didn't you kick him out?" Dr Sherwood asked Mr Tindal.

Captain Stevens forestalled the answer. "Well, you know, in his way the man was a genius. He was the typical exponent of 'the science of salesmanship'. He was untidy, not only in his clothes, but in everything. Wherever he went, he dropped papers, letters, and telegrams; but when one was needed, and the typists frantically searched for it in letter trays, on desks, in waste-paper baskets, he'd straighten his back and say, 'Just a mo!' And then he would delve into the capacious caverns of his memory and, a moment later, reproduce it verbatim. I don't think he ever made a mistake. Did he now, Mat?"

"Not to my knowledge," Mat said with vicarious pride.

"And did you ever know him to be late?"

"He was late once," Mat said with a senile snicker. "The last time I saw him."

"Tell us about it," the captain said, his old eyes twinkling.

Again a warning glance flashed from the wife to the husband; and when he tried to ignore it, there followed a stern, "Mat!"

But he was beyond restraint; he, too, had his memories. Testily he turned to her, saying, though in a voice unexpectedly mild, but drumming the knuckle of his middle finger on the board, "Anna, I'm getting tired of this everlasting repression. I am not a child."

Which, coming from a man in his second childhood—he was seven years older than the senator—was pathetic, if not ludicrous. There was, however, an embarrassed silence while plates were changed for the dessert, before the former 'realtor' went on.

"It was ten o'clock when Mr Ferguson came slowly and heavily up the circular stairway to the filing floor where I had my suite. As always, a black cigar, half chewed off, was hanging from the corner of his lips. His vast raccoon coat was buttoned awry over chest and stomach. He reminded me of a grade-three boy who has dressed without the help of his mother. On his huge skull a wide-brimmed hat sat at a rakish angle. He came in without a greeting; and I saw at once that, for the first time in my experience of him, he had been drinking. Downstairs, the typewriters had gone silent.

"'Well,' he said, dropping into a chair, with the first attempt I had ever known him to make at controlling his voice, 'up to you now, old horse.' He always had some outrageous name for me. 'I'm through. That piece of news you brought me, after the shareholders' meeting the other day, has knocked the bottom out of the barrel.' Perhaps I should explain. We had just bought a considerable new acreage for subdivision, paying a stiff price, on the strength of the expected expansion of the mill; building operations were going on there on a vast scale. But Mr Clark had refused to give details regarding his plans except to a shareholders' meeting. When, months later, that meeting was held, he had casually dropped a remark to the effect that the expansion would involve no increase in the number of hands employed. Pardon me, senator, if I say that much; without it, my story would not be clear."

The senator waved the hand of concession.

"But the boom we had launched rested on that expectation of an increase in population.

" 'As a matter of fact,' Mr Ferguson said, 'I don't own a qualifying share in this business any longer. Sold the last thousand dollars' worth to a guy in Vancouver who was fool enough to give me six thousand for it. Pays to sell on the crest of the wave.' "

At this point a cackling laugh interrupted the recital. With a shock the company realized that it came from the senator. It was not till he saw that all eyes were turned on him that he waved a hand. "Go on, Mat," he said. "Don't mind me. I was just reminded of something." This something was the fact that he, too, had sold out of Langholm Real Estate on the crest of a wave, without giving the principle the slightest thought; nor had he received such a price.

" 'Well, I'm off for pastures new,' Mr Ferguson added. I looked at him. Though I detested the man, I dreaded the thought of being left alone with a business on my hands into which I had been railroaded twelve years before and of which I knew practically nothing. 'Who's to look after things?' I asked.—'You, I suppose. I wash my hands.'—'The boom isn't over,' I said.—'Isn't it?' And Mr Ferguson took the cigar from between his lips, pointing the chewed-off end at my necktie. 'Listen, Tindal,' he said. 'If you want my advice, you won't sell another lot. Not locally. When that news about automatic operation gets about, people will jump to conclusions. You're a shareholder in that mill. Are people going to believe you when you tell them you didn't know? Besides, you're too white-livered'—his word for 'honest'—'to tell them such a thumping lie. They'd lynch you. Somebody will have to face the music, but you can bet your shirt it won't be me.' That was the first hint I had of things the man had done which weren't absolutely above-board. In fact, I didn't quite see it yet . . ."

A smile went around the board. Mrs Tindal lowered her eyes.

" 'Things are booming,' I said.—'While building's going on,' he replied. 'When that's finished, the whole floating labour supply which you call population will fade away and die. Of course, you can capitalize a slump as well as a boom; but it takes a sharp one if you know what I mean.' Excuse the vulgarity, ladies and gentlemen; they are his words, not mine. 'I never thought that mill would come through. Those Clarks surprised me,' Mr Ferguson continued. 'I had counted on a little boom of a thousand lots; it's run into fifty thousand. We've subdivided this burgh for a population of a quarter million. Sooner or later there was bound to be a collapse. But when a bone is picked clean, the wise dog leaves it to hunt for another.' He laughed' 'Investors!' he said. 'Suckers I call them.'—'Do you mean to say we've been overselling?' I asked.—I won't tell you what he did. Yes, I will. It shows the whole vulgarity of the man."

"Mat!" came Mrs Tindal's warning voice. But wine and good fellowship carried the day.

"He rose and came around the desk, bending to look at my legs. 'Hm . . . I thought I'd seen long pants on you. The way you talk . . .'"

Again a shout of laughter went around the board so that the wine glasses tinkled. Even Lady Clark smiled faintly, probably more at the narrator's simplicity than at his narrative. In spite of his age, Mat coloured; but the success of the story went to his head like wine.

" 'You wanted your money,' Mr Ferguson went on; 'same's I; and since you owned some of this real estate which we've been peddling about, you've made several times as much as I have. What's wrong about it? Sheep want to be sheared. It's a dirty business; but it's got to be done. If we hadn't done it, somebody else would. The suckers thought they could get something for nothing. So, for that matter, did you. But then you had me. For the rest of them the world isn't made that way. Is it my fault that they didn't know it? What good is a hundred and fifty each to fifty thousand people? We relieved them of what would have been of no earthly to them.' That phrase I remember with the greatest distinctness. 'No earthly!' 'Except to pay a hospital bill to help another sucker into the world? To us, the total's been a nice, tidy sum.' The man, you see, had no ethical standards. Suddenly I thought of another angle. 'Are you sure,' I asked, 'that nobody's got a legal comeback?'— 'Trust me,' he laughed. 'They'll try to kick up a row, of course. Don't worry. Only bunglers run foul of the law.' " Mat, in his white vest, sat and looked about.

"Well," Captain Stevens said, "he did run foul of the law at last. Come to think of it, there was legal trouble here, too, later on."

"No real trouble," Mat said. "Some cranks sued the company and lost their cases. One of them used expressions which forced me to bring a libel suit against him."

"That suit," the captain said, carefully drawing Mat towards a final exposure, "that suit you won, didn't you?"

Mat took the bait. "I certainly did," he said, poutering his chest.

Insidiously the captain went on. "If I remember right, you sued for ten thousand dollars damages, didn't you?"

For the third time Mrs Tindal's "Mat!" was heard. But it was too late, though Mat himself at last was shrinking.

"They cut that down a bit in court, though," the captain went on inexorably. "If I remember right, what you got was five cents."

The butler looked at the old man who sat there, immaculate, a millionaire. To him, at least, it was a dramatic conclusion to the tale.

The senator, trying to soften the impact of the poisoned dart, though he had never had any liking for Mat Tindal, had, in fact, called him and his associate 'sharks', raised a finger, nodding. "That collapse of the boom," he said, "was the direct cause of the first strike the mill had ever had."

Mrs Tindal's eyes darted a flame. "No," she said, "the direct cause of that strike was the conduct of Mrs Sibyl Carter."

Which, to some of the guests, would have been somewhat of a comeback had not Lady Clark at this moment risen, with a glance at Dr Fry. "I believe," she said, "we'll have a little music."

Even the men, with the exception of Captain Stevens, felt sufficiently with the Tindals to rise and join the ladies without sitting over their port.

For days Lady Clark did not betray how profoundly Mrs Tindal's asperity in contradicting the senator had shocked her. In the first place, anything said openly against Sibyl Carter reflected on the family of Maud Clark, a woman whom she had always wished to be able to admire; in the second, the tone had betrayed that, even in the small remainder of what had been Langholm society, envy of, and hostility against, the Clarks were still rampant.

But the very indignation which she felt against Mrs Tindal made her desirous of knowing exactly what had been the state of affairs prior to that strike. Since Miss Charlebois had told her of Sibyl's first appearance at Langholm, she had harboured a distinct aversion for even the memory of this woman. Since the day, however, when the whole reputation of the Clarks would be in her keeping could no longer be far off, she felt she must know what she could find out. She could not discuss Mrs Carter with her father-in-law; the less so since Miss Charlebois had hinted her belief that the woman had come near wrecking the senator's marriage. She was almost afraid of hearing details; but she felt she must overcome her disinclination. In Miss Charlebois, who had been an inmate of Clark House for over forty years, she had to her hand a living chronicle of events. Miss Charlebois had further knowledge. She must ask her for all she knew.

The occasion offered one afternoon when the senator, having caught a slight cold, was lying down. Dr Sherwood had been in to see him.

"Nothing serious, I hope?" she asked, standing in the gallery.

"At the senator's age anything may be serious," the huge doctor replied. "It's no more than a slight head-cold . . . now. I have given him a diaphoretic and a soporific. I think he'll sleep. His valet is in the dressing-room. I shall send a nurse for the night. Just as a precautionary measure. The chances are he will be around again in a day or two; but one can never tell."

"Had I better sit with him?"

"No. He is best left alone. Rest is the only prescription."

So, during the afternoon which the two women, as a rule, spent in reading, Lady Clark sought out Miss Charlebois in her sitting-room.

"I want to make you talk," she said with a smile as she sat down in a chintz-covered armchair.

"Certainly. What about?"

"You remember the night of the old men's dinner? Just before we rose from table there was an allusion to the first strike. I should like to see clear in the matter. Who was right, the senator or Mrs Tindal?"

"Both," Miss Charlebois said promptly. "Both or neither. There was no single cause for that strike. The situation resulting from the suspension of activities on the part of Langholm Real Estate was distressing; the men blamed Mr Clark for the collapse—not at all, of course, in the sense in which he was responsible for it; motives of wealthy men are usually misinterpreted as you know. The market for Langholm real estate had vanished. The men suspected that Mr Clark was manipulating that market to protect his interests in the Terrace. That was nonsense, of course, but it sounded plausible enough. The men did not know Mr Clark . . . You know the huge 'Hall' as it is called, below Hill Road, on the Terrace? Mr Clark had built it to give the men a sort of community centre, with a gymnasium, a swimming-pool, a library, and a dozen recreation rooms. It had as much to do with the strike as anything else."

"How?" Lady Clark asked, surprised.

"I am talking, of course, only of what I was told. The men said, 'It goes to show . . .' Meaning that it proved how enormous the profits of the mill must be if its owner could afford to give them such a gift."

"I see."

"Meanwhile *they* had lost their savings by speculating in town lots. Town lots, instead of making them rich, as Mr Ferguson had promised, were suddenly worth nothing. I heard Mr Selby, the former manager of the Commercial Bank, talk about it. They came to him and tried to borrow on their lots. Mr Selby had to tell them that Langholm lots were no collateral. Meanwhile, as you know, the building activities at the mill promised a fabulous growth of the town. By this time it was clear that the capacity of the mill would be four, five, six times what it had been. The new units would come into operation in 1901. Where were the men to live that were needed to operate them? How could the mill grow without bringing a boom? Had Mr Clark, at that time, frankly stated his aim, it would have prevented that strike. But that was a thing he could not bring himself to do. Whether it was his natural secretiveness . . ."

The women looked at each other. All the Clarks had been secretive.

"Or whether he had some definite purpose, I cannot tell. Since I have lived the life of the Clarks as a member of this household from my twenties on, I have given a good deal of thought to the problem. I have mentioned that at one time I thought of writing the history of the mill or the family. The historian has sometimes to infer motives."

"What did you infer?" asked Lady Clark.

Miss Charlebois sat pensive. Then she went on. "It is a matter of public knowledge that, by the time Sir Edmund took over, the mill was the exclusive property of the Clarks. There were no outside shareholders left."

"I know," said Lady Clark. "You mean to say he kept his plans a secret to be the more readily able to eliminate the others?"

"Exactly. Why he should have had that desire is beyond my guessing. At any rate, the collapse of the boom, the disappearance of Mr Ferguson, the mystery surrounding the expansion of the mill—it had helped to bring about the atmosphere in which a strike was possible. That it actually broke, and at the time when it did, arose from two things. In the first place, Mr Clark suddenly went to Europe, with his wife and little boy—I, too, of course, was with them. Again, I don't know whether it was by inadvertence or in pursuance of a definite policy that he left behind, in charge, the most unpopular man on the staff. . . ."

"I know. Mr Stevens."

"Yes. Mr Stevens had great abilities. If, during the strike, there was no break in deliveries, it was due to his foresight. All the subsidiary plants, at Regina, Calgary, Edmonton, Winnipeg were ready to run triple shift; and there were enormous reserves. Yet I should think he would have preferred to postpone the outbreak of the strike till Mr Clark had returned from overseas—unless he wished to prove his ability to cope with it in the absence of the president. There the second cause of the actual break between men and management came in. The installation of the machines began: trainload after trainload arrived from Europe; even the men could now see that automatic operation was coming. They felt threatened in their very livelihood.

"But even then it might not have come to the worst had it not been for the fact that Sibyl Carter first had her divorce suit and then became the object of the infuriated men's desire for vengeance. The revenge the men took for the woman's provocative conduct during the preceding years has always seemed to me to have broken their morale. It introduced a new spirit, a spirit of insubordination if you care to call it that; it was really an unleashing of primitive passion; the veneer of civilization which had overlain the manners and the ways of thinking of the mill-hands, wore off. Possibilities opened up of what is called direct action. And Sibyl Carter was just the person to show them that, instead of men against management, beast might stand against beast. But to the men, Mrs Carter was identified with the Clarks; she was Maud's sister-in-law; and I know there were those who asserted without hesitation that she had been Mr Clark's mistress...."

"Odette!" Lady Clark cried out.

"I know, I know. It sounds preposterous; it was preposterous. But the men believed it. They didn't know Mr Clark's profoundly monogamic nature. Has it struck you that the three women who have influenced his life all bore the name Maud? I often think that, in his present state, he is sometimes not quite sure which one you are."

Lady Clark smiled. "I am aware of that. Miss Dolittle, of course, was the second Maud? I know, no one better, in which sense you speak of her influence on him. But don't let us digress."

"I doubt whether you know what I mean. But it has nothing to do with our present topic. Let me explain what I said. During an absence of Mrs Clark's in the east, before the trip to Europe, Mr Clark showed Mrs Carter over the mill; and after that he was closeted with her in his office. It was not only the mill-hands who stood agog. The thing was discussed even among the servants of this house; it had raised such a train of comment and speculation. Nor have I the slightest doubt that Mrs Carter had set a deliberate trap for Mr Clark. She had been a daily guest here, going in and out as if she owned the place. There had been dinner parties, dances, picnics, in sleighs, on snow-shoes, a giddy whirl. Suddenly, with Mrs Clark's departure, it had all come to a stop. Mrs Carter had nothing whatever to do. Her husband was at Vancouver: the papers reported his movements in the social columns. Her parents faced the most spectacular bankruptcy in the Pacific lumber trade. That, too, was matter of public record.

"Everybody was watching for developments between Mr Clark and Sibyl Carter. But there were no developments. Instead, Mrs Carter vanished from the town. It was asserted that she had taken up quarters nearby where she and Mr Clark could meet. Those who knew him—but remember they were few— never placed any credence in these rumours; I didn't, for one. And to those who were not hopelessly prejudiced, Mr Clark furnished the best refutation of these slanders; he never left Langholm till his wife had returned; and then he went east, not west. What he went for, and where, I don't know. But it was while the divorce suit was on.

"Of the suit, too. I know nothing but what the papers reported. It caused a sensation. To the men, it seemed to lay bare the corruption of a whole section of society, including, of course, the Clarks . . ."

"Pardon me for interrupting. I don't even know who sued whom."

"*She* sued *him*. Though, before long, they were suing each other. The town seethed; it seemed too bad that the suit was brought at Seattle. There was a local paper at the time, the *Langholm Lynx*. But the news-stands were promptly snowed under by an avalanche of American papers from Chicago, Seattle, New York even; they were always a few days late, of course; but they were eagerly bought by mill-hands, clerks, and everybody. At noon, during the lunch recess, the men were sitting on the roofs of the mill and below, on the ground, and on the loading platforms, a sandwich in one hand, a newspaper in the other. On Main Street, in the lunch rooms, clerks from the Flour Building, the banks, the professional offices, the stores, barely took the time to eat before they immersed themselves in the reports. When, at Seattle, the court was not sitting, the papers were shrewd enough to make up for the lack of news by filling their columns with summaries and editorial comment. The case Carter v. Carter had national reverberations. Here at Langholm nobody seemed to talk of anything else.

"To come back to your question about who sued whom. Mr Carter, Dick Carter, as everybody called him, was, as far as women were concerned, Mr Clark's exact opposite. Many girls from the families of the mill-hands had had affairs with him. He was popular among the women, more so than among the men; and he *was* fascinating, in a crude, physical way. He had been free with his money till he got married. He was himself a hard-working man; yet pleasant to meet and to talk to, affable and good-hearted. To the mill-hands he appeared as the prince of good fellows, the idol of women. What if he *had* kissed the girls in his office? They had been willing. He was human, warm-blooded, susceptible to feminine charm. So were the men them-selves.

"Whereas Sibyl Carter had never spoken to anyone not in her set except in the tone of command. She had indulged in an ostentation of wealth beyond even her ample means; she had gone past the mill on her saddle mounts, a groom following be-hind; she had treated the town, with the exception of those frequenting this house, as though it did not exist—except, of course, where her sexual greed was concerned; it last, it seemed, she had 'vamped' the boss.

"The trial, with its amazing revelations, opened in spring.

"Assisted by half a dozen famous lawyers, Sibyl Carter con-ducted her own case. In court, she spoke with a startling frank-ness, airing her views of a man-made civilization in which woman was denied the right to live her own life while man did as he pleased. Worst of all, she seemed to carry with her the court, the papers, the country. By the court, the papers, the country Dick Carter was treated like an outcast—which in-furiated the mill-hands. Even the fact that Sibyl disdained to shield herself behind silence, which the court informed her, she had a right to do when awkward questions were asked, made her, in the eyes of the mill-hands and their wives, especially their wives, appear a shameless hussy. When the court declined to take her admission that she had not come to her husband a virgin as relevant, he having admitted that he had not been ignorant of the fact, the mill-hands said she had 'fixed' the court. When the defence marshalled facts to prove that, as a married woman, she had lived an immoral life, and she chal-lenged that defence to prove a single case of post-nuptial infi-delity against her, the mill-hands said—like Maud, by the way —'It wasn't that she did not try hard enough.' When the de-fence intimated that she had contracted her marriage for mer-cenary reasons, and she rebutted the charge by saying that, at the time, the Lanes had been vastly better off than Mr Carter was ever likely to be, it was surmised that, most likely, she had already known of the impending collapse of their fortunes which was now a matter of public record.

"She based her suit on one single case. But that case re-vealed an appalling story of physical passion for him on the part of a middle-aged woman of the highest society in the Washington city; and of the cold-blooded exploitation, by the man, of that passion. From the beginning there was no doubt, to the disgust of the mill-hands, that Mrs Carter would win her suit. Yet it dragged on and on, through the summer, degenerating at last into an undignified squabble over money.

"It appeared that, before the marriage, Mrs Carter had stipulated for the settlement on her of a life-annuity of $30,000 a year. Now she claimed an additional $30,000 for 'maintenance'. The settlement which guaranteed the annuity was produced in court; extracts were read and later printed in the papers, especially the clause stating that the annuity was in compensation 'for value received'. This expression brought a dramatic climax. Mr Dick asserted the value received consisted in her consent to marry him, which Mrs Carter flatly denied. When the defence challenged her to name the value which she had given, she, for the first and only time, refused to answer a question; and the court upheld her right to do so. Her lawyers argued that business relations which antedated the marriage could not prejudice her right to alimony as Mr Carter's wife. The defence offered to reveal the exact terms covered by the expression 'for value received' in a secret session; the court refused to close its doors. Only now, by the way, did it become known that, simultaneously, she was suing the co-respondent, a married woman, for an indemnity of $200,000.

"Next, Mr Carter put forward the claim that, to pay an additional $30,000 would bankrupt him. The plaintiff asked for an adjournment to prepare her answer and got it. Here, the Terrace resounded with protests. 'They want her to win,' the mill-hands said.

"Next morning, Mrs Carter filed a minutely itemized statement of Mr Carter's earnings for the last three years; they averaged over $150,000 annually, half of which had been derived from the Langholm mill; the other half was more likely to increase than to diminish, owing, the plaintiff said maliciously, to the free advertising the suit provided for.

"That day, the suit against the co-respondent was settled out of court by the woman's husband, for $175,000. Of course, it was mentioned in court; and it was the last straw. The verdict in the divorce suit gave Mrs Carter an additional $27,000 per annum.

"The mill-hands gasped; and then they howled. They were as much inflamed against Dick Carter now as against his wife.

"If a man, they said, connected with the mill merely as its architect, could draw a clear income of $75,000 a year from it, what must be the profits accruing to its owners?

"There was a demonstration in front of the vacant house

on Clark Street. On the hill-slope east of it, Mrs Carter was burned in effigy.

"The excitement was such that Mr Stevens took alarm. He was in charge of the employment bureau of the mill; and for the first time he placed large numbers of spies among the men.

"The consequence was that, next Saturday, many mill-hands found, when calling for their pay cheques, that their envelopes contained a brief notice of dismissal. I am convinced that Mr Clark knew nothing whatever of it. It had a tremendous effect on the men.

"Some of those discharged knew they had given vent to their indignation only among themselves, in strict confidence. They knew why they were discharged. But how, short of being omniscient, did the management know what they had said to fellow workmen? There was only one explanation, the correct one. They had spies in their ranks. Even the older, steadier hands were appalled. They looked at each other, shrugged their shoulders, and kept their mouths shut. I have heard Mr Clark say that all talk was driven underground. Even that was an understatement. I was doing social service work among the women; I can say that all talk ceased. The fact made the excitement explosive.

"I knew positively that the strike was on the point of flaring up. It was that moment which Mr Clark chose for leaving Langholm; he was away for two weeks, going east. I don't believe even Maud knew what for. She would have mentioned it to me.

"I do know that Mr Stevens, provisionally in charge at the mill, as Miss Dolittle was in charge at the office, expected the strike to break in Mr Clark's absence. The number of provincial police in the town was increased to ten times what it had been.

"And then Mrs Carter took it upon herself to save the mill once more."

Lady Clark gasped. "How?" she asked.

Miss Charlebois looked at her with a strange smile. "She ret'rned to Langholm," she said, waiting for the statement to take effect.

"Yes," she went on, "this woman who was the object of the men's intense hatred boldly walked into the lions' den.

"I hardly know how much to tell you of this amazing story. I did not witness what happened, of course. But everything became known in a few days, in the minutest detail. Some of the incidents I have from highly-respected women who came to see me for no other purpose than to relieve themselves of the burden of secret and exciting knowledge imparted to them by their husbands. These women who, a few months ago, had been among the envious admirers of Mrs Carter, took a fiendish delight in hinting at, or telling, what they knew."

"Well," Lady Clark said, "don't be afraid of shocking me. I am prepared for a shock. Mr Clark was away. How about Mrs Clark?"

"Oh, she was at home. So was I. Later, it gave me a queer feeling to reflect that the climax took place just outside the park, up on Hill Road, without our having the slightest idea of what was going on. The gardener saw at least part of it. But let me start at the beginning.

"Why Sibyl Carter returned to Langholm is of course mere matter of conjecture. At the time, the theory accepted was to a certain extent confirmed when, a few days later, Mr Dick, ex-husband, also appeared in town and went straight to the house on Clark Street.

"The theory was this. In going to Seattle, hot on the trail of her husband's infidelity, Mrs Carter had left behind, in the house, papers or documents which might have jeopardized her chance of winning her suit. The conjecture was based on fragments of letters found on Hill Road by the police, after the night of which I am going to tell you. It was assumed that, in fleeing from the mob of which you will hear, she had torn them up so as to prevent their falling intact into the hands of her pursuers. One of these I was shown by Mrs Tindal; it betrayed that the unknown writer had known Mrs Carter intimately, to say the least; but it was not in Dick Carter's writing. After the suit had gone against him, Dick Carter must have got wind of the fact that there had been such a correspondence; and he had started east hot-foot to recover it, hoping, no doubt, to reverse the verdict. But, as I said, this is mere hypothesis. The verdict stood.

"It was a cold day at the end of September. Nobody ever expected to see Mrs Carter again. But when the noon train pulled in from the west, lo and behold! Mrs Carter, clad in a sable coat, descended the steps of a Pullman car in which she had occupied a drawing-room. Behind her came her maid, a mature girl of fading charms well known in Langholm. At the end of the platform stood a hired carriage; she had wired the best livery stable in town.

"As always when the noon train came in, the platform was crowded with loungers. Apparently she had taken her ticket for Langholm only, though at midnight she intended to proceed to

Montreal; so she had to make new reservations and to recheck her baggage. To this end she turned into the waiting-room, bought her ticket, and reserved a drawing-room. All this was done before a crowd of eagerly-listening lookers-on. Inconspicuously, two or three members of the crowd disappeared.

"Leaving the office, followed by her sardonic and over-powdered maid, she went down to the carriage, stopping a moment to stare at the mill which, though an unfinished torso, was at the centre towering up to almost its present height; there must have been fourteen or fifteen stories bristling with steel skeletons reaching into the sky.

"The train had been late; one-third of the mill-hands was crowding every available roof; the men were taking their lunches.

"Nobody has ever explained how it happened; but at once a commotion arose in that throng. As the carriage rolled over the bridge, everybody up there rushed to the edges of the roofs to look down on the crescent of the driveway to Main Street as from a grandstand. Catcalls, whistling and hooting greeted the women as they emerged from behind the screen of the elevators. They looked at each other, shrugged their shoulders, and laughed. At which the noise from the roofs took on a threatening note.

"A moment later the carriage stopped at the main entrance of the Palace Hotel, still in view of the crowds. A liveried porter hurrying out of the revolving doors of the entrance, the women alighted and entered, followed by the porter who carried two handbags.

"It was observed that a lounger leaning against a lamppost came forward and engaged the driver of the carriage in talk.

"While Sibyl and her maid sat in the dining-room of the hotel, the news of her arrival spread through the town, electrifying it. Clerks hurried through their meals, at home or in the various restaurants, and returned to the streets. Not every day could a notorious woman be seen in town. They were rewarded. Within three-quarters of an hour the women re-entered the carriage which promptly drove east, to turn south on Argyle where the hill rose sharply, and east again on Clark Street; they were going to the house where Sibyl had lived.

"Sibyl's attitude was not calculated to regain lost ground for her. Looking down on the staring salesgirls and clerks who crowded the sidewalks, she ostentatiously remarked upon them; and her maid burst out laughing.

"At the entrance to the house, the last on Clark Street,

Sibyl spoke to the driver, giving him instructions about the carriage.

"Within a few minutes, these instructions as well as the arrangements made at the hotel were known at the mill. But nothing happened. At half-past six, in the last light of the setting sun, the women, leaving their bags, returned to the hotel whence, at eight, they were taken back to the house.

"At eight-thirty they and the whole east end of the town were startled by a tremendous noise breaking loose all about the building, which was separated from the nearest house to the west by three or four lots occupied by the disused stables of the property.

"In the now utter dark, hundreds of shapes had sprung up out of nowhere. Their voices, accentuated by whistlings, serenaded the temporary inmates of the house with bawdy songs. Sibyl tried to telephone the police but found herself disconnected.

"The police, however, already reinforced by reason of Bob Stevens's warning against trouble at the mill, were on the way: the town's chief and two provincial officers, all three on bicycles. At their approach, heralded by their acetylene lights, the crowd encircling the house vanished into thin air. Mr Burt, the chief, allayed the fears of the women and told Sibyl, who, as the bolder, had come to the door, that the provincial officers would remain at the house while he would line their route to the station with a cordon of picked men.

"All remaining quiet, the women, safe in the protection of the police, settled down to a patient wait for the carriage.

"Shortly after ten-thirty, wheels were heard crunching over the gravel outside; it was still more than an hour till train time. The women went out into the night. The man on the driver's seat was not the one who had driven them before; but that gave them no cause for alarm. Escorted by the two officers, the women went down to the road and took their seats; they were directly under the last street lamp; and the lights of the carriage pierced the sloping hillside beyond the house. Nobody thought of asking why the driver had not first turned the carriage; the street is wide; there was ample room.

"Now it so happened that, the women having taken their seats, both officers turned simultaneously to pick up the handbags inside the door of the house; and when a sudden noise caused them to leap sharply around, the carriage, its lights extinguished, was already wildly plunging on to the sparsely-wooded hillside as if the horses had bolted. The officers started in hot pursuit but soon saw it was useless. The night was pitch dark there; they had nothing to guide them but sounds.

"The women would have jumped; but before they could do so, the front seat of the carriage tilted up; and a man emerged out of the box underneath to hold them down. They screamed ineffectually.

"For several minutes the horses plunged over precarious ground; then, after a brief glimpse of the floodlighted mill, they dipped again into utter darkness and shortly came out on a smooth road. The women did not know it; but it was Hill Road, at the east end of the cemetery.

"Instantly the carriage was surrounded by a crowd of women resembling those of a witches' sabbath. The maid was held in her seat; Sibyl was rudely pulled out. The carriage departed.

"Hardly conscious of what was being done to her, and trembling with fear, Sibyl was pushed into the middle of the road, facing the radiance which the mill diffused into the sky behind the hill covered by the cemetery. She probably felt more than saw a vast crowd surrounding her in the night, weirdly silent though not motionless. A fist pushed against her shoulder-blades; and she was told, 'Run, if you want to catch that train. Run, you bitch, run!'

"And she obeyed.

"But the crowd ran with her, silent but fiendish. She had just got into her stride, for she was athletic, when she felt herself half arrested from behind by two or three hands reaching for the collar of her coat. Shouldering out of it, she sprinted along in a panic, gathering up her silk dress in front. But fast though she was, another woman caught up with her, inserting her hand in the neck of her dress. She was running uphill now, towards the light. Then came the screech of tearing silk; she came near falling, for the slipping dress impeded her feet. It was found there next day. She kicked clear of it, losing her shoes in the process and thereby increasing her speed on the grassy margin of the road, unencumbered except by her underwear. As she approached the crest of the hill, beyond which there was the direct light from the mill, the fun waxed fast and furious. All the time such of her pursuers as fell behind were replaced by fresher and younger ones. But she knew now where she was: in a moment she would be skirting the park of Clark House. Meanwhile new hands were reaching for her. Her petticoat fell; her vest; her drawers; and, just as she was topping the hill, coming into the direct light, she ran naked, save for her corset.

"At that, the utter silence was broken by a tremendous shout which we, Maud and I, and everybody in Clark House, heard distinctly, so that we sat up, breathless. It lasted for less than ten seconds; but while it lasted, it was a pandemonium of hilarity.

"Half a minute later she reached the carriage which was halted just above the gate, in full view from the gardener's cottage. Her maid was frantically waving and calling.

"At the head of the horses stood two masked men; the driver was the one of the afternoon, not the one of the evening. The mob, after the great shout, had vanished.

"As Sibyl tumbled into the back seat, her fur coat and her shoes were shied after her. The man holding the maid jumped out; the masked men in front leapt aside; the horses reared and plunged forward. The driver, braced against the dashboard, see-sawed at the lines.

"The horses paid no attention; in a stretched gallop they tore down Hill Road, the women clinging to their seats for life. But suddenly, reaching level ground, they realized that they must pass through the centre of the town. Sibyl jumped up. 'My coat!' she cried.

"Already the carriage was rounding the corner of Argyle Street where it abuts on the lake. Street lights were everywhere. But the driver could not spare a hand to reach for the coat which had fallen at his feet; there was danger of upsetting the carriage.

"Thus the apparition—it must have looked like one—was seen by the loungers at the corner of Main Street—and by Miss Dolittle who had been dining out and was going home, escorted by Dr Cruikshank.

"Not till they were passing the Flour Building, to enter the huge S-curve crossing the bridge, did the driver succeed in getting his horses under control. They were in plain view of the men mixing concrete on the scaffoldings surrounding the end of the mill. All work stopped; and then, as the driver at last handed back Sibyl's coat and shoes, there was another outburst of noisy hilarity. The mill-hands were in the secret, of course, and swarmed over the roofs everywhere.

"At the station, Sibyl Carter, clad only in shoes and fur coat—her tattered stockings she had discarded—was received by the two provincial policemen one of whom carried the handbags.

"When the train pulled in, this officer boarded it with the women, found them their drawing-room, and asked Sibyl to give him a few minutes of her time."

" 'What for?' she asked, smiling provocatively at the handsome man.

" 'To get your version of the affair, madam.'

" 'I don't think I have anything to say,' she replied, entering her compartment. From the inside—I have this on the best authority, that of the man himself; for we were all questioned next day—she smiled back through the crack of the door, bowed, laughed, and closed her door."

Lady Clark sat staring at the older woman opposite her. "Have you ever told that story before?" she asked with a peculiar smile. "To anyone?"

"Never," Miss Charlebois said. But an embarrassed smile trembling around her lips betrayed that she understood what Lady Clark's question implied.

THE senator, too, was thinking of that time, the winter of 1900 to 1901. His thought had been directed to the strike by the same remark which had occasioned Lady Maud's question.

If, in such a thing, one could talk of guilt, it lay partly at his door; his conscience would not let him rest. He had half welcomed the slight cold which gave him undisturbed leisure.

Would that strike, or would it not, have broken had he remained at home? Would it, or would it not, have broken if he had put someone else in charge?

His absence, that had given him a few months in which he had been happy because he had been able to forget the mill, had at least been a contributing factor in bringing about that disturbance. He had, of course, been only less unpopular than Mr Stevens; but at the worst he would have avoided the undoubted mistakes which Mr Stevens had made. Mr Stevens had been bent on making his power felt with regard to the men; bent also on proving to him, the president, that he was capable of running the mill. Under the peculiar circumstances of the time both had been dangerous ambitions. Mr Stevens had, of course, kept a minute record of all he had done; and when Sam, later, studied that record, he had been able, step for step, to pick out those decisions which had made the strike inevitable.

Why, then, had he gone away, leaving the mill at that moment?

His reasons had been almost too complex to unravel them at this distance of time.

His first absence, of two weeks, had been solely for the purpose of going to New Orleans where he felt sure nobody would as much as enquire into his identity. Under an assumed name, posing as the representative of another person, he had, through a lawyer, despatched an express parcel containing thirty-odd thousand dollars plus the interest at six per cent for twelve years, all in currency bills, addressing the parcel to the insurance company which had paid his father's claim at the time of the fire. There had been no indication, in or about that parcel, which could lead to the detection of the sender.

The senator, in his bed, almost chuckled to himself as he thought of that anonymous payment and the reports of it which had promptly appeared in the public prints. The insurance company must have been sufficiently startled. The reports had read as follows.

"For the second time in a dozen years, the XYZ Insurance Company of New York has received, through the public carrier, a parcel containing a not inconsiderable sum of money from a source unknown. The first time, in 1889, the sum amounted to $35,400; this time, to $51,600. In both cases, the company made the most searching enquiries; the first time at Montreal, Canada; this time at New Orleans. The origin and the purpose of these payments remain a secret."

At the time, it had taken him several weeks before he had realized that the 1889 payment must have come from his father who, as he could verify, had been absent from Langholm for eight days, while he, Sam, had himself been at Montreal, organizing his sales force.

Having returned from New Orleans, he had made up his mind to take Maud to Europe. Why?

One of the reasons had been the very desire to be away during the outbreak of the strike which he only now realized might have been prevented by his staying at home. At the time he had not thought so; the strike had seemed inevitable. The argument by which he had justified himself had run as follows. If the men struck in his absence, with Bob Stevens in charge, Bob would fight them uncompromisingly. Sam would have seen too many sides; he would have been tempted to yield to the men; and that would still have been a disaster to the whole industry. An outright victory for the men would have led to new strikes on the slightest provocation, not only at Langholm, but elsewhere as well. The world was not ripe for that; neither were the men ready to govern themselves. If he were not there, the strike would go on till the men were tired of it. If that state of affairs were reached before his return, the men would hail him like a saviour. He would settle the matter with a few trifling concessions; and he would gain an increment in popularity which he could gain in no other way.

That had been Machiavellian reasoning; it had been a reasoning which his father might have made his own. For better or worse, he had said to himself, he was his father's son.

When, months later, he had returned, fate had played into his hands: the Boer War had broken out. When he had told the men what he was and what he was not prepared to concede, the fact that England needed the flour had branded every grumbler as a traitor willing to leave the mother country, in her hour of need, in the lurch.

While thinking about these distant events, the senator was, however, quite conscious of the fact that his chief motive in going away had been entirely personal. He simply had to dis-burden himself to someone. Who was there on whom he could place the burden which he had carried now for nearly three years with greater justice than his wife? He had lived through a nightmare. She must know. It would not only free him of his load; it would solve her problem, too, perhaps.

He had never enquired into what had happened to Sibyl on the occasion of her last visit to Langholm. People would have been only too ready to enlighten him; but he discouraged them. All he knew was that there had been what the police called a riot.

A number of arrests were made; but every person arrested had an undoubted alibi. Few people, so far, knew enough de-tails to see clear in the matter; few people, even at a later stage, knew how much the incident had to do with the outbreak of the strike. Many questioned the driver of the carriage; but all he could tell was that, in the darkness of a lane behind the livery stable, he had been pulled from his seat and rushed to the cemetery by masked men. Obviously it was impossible to arrest the population of the Terrace. There were no clues.

Consequently, every arrest made irritated both men and management; it interfered with the smooth running of the mill; when substitutes were picked from the floating labour supply hanging about the north end of the town, they were, on the part of the men, under suspicion of being spies; whereas the management had to dismiss them when the arrested men had been released.

Watching these developments, Sam had chosen this precise moment for his departure.

The very next day the roofs of the old units were opened. For the first time the men had a glimpse into the new structures, access to which had been barred except to those employed in construction.

For over twenty months mill and town had, day after day, resounded to the deafening clangour of pneumatic riveting machines. Precariously perched on aerial seats three, four hundred feet above the level of the lake, hundreds of men had worked in feverish haste, nobody of the management inter-fering. That was the contractors' business; they, working to rigid specifications, acknowledged no one as their boss except Dick Carter who rarely showed himself and, when he did, left again by the next train. Since the divorce, he had not been seen at Clark House, nor at the office.

But the moment the president was gone, the acting general manager took it upon himself to find fault with the rate of progress. In the hearing of the men, Bob Stevens wrangled with Dick Carter's understudies. The work had been pushed forward at the utmost speed; for Bob Stevens it was not proceeding fast enough. It was his ambition to put the hundred-odd units in operation before the president returned.

For weeks before Sam's departure the German engineers, a whole staff of them, had been assembling machines. Between dam and mill they had built a spur of the railway; the flatcars loaded with parts were shunted in by means of a turntable, coming and going with the boxcars that brought the wheat and took the flour.

No provision had been made for increasing the capacity of the Terrace. There was much discussion on that point. So far, the theory was that the new units were to be left idle for months. But when, day after day, night after night, machines of an unfamiliar type were being swung up by means of specially-constructed derricks, and then carefully eased into place through the walls which were left open on the east side, things became puzzling.

Simultaneously with the opening of the roofs in the old units, certain machines of the so-called screen-house—the former top floor—were shut down, dismantled, and moved while screened and cleaned wheat reached the other machines from nobody knew where. The process involved the laying-off of small groups of men who grumbled but, so far, submitted; they were told to return to work after so many days. But when the process spread downward, involving larger numbers, discontent grew. Meanwhile the mill was under police surveillance. Not one of the squads hastily called in on the occasion of the 'riot' was allowed to depart. Uniforms were in evidence everywhere.

Then, the old roofs being opened at last, every one of the hands went to cast a glance upward through the openings; and what they saw made their hearts sink. Not one of the new units had so much as a floor; from their former top floor they looked up through many stories, through three hundred feet of empty space. Not yet did they grasp what it meant; but, in a technical sense, the word 'unit' had lost its meaning.

Here and there the dizzy height was broken by steel grids consisting of highly-polished bars two inches thick, accessible only by steel ladders of similar bars. Everything was dripping with oil.

Then, watched by the men, the installations began. Starting from below, machine after machine was added till there was a continuous chain from the top to the ground floor. Incidentally, in the centre of the cluster of cylindrical grain elevators, an enormously high but slender structure had been erected; and out of an opening in its east side, near the top, a movable pipe arm, similar to the straw-blower of a threshing machine, hung poised, reaching across to a similar structure above the new top floor of the mill. This linking-up of elevators and mill looked so bold, from the so-called crescent, that even the men felt a thrill of admiration and pride.

But that thrill soon changed into one of consternation. At last the meaning of it all became clear. The final installation in one perpendicular tier had proceeded with a speed which testified to the minute accuracy with which the whole thing had been designed.

One morning the hundreds of men on day shift were startled by a noise as of distant thunder. A few who were near the new line-up rushed over and looked up; and there, in a glass cage glued to the inner wall, they saw, about two hundred feet above them, Max Eckel, Mr Brook, and two or three German engineers, handling levers. High above these, through an opening in what the men called the turret, the end of the pipe from the elevators nodded down its hood and dumped a few tons of wheat into . . . what? Below, machines began to revolve and to shake; the movement was propagated downward; and within a quarter of an hour it reached the ground floor where a bagging-machine, with an almost human intelligence, by means of two hooks, was picking up a flour bag, to move it into place under a spout. The bag, filled, fell on its side, in place for the stitching-machine which closed it and tossed it to an endless conveyor which started it on its way to the boxcar outside.

Within half an hour the machines were stopped; this had been a test run. Mr Eckel, in his white smock, followed by the others, descended.

Such men as had been unable to leave their machines got the report at noon, when, in successive shifts, they took their lunch. Of every stage in the process of milling, they were told, samples had reached the laboratories through special chutes;

thence signals had reached the glass cage reporting the results of the analyses made. By-products—bran, wheat germ, gluten, screenings—had been bagged elsewhere.

All was clear. Flour had been made without the help of human labour though under human control. The work of transportation had been done by gravity; a horizontal alignment had been tilted into a vertical one.

Sam was in Italy at the time; but, to cap it all, the test run was made on the day when overseas news brought word that, in South Africa, matters were working up to a war.

Were these Clarks omniscient? Had they secret information of what was to happen years after? Here they were ready to multiply their output when the demand in England was going to multiply correspondingly.

Henceforth the men went, at the end of every intermission, to a point whence they could look up into this new assembly. Not a mill-hand was to be seen between ground and top floors. At dizzy heights two, three men were crawling about on steel grids and ladders, oilcans in hand, cotton waste dangling from their pockets. Swaying power cables and a battery of levers controlled everything. The men up there were at last willing to talk and explain.

Not one of those craning their necks spoke to his neighbour. Nobody knew whether he was standing next to friend or spy. Even the foremen were nervous. There was tension in the very air.

But for several days nothing happened. Then, by the light of powerful electric arcs, a second tier was tested at midnight. The noise, as of distant thunder, which had been punctuating the silence from time to time, doubled in volume. Within a few minutes another principle became clear. The screen-house, at the top, fed not one, but two tiers of machines which stripped the bran off the kernel of wheat; each of the stripping machines fed two cutting machines below, where the kernel was broken up into 'semolina', hard pellets; and so on.

Another two weeks went by. The new tiers were filling up. Then something went wrong. One day, certain readjustments having been made in the linking-up of the machines, Mr Eckel and the engineers climbed back into the glass cage. Throughout this new part of the mill reigned a dead silence. Then the sound of distant thunder came through; and, a lever being thrown in the cage, there was the noise of breaking steel and the clatter of falling parts.

The engineers found the place where one of the machines had been tampered with; certain bolts had been withdrawn.

In spite of the disquietude in which they lived, the older men were as indignant as the management. The only people who remained undisturbed were the engineers. Such things were expected to happen : the damage would be repaired in a day; there were plenty of spare parts.

But Mr Stevens was furious. A spirited exchange of telegrams between Langholm, Winnipeg, and Ottawa ensued; large reinforcements arrived for the police; every point from which the new tiers could be reached was surrounded with a cordon. The sedate element among the men approved; cynics sneered; the disaffected seethed.

At this stage the local paper brought the news that Mr Clark was in London, negotiating with the War Office. The War Office required for South Africa a flour which, while not too highly milled, would not sour in its passage through the tropics.

Last installations were rushed through. The machines went into full operation. A sample shipment was prepared, to be taken, from Halifax, to the seat of the war.

Mr Stevens hardly left the mill any longer; there had been a turn of the wheel in his favour. *He* was the man who, in the president's absence, was handling matters. The sample shipment went through; and Mr Clark cabled orders of such magnitude that, if they were to be filled without delay to ordinary deliveries, the automatic part of the mill would have to start continuous work.

Mr Stevens had a brilliant idea. Certain machines of the older units could be linked up with the new ones. It would be patch work but it could be done. The old units would have to be shut down for a week.

At that stage Mr Stevens made his mistake. All the men were affected. One morning, when the night shift went off, the day shift was told they were not wanted for six days to come. Their regular output was to be taken care of by drawing on reserves. It wasn't the thing as such; it was the abruptness and rawness of the procedure.

That night, the Terrace boiled over; nothing had been said about compensation; the men concluded they would lose a week's wages. The 'back-to-backs' buzzed like maddened beehives; the women 'saw red'.

On the morning when the work was to be resumed, not a

man appeared. The machines of the remodelled old units remained idle.

The intention of the walkout had been kept so secret that the management was taken completely by surprise. Mr Stevens was in bed, at the Palace Hotel, when the telephone gave him the news. In five minutes he was crossing the street to the Flour Building; in fifteen the wires to three capitals were humming; a cablegram was on its way to London, England. The police occupied the approaches to the mill; the area comprising mill and dam took on the aspect of an armed camp.

By night a trainload of strikebreakers arrived, to be housed in sleeping cars chartered from the railway; to be fed in dining cars on the fat of the land, engaged at a flat rate of $3 a day, all found. Provision had been made for their safety provided they stayed within the cordon of police. If they left it, they did so at their peril.

Since the automatic units were taking care of the overseas demand and reserves were ample, the bringing in of this handful of strikebreakers was branded as a needless provocation.

As for the strikers, the vast majority had never been in a strike before; most of them were well-intentioned; many considered the affair as a joke on Mr Stevens. When he crossed from the hotel to the Flour Building, he was greeted with cat-calls. So to him, the thing looked more serious than it was.

Eastern millers and even United States concerns flooded the mill with offers and were surprised at being told that no help was needed. Leaflets arrived from United States manufacturers' associations containing directions how to break the most stubborn strike. Mr Stevens, looking them over, found that most of the measures advised were already in operation; those that were not did not fit the case.

In town, an occasional strikebreaker ventured out of bounds and was molested by the crowd; the police made a few arrests. Once a shot was fired, but no one was hurt. The men themselves saw to it that order in any case was maintained.

But slowly the conviction gained ground that the joke was not on Mr Stevens but on the men. The streets became deserted; the mill-hands remained on the Terrace. Mr Inkster, a widely-travelled young man just settled in town, remarked that its sight reminded him of Pompeii, with the few townspeople to be seen in the streets representing the tourists gazing at sights that had been buried for two thousand years.

The thing was oppressive; the strike was a fiasco; the mill

kept functioning. In a spirit of defeatism the men wished they had not struck.

At this juncture the local paper brought the news that Mr Clark was on his way home.

When he arrived, ahead of his family, he had a conference with Mr Stevens before he even went to Clark House. A directors' meeting was called; everything was done in the most formal manner. Mr Clark had nothing but praise for Mr Stevens and his zeal. He outlined what concessions he was prepared to make and had them approved. Then he asked Mr Stevens to let the men know that he would receive a delegation at ten o'clock on Monday.

As the senator thought of that meeting, one thing struck him as peculiar; he had acted and spoken in a manner opposed to all his preconceived principles. He had always contended that, rightly handled, the mechanization of processes formerly performed by hand contained the greatest blessing that had ever come to mankind; every man formerly employed in industry was entitled to as many of the benefits which such a mechanization conferred as the owners of the plants. But the moment he faced the concrete problem, he instinctively denied these benefits to the men; it seemed imperative in the cause of law and order. Utopia would come in time, not now. If the men remained poor while the masters grew rich, it seemed a law of nature which he could not change. He arrived at this attitude quite instinctively, without conscious reference to his father. But he felt that he was a link in a chain. Do nothing now; or as little as possible; enough to win the good will of the men; more radical changes must come from the generation to follow.

The strikers' delegation, headed by Watson, the globular mathematician, waited on him in the boardroom where he received them standing. Watson being, unfortunately, one of the few men employed by the mill for whom he had an active dislike, matters came easily to him.

He read a written statement of the strike aims with great care. The men asked for the unconditional reinstatement of the strikers; for the immediate dismissal of every strikebreaker; for the withdrawal of the police; for an eight-hour day, for a raise of ten per cent in wages; for Mr Stevens's retirement as general manager; for representation on a permanent commission to handle 'hirings and firings'.

Sam knew that, if he had refused all these demands, the men would by this time have grasped at the chance of returning to work; they were aware that it was in his power to turn them loose. His problem was so to grant some of the demands that the peace he offered would retain the appearance of a dictated peace.

"You make it hard for me," he said, "to come to terms. This strike is silly; the quarrel rests on a vague grudge and on no real grievance. If the men had not been drifting towards a strike for months, the police would never have been called in. As it was, we had to protect the mill, in your interests as much as in mine or the country's. It would pay me to refuse to negotiate. If I don't, it is on your account, not mine. But it was your right to call the strike; it is mine to lay down terms for ending it. If I don't make them harder, it is because some of your demands would have been granted without a strike.

"As for the retirement of Mr Stevens, it settles itself. I am the general manager; in case of my absence, in future, I shall appoint as my substitute whomever I like. The men I shall reinstate as fast as it can be done without injustice to those we called in to keep the mill going. The police will be withdrawn from the mill; their withdrawal from the town is beyond my jurisdiction. Of the strikebreakers, I reserve the right to retain as many as I please. The men who were laid off may call at the pay office; they will receive cheques for time lost up to the walkout. Wages will be raised only if output increases. You will be competing with a new line-up; henceforth wages will be based on the ratio your output bears to that of automatic machinery; I hope we shall be able to raise them. As for a commission to handle employment, I agree in principle; the details to be worked out jointly. I grant the eight-hour day; but the output must not suffer. Remember that the machines will set a new pace.

"Those are my terms. Here is a paper in which I have taken up your demands point for point. I want the decision of the men by five o'clock tonight. If it is adverse, I shall, by cable, order what is needed to complete the automatic line-up for the whole mill."

Having finished, he turned to his private office with a nod of dismissal. He almost hated himself for having wound up with a threat. Yet he had been unable to suppress it.

At five o'clock a new delegation was in the boardroom to submit the unconditional surrender of the men and, what was worse, their thanks.

CHAPTER

XV

THE senator's condition was rather low; yet Dr Sherwood could find no reason why it should be so. The fact was, the cause was mental.

He was reviewing his trip to Europe and those months which were followed by the long-drawn agony of Maud's pregnancy and her death.

The opportunity to disburden himself to her came as the liner carrying them was nosing its way out of the Gulf of St Lawrence into the open Atlantic. They were still in the shelter of the land; and he had taken two deck chairs into the prow of the boat where a solid railing enclosed the stem. It was pitch dark, for a storm was threatening; and for quite a while he and Maud sat in silence.

Suddenly, his voice coming out of the night as if disembodied, he began to speak, telling in minute detail of the burden which the days after his father's funeral had placed on his mind. He spoke quietly, without emphasis, intent only on making clear the implications of every word. She listened in a silence which, at moments, made him doubt whether she was still there.

It was the first time that he let her divine how much of the constructive work that had gone into the making of the mill had been his; and there was something new in her voice when she said, in a pause after he had told her of his first conception of a mill run automatically, "I understand at last why Dick spoke of you as a genius."

Her tone encouraged him in unfolding to her just why, after his father's death, he had gone on carrying out that father's wishes, namely, from the necessity of protecting his name, and thereby hers and little Edmund's. There was another new note in her voice when she said, "And through all these years you have lived with that on your mind, without sharing it?"

A long silence followed, accompanied only by the unbroken swish of the waves against the bows of the ship. At last, divining her thought, he said in a husky voice, "I have just refunded, anonymously, the excess indemnity received by my father. That's what I went south for."

"You couldn't do less," she said. "Doesn't that settle the matter?"

"I don't know," he said. "I had no idea, of course, that my father had already done the same thing."

Maud laughed. "He might have marked that down in the account book. It would have clarified matters. I understand him better now, down to his refusal to admit you into the administration."

"He admitted others," Sam said unhappily. "Mat Tindal was a director."

"Mat Tindal was a dummy."

"He was at least that. I was nothing."

"You were his brains. I always thought he was yours."

"And you despised me a little," he said under his breath.

Again there was a long pause. The utter blackness of the night was barely relieved by the lights of the liner which was just then meeting the first long swell of the open sea, dipping reluctantly.

Spray dust went over them.

Maud shivered and rose, holding on to the railing. When she spoke, her voice had again the old ring of cold irony. "Oh, Sam," she said, "I wish you had been born with a robust conscience. I hope I gave Edmund one. Mine is pretty robust."

She stood within the faint radiance from a red sidelight of the boat—a silhouette swaying to its motion.

A pitch of the boat caught her, tearing her hand from the railing; and she vanished; for, before Sam could grasp her arm, she was forced, in order not to fall, to run aft, towards the bridge.

Sam was in a mood in which everything seemed symbolic. Yet he knew that her run, away from him, had been entirely involuntary. He remained behind, feeling helpless and deserted.

When, half an hour later, he went below, he cautiously tried the knob of the door to her stateroom. Finding it locked, he entered his own quarters opposite and undressed to go to bed. He took a book from a suitcase and laid it handy, expecting a sleepless night. But when he had lain down, leaving the door unlocked for the valet in the morning, he felt unexpectedly drowsy. Having disburdened himself, his mind seemed vacant. He switched the reading-light off again and turned to the wall. But he had hardly done so when he heard the click of his door; and as he sat up in his bed, his head brought up against Maud's bosom.

"I am seeing ghosts," she said. "Let me come into your bed."

Every now and then, during this second honeymoon, she came back to what he had told her, abruptly as a rule, without introduction.

"It was like borrowing money," she said one day in the Louvre at Paris. "It has been repaid, with interest."

"Twice," Sam said.

She laughed gaily.

"Or," he went on, "like embezzling and replacing the money before the defalcation was discovered."

"If it were discovered afterwards, what would happen?"

"Nothing. Except that if the embezzler were an employee he would be discharged as an untrustworthy person."

"Well," Maud said with sudden impatience. "It wasn't you who proved untrustworthy. Why worry?"

And he did cease to worry. But it seemed criminal that, with such a secret on his mind, he should live the life of a lover.

One day, in their rooms at Marseilles this time, he asked, "Can one be descended from a tainted stock and not be tainted?"

"What do you mean?" she asked.

"How about Edmund?"

When she grasped his meaning, she towered in anger. "This is vile," she cried. "I will not bear it. How can you allow such a shadow to darken your life?"

"I won't if you'll help me."

"Face the present," she said. "Don't face the past. Besides . . . If you believe your father foresaw the growth of the mill, you should draw the conclusion that he was right in doing what he did. To every great man the end justifies the means."

At Florence, at last, she swept him off his feet. "I never thought," she carolled with a note of triumph in her voice, "that *you* were the great man. Dick did. But I didn't believe him. As you said, I've always despised you a little. It was your own fault. To listen to you, it was always your father who did things."

"It was," he said.

"Of course! He didn't dare to let you see how much you led him."

"If you despised me, why did you marry me?"

She looked at him sideways and laughed. "One doesn't need to respect a man in order to love him."

"You resented it when I withdrew after my father's death. Yet you never said a word about it."

"Of course I didn't. You withdrew. There was Sibyl."

"There was Dr Fry," he said.

And both laughed.

And then she told him that she was pregnant.

Sam was frightened. For the first time he disclosed to her that Dr McIntosh, the Winnipeg surgeon, had told him, the night of Edmund's birth, that it was unlikely that she would ever have another child; what was more, she mustn't.

She scoffed. "It's what I've wished for throughout the years."

"Forbidden fruit!" Sam cried.

"Let them die that can't live!" she protested. "I'll fight; but if I can't win . . ."

"How about me?"

She rose to ruffle his hair. "There are other women. Better women than myself."

A few days later they hastily returned to England; it was war in South Africa.

The senator who had stayed in bed to dream himself back into those few, brief months found that he could not bear to think of them. His throat choked.

In the following spring, Clark House having been converted into a hospital, with Dr McIntosh in charge, a girl had been taken from the mother's womb, by means of a Caesarean cut; and the mother had survived the operation by only three hours.

PART TWO

Resurrection of the Master

We must reform and have a new creation
Of state and government, and on our chaos
Will I sit brooding up another world.

CHAPMAN

CHAPTER
XVI

"I BELIEVE," Lady Clark said to Miss Charlebois—they were sitting in Lady Clark's open living-room upstairs, "that you are indeed the logical person to write, if not the history of the mill, at least the senator's biography."

"I know nothing of his early youth. I never met him till he was forty."

"Does it matter? It was at that age that he began to direct the fortunes of the mill. It would be the mill which would stand in the centre of even a biography."

Miss Charlebois mused. "Yet, what do I know of the mill except what everybody knows? How it grew; how it passed from Mr Clark's hands to those of his son; and back again into those of the senator. What I know about is the history of the family; and even there I am conscious of gaps."

"Name them."

"The relation of the senator to his son. The senator is so reserved that one can only conjecture. He was and is an enigma."

"Everybody is. But he is a national figure; every ray of light must be welcome."

"As I told you, I have thought of it. I have tried to interpret what I saw. To some small extent I have been an actor in the drama; an actor necessarily sees only part of the play."

"Even though you may shrink from publication, write things down as you saw them. They will form material for the future historian."

"I knew Maud, for instance, the senator's wife. But there were three Mauds; when I look at his life as a whole, I doubt whether one of them is more important than either of the others."

"I being one of the three," Lady Clark said. "And Miss Dolittle the other. But Miss Dolittle cut more effectively across my life than his."

"Are you sure?"

"It has often puzzled me why you didn't become a second Mrs Clark."

The effect of this remark was striking. Miss Charlebois blanched; and her hands trembled. But, keeping her eyes on her embroidery, though her needle remained poised, she said slowly, "That is part of the story of the seventeen years that followed Mrs Clark's death."

"You mean to say . . ."

"Does it surprise you?"

"No. But I don't see clear."

"If you reflect a moment, you will see that it was the natural thing for the expectation to arise. I was keeping his house for him. I presided at his table. I very largely raised his children. When some sort of normal life was restored after Maud Clark's death, Mr Clark insisted on my acting as the lady of the house and on my being treated as such . . . As for the children, especially Ruth, of course, nobody had any influence over them but myself. Both Edmund and Ruth were Clarks; there was little of the mother in them. Within the Clark tradition, Ruth resembled her father more than Edmund did; as everybody agreed, Edmund was his grandfather resurrected. Ruth was a rebel. As for Edmund, I believe it was part of Mr Clark's deliberate method to abstain from asserting any influence which he might have had; against Ruth he held that grudge . . . If it had not been for me, she, at least, would have grown up wild. Since everybody knew of her father's attitude, there was always the problem of keeping her out of his way. From an early age she seemed to live under cover; her chief problem was to eclipse herself. Even after Master Edmund was sent away to school . . .

"It was at that time that this house saw once more some sort of social life. But Mr Clark barely took part in it. He insisted on having young people in; crowds of them; and it fell to me and Miss Dolittle to entertain them. Mr Clark spent most of his time in the library, appearing for minutes only. But after Mrs Clark's death Maud Dolittle was always here—I mean when there was company. It was I, of course, who asked her; and she was glad to come."

"How old was she at the time?"

"At what time? We are talking of decades."

"Well . . ." Lady Clark laughed. She divined that Miss Charlebois suspected her of thinking of a later date when Miss Dolittle's relation to her own husband had taken on the tinge of an open scandal. "Let us put it in this way," she went on. "How did Miss Dolittle's age compare with that of Maud Clark?"

"She was younger by a few years. Mrs Clark was almost exactly my age. When Miss Dolittle began to frequent this house, she made the impression of a young girl in her twenties."

"She did that when I saw her. No, not her twenties; her thirties, I should say, the early thirties. I saw her on one occasion only, in the railway station at Montreal. I was amazed. I knew that she had been working for the mill for over twenty years then."

"That was when you were engaged to be married to Sir Edmund?"

"Exactly."

"In 1920, to be precise? I thought so. She must have been between forty and forty-five. She became Mr Clark's private secretary in 1896 or '97."

"And that was how many years before Maud Clark's death?"

"Maud Clark died in the spring of 1902, Miss Dolittle was one of those women who, after a given age, hardly change for the next two or three decades."

"And you mean to say that nothing resembling an attachment had arisen between her and Mr Clark in Mrs Clark's lifetime?"

"I am positive about it; not on Mr Clark's side. He liked her, liked her very much; and he admired her very great ability. He listened to her advice. But, if anything, he looked upon her with the sort of affection a father has for a favourite daughter. Yet I am equally positive that Miss Dolittle had all along found her inspiration in her employer; he had been her god."

"But such a sentiment did spring up in him, too, at last?"

"When it was too late, yes . . . I will tell you," Miss Charlebois went on after a pause. "I remember the occasion as if it had been yesterday; and I will also tell you why. It is all so long ago that I can laugh at my own folly. That occasion marked the end of all my hopes.

"I had been an inmate of his house for sixteen, seventeen years. From the way the management of the household had been left in my hands, since Maud Clark's death; from the way in which Mr Clark treated me and insisted on my being treated by others, I don't believe I am going too far when I say that the servants and everybody who frequented this house expected that, sooner or later, Mr Clark would ask me to take his wife's place, if only as a matter of form. I had no illusions; there was no love on his side; I could never have replaced his wife; but

I could have lived with dignity as Mrs Clark. Rumours in town, of course, had it that some such acknowledgment of my position was no more than my due. My own acquiescence in the arrangement as it stood left no doubt about it that I should accept if an offer were made. Ruth would certainly have benefited from the change; so long as I was no more than Miss Charlebois, she remained of necessity fundamentally alone. . . .

"One day, Master Edmund being at home for the Christmas holidays—it must have been in 1912, for he was about fourteen—a young people's dance was arranged for. It was my suggestion; but when I mentioned it over the dinner table, Mr Clark fell in with the plan at once. 'Better ask Miss Dolittle to assist you,' he added. I will not deny that, at the stage which matters had reached, it wounded me; in spite of the fact that I should have asked her of my own accord. As it was, I did not ask her to assist me; I invited her as a guest.

"The evening of the dance, Mr Clark made it a point, as carriage after carriage, car after car rolled up under the *porte cochère*, to receive the guests, children, adolescents, and grown-ups himself, standing near the vestibule in the hall. I, too, of course, was there. In the vestibule, maids and footmen were divesting the arrivals of their wraps; and Master Edmund and Ruth were similarly employed. There must have been over sixty young people and some forty adults, mostly mothers. I do not remember a man among the guests. All the ladies, including myself, were in semi-formal dress.

"Then, just as the music intoned the first march, and the doors of the ballroom were thrown open, there was something like a sensation.

"Miss Dolittle arrived.

"She entered with an embarrassed laugh, seeing at once that she was the only person in full evening costume. She looked as if, by some miracle, she had been able to turn back the hands of time on their dial. She did not seem a day older than twenty. Yet she did not look like a *jeune fille*; rather like a young matron; and not so young, either, somehow. It is very hard to explain. There was something of maturity about her, in spite of her dazzling looks; she looked twenty; but inevitably she recalled Balzac's title *La Femme de Trente Ans*. They say that, in later life, after her connection with the family ceased, she became stout.

"From the moment she entered, exclaiming over the enormous Christmas tree at the far end of the hall, in the northwest corner, nobody had eyes but for her. She did not go out very much; nobody knew anything of her private life except that she had her own house in the west end of the town, overlooking mill and river valley. I knew that she kept three servants, cook, parlour maid, and soubrette. I also knew that she was always marvellously groomed. This night she was radiant.

"It was most striking to see how Master Edmund at once began to dance attendance on her. Throughout the evening, I believe, he never left her side, dancing with none but her, monopolizing her during the pauses, waiting upon her during the midnight supper in the large dining-room. I will admit that, seeing it all from the corners of my eyes, I was frankly jealous; for Mr Clark, too, seemed to see only her. He did not remain in the hall; I don't think he ever entered the ballroom; but whenever he came to look on, from the door, he came, driven by one desire, to look at her.

"No doubt he saw others; one could not help doing so; there were so many charming figures. It is over twenty-five years ago; but I still remember with great vividness that of a little girl from the east, a friend of Ruth's, from the boarding school where, at my suggestion, she had been placed for a term; she did not go back; she begged off. That little girl, twelve years old perhaps, was a perfect picture, looking like a life-sized statuette from the days of Watteau. I remember her first name was Sandra. There were others; the whole affair was utterly charming. But for me it was spoiled.

"Not but that I admired Maud Dolittle as much as anyone did; but I could not forget the glance with which Mr Clark followed her whenever he appeared in the door, small, grey, distinguished. Over the heads of the boys and girls he looked only at her; and now and then their glances met; and she smiled; for she was in the arms of his son.

"Perhaps that should have reassured me; for there could be no doubt that the precocious boy who was her inseparable escort was swept off his feet. Her expression, when she looked at the child, was that of a maternal good will. But she could not deceive me. She was aware of that child in a peculiar way. She herself was fresh, virgin, untouched; but when she danced, she was transformed; it looked as if she made it a point to intoxicate the boy. If she did, she succeeded.

"But I watched Mr Clark. He, too, was intoxicated. Anything might happen. Her essential life was unlived but called out to be lived at last. Like a rose opening up she was one single appeal. Yet, seeing what I saw, I knew nothing would happen.

From that evening on it was too late. Her feeling for the boy was more than maternal."

"Would Mr Clark see it?"

"Apparently he did not. Again and again he came out of the library to look on.

"At midnight the large dining-room was thrown open, set with some fifty small tables, each with covers for two. Perkins, our butler, helped me to supervise. Miss Dolittle did not assist; she was not one of the hosts; she was a guest.

"It was one of the strangest sights to see her and her cavalier. Young Master Edmund was gay, radiant, reckless, brilliant. He and Maud Dolittle seemed to be natural, complementary partners: a pair that had stepped out from some rococo canvas, bowing, curtseying to each other, in what looked like an artificial stage abandon. What made it look artificial was, however, nothing but the difference in age between them. Well, there was a considerable difference in age between her and Mr Clark; there had been almost the same difference in years between him and his late wife. . . .

"Again I asked myself whether Mr Clark saw it. Well, he did. From the moment when he looked at them in that dining-room milling with children, I knew that Mr Clark would never marry again. Had he offered himself, that he saw at last, Miss Dolittle who, a year ago, would have fallen into his arms, would no longer have accepted him. But *me* he no longer noticed. That was my end of it. As for Maud Dolittle, he would not offer himself; his expression showed that he knew she had passed beyond him.

"For an hour or two, I feel convinced, he knew keen suffering which I should willingly have spared him. For I suffered, too; but I did not hate her any longer as I had done for moments that night. I resigned myself to become what I am."

"I see," Lady Clark said. "I understand . . . Tell me all you know about the boyhood of my husband."

"There is little to tell; little at least that I know. He had all the advantages, and the disadvantages as well, of the children of the very rich. From an early age he was in the constant company of a tutor; under constant supervision. That made him shy in his relation to his father and secretive with regard to anyone else. Among the servants of the house he became a patient listener. For a short time he became a hero-worshipper."

"Of his father?"

Miss Charlebois remained silent for a moment, pensively looking at Lady Clark. "No," she said at last. "Apart from myself and Maud Dolittle, there was nobody who saw in Mr Clark a great man. And the time came when Maud Dolittle ceased to hold that view of him."

"It was the grandfather who had become the legendary figure, was it not?"

"Exactly. It was, of course, largely Mr Clark's own doing, both in a positive and a negative sense."

"How do you mean?"

"In the first place, he never spoke of his father except in a panegyric sense; in the second place, he forbade those dependent on him to speak of the dead man in the child's presence. Among the older servants who had known him there was, naturally, a good deal of talk going on about him. They knew he had been a working miller. His rise to wealth and power had been phenomenal. He was still being talked of in town. So, whenever Master Edmund, as a child, appeared among the servants, there was a sudden silence, on account of Mr Clark's prohibition.

"And then there sprang up that strange friendship between a middle-aged man and the boy which led to his being sent away to boarding school in the east."

"A friendship? With whom?"

"With Mr Stevens."

"I see," Lady Clark said slowly.

"In a way it was very natural. Mr Clark began to live largely at home. The mill ran itself; it had become an independent thing. There were details to be looked after, of course. Well, Mr Stevens, in charge of production, and Miss Dolittle, in charge of distribution, looked after them. Mr Clark got into the habit of having these two report to him, ordinarily over the telephone, occasionally here at the house. I believe the conversion of the mill to automatic operation was responsible for the change; the twenty units which were still operated by hand had lost their importance. Mr Clark indulged in his new hobby."

"Which was?"

"Botany. He laid out the arboretum which is still the pride of the park. Soon he had callers from all over the continent and even from Europe. He put a noted horticulturist in charge of his plantation—a Mr Magby, who is dead now—and at all times experiments were going on, directed by the biologists whose Maecenas he became, and closely watched by himself. He built greenhouses and laboratories for them and endowed the botanical departments of several universities. For years it was rare that the house did not harbour some noted biologist; often there were half a dozen here at a time; and endless arguments were proceeding in the library, often lasting through the night.

"It was a weird life. The two children were living underground, so to speak; their father often did not see them for days together. We kept them out of his way.

"He also began to indulge in large-scale philanthropy. A special office in the Realty Building was in charge of an expert actuary. Mr Clark must have spent millions in that way.

"And he began to collect his few pictures; he had his agents in all the large cities of Europe. He bought many which he did not keep. His purchases were shipped here and inspected; he kept only those which specially appealed to him; the rest he gave to public collections.

"The grounds also demanded a share of his time. You know, of course, that, by the will of old Mr Rudyard Clark, this whole property was reserved for the wife of the oldest son of any Clark whose wife was no longer living. You hold the property by that title yourself. You also know that there is a special fund set aside for the upkeep; it has been accumulating for decades. Mr Clark never touched it; as a matter of fact, he could not. But he faced all the retaining walls and the landing stage at the lake with marble; and he finished the circular swimming pool at the end of the lane.

"All these things occupied him; but they occupied nobody else in this house. As I said, it was a melancholy sort of life. One could not help pitying him; he was so shut up in himself. You must also know that, towards the end of her life, Maud Clark had changed towards him. The ironical condescension with which she had always treated him disappeared; as if she had foreseen her end and wished to leave him with a new picture of herself. I have just told you how that children's party put an end to a period of his life in which the essential impulses often appeared to me to be sunk behind the past. It was the past that ruled him. Even his botanical interests had been a legacy from her; like his music. Perhaps I should have mentioned that no famous musician ever came to Canada without being invited to come to Clark House, often receiving fabulous fees for his consent to do so. From all which, at that children's party, he seemed to awake.

"I mention all this merely in order to explain how Captain Stevens—or Mr Stevens as he was still called—became acquainted with Master Edmund. He met him at the house, of course. The boy was most attractive, physically as well as otherwise, though excessively shy. Then he met him in the grounds, by chance at first, I have no doubt. But soon he began to come to the park without calling here, with the undoubted purpose of attaching the child to himself. When I asked myself why he should wish to do so, I found only one possible reason. During the last years of Mr Rudyard Clark's life, Mr Stevens had become the old gentleman's right-hand man; he knew that the development of the mill was still proceeding largely along lines laid down by old Mr Rudyard; in Mr Samuel Clark he saw only the man who carried out another man's bidding; he did not know that, essentially, all Mr Rudyard's plans had been determined by his son's forecasts."

"How do you know that?"

"There are papers in existence which prove it. One day, during the years I am speaking of, Mr Clark turned them over to me, with the request to put them in chronological order. While I did that, I studied them in some detail.

"Somehow I found out, by overhearing casual snatches of their conversation, what Mr Stevens and the child were talking about: it was always the grandfather. They walked and they talked. At last Mr Stevens began to relieve the tutor in taking the boy on long horseback rides. I often thought about it. Was it my duty to tell Mr Clark? I didn't; and it went on for several years before Mr Clark found out of his own accord; when he did, he promptly ended the relation by sending Edmund away to boarding school. No doubt Mr Stevens laid, in those years, the foundation for his later position of power. You know that, when Mr Clark turned the presidency over to Sir Edmund—or, come to think of it, even before that: when Mr Edmund began to concern himself in the administration of the mill—Captain Stevens at once became general manager.

"To be sent to boarding school, at the age of eleven or twelve, did the boy a world of good. He lost his shyness. When he came home for his holidays, he was a different being: frank, boyish, almost manly. I liked him tremendously then. . . ."

"Till he went to the wars?"

Miss Charlebois felt thrown on the defensive. "Well, when he came home late in 1918, immediately after the armistice, though not yet of age, he was no longer child or boy or even youth. . . ."

"I know," said Lady Clark. "The war did that to the young people; and twice he had been very near death."

"The world was changed for them. And you know, of course, that, in France, he and Captain Stevens had met again?"

"Yes. And he had conceived a plan to make use of Mr Stevens's very considerable abilities. . . . How about Ruth meanwhile?"

"Poor Ruth!" Miss Charlebois said. "She became hard, callous, cynical; and all in consequence of the knowledge which weighed on her that she had been the cause of her mother's death."

Lady Clark shuddered. "Who could have told her that?" she asked, with the emphasis on the last word.

"A *bonne* whom she had tortured into exasperation. She was at once dismissed, that goes without saying; but the damage was done. . . .

"And meanwhile the mill went on. Somehow we were all living under the shadow of the mill. It went on like doom, ever growing. The twenty units still operated by hand, as they had always been, gradually assumed to us something in the nature of a feebly-beating heart within that colossus. The rest, the automatic part, seven or eight times as large, seemed withdrawn from human control. It was the strangest thing to hear those reports of Mr Stevens, as I sometimes had an opportunity of doing : they concerned themselves always with those twenty units; and I know, from casual remarks he dropped, that Mr Clark himself, when thinking of the mill, was always thinking of them : only *there* were human destinies at stake; the rest did not count. As a matter of fact, I believe, control over the automatic part of the mill had gradually slipped out of the hands of the administration into those of the engineers. Changes were reported, of course; but they were only reported; they were not submitted for approval or disapproval. To us, looking on from this side of the lake, it seemed as if no human will could stop it; as if, even though the whole population of the earth perished, it would go on producing flour till it had smothered the globe."

"It is a curious thought," Lady Clark said, "that of the two thousand men slaving away there, trying to keep pace with automatic machines and not quite succeeding. Was there never a change among *them*?"

"Oh, there were changes," Miss Charlebois replied, "even there. I don't know a great deal about them. I do know that, whenever a vacancy occurred, through the death of an operator, or through somebody's throwing up his job, that vacancy was never filled. A change was made in the line-up, by the engineers, which made it possible to dispense with the services of that operator. That gave the process of unbroken if slow growth the weird appearance of a decay. That the units operated by hand were preserved at all must have been the direct doing of Mr Clark, of course; for the engineers were always ready to eliminate any number of workers. The town, still apparently prosperous, seeming prosperous to any outside visitor, at least, had long become aware of its own approaching death. The time could not be distant when it must shrink in size, shrink, shrink. And it was on the gradualness of that process that Mr Clark relied."

"It was like a mining town when the vein whose discovery had called it into being became exhausted."

"Yes. Only that here the vein produced more and more abundantly, though by itself. Thus it went on till the Great War broke out, when there was a brief revival. For, what with enlistments, the old units became depleted at a rate faster than it was possible to switch over to automatic operation; and that at the very time when a speeding-up of production was imperatively called for. Then women took the place of the men."

"As everywhere," Lady Clark said. "As far as possible, I presume, the women were, by Mr Clark's order, taken from the Terrace, so as to keep the jobs open for the men when they returned?"

At this moment the senator, recovered from that slight, insidious cold, passed along the gallery on which the living-room opened. Frowning, he stopped.

"Will you join us in a cup of tea, Father?" asked Lady Clark.

"I might," he said absent-mindedly and sat down.

Lady Clark rose to press a button. "We were talking of the mill and the town before the war."

"Were you?" he said; and, visibly, his inner eye focused itself on that time: it looked as if his bodily eyes were withdrawn within his skull. Then he shook his head.

"It's a crazy world," he said.

It was rare that he spoke so directly; and he looked at his daughter-in-law as if realizing that she could not possibly understand all he meant to express. She had been born into a time when the change from the nineteenth century to the twentieth had been well under way. She had barely known an age without motor car and aeroplane; she had probably never been conscious of the acceleration and shallowing of all life-processes that had taken place as a consequence of their coming.

"Do you often sit here?" he asked, looking about; for this had been his own and his wife's sitting-room; so that, for the moment, he was not quite clear in what part of his life he was living; nor who this woman was: which one of the Mauds. Such lapses came over him more and more frequently. The difference between past and present vanished; in some new world everything seemed present.

And then he saw the picture over the mantelpiece, the picture of Stella, indistinguishable, down to the expression of the face, from a portrait of his daughter-in-law as she had been in certain moods ten, fifteen years ago. He recognized it; and the recognition gave him a shock.

But before the tea which Lady Clark ordered, meeting the butler who came in response to her bell on the landing at the head of the grand stairway, had been brought by the footman, both Lady Clark and Miss Charlebois tiptoed out; for, as often happened, in daytime, when the senator was less restless than he was apt to be at night, after dark, he had fallen asleep in his corner of the chesterfield; but not before, in some mental twilight, he had absorbed what his daughter-in-law had said about the town and the mill.

In fact, he was positive that he was not asleep at all, though he knew he was dreaming. It was a half-waking dream of whose nature he was fully conscious. He even knew that the women were leaving him under the impression that he was sound asleep; and he felt as if he were playing a trick on them by letting them depart with that impression.

What in the world was wrong with the mill? What with his own family? What with the town? The senator saw scenes. Standing half in, half outside his dream, he was not sure, at times, whether what he saw was before or during the war. It was all such a wild, chaotic confusion.

Of course, when he thought or dreamt of the mill, it was always that part of it operated by hand he had in mind. The rest had nothing to do with him any longer, even though, to the world, that rest was 'the' mill.

Reports spoke of seething discontent again, of agitation, of propaganda for something called socialism; of an attitude generally hostile to the management; yes, hostile to him who considered himself the best friend the men had anywhere: he had raised wages in the face of the fact that automatic production was cheaper now than hand production; he had lowered rents; he had established company stores where all the necessities of a mill-hand's life were sold at cost. He had made, he had anticipated the demand for, concessions. Against his will, against his reason, he found himself driven into an attitude of defending class interests instead of preparing a new world order by eliminating human toil. He tried to understand; he had always tried to understand; he had never succeeded; he did not succeed now.

He asked for an explanation from Mr Brook who was still superintendent of works; but Mr Brook knew no more than himself, except that there was a spirit abroad which was most disquieting. Being pressed for definite answers to definite questions, Mr Brooks had recourse again to the ancient device of placing 'confidential men' in key positions where they would be able to pick up information. He could readily do so; he was chairman of the commission controlling employment.

When these men reported that Bruce Rogers—a foreman at that—was responsible for much of the dissatisfaction, Mr Brook proposed to have him dismissed; he would have done so on his own responsibility had not the promotion of the man been due to a direct expression of the president's will. Mr Clark vetoed that procedure. "No," he said. "Tell him I want to see him."

Just before the interview took place, a terrible thing happened at the mill. An elderly workman was seized by a belt, hurled aloft, thrown to the floor, and instantly killed. On a fatal scale, it was a repetition of the accident which had crippled old Mr Rudyard Clark. Hearing of it, the president at once sent word to the widow that she would be taken care of by the mill. It was the first immediately fatal accident the mill had had.

The hands felt unnerved; they blamed the 'system'.

Bruce Rogers was now himself in his forties, married, father of a small family. When he entered the presidential office where Sam had gone to see him, he was sullen at first, reluctant to say anything whatever. But Sam, who had always had a liking for him as well as for his aged father, told him to sit down, discarding the testy tone in which he was known to speak to subordinates.

"Surely," he said, "I've shown myself reasonable enough. I gave you all you asked for in 1901. I have raised wages beyond what was advisable. What is it the men want?"

"They want a bit of what you'd call life, I suppose."

"Life? What do you mean?"

"They want to feel human. They're slaves."

"If to have to work for a living can be called slavery, then we are all slaves."

"It's hard to explain," Bruce evaded.

"Come now. I won't let you get away with that. Give me something concrete. It's hard to explain, you say; but unless it's explained, I can't do anything to help."

Bruce observed a discreet silence. At last he said, "I don't suppose there is anything concrete. It's the system."

There was that word again; and it made Sam jump. "Will you be good enough to tell me what you people mean by 'the system'?"

Bruce looked up at the change in tone. But it roused him. "The inhuman grind," he said. "I'll tell you one thing. Do you know what is the most prevalent disease on the Terrace?"

"Disease?"

"Disease. It's insomnia. Ask Dr Wellwood or any of the other doctors. Ask the dispensing clerk at the company drugstore. They'll tell you that the use of sleeping tablets is extraordinarily prevalent."

"Is that so? How do you account for that?"

"As I said. The men are slaves. Slaves to the machines. They must keep pace with the machines; or something happens. When they quit, at the end of their shift, they are deadbeat. . . ."

"That doesn't seem to agree with the fact that the moving pictures do a flourishing business. Why don't they go home and rest?"

Bruce looked at his employer and once more observed that discreet silence. It lent the statement when it came an extraordinary force. "It isn't that kind of exhaustion. It's a nervous exhaustion. Physical rest doesn't remedy it."

"I see."

"Look at this death," Bruce went on, won by his interlocutor's undoubted sincerity, expressed in his tone. "We've got more safety devices than we've ever had. Anybody at home in the mill should be able to take care of himself. The trouble is that nobody feels at home there. I wonder to what an extent you realize that, whenever some new automatic link is established, the pace is affected, be it ever so little? When the men go to work, they should be going to an ordinary routine; but they don't. Even an ordinary routine is a lifeless thing; but what they are facing is infinitely worse. They've got to key themselves up to their work. There's a girl on the bagging floor. All she's got to do is to see to it that the open end of the bag falls in the right position under the stitching machine. The bag travels on a conveyor; the stitching machine runs of its own accord. All she needs to do is to stroke the empty end of the bag so it lies flat, and that only when it accidentally happens that it doesn't. But watch her. Her whole body is working all the time. To look at her work, you'd think she could carry on a conversation at the same time. But the bags come so fast that she's got to keep up a steady rhythm. She strokes every bag, whether it needs it or not. They come so fast that her eye is not reliable, her muscular response not quick enough. So her whole body works. She beats the rhythm with her knees. Both her elbows swing as if she had St Vitus dance. If they didn't, her fingers would get caught by the needle; for it is a question, not of seconds but of a hundredth of a second. . . . She's an extreme case, I'll admit. But more or less they are all like that. The thing is inhuman; and the worst of it is there is no way out."

"What do you mean by that?"

"Suppose a new hand starts work with us. He's an ordinary human being; he laughs and jokes as he goes to work. But within less than a year something comes over him. Whatever he does, he seems to do automatically; in reality, the pace forces him to be constantly on the watch; it isn't that he becomes a machine; that would be tolerable if undesirable. What he becomes is the slave of a machine which punishes him when he is at fault; the machine seems to watch for the chance. All the time. The men are tempted to yell and to curse at it. And then he is spoiled for anything else. . . . Meanwhile, he gets up and lies down. Between the two things time disappears. It is nothing but a nightmare. It's always time to get up; it's always time to lie down. That's where the movies come in. They're a drug; and all drugs, of course, do harm. Even accidents will become routine; there has been one; there will be others."

"Don't say that. Is there nothing we can do?"

Bruce shrugged his shoulders.

"There's no way out, you say. You were a mill-hand; you're a foreman now."

"I know whom I have to thank for that. If I hadn't happened to catch your eye one day . . . What you say is exactly what my father says. But before the machine we're all equal, as we're supposed to be before the law. My father thinks we're still working under the eyes of a boss who appreciates good work. But the machine is the boss now; it doesn't promote; it just exacts motions. Besides, there's no room at the top. When my father was young, he was foreman over three, four helpers; now we have a gang boss to every twenty-five hands; and a foreman for two or three hundred."

The president rose. "I'll think this over, Bruce. You've given me something to go by. . . . By the way, they say you're agitating among the men."

"It's not true," Bruce said angrily as he, too, rose. "I'm trying to explain matters to the men. I'm telling them that the whole thing can't be helped; that it is nobody's fault; that strikes and walkouts are of no use. That there's only one way out: to leave the machines to themselves; or to the engineers. . . ."

"That," Sam said, "would turn the men adrift; and it's been my whole endeavour to prevent that."

Bruce, stopping at the door, shrugged his shoulders. "I suppose the State or what they call society would have to see them through. . . ."

Whenever, at that time, the time of the 'troubles', he had thought of his daughter, he had mentally averted his eyes. With regard to her he had a bad conscience. But other girls were orphans and had to live as best they could. He could not help himself; just as Bruce said there was no help for the mill.

The mill!

Ninety per cent of the country's need for flour was being supplied by that mill. Slowly but inevitably it had reached that figure. But only that figure. It could have supplied five hundred per cent. That it remained below the hundred mark was due to the fact that a few independent mills were still hanging on; and Sam was careful, always, to spare their existence. He knew that Maud Dolittle criticized him on that score. Only by sweeping them out of existence first could he hope to do those other things which, in the past, he had dreamt of. His son was growing up; it was that son who would have to see to further changes. His own arteries, spiritually, had hardened. He had had to live in a system so long that he had become powerless to change that system.

By 1914, the mill, as it stood, had been completed: one hundred and seventy units were grinding out flour for Canada, for Britain, for part of the United States, for Italy, France, Spain; and, later, after the war, for Germany. The growth had been automatic and inevitable: as if from below, from out of the still plastic igneous bedrock of the earth, new units had been pressed up like intrusive dykes, hardening on exposure to the air, and cooling. This impression had been enhanced by the fact that for the last eighty units or so not even an architect had been employed. If further growth there was to be, it would have to be elsewhere now. But further growth would mean monopoly.

Monopoly Sam had always dreaded; the fact was that he had lost his courage and faith. Maud Dolittle knew it; and she was pressing for monopoly now; or not pressing; for she never used the word; but she looked at him, and her eyes suggested it: they suggested *what he might have been*; suggested also what he might have been to her if he had not lost courage and faith. No. And he knew that he was writing his own verdict and the verdict of the Victorian age. Monopoly meant new and wider problems with which he dared not cope.

It was true, he had striven for monopoly of ownership. Slowly he had united all but three shares held by Miss Dolittle in his own hand, always excepting that single block still held by Mr Cole, the shareholder who had given his father trouble before him. Though, apart from the tenacity with which he held to that block of shares which he refused to sell, Mr Cole gave no trouble any longer; he acquiesced in everything. The control of the Clarks was too unquestioned: it was based on the ownership of ninety-odd per cent of the stock. . . .

Suddenly the senator, half asleep, half awake, or perhaps dreaming within a dream, saw a scene in which Mr Cole was the central figure. Again, as at that shareholders' meeting in his father's lifetime, Mr Cole exploded; but he exploded against Edmund, his son, not against his old father. . . .

He had just been thinking of Ruth. . . .

Within his dream the senator tried to adjust the chronology. The interview with Bruce Rogers must have taken place in 1912; the explosion of Mr Cole came in 1923 or '24. Ruth had gone to Europe in—1921, was it? Somewhere there was something radically wrong. In seeing Mr Cole, in that last explosion of his, he heard his son called Sir Edmund. Charles Beatty was standing in a large and lofty room crowded with brilliant figures, for Sir Edmund was playing a political as well as a financial game. By some trick worthy of his grandfather, Sir Edmund was ousting his father from control. . . .

But the chaos became so chaotic that it woke him. With a start he sat up.

The room was in darkness. Nobody had seen fit to come and switch on the light. Suddenly he was conscious of the fact that he was an old, old man, burdened with responsibilities beyond his power to bear. He rose and went to his room to go to bed.

Within half an hour Lady Clark followed him; and, finding him seemingly asleep, she sat down in the sitting-room adjoining his suite, leaving the doors between it and his bedroom open.

CHAPTER

XVII

EVERYBODY in the house was aware of the condition of the senator. But the two ladies were the only ones who understood that he was tracing the history of his soul, in an attempt at self-justification. None of us can live unless we stand justified in our own eyes; not even those among us who are murderers or thieves. . . .

In this attempt, so at least Lady Clark realized, nothing was quite as puzzling as the time element. She knew he was simultaneously the man who lived through a crisis after his father's death; the man who was everlastingly worrying about the mill; the man who wished to shift his responsibilities to younger shoulders but dared not quite do it; and the man who was sitting by the dead body of his son, trying to discover some vista into the future along which he could either go himself or point those who must follow him.

Lady Clark saw much; yet she wished to be able, by some magic, to peer into that soul. She wished to do so without fear; she was convinced that she would have to witness nothing base: nothing that could have revolted the most delicate sensibility.

She went so far as to wish she knew all Miss Charlebois knew. Within the space of weeks, or months at the best, she would have to assume those responsibilities which nominally still rested on her father-in-law. Already it was she who held a control which she dared not exercise; shortly, if she was the senator's heiress, she would be the absolute owner of the mill and all its subsidiaries, the mill at Arbala, built by her husband, not excepted. Her sister-in-law, Ruth, the *Marquise* as everybody called her, had been fully compensated for her surrender of any voice in the affairs of the mill. Why, she wondered, had she agreed to that? Did she share her mother's attitude to the mill?

Lady Clark made up her mind to ask Miss Charlebois. She did not wish to appear unduly inquisitive; but she must know more than she knew at present. Sitting in that living-room leading to the senator's suite, she pondered deeply in order to find the most trying gaps in her knowledge.

As for her dead husband, she knew enough to piece matters together.

When the war broke out, Edmund had been only sixteen, just ready to enter college. But college as such had held no lure for him. It so happened that, in the summer of 1914, he had, with some classmates, been on a cruise in the West Indies. The yacht on which he had been a guest had at once returned to England where it was owned by the father of one of his friends. This friend, two and a half years Edmund's senior, had, after several expulsions in England, been sent to Canada, in a futile attempt to force some measure of standard education down his throat; now he had promptly gone to his grave in France.

Edmund had willy-nilly returned to Canada where, at Toronto, he and she had met on occasion, little thinking at the time that one day they would be man and wife. She, like the friend, his senior by two years, had been among his distant admirers, for he had begun at once to train for service in the air.

More than once she had been among the crowds that watched him when he flew; for from the start it had been apparent that he would be the most daring if not the most competent flier to come from this continent. Whenever he appeared on the flying-field, he was cheered; he was cheered again whenever he landed. At the age of seventeen he had been a flight commander.

She had met his father, too, at the time; casually, as she had met Edmund, for she had been 'in the swim', or, as she still expressed it to herself, after the lapse of a quarter century, 'on the market'.

The moment Edmund had completed his eighteenth year, he had gone overseas, to establish for himself that record which remains written into the history of Canada in the war. Every now and then she had heard of him, in a roundabout way or through the press; had heard of exploits so daring that he became internationally famous. Twice he had been wounded; once to return to the front after four months; but the second time so severely that he had to accept an honourable discharge.

Yet he had remained overseas, in England now, where, with the help of Captain Stevens and another man whom he had met in France, a Captain McDermot—a huge man who, in spite of his cumbersome physique, had led a most adventurous life—he had built a factory for the production of aircraft, revolutionizing the construction of flying machines. At the end of the war he had given this factory to the nation, thereby qualifying for his knighthood. This knighthood had first been offered to his father, who had financed the enterprise; but, being declined by him, it had, on his majority, been given to the son.

All this she knew and had known at the time; it was a matter of public record. When he had returned to Canada, they had met again, first casually, then on purpose. Having come into the fortune left him by his mother—which, under the careful administration of Charles Beatty, had more than trebled—he had built the marvellous mill at Arbala in Ontario, with the set purpose of ousting such milling enterprises as still remained independent; till there had been left, throughout the country, no more than three great milling concerns, all owned by the Clarks: the mill at Langholm, the greatest of them all; the group of four mills comprised under the name of Western Flour Mills; and the new mill at Arbala. What she did not understand was why these three concerns should have been competitors engaged, more than once, in price wars. She had come to divine that, between father and son, there was a profound division; and it was the son who had schemed for control of the manifold 'interests'. Even she, Maud, had been a pawn in this game of chess.

Though she had not seen clear at the time and did not see quite clear now, she had pieced together a picture of the situation which she felt to be essentially true. She had, at the time, been sorely tempted to break off her engagement; but there had been the fascination of coming events of world-wide importance; today, she admitted to herself, somewhat ruefully, that hers had also been a plan to strengthen the hand of the father rather than that of the son—which had been the reason why, on the eve of her marriage, she had accepted the profound humiliation to which she had been exposed.

As she sat in the room adjoining the senator's suite, that night, she thought it all over. The house at Arbala had been building; her father-in-law, happening to be in the east, to see his daughter Ruth off, on her way to Europe, had run down from Toronto with his son who was also leaving for England—a trip from which he returned as Sir Edmund. She herself had been living at Whitby, with her sisters, in the house which her father had acquired on his retirement as president and chancellor of the University of Eastern Ontario. A telephone call, followed by the despatch of a car, had summoned her to join them at Arbala; and there she had met Mr Clark and his daughter, for the first time since her engagement.

Having inspected house and mill, her father-in-law, on the point of being called to the senate—it had been Edmund's doing —had invited her to spend the few days remaining before the boat sailed with him and his daughter at Ottawa. There, Edmund would meet them in time to catch the boat; and his father would take her home.

What had struck her on that occasion was the utter detachment in which father and son faced each other. It had been a puzzling thing; but, of course . . .

"What," so she asked of Miss Charlebois, late that night, when the senator was quietly sleeping, "was known at Langholm of the Arbala mill, at the time before my marriage?"

"Let me see," Miss Charlebois said. "It was a strange period for us all; there were so many developments. One might have thought we were living on the eve of a revolution. . . . Oh yes," she went on after a pause, "it was Mr Inkster who brought the tale."

Lady Clark smiled. "He would make an effective thing of it."

"He did. I remember the occasion most vividly now. I was still in charge of this house, of course. A rumour of what Mr Inkster was telling around town had reached us; I shouldn't be surprised if I were told that Mr Clark arranged for that dinner party on purpose, in order to have a chance to hear it from Mr Inkster's own lips. The senator asked no questions; he left that to others. But it was a foregone conclusion that such a question would be asked where Mr Inkster appeared. Dinner over, Mr Clark merely watched and drew near the edge of the group of which Mr Inkster soon formed the centre.

"Suddenly, from that group, I heard the word Toronto; and I, too, drew near to listen. If I remember right, Mr Inkster had gone there to argue a case.

"Then, 'At Toronto,' Mr Inkster said, 'I heard interesting rumours about young Clark's new mill; and, being his father's legal adviser, and generally interested in anything the Clarks did, I became curious to see that fabled structure. Well, I went . . .'

"He looked about at his audience, huge even then, as you know him, ponderous, impressive, ironical. I have often thought that the lawyer's profession has a good deal in common with that of the actor: you can always tell either the way in which they seem to draw the eyes of an audience before they speak.

"And then he went on. 'At the office building at Arbala I was left to cool my heels for close to an hour, in the ante-chamber of the superintendent, a Captain McDermot. His first name was Cyril.'

"Again he looked about, smiling sarcastically; I didn't know why. It gave the impression that he presumed vast and significant conclusions could be drawn from the name.

"'From the windows of that room,' he proceeded, 'I had a magnificent view into the valley of the Arrow River and up the wooded heights gorgeous in the colours of the fall. On these slopes stood a few sumptuous villas; but there was no town; no village even; nothing resembling any sort of settlement. In coming along the road, in a rented car, I had noticed to one side a small farm-house which bore the name "Arbala", blue on white, proclaiming it to be the post office of a district which, as a district, did not exist. The mill *was* the district.

"'The office building, of grey limestone, not so very large at all, but lofty inside, and more spacious than you would have expected it to be, with wide, spotless corridors, snow-white, and fine rooms, most of them empty, stood a few hundred feet south of the mill which barred the valley, approached by a circular driveway through freshly-planted shrubberies. So far, inside and out, I had not seen a human being apart from the telephone operator at the entrance who, after a word or two into her transmitter, had said to me, "Third door to the right, please. Mr McDermot is busy. If you care to wait . . ."

"'Well, I waited, having the impression that I was in a void peopled by superhuman intelligences. The silence throughout the building was absolute.

"'Thus the hour went by. Then, startlingly because soundlessly, a young lady condensed out of the ambient air. Without a word this houri, a marvel of impersonal elegance and flawless perfection—where was the beauty shop?—conveyed to me by a smile and an inclination of her permanent wave that I was going to be admitted into the presence.

"'In the inner office, Mr McDermot, impassive and motionless, received me without rising, but laying down the transmitter of a dictaphone. He subjected me to a cross-examination conducted in a dispassionate voice that knew no stresses : as to my antecedents, academic and professional, my business, my future intentions; above all, why did I wish to see the mill? He did not ask me to sit down.'

"Again Mr Inkster looked about his audience. He was, as he is today, the personification of the dignity of the law, accustomed to see others wilt under his trenchant questions; never before cross-examined himself. Those surrounding him smiled at the picture which, with a few deft touches, he conjured up before them.

" 'Well, Mr Inkster,' Mr McDermot went on at last, 'we are not in the habit of showing callers about. But, since you give me your word of honour—and if I am any judge of men, I can rely on it—that you are neither a miller nor in any capacity employed by a mill . . .' (here he made an impressive and questioning pause) 'we shall make an exception in your case.'

" 'Now mind you, I was not aware of having given any such assurance; but since, had I done so, it would have been in literal accord with the truth, I nodded. "Very good of you, I am sure," I muttered.

" 'Whereupon Mr McDermot pressed a button under his desk which summoned a young man in a spotless white smock, worn over a faultless dark business suit. He had a pleasant face and gave me a gold-filled smile. This, Mr McDermot said, is Mr Inkster, K.C., of Langholm, Ontario—or is it Manitoba? He wishes to see the mill. Will you be good enough to show him around, Shaw?

" 'To cut a long story short, young Shaw took me across a parklike expanse to the towering structure of the mill, twenty stories high and perhaps three hundred feet square. Like the mill here, it stood with its back against a dam; but the railway tracks ran through it lengthwise, not crosswise; unlike it, its outline was not that of a pyramid. Inside, everything was white, spotless, silent, and seemingly motionless. I half thought they had stopped the machines for my benefit. In reality, all motion was internal and enclosed.'

"Mr Inkster paused and proceeded only when one of the audience asked, 'Well, what did you see?'

" 'Nothing. Throughout the building there were not more than half a dozen men about. There were no elevators, no stairs, no floors. We climbed over steel ladders to the third tier of windows; and then, not being a mountaineer, I said I had had enough. There was nothing to see in any case. The place was like an enormous well into which all sorts of puzzling machinery had been suspended. Here and there a man with a mop of cotton waste was hanging in mid-air; here and there another was crouching on a grid, wiping flour dust. Everything glittered; everything felt and smelt oily. At various points, far overhead, pipelike tubes entered and, from minute to minute, discharged, with a sound, first of hissing, then of rumbling, what I presumed to be a few tons of wheat which came I don't know whence. Below, unattended endless conveyors carried unbroken rows of bags full of flour, carried them into specially constructed boxcars, all painted white, inside and out; when these were filled, they were noiselessly shunted away by electric motors.

" 'You may say, of course, it is much the same here; but it is different, too. For one thing, there is the town; the mill is not surrounded by an interstellar vacancy; for another, there are men in this mill, at least in spots. At Arbala, everything proceeded as in a void; no vestiges of the past were to be seen or inferred. It was uncanny. Though it was much smaller than the mill here, it was the pure essence of the thing.

" 'One trifle interested me. On the lake behind the dam of which I had a glimpse through an upper window lay a fleet of perhaps a hundred giant seaplanes. What they were there for, I couldn't guess. I asked Shaw. He muttered, I know nothing about them. It's Mr McDermot's hobby. It was a pretty sight.'

"As I said, the story was effectively told. It made all who heard it shiver."

"I can imagine," Lady Clark said. "The strange thing is that I have seen the Arbala mill a dozen times; but I now realize that I had never really *seen* it. Even at second hand Mr Inkster's tale has opened my eyes."

"He has a graphic way," Miss Charlebois said.

Both women had the peculiar feeling as if, in thus resurrecting the past, they were holding an autopsy over a corpse. Yet they could not get away from that past. There was nothing to talk about in the present. Each of them knew that the other was anxious to ask further questions; each was searching for some seemingly aimless and artless way to make the other talk. At last Lady Clark felt that, if either must let the other see what was in her mind, it had perhaps better be she. She had the advantage of position on her side.

"Tell me," she said, "how Ruth came to go to Europe."

"Poor Ruth!" the Frenchwoman exclaimed again. It seemed as if, whenever she had to mention her, the epithet 'poor' came to her lips. After a while she added, "I suppose you have been in a finishing school yourself?"

"Have I?" Lady Clark said, smiling to herself.

"Do you know that you and I have much in common? Though, of course, your case and mine cannot compare. . . . But Ruth went successively to half a dozen."

"Half a dozen!"

"Yes. Invariably she was at last 'let out', to use the vulgar phrase. I believe she played deliberately for her expulsion. Long before the war she anticipated post-war attitudes: defeatism and cynicism; she refused to accept age-hallowed standards. Long before it became fashionable she adopted that lounging, slouching carriage, flat-breasted and curved in the spine, with a masculine affectation of speech. She was in revolt; and no wonder."

"And when she came home?"

"Utter boredom."

"Yet," Lady Clark said, "from the brief glimpses I had of her when she came here with her husband, on her trip around the world, I arrived at the conclusion that there was in her . . . I don't know what to call it . . . some sort of depth . . ."

"Oh, there was. She could not help betraying it on a thousand occasions. She suffered. Her airs were a mere camouflage, as they called it after the war. Except, of course, in one point."

Lady Clark looked up, a question in her eye.

"She was without sex."

"I felt something of the kind, it puzzled me at the time. But it also attracted me. Her marriage, with that ancient marquis, was a camouflage as well."

"A defence; or whatever you care to call it. Her title protected her. Before her marriage her notorious wealth had made her a target. After it, her position in European society, as a *grande dame*, made her affectations seem mere eccentricities; it removed her from the front line of attack. It was her marriage with a man who, under human limitations, could not be expected to live much longer which interpreted for me her last year at home. What she married was not a man. It was immunity. No matter what you say, a title, especially a great title, lifts you beyond the reach; even today . . . Did she tell you of her step-sons?"

"She did. One a general, the other a colonel in the French army; one fifty, the other forty-five when their stepmother was twenty-one. But it was on their account that her husband had agreed to the arrangement."

"Was it? Now there is something I didn't know. I was afraid he was an old debauchee."

"No, no," Lady Clark exclaimed and repeated, "Oh, no! The war had ruined him. Or was it the peace? I forget. He had a magnificent place in the *Dauphiné*; but it was mortgaged to the hilt; and the old man lived there, with his valet Jean-Jacques, as old as he, in a single room, on something like twenty dollars a month, contributed by his sons. It was Ruth who proposed to him. She simply bribed him into consenting. She settled half a million francs annually on him and promised to keep up the estate for the sons. There were some picturesque details about the affair; but on his part it was a purely commercial transaction. She told me, though, that he was very fond of her, as of a grandchild; he would have done almost anything for her. But, of course, the marriage was never consummated.

"I remember the occasion when she told me all this," Lady Clark went on reminiscently. "It must have been in 1923, for she was of age. In fact, she had come over to arrange for the transfer of her fortune to her own name; and she had to see her father and Charles Beatty who had been administering both what her mother had left her and what her father had set aside for her on his son's majority, or rather at the time when the settlement was made before Edmund and I were married. He had, at that time, insisted on her being excluded from any share in the mill; and that fact, the mill being a fabulous asset, gave her a certain bargaining power in the final settlement after her majority, a power which she used exclusively for the benefit of her step-sons.

"There had been a last conference between her and the two men in the library; and Ruth had come out somewhat flustered, though, on the whole, I believe, triumphant. She never told me anything of these money matters. . . . I was sitting on the veranda, for it was early summer; and after a while her father and Charles Beatty followed her into the hall. Promptly she came out and took my arm, a flush on her usually pale cheeks. The marquis, of course, was upstairs, resting. By the way in which she came up to me, as if fleeing from those two men one of whom was her father, she intimated to me without a word that she wished me to rise and come with her. When I was on my feet, she took my arm and drew me on, and out on the lawn, where, after a moment's hesitation, she took the road to the car sheds. Still without a word she backed a car out while I waited for her. When I had joined her in the front seat, she drove up the hill.

"Then, without disguising the fact that it was a mere pretext, she alleged that she needed something or other for her dressing table and turned down Hill Road towards town. You know, of course, that she was a daring and skilful driver. Seeing her coming down Main Street, most other cars stopped as they do for a fire engine. For a moment she disappeared in one of the shops and then returned, tossing her purchase into the car which was parked at the curb, its engine running.

"It was between five and six in the afternoon, the hour when offices closed; and the car stood on the south side of the street, headed east, near the intersection with Argyle, the busiest point. It was, as you know, before the final decay of the town. On both sides of the street there was a stream of young people released from the work of the day, hurrying home.

"For a moment Ruth stood, looking about at them all; and then she laughed. She took a case from her purse and lighted a cigarette; and thus, still betraying agitation, by the speed and quality of her movements, she raised one foot to the running board of the car, leaned an elbow on her knee, and began to talk as if we were alone in the world, every now and then flicking her ashes to the ground, and staring at every passer-by whether clerk or workman, male or female. The picture impressed me so vividly that I see it before me in all its details: the marvellously tailored suit from Paris; her pale face with the brightly-rouged cheeks and the brilliant lips; her tired grey eyes; her coquettish hat; and the expression that lay over it all, of a profound, if smiling weariness with life and the world.

"And there, in this crowded street of the small industrial city, she poured forth to me the story of her marriage and the motives which had guided her in contracting it, touching on her husband with delicate touches of humour, it is true, but also with a sort of compassionate tenderness which, more than once, caused her deep, throaty contralto to drive the tears to my eyes while, at the same time, I could not but laugh at the drollery of her expressions. She never called her husband anything but *cher Henri*, half making fun of him, half defending the purity of his motives. She made no secret of it that in certain ways she pitied him, pitied him even for the fact that he, older by decades than her father, was being dragged around the world. He would have much preferred to remain at home, of course, awaiting the end in sequestration. She had persuaded him to come with her by the tale of what she would do for his sons. Well, she added, she had done all she had promised, and more. But it seemed a pity that in order to do it she had had to take him out of France to circle a shrinking globe. On one occasion she had coaxed him into a passenger plane. Everywhere, of course, people started at this pair, having ascertained, from the hotel registers, that they were man and wife, not grandfather and grandchild. At times I was not so sure but that this sort of sensation which they created had been among her reasons for marrying the old man. . . ."

Since Lady Clark ceased pensively, Miss Charlebois nodded

slowly. "No doubt," she said. "She did many things because she saw herself in a stage part . . . I know," she added, seeing what amounted to a motion of protest on the other woman's part. "She would have repudiated the very idea of it; but so would nearly all the members of her generation. They felt themselves so utterly sincere. Yet, is not most of our life up to our thirties imitation?"

"Mine wasn't," Lady Clark said. "But we are straying from the point. I see Ruth perfectly as she was after her marriage, still in many ways immature; wrapped as it were in the armour of her cynicism; yet easily wounded; altogether tragic. But I don't see her at all as she must have been when she came from school and buried herself in this mill-town where nothing interested or attracted her. Her brother was away; and they had nothing in common anyway. . . ."

"I am not so sure of that; they understood each other."

"Yet they went in opposite directions. Besides, her problems were personal; his were social and even political. And there was the father who, in this respect, had a blindspot; he never could understand his children. . . ."

"True enough. Yet, tell me, where should she have gone? What could she have done with herself? Her very wealth removed her from most who were of her age. With the keenest curiosity about life she had a profound aversion for what is commonly called education, an aversion which amounted to inhibition. Hence her expulsions. She was not merely indifferent; she was hostile to those who insisted on instructing or training her. Strange to say, that was the very reason why, in interview after interview, I had urged her father to send her away. I feared I might be included in that aversion; it would have deprived the poor child of her one precarious anchorground. I wanted to retain my slender hold on her affections.

"When she returned for her final stay, I could do that only by leaving her conduct entirely to herself. It seemed that what I have called her being without sex would protect her; and in that at least I was right. When, soon after the war, she made up her mind to break away by going to Europe, to South Africa, South America, Australia, anywhere, it was I in whom she confided; she left it to me to get her father's consent; and I got it. It was her wealth which disgusted her; she could never be she; she was always the heiress; she wanted to go where her wealth was unknown. She wanted to face life without that barrier between her and reality. Her marriage she contracted only when she had seen that it was impossible to divorce herself from her wealth.

"Let me tell you what cut her adrift.

"It was after the war; and the temper of the mill-hands was getting brittle; that was perhaps why Mr Clark, not yet the senator, took things as he did and agreed to Ruth's leaving Canada. There had already been a certain amount of gossip about young Mr Edmund; he had not yet been knighted. In connection with his children as with anything else it was never the thing itself; it was its effect upon the labour situation which worried Mr Clark. He was, I believe, still adhering to his policy of gradualness. I don't believe he even saw the tragedy through which Ruth was living; nor that of his son. He always looked at the wider issues. To him, the mill was the only reality.

"Well, one afternoon, the chief of police of the town called here at the house, asking for Mr Clark. Mr Clark was not in; so I told Mr Burt to sit down and wait in the hall.

"Perhaps I should tell you that this Mr Burt was an odious man; he is dead now, or retired, I don't remember. It was he who, before the first strike at the mill, had called in so many provincial policemen, though Mr Stevens had suggested it. He was a tall, flat-breasted man, cavernous when he stood in front of you. Apart from the members of this household, the executives of the mill, and a few wealthy and influential people, I believe he considered the population of the town more or less as his subjects.

"One day there had been an accident on Main Street, and its whole south half was blocked, just at the time when a shift at the mill was coming off duty. Naturally, Mr Burt acted as traffic officer. It so happened that I had been out calling in the west end of the town; and before I realized it, I was caught in the jam. In front of my car was a dilapidated old Ford driven by a mill-hand. This man, apparently, knowing nothing of the accident, and anxious, no doubt, to get through to the Terrace, shot over to the left; and my chauffeur followed him closely. Burt stopped the mill-hand and gave him what I can only call a bawling-out, in the most galling manner, while he took the man's name and license number. My chauffeur sat impassive, relying on the immunity of privilege, though his offence, if offence there was, could be no less than that of the mill-hand; you know the snobbery of dependents. I had lowered my window, to give what information or apology might be required. But as soon as the mill-hand was out of the way, the chauffeur shot forward, paying not the slightest attention to Burt. To my amazement, the chief, recognizing, with a still irate glance, a car from Clark House, dropped his manner like a cloak and, bowing obsequiously, waved his hand, with a bright smile, for us to proceed.

"I tell you this in order to explain Mr Clark's reaction when he came in. He, too, knew Burt. It so happened that I was passing through the hall; and, seeing Mr Clark, I stopped to say a word in explanation. Mr Clark, hearing, in the man's first words, his daughter mentioned, looked at me, detaining me by that glance and nodding towards a chair. He knew, of course, in a general way, about Ruth's life; we had talked about her; and I believe he held me more or less responsible for all she did, though he had more than once admitted that I could not be blamed. Burt, of course, had risen and was standing in the attitude of a subaltern before a superior officer.

"What Burt had said in that moment before Mr Clark detained me was, 'I don't know, Mr Clark, whether your daughter has seen you yet.'

"'Seen me? What about?' Mr Clark asked testily and in sudden misgiving while I sat down.

"'About what happened this morning.'

"'I know of nothing that happened this morning.'

"'I wasn't at the station myself, at first,' Burt went on, meaning the police station at the upper end of Main Street West, next to the Realty Building; I don't know whether it is still there. 'But as far as I could make out . . .'

"'Save your preamble,' Mr Clark said impatiently, sitting down himself and leaving Burt standing.

"Whereupon Burt precipitated himself into a recital to which Mr Clark listened without moving a muscle in his face, without even smoothing out his initial frown.

"Shortly before six o'clock in the morning, it appeared, just as the day shift was going to work at the mill, a high-powered car with which something had gone wrong had crazily come down at high speed from Main Street East and probably beyond from the open country, via Hill Road. In front of the Realty Building, just east of the police station, both brakes being applied, the car, swinging from side to side, and skidding out of control, had been brought to a sudden and jerky stop against the curb, the mill-hands dodging to make room for it on the sidewalk; for the car threatened to jump the curb.

"From the car, Miss Ruth Clark had alighted, in evening clothes, a white ermine wrap over her shoulders. With a white-gloved hand she had opened the hood and peered in; then, closing it, she had resumed her seat behind the wheel. Since, like any inmate of Clark House, she was an object of curiosity to the men, some of them had stopped and stepped up to offer assistance, at the obvious risk of being late at the mill. She had merely stared coldly at them through her window.

"Restarting the engine, which ran smoothly enough, she had thrown the lever, first into low, then into second gear, tentatively engaging the clutch. The engine had roared; but the car had not budged. The men, feeling her hostility, had laughed. Viciously she had thrown the lever into reverse, stepping on the accelerator as, for the third time, she engaged the clutch.

"The car had leapt backward with a lurch; but, as the steering gear was out of order, it had turned at right angles to the street. She, losing her head, had frantically but ineffectually pulled at the wheel and, instead of applying the brake, had jammed her foot down on the accelerator—with the result that, with another leap, the car had jumped the curb on the south side of the street, vaulted the sidewalk, backward, and crashed through the plate glass window of the Chevrolet showrooms, landing in a precarious equilibrium between two demonstration cars which had both been damaged but were holding her Cadillac off the floor, rear wheels spinning.

"In the early morning light, the men on the north side of the street had been standing convulsed with laughter.

"It was a marvel, Burt said, that the young lady had not been struck by the flying glass.

"Gingerly, having stopped the engine, she had alighted first on the running board of one of the demonstration cars, then on the floor to pick her way through the wreckage to the street, at the precise moment when a sleepy night clerk, rudely awakened from his rest on a couch in the inner office, had emerged through a door behind. Seeing who was responsible for the destruction, and frightened by the angry scowl on her face, he had discreetly held back.

"At this moment Burt himself had appeared on the scene, just in time to hear one of the mill-hands shouting after Ruth as she turned up the street, 'Never mind, miss. We'll work a bit harder, so papa can pay for the damage.' Whereupon Burt had dispersed the crowd.

"All the time, during this recital, I had held my eye on Mr Clark. I could see how he felt. He was looking into a void. He controlled himself with an effort. Yet even now he was thinking, I felt sure, only of the effect the scene would have on the men; not of his daughter.

"I was also puzzled to probe the exact spirit in which Burt was giving the tale. Superficially his voice held all the deference due to the first citizen of the town—a man who wielded the most colossal economic power in the whole country. There was, in addition, something of that sympathy in his tone with which one father tells another unpalatable truths about his child. But, in spite of all that, there was, pervading it in the careful elaboration of detail, the hidden triumph of the man of the street who had caught a member of this great family 'out'.

" 'I thought,' he went on, 'I'd come and tell you myself. Those are the facts. Naturally, every correspondent of every yellow paper in the country has tried to unearth them. I've seen to it that they got nothing but the report of an accident which was the consequence of a broken steering gear. Those Chevrolet people, of course, will expect to be indemnified.'

"Mr Clark rose in dismissal. 'Tip them off, Burt,' he said curtly. 'Let them send me the bill.'

"Burt nodded and turned away.

"He had hardly left the house when Mr Clark looked at me out of haggard eyes. 'I think,' he said, 'this is a case for you to deal with.' "

Lady Clark had listened in silence. "What did you do?" she asked.

"What could I do? I talked to her in the most forbearing way, telling her about Burt and his errand; and, yielding to my obvious sympathy which she was well aware she had always had, she told me the whole story.

"I'll summarize it for you. For years, even at school, she had wished to escape from what she called the bondage of this house. Shackled by her wealth, which she called herself a coward for being unwilling to surrender, she had seen no escape except by marriage. She had dreamed of disappearing, of changing her name, of taking a job. She had come to the conclusion that she could not do it. After all, she had, throughout her life, been used to having luxury and service at her command. In that, the mother came out in the child. Like all the Clarks she had a high endowment of native intelligence; but, like all the Clarks, too, with the one exception of the senator, she despised academic proficiency. School she hated; so, she said, she had courted expulsion by refusing to obey regulations.

"At bottom I thought it was simply the inability to bear institutional life. I believe her instructors suspected her of outright immorality. I knew, of course, and you have divined, that there was never anything of the kind. What had happened immediately prior to that morning confirmed it.

"Among all the young men who had courted her, there was only one, by name of Magnus Wright, with whom she had tried to persuade herself she could live in that daily intimacy which marriage implies. She had met him in the east. He was moderately well-to-do himself and an artist; and these two facts were in his favour. At least, so Ruth reasoned, he was not after her money but after her. She corresponded with him; and he moved to Winnipeg to be nearer to her. At last she asked him to come down to Langholm. He was to stay at the Palace Hotel till she had made sure that she wanted to invite him to the house.

"He came; and an appointment was made over the telephone. He was to meet her at a certain corner in the eastern outskirts of the town where she would pick him up in her car, after dark, when they could no longer be recognized where there were no street lights.

"I asked her whether he had ever actually made love to her; had kissed her, for instance.

"In the ostentatiously vulgar way which she always assumed when anything embarrassed her, she said, 'Oh, damn it, he'd been holding my hand. No, he'd never kissed me.'

"From the start, there was trouble with the car; but they got out into the open country east of here. He tried to put his arm about her waist; and she took a sudden dislike to him. She'd always been unaccountable, you know, in her impulses. She told me that there had been just enough light from the panel for her to see that his lips trembled. He proposed to turn and go west, towards Winnipeg.

"She assured me that she had no desire to whitewash herself; she said that, if she had liked the look in his eye or the touch of his arm, she might had gone. But she was suddenly convinced, as she expressed it, that, no matter how many conventions she cast overboard, it would not cure her boredom; she felt sick of herself, of life, of everything; she wished she had been born a working girl; and after she had seen him like that, with the lecherous jaw quivering under his blond beard . . .

"Intentionally she stalled the engine, just to get him out of the car and leave him there, twenty miles from town, to walk back if he cared to. He couldn't find what was wrong with the gears. So she got out, too, and poked her finger under the hood, at random. Something clicked. She told him to wait and re-inserted herself behind the wheel. The engine started. He tried to get in; but again she told him to wait. Pushing the clutch in, she went into low gear; the car did not move; into second, with the same result. He stepped up on the running board, by her side, and tried to kiss her. When she turned her head away, he tried to get his arm about her again, through the window. She slipped into high gear and stepped on the accelerator till the engine roared; and as she engaged the clutch this time, the car began to crawl forward.

"Straight ahead, there was a bump in the road, and at last the clutch took full effect; the car slipped smoothly away. He was still on the running board; but the bump, combined with the sudden acceleration, made him lose his footing; to steady himself, he clutched at her. This made her furious; and so she gave him a push with her elbow which catapulted him into the ditch. She slowed for a moment, saw him jump up, and knew that he was not seriously hurt. So she stepped on the accelerator again; and after that she never turned to look; she did not want to see any more of him, ever. She drove all night, partly because she could not conquer her disgust and agitation; partly at last because she dared not stop the car to turn it. She went on and on over bumpy bush roads; the Loop, of course, had not yet been built. And when, towards morning, she managed to get back to Hill Road, she found herself unable to take the turn through the gate, down into the park for the car refused to travel slow. By that time, the steering gear, too, had gone out of commission beyond a certain radius; and she could hold the car on the road only by constant tacking. It was a very old car.

"When she had finished her tale, broken more than once by impotent, explosive sobs, she was leaning against the mantelpiece in my room and dabbed her eyes with her handkerchief. Suddenly she sat down.

"I felt it to be imperative that I should find the exactly right word to say, or the exactly right gesture to make. I went over to her and put my hand on her head.

"She clutched at it and cried, 'Please, please, help me to get away.'

" 'Where?' I asked.

" 'Anywhere. To Europe, Africa, China.'

" 'What for, child?'

" 'To get away from myself.'

" 'We don't get away from ourselves by moving about on this earth,' I said as softly as I could. 'But I'd do anything to help you.'

"After a pause she got up. 'If I were a man I'd know what to do.'

" 'And what is that?'

" 'I'd make a bomb big enough to blast such abominations as this town into nothingness.'

"I shuddered. . . .

"But I approached the subject of her European trip with Mr Clark; and he agreed to everything I proposed."

CHAPTER

XVIII

THE senator stayed in bed only in order to remain undisturbed.

One problem absorbed him: how had he lost control? He was under the sway of his father who, in his will, had imposed it upon him as his supreme, his most sacred task not to let go of his control of the mill. For more than two decades he had constantly kept that aim in view, pursuing it by the purchase of every share in the business that had come into the market; using, on occasion, persuasion and even pressure—with such as Art Selby, the banker; Rodney Ticknor, the general merchant; Mat Tindal, the 'realtor'—by offering inducements in the stock market for a surrender of their shares in the mill. One man, Mr Cole of Winnipeg, he had never been able to get rid of; and his resistance had forced him to leave the business in the status of a stock company with limited liability—which, unfortunately, demanded the publication of statements. Then, Mr Cole being eliminated, not by himself, but by his son, it was not he, it was his son who had held control.

Now it was Lady M. Clark; and she had gained control of course, through the death of her husband who had died intestate. How had that husband succeeded in wresting control from him? He had done so by means of an intrigue; and that intrigue, worthy of old Rudyard Clark, the senator now tried to unravel.

He did not succeed just yet. But, in his endeavours to clarify the thing, he suddenly remembered a day, two or three years after Edmund's return from overseas, and shortly after his majority, when they had once more talked of the old man in his grave. Once more? No. For the very first time. . . .

Yes, it had been the day after a shareholders' meeting at which Edmund, supported by Mr Cole, of all men, had unexpectedly moved and carried a measure depriving his own father, not indeed of control—the time for that had not yet arrived—but of his nominal office as general manager. It was all so puzzling. But that conversation stood suddenly out with the greatest distinctness and in considerable detail.

It had taken place in the library. Captain Stevens was, at

the time, general manager of the mill at Arbala; although Sam had offered him the opportunity, he had refused to return to Langholm unless he were given supreme authority. It was this measure—the recalling of Mr Stevens—which Edmund had carried through with the help of Mr Cole.

For several days before that shareholders' meeting there had been tension between father and son. It was the first time that Edmund had come to Langholm after his elevation to the knighthood; and that fact dated the occasion for the senator now.

After the son's *coup d'état* the tension had become so pronounced that, as by common consent, they had, in the afternoon, withdrawn to the library to 'have it out'.

"I thought," the father said as soon as they were alone, "you had more or less lost interest in the Langholm mill? Since you built the new mill at Arbala. . . . Sit down. Let's talk this over."

"Thanks," the son replied. "I prefer to stand." And he began to pace about in his restless way which stood in such strange contrast to the stoniness of the expression in his pale face which twitched from time to time with pains left behind by his wounds. "Lost interest, you say. No. On the contrary. The mill at Arbala was built for a single purpose; and that purpose has been served. It is the Arbala mill in which I have lost interest."

The father betrayed his surprise by no more than a gesture. He drew his right eyebrow up till half of his forehead was puckered in countless parallel, curved wrinkles which left the left half perfectly smooth. It was a gesture hereditarily characteristic of the Clarks. Rudyard had had it; Edmund had it, though, in the latter's case, the wrinkles were, so far, barely indicated as such. "The mill at Arbala," the father said at last, "you say was built for a purpose. What was that purpose?"

The son paced about more swiftly, as if he resented the fact that he was called upon to explain. Then he stopped. "You know as well as myself that the share of the Langholm mill in the flour trade of this country amounted, even after the war, to no more than ninety per cent. We had more than fifty per cent of our output to spare for export; but in the domestic trade we held no monopoly. I had no power to influence the policy of the Langholm mill. So I built Arbala and forced the Langholm mill into a price war. The consequence was that Langholm and Arbala, between them, shortly possessed that monopoly. Arbala had become necessary because you did not choose to admit me into the administration. Because you mistrusted me."

The father blanched. Was the tragedy of his own youth, the tragedy of the division between father and son, to be repeated between Edmund and him?

Pacing about again, the son went on. "I know more of the history of this mill than you think. I know that, during your father's lifetime, you were in revolt against him because he held you in subordination. I also know that you made up your mind to act towards me as he had acted towards you."

"You say you know. How *do* you know? As a matter of fact, it is not the case. I never made up my mind, as you say, to any such thing."

Again the son paced about in silence for a moment. "It is the most charitable interpretation of your actions," he said at last. "Bob Stevens, of course, had told me much; more than he ever thought he was telling me." Suddenly, a spasm passing over his face, he turned to a chair and sat down. "Do you remember the time when I was a child in this house? It was inevitable that you should overhear things which went on between my tutor and myself; and you suspected Bob Stevens. It was quite true, too; I wanted to ask questions which were often not easy to ask. Bob Stevens anticipated them. You prevented me from seeing Bob; I knew at once why you sent me away to boarding school. Whenever you talked of my grandfather, there was that in your voice which told me that what you said was meant to prevent me from investigating on my own account; and yet it betrayed that there was much to be found out. No doubt you acted, at that time, with the best of intentions. It is always the well-intentioned that do the most mischief. But all you did had, for that very reason, an effect diametrically opposed to the one you aimed at. There came a time when you never mentioned my grandfather to me; and your very silence told me a great deal: there was something that must be concealed. I was precocious, and I wanted to grow up. You, more than anyone else, should have enlightened me. But you didn't. Why not? Instead, you tried to influence me through others; first through that tutor of mine; then, when I was of age, a grown man, old for my years—because of the war—through the woman that was to be my wife."

The father remained silent. This indictment he could not deny.

"Let me remind you," the son went on after a pause, "that it was you who led up to this explanation, not I. It was that latter fact—that you tried to place me under the tutelage of my prospective wife—which, more than anything else, drove me to make one last attempt at persuading the other Maud, Maud Dolittle, to remain with me; to marry me. It was I who had called her to Montreal, though the meeting there was not of my planning; it came about through the crossing of two wires. I was even then willing to break off my engagement, which I had entered into very largely because Maud Dolittle wished me to. She understood the whole complexity of the situation. She would have been a tower of strength to me. But she could never forget that she was more than twice my age; in spite of the fact that, as lovers, we had been supremely happy. Since she insisted, at the critical moment—in order to coerce me—on disappearing from my life, I married the one woman whom I had met whom I could imagine as being capable of bearing the burden of marriage with me. I thought so highly of her that I married her in spite of the fact that I knew you were trying to make her your tool."

"Is that just?" the father cried in distress.

"Perhaps not from your point of view. You would probably say that, in keeping me in ignorance, you wanted to leave me free to face my task without prejudice; you wanted to safeguard the freedom of my decisions; you wanted me to have a clear conscience. But look what you did. Being a miller yourself, being the son of a miller, intending me to take over the mill one day—an inheritance like that one cannot decline—you brought me up as though I were to be anything but a miller. Almost as if I must be a financier. Well, a financier I have become, willy-nilly. To do what I wanted to do, I had to have millions. Yet, even as a financier, you did not leave me alone. Mistrusting me as you did, you would not stand back. You tried to direct me, from behind the scenes, through my wife."

The father sighed. "It is the father's lot, I suppose, to be tried, judged, and condemned by his son. The younger generation never sees all the facts."

"Whose fault is it? Yet, let that rest. We see more than the older generation thinks we do. I assure you I have suffered from being a son; and more than once I had sworn to myself that I would not be the cause of anyone suffering as I had suffered."

Appalled, the father stared at his son. "What do you mean?" His voice was a stammer.

"What do I mean? Can't you guess? Maud knows. She and I have been married for two years. There is no sign of a child; there never will be. If I had not come to love, I have almost come to revere my wife for understanding why that can never be."

"And you blame me!"

"Blame!" said the son with a note of impatience. "Life is a concatenation of events beyond praise or blame. But the fact remains that you are the cause of it all."

"How so?"

"Must I explain? I will give you one example of the sort of thing I have had to live through. You remember the lawyers' meeting at Toronto when the marriage settlement was made? When Inkster read out, point for point, what you and he had agreed upon—and splendidly generous would it have seemed to any outsider—I reached for a pad of paper and did some quick figuring. I had, by that time, what mother had left me; and so had Ruth, though she was a minor; and Charles Beatty still administered it for her. To her the mill was a horror; so, perhaps, it was justified that she should be excluded from any share in its ownership. But to me it was a severe blow; for I could always have co-operated with her; we understood each other. To Maud you gave, on the day of her marriage, this property—in that you were bound by my grandfather's will; but you also gave her half a million in shares of the mill, par value. I don't mean to say, of course, that the market value's being many times that much mattered in the least; certainly not to me. I wanted my wife to be a rich woman; she had been poor long enough. But the moment Inkster read out what you settled on me, the whole plan which you were trying to disguise became patent. Need I tell you? You left me short of control by exactly the share you gave to Maud. You did not wish to retain control in your own hands. You saw what was bound to come. . . ."

"Exactly!" the father cried with passionate emphasis.

The son, disturbed by that tone, rose in agitation. "What do you mean?" he asked in his turn.

"Control in one hand was a dangerous thing."

"You say, in one hand. You mean, in my hand."

"Perhaps."

"Dangerous or not," the son went on, "in order to be effective, it had to be in one hand, as you will see before long; for the issue is whether ignorance or knowledge is to govern this country; and, wheat being its principal product, control of the mill, in the long run, means control of the country. Of that control you left me just short. What was the meaning of that? There could be only one meaning. You wanted me to be dependent on my wife's support. Between us, my wife and I held control by just one per cent. But, don't you see that, control of a thing of the size of this mill, this industry which controls the nation's food supply, being a dangerous thing, I could not possibly go to my wife and ask her to share the responsibility with me? And there you have the reason why, at yesterday's meeting, I won over, not you or my wife, but Mr Cole, to my support."

The father looked at his son out of pensive eyes.

The son went on. "If, instead of Maud Fanshawe, I had married Maud Dolittle; and if she had held the key to control in her hands, I should not have hesitated for one moment: she was a woman born to bear responsibilities. But she shrank from being more than my mistress. She should have been your wife and my stepmother. She was, she is, a woman fit to be the mother of kings and rulers of empire. . . . What I mind about the whole thing," he went on in a different tone, a tone less exalted, "is that I shall willy-nilly have to act the part of a traitor."

The father looked up.

"Yes. A traitor, I said. Mr Cole supported me last night. Tomorrow or the day after, or perhaps a year from now, whenever the opportunity offers, I must oust him as a shareholder. I shall need his vote even against him; and it cannot be done any other way. The very man whose vote enabled me yesterday to take the general-managership from you, I must strip of that vote, . . ."

"Suppose," the father said, clearing his throat, "I gave you control today?"

"It is too late," the son said icily. "The plan is laid; the wheels are turning. Now I prefer to go on without help. Like my grandfather I must go crooked ways to reach a straight goal."

"What do you know of your grandfather's crooked ways?" the father asked with a startled upward look.

"Exactly. I know all about them. Must I explain? Very well.

"It was inevitable, of course, that I should meet Bob Stevens in France; I was bound to look for him; and it was equally inevitable that we should resume our relation where you had interfered to break it off. There was only this difference that, before you sent me to boarding school in Ontario, I had been a child; when we met again in France, I was a man old for my years. You said just now that the younger generation never sees all the facts. Why not? I asked. Because the older generation, in its infinite wisdom, tries to conceal them till they are found out. Do you wish me to tell you in detail how I found out?"

"I have nothing to hide."

"But the conclusion at which I arrived was precisely that you had something to hide; and the irony of it is that I was right. It was not my fault that I had to pump information out of Bob Stevens; it was yours. I asked him at last what had enabled my grandfather to become, from a working miller, the commanding figure he became in the industrial life of this country. He had a long story, of course, about the opportune fire and the man's transcendent financial ability. I laughed and came to the conclusion that, about the essential facts, he knew as little as I did. Quite casually, almost inadvertently, he mentioned the name of Bill Swann as that of the only man alive who, in association with my grandfather, had lived through the whole of that amazing development. Bob said the man had been a sort of lieutenant to my grandfather throughout. Naturally, I asked whether he knew where this man was."

"And did he?"

"He did not."

"But you made it your business to find him?"

"Who wouldn't? The surprising thing was that it was pure chance which placed the man within my reach. Living as he did—a widower with an unmarried daughter—retired from business, in the neighbourhood of the base hospital in Devonshire where I was taken after my first wound, he, recognizing my name, and reading of me in the papers, inscribed his name in the special visitors' book which was kept for me on account of the many illustrious names that were thus collected; and as luck would have it, one of the nurses mentioning the many enquiries after my condition, I asked to be shown that list, a day or so after his call. There I saw his name and knew at once, intuitively, that he was my man. I asked that, if he called again, I be allowed to see him. He did call again and was shown in. I was very careful not to ask any indiscreet questions so far, for Stevens had told me that you had dismissed the man a day or two after your father's funeral. Having found him at last, I was in no hurry; he was a hale and hearty old man of sixty-five or so, rather fat, but in excellent health.

"It was nearly a year before I came to Devonshire again, this time disabled. Again Swann called; and I elicited the information that, during the last fifteen or sixteen years, he had made a small fortune enabling him, on his retirement, to buy a little place in that neighbourhood. You came over to England again and stayed a long while, till I was on the road to recovery. All the time I was in constant fear that the two of you might meet in the halls of the country house. But as luck would have it, you didn't; I feared it because I felt sure, if you did, you'd prevent me from seeing him again. At last Swann's and my parts were reversed: I was on my feet again and allowed to have drives and short walks; he, one night, had been knocked over by a motor car as he turned the corner of a lane near his place.

"A few days later, having seen a report of his accident, I had myself driven over; and, seeing at once that he was most unlikely to recover, I asked him point-blank whether he did not wish to disburden his conscience. I had no intention of spying on you or anyone living. The only person I was interested in was my grandfather. You can imagine that my association with Bob Stevens had not tended to diminish my curiosity about, and my admiration for, him; and I had an idea that his real story would be an encouragement to me in the plans which I was even then forming. I knew, of course, that it was the theory current at the time, still current for that matter, that all great fortunes had been made by chance. Some opportunity had offered and had been blindly seized; and those who seized it were borne forward on the wave of expansion, especially in colonial countries. Such things have happened; I had seen them happen; if I had not been a minor in the legal sense, I could have made a fortune myself out of the war. But somehow I was convinced that that was not my grandfather's case; too much seemed to concur to be explained by mere chance; and something in the man's behaviour told me that Swann held the key to an understanding of my grandfather's true greatness."

"And he told you?"

"He told me. You know all about it, of course. Though I never could quite understand why you dismissed him."

"I'll tell you. He had embezzled funds entrusted to him. If anyone but myself had found out, there would have been a prosecution."

"So that's it, is it? That explains why you dismissed him. It doesn't explain why you let him go free."

"He had been blackmailing my father."

"And you wanted to protect your father's name? All right, that makes the last thing which was doubtful clear. But why did you keep this from me? Why did you interfere between Stevens and me? Stevens knew nothing. Yet, without that interference, I'd have accepted his view of the matter. I can understand that you did not think it wise to let me know too much while I was a child. But as I grew up, I was entitled to know."

"I'll tell you why," the father said, his voice trembling. "This thing had spoiled my whole life. I was not going to let it spoil yours. I wanted you to face the mill with a clear conscience—which I had never been able to do. My father had succumbed to an overwhelming temptation arising out of the mistake of a clerk. The fact was best forgotten."

"And you became the keeper of a secret?"

"Exactly. That had been my life till I told your mother."

"I had read you right, then. What did my mother say to it all?"

"Is it relevant?"

"Perhaps not. Let it go. But it is natural that I should ask; I am her son as well as yours. But even if you condemn my grandfather from a moral point of view, you have to admire what he made of his opportunity."

"By creating the mill?"

"Yes. Or by making the creation of the mill possible."

"Wherein lies the distinction?"

"In this. The mill could have been created by means of borrowed money; the plan alone, communicated to the right people, would have produced the capital needed. But like myself, my grandfather wanted control. Who but a great man would have seen in a flash what this mistake of a clerk, as you call it, might mean to him if properly used? Who but a great man would, without a moment's hesitation, have acted on it?"

"Acted? All he did was to keep silent when the fire came."

This, so the senator remembered, had slipped out of him because, during the years and the decades, he had so passionately repeated it to himself; but, of course, he had never said it to anyone before. The moment, however, it was uttered, he had a premonition of the fact that it was going to be refuted. It was.

"You *don't* know, after all!" cried the son. And then he laughed, restlessly pacing the floor.

Very slowly, aghast at the vista opening before his eyes, the father asked once more, "What you you mean?"

The son shrugged his shoulders. Then, as if changing his mind, he stopped. "Of course," he said, "it all hinges on the fact that the day was a Sunday. My grandfather went to the office late at night; there he found Swann's statement; and he must have spent a few agitated moments. For he saw that, if the mill burned down at once, while this statement was the only thing on which to base an estimate of the loss, he would have the exact minimum which he had long since figured out would be needed to put that mill on an entirely new basis by building the dam. Everything depended on that dam: that dam must be his or at least under his control. Even before Swann told me of that nocturnal visit to the little office on Main Street I had said to myself that such a concurrence of opportunities does not happen fortuitously; it is made."

The father felt his knees going weak. Here was what he had dreaded; what he had refused to believe; what he had avoided looking into. The certainty came from the son whom he had tried to keep in ignorance. "What did Swann tell you?" he asked at last.

"At night, having been out late," the son went on, "Swann felt vaguely disturbed in his mind; he had deliberately left a false statement on the table in the office; and it suddenly seemed as if, from that, incalculable consequences might follow. So, after having gone to bed and found it impossible to sleep, he got up again to go down to the office in order to rewrite that statement and to correct the figures in the warehouse voucher which he had forged. But when, on Main Street —it was after midnight—he was within a hundred steps of the office, he saw your father coming out of its door. There was a street light in front; and he recognized him distinctly. Swann eclipsed himself behind the wall of a blacksmith shop, waiting there, in impenetrable darkness, to let your father pass. But he did not come. After a minute or so of waiting Swann peered cautiously round the corner of the shop; the street was deserted. There was only one place the old man could have gone to; he was not given to nocturnal walks over the hills; that place was the mill. I don't know much, of my own knowledge, of the vanished topography of the town; but Swann must have been able to go down, behind the blacksmith shop, to what was still the bank of the river. A suspicion had come to him; and after a long while, the waning moon having risen in the interval, he saw your father coming back from the mill. He did not go by the street—another suspicious circumstance. He, too, came along the river, over rough and treacherous ground often flooded at that time of the year; and he passed Swann who was hiding behind some willows within twenty feet. Swann never stirred.

"When your father was out of sight, Swann was tempted to go to the office; he had a key. But, suspecting what had been done at the mill, he feared, if he was seen, that he would fall under suspicion himself; and so, hurrying now, he went home in the wake of your father; they lived near each other, along the same street; not to sleep now, but to await the development which he expected. Strange to say, he said, it was over an hour before the alarm was raised."

When the full import of his son's recital came home to the father, he covered his face with his hands. But Edmund went on, something like exaltation now blending with cynicism in his voice.

"This overwhelms you? . . . Think for a moment. The old man had the courage to sweep a worn-out world into limbo. He had long wanted to shape the mill to man's ultimate purpose. In him he felt the power to make nature subservient to his design, to the design of man himself. Man is *homo faber* as someone has said. Nothing stood in the way but a heap of rubbish which flames would readily consume; it was worthless to him, in the light of his aim. But if flames consumed it, it would suddenly be worth all he needed. He put the match to that rubbish, and the result is the flawed marvel of the present mill.

"It was against man's law; granted. He obeyed a higher law. No great man has ever hesitated about breaking man's law when a greater purpose was to be served by its breach. He needed money; not for the sake of money or for himself; what money he made, he risked more than once; he was always playing a dangerous game. In twenty-one years the mill had paid more in premiums than he would receive by way of indemnity. Compared with the premiums the new mill would pay, the sum was trifling. Besides, he could refund it later on. There lay the capital needed, ready to hand, yet worthless, sterile in the shape it had. Consumed by flames it could be fertilized. The end justified the means; it has always done so; it will always do so. Why in the world boggle at it?"

"Because it made us rich; because it gave us power."

Edmund laughed. "I have said that myself, of course. It is wrong. There is a plan and an end in all this. What it is I don't know; at least not yet; perhaps it will unfold itself in time. I was tempted to find out, of course. I built the Arbala mill. Personally I care as little for mere wealth, for pomp and circumstance as my grandfather did. I'd be glad to retire and work on a farm like a numbskull. But, like my grandfather, I am a tool of destiny; and I was born to wield power . . . Let all men be equal in an economic sense, and one incitement to live is gone. Man wants to be able to worship power; and power, today, means enormous wealth : wealth that gives him all he needs. He does not want to take, or to conquer it; he wants to receive it as a free gift.

"They talk of capitalism and don't know what they mean; they talk of socialism and know still less what they mean. They say men are born equal . . . Most of them are equal only in this one respect that they can't look after themselves. They'll show it when it comes to the final struggle. If they came to power, the masses I mean, the first thing they'd do would be to destroy what we have achieved. They have shown it in every revolution that ever broke out. They'll try to scrap civilization."

"What is civilization?" the father asked scornfully rising.

"Exactly. It needs redefining." And suddenly the son changed his tone and spoke as if he were pleading. "We are sitting at a table and playing a game of chance the laws of which we don't understand; and somewhere around the board sits an invisible player whom nobody knows and who takes all the tricks; that player is destiny, or God if you like, or the future.

"It was the Victorian attitude, and it was yours and your generation's, to mistrust the future as you mistrusted me. So they fought the coming of that future with laws and guns; and finally, seeing that they could not shoot holes into a tide, they fought it with concessions to the rabble, designed to retard the coming of the tide. They were intent on saving their skins. They did save them, for the moment. But what was their answer to the question asked by the centuries, the question asking for justice? Their answer was the *status quo*. But, hold on to the *status quo*, and you strangle life. Throw the mob your crumbs, and you head for destruction. From the crumbs the mob merely draws one unfailing conclusion : it infers what you have on your table and what you want to consume yourself. At the end of all your concessions stands revolution and bloodshed. The very fact that there still is a mob, indicts you. You have crippled mankind by making it three out of four cogs in a machine which the fourth one runs. That you call democracy. What utter nonsense!"

The father looked frightened. "What do you propose to do?"

"I? Nothing. I am humbly content to be the tool of evolution; or, if you prefer, to experiment. I want to go forward, not turn back, no matter where. It will involve suffering; it may involve bloodshed. It cannot be helped. Every revolution has involved suffering and bloodshed; but, so far, every revolution has sooner or later turned back. The equilibrium that had become unstable was merely made stable again, with a slight displacement of power. That was because those who conducted it became scared. No revolution has ever based itself squarely on what the past had achieved; if it had done so, it would have ceased to be revolution; it would have been evolution instead."

"Do you know," the father asked irrelevantly, "that, here at Langholm, you are threatened with a strike?"

The son shrugged his shoulders. "Strikes," he said, "are part of the pattern. This one won't come just yet. I heard them cheering a while ago, on the Terrace. They are holding a meeting there and listening to nonsense. The strike will come when I want it."

"When you want it?" the father asked, appalled.

"Don't you see that things, through your own mistakes, have gone too far to be adjusted without some sort of clash? The logical time for the final conversion of the mill was at the outbreak of the war. When the men returned, it would have been the Dominion that would have had to look after them; for it was the Dominion that had got the country into the war. To repatriate them on any assumption but mine was a needless cruelty. Suppose I were to announce today that completely automatic operation were to begin? In 1914, the change would have been hailed as a patriotic triumph. Today there would be an outcry; there would be an attempt at destruction; for we are living in chaos, without plan or aim. Public opinion—that is the opinion of the mob—would demand my head; yet I am at present, it seems, the only one capable of keeping his head. The mob has always demanded the heads of its benefactors. But if the men strike; if they walk out; and if, when they want to give in, they find their jobs gone, public opinion will condemn *them*. It serves them right, people will say; and, in a chastened mood, the men will be glad to take what they can get—which, for the moment, will be the dole."

"They won't. They will storm the mill."

"That is where the old methods will have to function once more. Police and soldiery will have to protect that mill, with machine guns and tanks if need be; for the good of the masses themselves."

"What if the soldiers refuse to fire on their people?"

"You have trained them too well. The armed force of the nation, being used to eating their bread as parasites, can always be relied upon to defend what they think is the *status quo*, even though it be only a tightening of the bonds of their slavery. That is the paradox you have brought about. It resembles that other paradox that, for the forging of the new order, something so illogical as money, money, money is needed."

"And what will the new order consist of?"

"I can't so far tell. But it will be the dictatorship of mind over matter. Already I control, or a company which I control in its turn controls, two-thirds of the industries of this country. Many of these industries are not yet aware of it; the government of this country is not yet aware of it; it still thinks it is carrying out the wishes of a majority of the vested interests; but the moment I care to show my hand, the new power will be revealed as a state within the state, ready to replace that state as it stands today. It will then appear that, essentially, the state is an economic organization and has always been so, not a political one. The word freedom will become meaningless; or rather it will change its meaning to that of a freedom from economic distress. Very largely, of course, that freedom will result from a shrinkage of world population. It has been a consequence of the insane way in which you have organized matters that the man fit to propagate himself begets one or at most two children; whereas the morons pullulate with a dozen or more. If there is to be progress, we shall have to reverse that."

"How?"

"I don't know. Perhaps sterilize those who live on the dole; or make an increase in the dole dependent on their consent to be sterilized. We shall find some way.

"Though, speaking generally, the danger arises from the fact that a thousand problems cannot be solved till they arise. Human ingenuity can neither foresee the problems nor their solutions. For the moment the dominant question is the food supply of the nation; and it depends on the merging of the mills. If I, by myself, can feed the masses and do so, they will give me a chance. If I can't there will be a cataclysm; and the whole industrial revolution will be lost to mankind."

There was a long pause. Till the father asked, "Why, then, if your plans reach so far, do you refuse the control which I offer?"

228

"I will tell you that, too," the son said in measured tones. "If, when you gave me a share just short of control, you had given me the whole of it, I should have considered it as implying a mandate. You and I, in spite of all that divided us, should have stood together. As it was, you threw me back on my own resources. I am glad of it now. After all, I may unite the brute force of a world against me; if I do, I prefer to fall alone."

"Your plan is to divide mankind into two classes?"

"The rulers and the ruled; the masters and the men; those who control the machines and those who benefit from them."

"Benefit?"

"Yes. Don't you see that, when the process is finished, they will live in a toilless heaven?"

"How about the farmers?"

"There will be nothing but farmers, held in subjection by the life of ease they will live; and by mental and emotional suggestion."

"In other words, by material welfare?"

"Exactly."

"To put it plainly, then, matter will rule over mind."

The son laughed briefly. "But the masses will be ruled by mind."

"Not their mind, though; the minds of others; and you think they will acquiesce?"

"I do. Material ease effectively dulls ambition."

"And you think you can persuade Mr Cole to go with you?"

"Mr Cole!" Edmund said scornfully. "He is one of those who question no system which brings them profits."

"So, if you leave the word 'them' out, is your right-hand man Captain Stevens."

"That is why he is not my right-hand man but my tool."

"You'll never coerce Mr Cole."

"I'll eliminate him. The plot is laid."

"Does your wife know of all this?"

"The greater part of it she has known for years; and she is willing to give me my chance. I don't want her to do so blindly; she must see what it involves. But at the same time I want to leave her as well as you unencumbered with responsibilities. So that, if I fall, you can reassemble the wreckage."

"I see," said the father. "I see."

CHAPTER

XIX

LATE at night, Lady Clark sat for a while by the senator's bed. She looked at him as he lay there, frail, almost insubstantial, yet still a mind; and that mind troubled, as she divined, by his one-time relation to his son. She, too, was troubled by such a memory. All who had known him were. Extraordinary men, she said to herself, cannot be measured by ordinary standards; one does not apply a foot-rule to the speed of light. Yet both she and this old man had tried to do just that.

Whenever she thought of her husband, in the later stages of her brief marriage to him, she felt at the same time frightened and fascinated. Frightened, for he had always trodden under foot such rules as served to judge smaller people. Yet, what she had seen of him had been trifling things. His real mind had been hidden from her. She could not help herself: she pondered the trifles.

And suddenly, by a sort of transference of thought, she became aware that the visions, hers and the old man's, had merged; as if their blood were beating in a common pulse. She knew that he saw what she saw. . . .

Many years ago, at Montreal, when Ruth and Edmund had embarked for France and England respectively, the same fusion had taken place. It had had a different climax; for one of them was a woman, the other a man; one had been young; the other, far advanced in middle age; in fact, he had been over sixty, as compared with her twenty-four.

Since neither spoke now, since neither had spoken then, neither had given, or gave, the other the impulse needed to bring about an exchange of visions; and, for the moment, the paths taken by their thought diverged again from a common point.

What she saw, with her mind's eye, was that scene in the train shed of the station at Montreal where she, her prospective father-in-law, Edmund, and Ruth had just arrived, coming from Ottawa.

Things had not originally been planned thus. The plan had been for her father-in-law to take her home to Whitby by the direct road from the capital, after parting from the voyagers there. The last moment her father-in-law had changed that plan, proposing that they all four go down together to Montreal to see brother and sister off. The reason, so she divined, was that the older man wished to prolong his contact with her who was his prospective daughter.

It had so happened that, when this change of plan was proposed, in the lobby of the Chateau Laurier at Ottawa, her eyes had been resting on Edmund. While he had raised no explicit objection, he had frowned ever so slightly and then had turned away to go to the telegraph office: the change of plan had necessitated a readjustment.

Yet when, in the Montreal station, they had, a few hours later, to their surprise, run into a lady apparently known to everyone of her party except herself, she had not at once connected this meeting with Edmund's frown in the lobby at Ottawa. It was only when she saw the swift play of changing expressions on the woman's face that her curiosity was aroused; and that curiosity had become a suspicion when the stranger, with a slight precipitancy, had plunged into an entirely unnecessary explanation of her presence: she was on her way back to Langholm, she said, whence she had been called to the seaboard by the necessity of rearranging a contract.

It sounded all quite plausible; and it would have passed unchallenged if it had not been for the fact that her explanations were obviously meant to give Edmund a lead. Besides, through her sisters, certain rumours had already reached her, Maud Fanshawe, of an attachment between Edmund and a woman much older than he who was one of the executives of the Langholm mill.

Many a time, of late, she had been tempted to ask Miss Charlebois another question about the relation between Miss Dolittle and young Edmund. No occasion had offered.

At the time, at Montreal, the name Miss Dolittle had meant nothing to her; but, being warned by her previous observation, both of Edmund and of the woman's momentary discomfiture, due, no doubt, to her being unexpectedly confronted with this party, she had become clairvoyant, divining the very thing which Edmund's motionless detachment was calculated to disguise.

When, by way of introduction, her own name was mentioned, that of Miss Maud Fanshawe, there could be no doubt about it that Miss Dolittle knew who she was and what was her relation to Edmund Clark.

For the fraction of a second the two women looked at each other, each measuring and weighing the other. There was a flutter of eyelids; then, on her own lips, the ghost of a smile, answered by an almost furtive curving of the other woman's lips; lastly, an all but confidential nod. Whereupon the avowal was complete: the prospective bride and the mistress about to retire from the scene were facing each other.

Miss Dolittle was the first to recover her presence of mind; for from the door of the waiting-room came the stentorian voice of a station guard announcing the impending departure of a west bound train.

"There they are," she said. "I haven't my ticket yet." She shook hands easily, wished Ruth *Bon Voyage*, and turned away.

Knowing that this sudden departure must have been determined upon on the spur of the moment. Maud admired her composure, especially since she even then divined what was going on in the woman's mind. The plea of the contract needing adjustment was, of course, pure invention. She had come to Montreal to meet her lover for a last time before his embarkation for England. Having, by this chance encounter, the consequence, no doubt, of some mishap, come face to face, if only for seconds, with his future wife, she was confirmed in her resolve to vanish from his life. In that moment when she turned away from the group in which everyone except Ruth was visibly a prey to anguished thought—for even the father divined what that motion implied—she was making a supreme sacrifice by handing the man she loved to another woman.

Edmund, saying, "Wait," to Miss Dolittle, forestalled her and ran to attend to her booking. When he returned, Miss Dolittle had already detached herself from the group; but, instead of merely handing her the tickets, he fell into step by her side; and, as if to confirm Maud in all her misgivings, she observed only now that there was an entire absence of baggage.

Then something extraordinary happened. Her father-in-law was transparently trying to divert her attention by trivial conversation. But Maud, looking, as if absent-mindedly, after Edmund and the other woman, became startlingly aware that these two were engaged in a rapid, excited, yes, passionate exchange of words. Miss Dolittle kept shaking her head; and when she reached the steps of her car, she extended her hand in an unmistakable gesture of finality. Edmund turned angrily away, refusing to take that hand. The train began to move, Miss Dolittle still standing on the lower step of her coach and looking back at him, stirred to her very depths, for she did not see that she was preventing the coloured porter carrying his stool from boarding the car. She forced him to run alongside till they had disappeared around a curve.

Edmund returned to the group. By the time he reached it, he had regained his composure to the point where he could advance a pretext for the oddity of his conduct: Miss Dolittle's baggage, he said, had failed to arrive from the hotel; and she had given him directions for forwarding it.

At the hotel, they had dispersed. But she, Maud, had hurriedly dressed to descend again; for what she had seen had excited her. The four of them had agreed to meet in the lobby before entering the dining-room.

Almost at once she saw Edmund at the cashier's wicket; and his father was lingering near him: they, too, must have hurried, for they were in evening dress. Edmund was settling an account and giving directions to the obsequious clerk. Neither he nor his father saw her. Ruth had not yet come down.

When Edmund had attended to his business, father and son faced each other, the former showing signs of being more or less upset.

Approaching, she heard the father say, "Perhaps Maud would like me to motor her home?"

Edmund looked blank.

"I mean Maud Fanshawe," the father said pointedly.

Edmund gave no start; but it was a second before his lips curled in a peculiar smile. "Just so," he said. "We'll ask her." At that moment he caught sight of her; and at the same time Ruth emerged from the elevator.

But, being surrounded by a crowd, the father had not yet seen either. "Is it fair?" he asked.

The son's only answer was the bow with which he turned to her, as if to warn his father not to proceed.

In a flash of insight she had, in that brief moment, seen many things; and suddenly it was clear to her that the engagement between her and Edmund must stand. So far she had wavered, under the impact of the revelation which she had received. Seeing Edmund's look, which presumed her knowledge and asked for her sympathy, she had become aware of a task ahead.

She knew that, before the boat sailed with the tide, shortly after midnight, father and son had had a brief interview. Something the father had said next day, while they were motoring up the St Lawrence, implied as much. He, too, had taken her knowledge for granted and tried to make the meeting seem less of an insult by explaining that two wires had crossed between Ottawa and Montreal, neither reaching the one to whom it was addressed in time.

To the woman by the senator's bed, the scene in the car, on the day which followed the departure of brother and sister, came to mind but briefly; yet the fleeting thought of it seemed once more to make one mind out of two.

The senator, his eyes wide open, almost dilated, and directed towards her own, for he was not ill, seemed mentally to have been as far away as she.

Suddenly his lips muttered; and she caught the words "Maud Fanshawe" spoken in a tone which was a revelation to her.

That revelation shook her to her depths. The young man who had become her husband had been in love with a woman twice his age; his father had, so that voice betrayed, once dreamt of being to her what his son had become. What would have been the course of events if each of them had been able to obey his heart instead of his reason?

The things that had actually been said, during that drive up the St Lawrence River, mattered little. She had intimated to the man by her side that she was determined to adhere to her side of the engagement; she had let him see that she had known of the attachment between the boy and the mature woman; yes, that, since she had met that woman, if ever so briefly, she approved of it because she understood what it implied.

He had told her how he had come to know of it.

Her mind went back. There lay the man who had spoken to her; and he would shortly face death and the cessation of things; the very nearness of the approaching end made the vision which had come to her indirectly, through him, the more poignant; for it was only now that she understood what it had meant to him, namely, the end of a dream. This was what she saw.

Again there was a great party at Clark House, this time to celebrate Edmund's majority.

The town was still the swarming, crowded little city between east and west; and once more, as so often in the past, every suite in the Palace Hotel as well as every guest room at Clark House was filled with people who had come from a distance, lured by fabled stories of the hospitality dispensed by the Clarks. And there were more local guests than there had ever been in the house since Sibyl Carter had left town.

Throughout the house there were the usual social activities. In the ballroom there was a dance, overflowing now and then into the hall; a famous string quartette was playing. Bridge tables had been set on the gallery as well as in the drawing-rooms downstairs; lovers were sitting in pairs on the stairway, displaying or hiding their happiness. In both dining-rooms a buffet supper was laid, with a multitude of small tables to sit at. Only in the library and the music room no provision was made for the entertainment of special groups. In the library a few of the older men were engaged in discussion; in the music room a few of the older women had sat down.

Among these women, as if to use them for a foil, Miss Dolittle sat alone on the chesterfield facing the fireplace, wrapped in a dream.

There Mr Clark had seen her; and his thought had gone back to that other occasion of a children's ball, seven, eight years ago, when she had played on Edmund's boyish infatuation, thereby thwarting a dream of his own.

As, on this evening of his son's majority, he had looked at her from the door, it had seemed to him as if she had about her something of the heart-rending beauty of the woods in the fall, gorgeous and ostentatious, as if in protest against the coming of winter. As though, standing already half behind a curtain, she were turning back for a last glance, fascinating still, in the glory of tragic beauty. He was aware of the fact that she had taken special pains with costume and make-up. Yet, instinctively, he knew it was not for him.

Strangely, the very fact that she was not at all impersonal, as she was apt to be to those who met her casually, in the street or the drawing-room, kept people away, kept him away, as if it would have been an intrusion merely to speak to her.

The smooth pallor of her skin was suffused with nobody knew what trace of colour; her glance, commonly steady, was evasive or trembling; her dark-brown hair electric with a metallic sheen enhanced by the rubies scattered through it and burning with the glitter of dark flames; her body, encased in a coal-black gown of chiffon-velvet, had thrilled to something which sent emanations about her like an aura; her lips were a miracle of freshness made sensitive by expectancy.

The memory of that sight as he spoke of her, during the drive from Montreal to Whitby—so that Maud Fanshawe would know all the facts before she made her commitment irrevocable—was still as startling to the aging man by her side as her actual aspect had been on that night. He frankly told her that, more than once, he had used a pretext to go into the hall and to look at that woman from the door of the music room.

He had felt disturbed. He had thought of that previous meeting between this woman and his son as a thing of the past of which it had formed a fleeting if, in one sense, decisive episode. And here the past had re-arisen.

At last, long after midnight, he had seen Edmund going into that room where the woman had sat throughout the evening and which, so far, he had seemed to avoid.

He had promptly followed his son to the door.

Maud Dolittle could not possibly have seen the young man enter; but her senses, made responsive by what was within her, had made her aware of his approach; her every quality had seemed intensified; till at last she had turned her head to smile up at him, as if she had asked, 'Are you coming?'

His outwardly imperceptible response had isolated the two from the rest in a sudden flare of intimacy and passion.

A moment later Edmund bowed to her, punctilious in the pretence of ceremonial formality. "May I have the pleasure of setting you down at your house? I have a car waiting at the door to the veranda."

Under any other circumstances this would have been a rudeness; for it amounted to a hint that it was time for her to go. As it was, it sounded like a call to a feast.

Miss Dolittle rose; and as she did so, the father, standing perturbed, small, grey, followed every motion of hers with his eyes. She was transformed by the elaborate and yet nonchalant grace with which she handled herself, as if she were looking on at herself from the outside; as if she were entering a magic path in enchanted woods, knowing it to be a path at once full of danger and of glory. There could be no doubt; she was conscious of the seduction of her snow-white shoulders and the straight, bare back. No one who had known her in the past could help asking himself what had happened to her : her swimming look was all submission to one, all haughty triumph to the rest of mankind. She smiled at those whom she left behind in the room; but she did not see them; she was gathered up into a different world.

Without quite knowing what he was about, the father followed her through the crowded hall to the door of the ladies' cloak- and dressing-room, encountering on the way his daughter Ruth who stood leaning against a doorpost, looking on, dark, cynical, smiling, a half-burned cigarette between her lips, her face screwed up in defence against the rising smoke. Then he eclipsed himself among the men who were donning their wraps, taking hats and coats from the hands of the footmen.

Miss Dolittle entered the ladies' room where two maids were in attendance. By reason of a chance obstruction the door remained half open; so that he saw her as, bending her head with a leisurely smile, she looked at herself in the large pierglass between two electric lights. A moment later a maid was holding her white fur wrap for her; and slowly, with voluptuous languour, as though revelling in the very maturity of her body as in a supreme luxury, she shrugged into its enveloping folds. Then she bent down to gather her train; and, half turning as she did so, she noticed at last that the door to the dressing-room had remained open. A shadow of dismay flitted over her features and melted into a smile of surrender. Following the direction of her eyes, the father saw his son entering the vestibule from the outside door—a confirmation of what the telltale light in her eyes had betrayed.

Edmund was very pale; his brown eyes glittered; over his narrow, straight shoulders, twitching as with pain from his wounds, a black Inverness cape was loosely draped, leaving his white, stiff shirt front exposed.

As, with her gloved hand, she gathered fold after fold of her train, she seemed deliberately to hold her pose. Her very thought became visible on her brow. Scruples? Nonsense. She was sipping a heady draught. She knew no scruples.

Edmund with a formal bow from his hips, acquired in France, held the door for her, waving a footman aside as she passed out; and the men in the vestibule fell back, making room for her and her escort into whose elbow she had inserted the tips of her fingers. . . .

From that night to the meeting in the station at Montreal —for three years—the young man, barely more than a boy in years, and this mature woman, so Maud inferred, had been lovers.

She shivered; never had Edmund behaved thus to her. . .

237

As her father-in-law had sketched the story, to warn her before it was too late, it had not been so circumstantial; it had lacked detail; it had consisted of hints and flashes. But she, Maud Fanshawe, endowed with a lively and benevolent imagination, had filled it in.

Strangely, it had convinced her all the more that she must accept what she felt to be almost a task transferred to her by the older woman who, after the meeting at Montreal, had disappeared as if the world or the sea had swallowed her up. Rumours had reached Langholm shortly that she was living somewhere in France.

What, with her mind's eye, Maud saw, sitting by the side of the bed on which the old man lay, was not seen in any great detail, either; it was a rapid succession of visions informed with emotion. Feeling that something unusual was coming, flowing from the mention of her name, in that strange tone with which he had spoken it, she nodded to herself, her nerves tensing.

And then it came. "Maud," the old man said, "tell me how you came to marry Edmund."

The question had the effect upon her as if she had been challenged to open the door into a secret room which held the instruments of a torture chamber and which had not been opened for decades. Her heart sank within her; she felt cowed as under the expectation of a blow. For years, many years, she had expected that question as something compliance with which might, in the estimation of this old man, undo her. For at least a minute she did not answer but fought to regain her composure which had been shattered. Her limbs felt weak; her fingers trembled. But not for a moment did she think of escape. The old man was entitled to know; if only because, being engaged in the task of reviewing his life, he must see clear in even such details as seemed to concern only her.

"Give me time," she said. "I will tell you."

And the old man closed his eyes as if to permit her to compose herself without witness.

When Lady Clark spoke and the old man reopened his eyes, her voice had that beautiful contralto which he had always loved.

"I shall have to go far back in time," she said, "so that you may understand. You know something of my father, the president, and later the chancellor of the University of Eastern Ontario. What you can hardly know is that he was the least provident of men. Even before his retirement, even before the death of my mother, there had always been financial difficulties, due to my father's lavish habits. A word of distress on the part of a poor student was a sure passport, not only to his heart, but to his purse. When a friend approached him with the request to endorse a promissory note for him, he could not resist. And no matter how many such notes came back on him, he would never learn caution.

"When he retired, having bought the house at Whitby which you know, the difficulties multiplied; and when he died, my sisters had to sell the town house at Queen's Ferry, with all the treasures accumulated in half a century of collecting in Europe and the other continents of the Old World. The proceeds barely covered his debts. I was a child at the time and knew or realized nothing of all this.

"Of my two sisters, Lillian and Agnes, Lillian, the younger, was recently married at the time but already involved in divorce proceedings which were to ruin her life. My brother-in-law, the respondent, was a man of magnificent physique and great administrative ability, employed in the Civil Service of the Dominion. But the scandal cost him his position; and when the verdict gave my sister an annuity of two thousand dollars, he stepped in front of a fast train at a level crossing. When my father's and my brother-in-law's estates were finally wound up, my sisters and I were left with nothing but the country house at Whitby and a life insurance policy of twenty thousand dollars. The house had so far, when occupied, required a minimum of three maids and one man servant. These servants were promptly dismissed.

"I leave it to you to imagine the atmosphere of continual sacrifice, of unremitting economy, of desperate efforts at making both ends meet, in which my childhood was lived. Yet my sisters sent me to an expensive boarding school at which only daughters of very distinguished or very rich men were admitted. To get me received at a rebate, use was made of my father's name. For many years I knew nothing of this; nor did I know at the time that, for months on end, to make it possible, my sisters never ate anything but oatmeal, three times a day.

"I was eighteen before the contrast between, let me say, their wardrobe and mine struck me with sufficient force to make me enquire; and then my sisters put me off without telling me the truth. That was in the first stages of the war; and perhaps I should mention that now and then I met Edmund at social functions; he was beginning his career as an aviator. Whenever I was at home, there seemed to be an abundance of the necessities; my sisters saw to that; and there was some social life, drawn from two universities and staged for my special benefit.

"The truth, however, was that, between them, these sisters had spent on me nearly all they had: their shares in the twenty thousand, interest and capital. They tried to sell the house, to move into more modest quarters. But the property, huge and cumbersome, found no buyers. Agnes, my older sister, short, plump, and old-maidish, as you have met her, twenty years my senior, would never have let me know of their difficulties. But Lillian made up her mind to take me into the secret, not in order to make me decline further sacrifices, but to secure my irrevocable adhesion to their plans. These plans were to exploit my good looks, my accomplishments, my social prestige by a wealthy marriage. I soon saw that it was too late in the day for me to rebel. I was on the point of graduating from college; and I went back to finish my course. But from the day of my graduation I was in the market for the highest bidder. That, for years, was my life; it was my profession."

The old man on the bed raised a transparent hand in mute comprehension, thereby showing that, no matter how frail he was in body, his mind was fully alert.

Lady Clark, as if to subdue the emotions reawakened in her by her memories, made use of the interruption to re-compose her voice before she went on.

"We had connections, of course. My father's name counted for a great deal. He had been a brilliant figure in his day. When, in the beginning of the century, the late King George had come to this country, he had insisted that it was he who should call on my father, not my father on him. In England, he was, among scholars, considered one of the significant men of his age. Oxford and Cambridge had vied with each other in attempts to bring him back. As you know, he had been knighted. Eastern University is still dominated by the tradition which he established; other universities stood under his shadow; at Toronto you can conjure with his name.

"As I said, apart from the life insurance, the only thing saved out of the wreck was the house at Whitby which proved a white elephant. But, it being less than an hour's run from Toronto, it was in that city that I was launched.

"Even then many men had filed past me, had been paraded

before me. On his belated and brief marriage with the widow of Sir Philip Ventnor, Dr Newcombe, friend of King Edward and King George, and my father's most intimate associate, though his junior by some ten years, had just moved there from Queen's Ferry in order to be more readily able to conduct an occasional symphony concert for the Philharmonic Society; and he as well as, I have no doubt, numbers of others were taken into the secret. By this time Edmund was overseas.

"I felt it to be my duty to restore the family fortunes and to compensate my sisters for the sacrifices they had made; though I never could acknowledge that they had made them for me. I felt the victim of circumstances.

"Dr Newcombe and many others reorganized their whole social lives with a view to furthering my ventures as a fortune huntress. I single him out because, as a musician of international fame who, incidentally, had married one of the great fortunes of the continent, he had more opportunities to help than anyone else.

"To my consternation, when, after a year of this, I came of age, I found that I had acquired an amazing record. Whenever it came to the point, I simply could not do it; I had declined scores of offers. The moment a nice young man approached me, I began to hold back; the thing was stronger than my will. From a distance, let me say, I had liked this one or that one; I had tried to persuade myself that I could come to feel more for him than the sort of vapid friendship which is the rule between young men and women. The moment he came near enough, I felt that surely he knew what I was after; and I became cold. I attracted some less desirable men, too, of course; when they became bold, I imagined myself living with them in the sort of intimacy which marriage implied; and I took fright. When an actual offer was made, I lost my head and declined. Soon rumour had it that I was not the marrying kind.

"All these men were hand-picked, of course. There was always the fear that I might actually fall in love with an impecunious young man; and that, in the view of my sisters, and of those whom they influenced, would have been nothing short of disaster. When I think of it today, the whole thing seems vile to me.

"Then all offers ceased. For a year or longer no one approached me in any but the most formal manner. I was unhappy. I seemed, to myself, to be constitutionally incapable of falling in love; I was never swept off my feet.

"To top it all, a great lady, wife of the then Governor-

General, took it upon herself to speak to me, Dr Newcombe must have taken her into his confidence. She frankly told me I was being discussed; young men were afraid of me; they dared not come near. In her mistaken kindness she added that, if I were an ordinary coquette or a silly girl, there would be nothing to say; but she assured me that she was taking a genuine interest in me because I deserved it and because I was a great beauty, meant by providence to play a part in the world. How I have cursed that beauty! It was at the bottom of all my troubles. And then she laid down rules for my future conduct. I am afraid I cried. That was in the winter of 1918 to 1919, after the armistice. When she wound up by inviting me to spend a few weeks as her guest at Government House, I could no longer control myself. I rose and left her.

"The consequence was that I remained still more alone. I was now being classed with the older girls, those beyond the marriageable age. Often, at a dance. I was without a partner till married young men took pity on me.

"And all the time I knew that, among the offers I had had, there had been one or two which, under different circumstances, I should have been glad to accept. But I was too inexorably in the market to let myself go. I never gave any liking, any incipient inclination a chance to ripen. The very necessity of an immediate marriage prevented that marriage from coming about. At the same time I knew that, in the eyes of the world, I was, in return for what my sisters had done for me, under an obligation to do this for them. Failure to do it was moral treason. We were now living on my share of the capital which, so far, could not be touched because I was a minor. Agnes and I were nearly always at Toronto, staying with friends and spending money with extreme caution, most of it on clothes for me. Lillian lived at Whitby, on a mere subsistence.

"The rest of that winter was a nightmare for me. I wanted to go out to earn money, as a stenographer, a salesgirl if I had to, a private secretary if I could. But the old-country, pre-war tradition of what my sisters called a great family stood in the way. They were startled at the mere fact that I could suggest such a thing. If I had done it, it would have driven them in shame into retirement. Neither of them knew how often I had betrayed them by discouraging a financially brilliant match. Agnes was over forty now.

"It was at this stage that I met Edmund again.

"He was the first man of his type I had seen. I mean the type of man that had gone through the war with eyes and mind open, coming out tempered, not softened. He saw the war as a business venture which had failed for both victors and defeated. His disillusionment and aloofness struck a responsive chord in me. The mere fact that I was two years older than he seemed to eliminate any relation other than that of a frank friendship. My first feeling for him was of pity; I knew instinctively that the war had shattered all his ideals; and, incomprehensively, my own experience had strengthened mine. I became interested in his social views; they were at least utterly unsentimental. I found out what was his attitude towards women; even it attracted me. He was the first man I had met whom I could bear to see exactly as he was and to whom I could show my-self exactly as I was. Physically, he was not repulsive to me, in spite of his disabilities.

"To begin with, we met rarely; but when we did, he promptly came to me with evident pleasure. We found we had a great deal to say to each other. When he went home for his majority, he told me frankly that, for many years, he had been impatiently waiting for that event. By using the fortune which his mother had left him he meant to prove, to himself as well as to others, that he had the rare gift of multiplying money, of using it strategically to gain control over various industries. I wanted to see what he would do with it. My curiosity was awakened.

"But what attracted me more than anything else was the way in which he took it for granted that I knew that he knew all about my private predicament. He made me feel that we could have discussed the matter with perfect frankness; he had the knack of making me look upon it as a natural thing which had nothing that need humiliate me. I was like a cripple; he like a man who does not for a moment think that the fact needed concealment or disguise. And so I could be quite natural with him. I was grateful for that; I began to like him tremendously; but I did not love him.

"Even the fact that my sisters who watched us began to consider my previous failure as providential—for here was the greatest fortune of all—did not interfere with my liking of him. Nor did the fact that, when he returned from the west, I knew at once that a woman had entered his life in a sense in which I could never be a woman to him and in which no woman had ever held him. I speculated a good deal about this attachment of which he never spoke. I came to the conclusion that its object must be a married woman; it never struck me that she might simply be twice his age. But somehow I knew also that

243

this attachment did not interfere between us; I even seemed to feel, *grande passion* though it might be, that it was nothing final: that it would 'form' him; that it would make him more 'he' than he had ever been; but that from the beginning, it was doomed to a tragic end.

"One day my sister Agnes told me that he had given her advice with regard to a speculation connected with a Montreal power project. She was to buy stock in a defunct enterprise, to be had for a song; she was to buy as much of it as she possibly could, on margin; and she was to hold it till he gave her the word to sell; but she was to do so only if she fully trusted him. You know how mature he seemed at the time, in spite of his youth. She came to me to ask my advice; for the little she had to invest was mine; and unhesitatingly I said, 'Do!' Within a few weeks she cleared more than the whole life insurance had amounted to. It was the beginning of that affair of Montreal Timber Limits of which, years later, you must have heard at Arbala House.

"Another year went by. No idea of Edmund's becoming anything more to me than my very good friend had ever entered my mind; nor his, I believe. But friends we were very definitely; and he helped me, by various hints, to restore to my sisters some measure of security, so that the tension under which I had lived relaxed. Financial troubles seemed to be at an end; and I welcomed the fact that I need not stand in the market any longer unless I wished to.

"Then, unexpectedly, a new element entered into the situation. In a sort of detached, half-jesting, and altogether experimental way Edmund began to court me. I wondered whether the other attachment was at an end. Today I know, of course, that his mistress was maternally steering him into matrimony; she must be an extraordinarily wise woman. He never gave me to understand that he loved me. I knew that, in the accepted sense, I did not love him. His presence gave me no thrill; his absence did not make me dream. Neither of us ever lost his head. Yet certain things came to be understood between us. Often now our meeting at a social function was not accidental; we met as two associates who liked each other's company and conversation; at last we met definitely by appointment. We talked our engagements or invitations over beforehand and ceased to go anywhere unless both of us had been asked.

"The strange thing was—and not so strange, either—that our friends, Dr Newcombe among them, insisted on interpreting things in their own way. Had our relation been a sentimental one, as they supposed, their behaviour might well have served to separate us. Wherever we appeared, the word was passed around. Perhaps I was, in some gathering, surrounded by a crowd of young men and women—for they were no longer afraid of me; I could be perfectly natural again. Edmund entered. The group melted away; the order was that we were to be left together, alone.

"What saved the situation was Edmund's utter frankness. 'There they go,' he said one night, laughing. 'You and I must not be interfered with.' And I, too, laughed without the least embarrassment.

"When, however, a year or two later, he came to the point, he did so in his own characteristic way. By that time he had built the mill at Arbala; rumour had it that he was edging into the automotive and aircraft industries. He had told me of the house he planned to build at Arbala, ironically, as always, speaking of a certain possibility which he had in view—the possibility, I presumed, that he and I might become man and wife. Before it was even designed, he made fun of that house: it was to be a sort of ostentatious private hotel, meant to dazzle people whom he wished to draw into his net by offering them social opportunities. He mentioned names; of men in high office or of great prominence in the world of finance. Among the latter I remember Mr Rosenbaum, the Jewish Montreal millionaire whom you met a few years later. Having played that idea up for a while—I remember it as if it had been yesterday; we were dancing—he suddenly said, 'The moment I met you again, after having returned from overseas, I knew that you are the only woman in Canada whom I can imagine myself as introducing to others as my wife.' And then, looking me in the eye, steadily, almost probingly, he added, 'Apart, perhaps, from one other who does not want me in that way.'

"I felt as if I must sit down; on Edmund's part, this was undoubtedly a definite offer. But the perfect detachment in which it was made restored my self-possession. 'Does that include all you have loved?' I asked. 'It does,' he said without flinching. 'But in contemplating this possibility, I have always said to myself that I could shut them away in a harem.'

"That was Edmund. He did not care to deny that he had loved others; he frankly admitted that, in an entirely new sense, he still loved one other. But without expressly saying so, he had promised me, if I accepted him, that they would never appear to embarrass me.

"For weeks, perhaps for months, nothing more was said. But Arbala House was building at last; and meanwhile, when we met—and we met with increasing frequency—he talked business and politics: business of a pattern new to me, and politics of a kind that would have made our legislators' hair stand on end. He opened amazing vistas, speaking of national and international affairs with a startling frankness. He predicted to me almost every major development which has since come about. He denied, for instance, that the treaty of Versailles had, in any legitimate sense of the word, been a treaty. A treaty, he said, implied treating: that is, mutual consultation. He said that the mill at Langholm would necessarily, in the long run, form the kernel of a political and economic dictatorship. To bring it about would be a tremendous task, he said; but it was the only way to avoid utter chaos. It would be a dangerous task, he added; whoever undertook it would have to be willing to stake his life. 'If I undertake it,' he said, 'it will appear as if I were bent on my own aggrandizement; wherever I go, daggers and hidden guns will lie in wait for me. It does not matter; the task is not mine alone; it is the task of several generations; but I must lead the way. It may well be that, at the end, there will come a state of affairs in which there are two classes, both slaves, one, the larger, subject to the other; the other, insignificant in numbers, subject to the machine. The machine may come to be worshipped as the god of a new universe, dispensing the good and the evil. What I have in mind may be desirable or not; but it is logically in line with all that has preceded it for millennia. Every other plan runs counter to it. And we have reached a state of affairs where experimentation on the large scale becomes, not only possible, but a duty.' I have since come to understand a good deal that was obscure to me at the time.

"One day he casually called at Whitby, throwing my sisters into a flutter of confusion. But he had been in the drawing-room for no more than ten minutes when he asked me whether I cared to see Arbala House which was nearing completion. I rose and left the room to dress for the drive. When I returned, I knew that he had formally advised my sisters of what was afoot.

"Throughout the drive, and after, we hardly spoke till we had been through the house. Then we both laughed. 'This,' he said, 'is the sort of thing which captivates the colonial mind. It's the past. The mills are the future.'

"We returned to Whitby; and there, on the steps in front

of the house, he asked, 'Do you think you would be willing to share the task, the danger, and the most problematical glory?'

"I hesitated about the form, not the substance of my answer. 'I want the task,' I said. 'I don't mind the danger. For the glory I do not care. If anything more is needed, I might add that I don't know whether you are right. But, right or wrong, I believe you are a great man.'

"He shook his head. 'The problems are great; not the men who tackle them. Nobody can be sure in advance that he is right. But he who is, and he may be very small, will go through history.' He bent down to kiss my hand, in the way which he had brought back from Europe. 'I count on you, then,' he said and left me.

"The next day he went west; a week later the announcement of our engagement was given to the press by my sisters.

"That, briefly, is the story of my marriage. The next step was the lawyers' meeting at Toronto when you proposed the settlement."

CHAPTER

XX

THE senator was up again and had resumed his old routine. In the morning he rose around eight o'clock; at ten he listened to Captain Stevens's report; at eleven he went out for the drive with his daughter-in-law; after lunch he lay down for a nap; and in the evening he walked about in the house, often till midnight; and when he went to bed, there were days when he had not spoken a word to anyone.

All which was as it had been for years, more or less; yet he was not the same as he had been before his brief illness. At his age even a trifling indisposition was bound to leave its effect behind.

Those who watched him had a peculiar impression: as if time were accelerated in passing by him; as water flowing in a stream is accelerated when it approaches a narrows. His own functions had slowed down, while those surrounding him went on at their usual rate, so that they overtook him unawares. This fact he betrayed by occasional brief remarks of surprise. "What? Already?"—when his daughter-in-law took his arm to lead him in for dinner. "It can't be time yet for Stevens?"—when a footman appeared to apprise him of Captain Stevens' presence in the library. Or, "Another week gone?"—when, on Sunday, he had not been summoned for that report, though there was never really anything to report except some minor repairs effected before they were needed.

Once when, in the mill, a cable running over two grooved pulleys and acting as a drive-belt had to be replaced, he betrayed annoyance.

"They told me," he said in his newly cracked voice, "that cable would last for twenty-five years."

"Well," Captain Stevens said as if he were set to watch over this ancient in his second childhood, "it's done better than that. It's lasted over forty."

"What!" the senator cried, his voice snapping from one key into another, with an almost comic effect.

But then he went silent, staring straight ahead, out of watery eyes, his thin lips moving in his hollow and newly discoloured face as if he were doing a sum in mental arithmetic. During the rest of the captain's stay he did not say another word, as though injured. In reality he was sunk in the pit of a bottomless amazement: he had been forty-three when that cable had been installed! *Over forty?*

Captain Stevens felt called upon to report this incident to Lady Clark, as if under orders to give her due warning of new developments.

Lady Clark nodded sympathetically. More than anyone else she was aware of the chronological confusion in the old man's mind. Thinking for a moment, she tried to guess at the time within which the old man was living just then in his memories.

Suddenly she realized that Captain Stevens was the very man to help her in piecing together certain phases in the history of the mill which, in her mental picture of its development, still remained unresolved.

"I am wondering, Captain," she said, "whether there are any documents, reports and the like, which would throw light on the reasons for the last strike at the mill?"

The captain looked up. "You, too, bothering about the mill?"

Lady Clark smiled. "Naturally. Sooner or later I'll have to own it."

"Sooner or later," he repeated, speaking as if he were disgusted. "Well, as to your question, yes; there are many reports, clippings, etc. Ever heard of Arbuthnot? Well, if you haven't heard of him, you've met him. Down at Arbala House. He was the man I sent there by aeroplane to give the late Sir Edmund the news of the walkout."

"Oh yes. A little man with crooked and pointed teeth and a hatchet-shaped head?"

"That's the chap. He's living in Boston now, as a writer, quite prominent, I'm told, in what they call Proletarian Literature. For a short time he had been in the war where he met Sir Edmund in one way or another. Sir Edmund met him again in this country when he was a service man in a gasoline station, already trying to write. He sent him down here. The man left numerous reports; and since I'm engaged in writing the history of the mill from 1898 to 1924, the crucial period, I've been in touch with him. Above all, however, there was, of course, Miss Dolittle who, between 1914 and 1921 when she suddenly resigned, knew more of the mill than anyone living; for *I* was first in France, then in England. I don't know whether you know of her?"

"I do."

"Well, in 1921 she went to southern France to live; but, soon after Sir Edmund's death, she came back to Canada and wrote to me about something or other. I've been in touch with her ever since. She's an old lady now, of course. She lives, by the way, in the upper Gatineau Valley."

"I see," said Lady Clark. "You have her address? Let me have it, will you?"

"Certainly. She had lots of material, of course, most of it in her head. But she's jotted a good deal down and turned it over to me. So I can pride myself on the accuracy of my chapters dealing with that time. Would you care to read them?"

"I'd like to, of all things."

"Let me see . . . I'll have them typed out for you. What you are specially interested in is the time . . ."

"From the end of the war to the strike."

The captain pondered. "Yes," he said; "all that's in a single chapter, and it's finished."

And with his usual and ostentatious gallantry he bowed over the hand of the woman before him. They were in the hall, for Lady Clark being told that Captain Stevens wished to see her for a moment, had come from the music room where she had been practising. Now she looked down on the little man who, grey Fedora hat, lemon-coloured gloves, and gold-headed cane in one hand, rubbed his forehead as he stood for a moment.

"I'll have those chapters ready for you, Lady Clark," he said. "They'll have to be typed; it'll take a day or two."

XXI

*A Chapter from Captain Stevens's
History of the Langholm Mill*

THE management placed many men in confidential positions; some of them without any definite circumscribed functions—as repairmen, trouble hunters, etc., who could circulate through the mill without arousing suspicion. They were actually placed by Mr Brook, the superintendent of works, who could readily do so because he was chairman of the Employment Commission which, in addition, consisted of two members chosen by the men and two appointed by the administration.

The men, of course, read the papers. According to these papers, the war had been a war to end war; a war also to prepare the way for a new system which would do away with what the men called special privilege. According to the demagogues writing in these papers, the war was to make the world safe for democracy, whatever that might mean; and to usher in an era of peace and universal brotherhood. What those who used such words of wide and undefined meaning meant by them it would be interesting, if difficult, to investigate.

The war was over; it seemed the time had arrived to fulfil those promises made by irresponsible scribblers. The great liberation of the masses must come. When men had given their lives or their limbs, when women had given their husbands, their sons, and their homes, they claimed they were entitled to determine their fates.

I am merely quoting, of course, what was being said. I never shared such vague aspirations.

It was also the time when the more or less democratic railway train was, as a means of transportation, displaced by the more direct motor car; and the worst about these new developments was that they brought wealth into the open as nothing else had ever done. In the past, all information about the lives of the wealthy had come second-hand; it had chiefly come from the gossip of servants. Now, the luxurious vehicles of the great of the world who, in doing something for themselves, had done something for their country, gave the lower classes a concrete standard of comparison.

In the first place, there was the number of cars kept. At Clark House, very naturally, there was at least one car for every member of the family. Besides, there were two or three cars needed for occasional company. There were also the cars for the upper servants whose duties required them to go to town on frequent errands. Miss Charlebois who, for years, had presided over the household, had her own car, of course; though she was the only one who, when she went shopping, was accompanied by a footman to carry her parcels. Perkins, the butler, had another car, less pretentious perhaps; and he took no one along to wait on him; but the tradesmen in town did all the waiting on him that he could possibly require. There was the head gardener, the under housekeeper, and many another who was supplied with his transportation by Clark House.

Perhaps half the mill-hands, too, owned cars; and those who did not, came to their work standing on the running boards of those who did, often closely crowded. These, of course, were T-model Fords, bought second- or tenth-hand, rarely washed, never polished: the workman uses his car up; he does not thriftily take care of it; he claims he can't. And thus there was the contrast, visible to all. For the cars from Clark House were huge machines, glittering, first with brass, then with chrome-nickel, and always with polish.

In the corner between mill and Flour Building a garish service station had sprung up; and it had become the favourite resort of many men during the recess for lunch; at other times, too, it became something of a social centre. Every time the great Lincoln or the older Mercedes or Rolls-Royce from Clark House drove up there—it did not happen any too often, for, of course, there was a gasoline standard on the premises— the men made their remarks. "Look," they said, "she swallows twenty gallons at a gulp; and the flunkey merely says, 'Charge!' "—The men, of course, bought only two or three gallons at a time; and of necessity they paid cash.

This could be watched by anyone. Our confidential observers supplemented the picture by their reports. Perhaps one of the lookers-on had bought, likely on the instalment plan, a twelfth-hand flivver for a hundred dollars. The Lincoln had cost over eight thousand, custom-built. What with the tremendously stimulated interest in automotive transportation, these prices were matters of public knowledge. The men next divided one hundred into eight thousand and multiplied the quotient by their annual incomes. The product was, of course, still below the mark of Samuel Clark's income; and it was not long before someone pointed it out to them. So they added up the capital costs of the twenty-odd cars kept at Clark House and repeated division and multiplication, wondering whether they still remained below the mark. They did.

Watson, the rotund, rabid little socialist whom his twenty-odd years at the mill had raised to a position no higher than that of a gang-boss and whom Mr Clark would not have discharged, for the very reason that he disliked him, laughed when he heard the men. He made a new calculation intended to prove that Samuel Clark's income ran into seven figures, as it did.

One of the hands gave a slogan to this element of discontent among the men; he was one of a small group of French-Canadians. *Ça me donne furieusement à penser*, he said; and this, translated word for word, became a tag, received with laughter whenever used, whether appropriately or not. "That gives me furiously to think!" Whether appropriate or not, it always served to remind the men of the contrast between their own incomes and that of the boss. I had more than once advised Mr Clark to make his home elsewhere.

Disaffection had spread into Mr Clark's own household. Before the war he had built, within the gymnasium erected by his late wife, an inside swimming pool, to be used by his two children. His son being away at college, it was chiefly or exclusively used by his daughter and her occasional girl friends. One day, one of our confidential men brought the news of a new topic of conversation. Some of the under-gardeners at Clark House claimed to have seen Miss Ruth Clark and other girls disporting themselves there without bathing suits, for the walls of the structure were of steel and glass. An old mill-hand, thinking of certain happenings among the dwellers of the Terrace, said, on hearing this, "Who lives in a glass house shouldn't throw stones." A jester in the group which heard this amended him. "Who swims in a glass house shouldn't be without a bathing suit." That, too, became a tag and was quoted on all sorts of occasions.

When Mr Clark's son Edmund returned from overseas, rumour at once busied itself with him and Miss Dolittle who was vice-president of the company at the time. Mr Edmund, it was said, often visited Langholm secretly, without alighting at Clark House; he and Miss Dolittle were said to keep an establishment resembling a fairy palace at Whitehead, twenty miles west of Langholm, where they went by car, over a corduroy trail.

All which it would be unnecessary to mention had it not led to certain developments on the Terrace. For Mr Clark, perhaps not fully aware of what was going on, chose in 1920, a moment when economic dissatisfaction reached its peak, to introduce another of his philanthropic measures.

There had already been a tendency among the younger men employed at the mill to go camping along the north shore of the lake. A few of them lived there throughout the summer, with their families, in tents; others visited the place on Sundays and such rare holidays as the summer afforded: Dominion Day, Bank Holiday, and the Civic Holiday which the mill observed.

This being reported to Mr Clark, he laid out, at the head of the lake, or at its extreme east end, a regular camping-ground with roofed kitchens, playground equipment for the children, wooden floors for the tents. Partly, no doubt, he did this in order to get rid of the noisy campers on the north shore, opposite Clark House; and if that was the case, he achieved his purpose. But in various ways he went beyond it. Thus he introduced the forty-two-hour week-end; and, while the men still furnished their own tents and beds, he arranged for half a dozen of the huge mill trucks to establish a regular transporation service between the Terrace and the camping-ground, via the north shore of the lake where the trucks soon wore a beaten trail into the hillside. By the middle of the summer there must have been close to five hundred tents at the head of the lake. Cooking, by the way, was done by electricity; and there was no charge for current.

This had been going on for some time when an amazing plan took shape among the younger men returned from France.

The proposal was to heighten the pleasure derived from these outings by inducing those among the young married couples who had not found all the satisfaction they had expected from the state of wedlock to exchange wives for a week-end. It seemed a huge joke. The young men laughed at the idea while discussing it, rather to make the young women blush than to carry it out. But the mere discussion corroded ancient sanctities.

Why not? they asked at last.

Such as were mismated or thought they were began to cast covetous glances on the wives of their neighbours. Young women, when meeting young men not their husbands, but by whom they knew they were being discussed, took to lowering their eyes and perhaps, if they were willing, to giggling; and suddenly the memory of Mrs Sibyl Carter re-arose among them; they began to watch Miss Ruth Clark who had adopted post-war attitudes resembling those of Mrs Carter. The young women of the Terrace took to walking, talking, sitting more boldly. The young men, watching them, repeated, "Why not?" The thing had a cumulative effect. Certain women became increasingly provocative; certain men, increasingly pressing in their response. Men challenged; women lured.

Nobody, of course, was prepared to take the responsibility for what was brewing; many withdrew from the camp; but by the very fact that their resistance was removed, the thing seemed to become the more readily feasible.

And then it was done; and the heavens had not fallen.

Households, it was true, were loosened in their joints. Terrific 'scenes' were enacted between husbands and wives. Women as well as men made comparisons; quarrels, carried on half in public, took place; there were recriminations; there was genuine suffering here and there; but economic pressure sutured even violated bonds; what could the passive sufferers have done, especially among the women?

Over the whole Terrace, like a dismal sky, lowered an atmosphere of defilement and sin. Yet the world wagged on. At last, once more, it seemed a huge joke.

Since scores of families were involved, the thing could not be kept secret. Young women known to each other exchanged glances, furtively at first, then brazenly; and finally they compared notes.

Among the older, steadier mill-hands, there was an outcry; the section of the Terrace whence the offenders hailed was put under a ban.

Yet, taking the Terrace as a whole, the germ of immorality grew as if planted in a culture medium. If it led to nothing else, it led to a freedom of speech and criticism unheard of in the past, and listened to, by many, with anticipatory shudders. The local drugstores began to do a flourishing business in contraceptive devices; the adolescent population pricked its ears. This so-called new freedom had the effect of a dazzling initiation.

But in the eyes of all who disapproved, it was shortly regarded as the result of the degeneration of the upper classes. An ever-growing pressure of disapproval gathered against the Clarks. "Sure," it was said, "it's them that's to blame."

At this point, young Mr Clark, not yet Sir Edmund, took a hand. He knew of the atmosphere prevailing over the Terrace;

and he made up his mind to utilize it for his own far-reaching plans. By this time the present writer was general manager of the mill and, indirectly, of all its subsidiaries. Young Mr Clark took him into his confidence, at least up to a certain point; and between them they consulted old Mr Charles Beatty, the solicitor for the mill, and one of the most level-headed men in its employ. Many called him crafty.

Mr Edmund Clark's plan involved the necessity of a strike. Discontent alone, Mr Beatty argued, was not enough to bring it about. In the face of the certainty of defeat, there would be no strike. Discontent would have to be strengthened by a feeling of power. It was he who, from the beginning, had pointed out that, if the conversion of the twenty units still operated by hand was to be achieved without rousing public opinion against the owners—while public opinion was still a factor—it must be undertaken during a strike. The problem, then, was not to let this spirit of independence and mistrust die down among the men; to feed it, rather.

A semi-political issue happened to define itself just then. It took us some time to work out a scheme whereby we could utilize it. But Charles Beatty was equal to the task. The issue developed as follows.

The population of the town was slowly dwindling; but for the moment it stood stationary at about twelve thousand. The area surrounding it had, by the activities of Langholm Real Estate, been subdivided for a population of a quarter million.

Now, while a reasonable surplus of unimproved, or improved but vacant land is an asset to any town where poor people become well-to-do, and well-to-do people rich, so that they can hand over to tenants such dwellings as, up to a certain point, had served their purposes, they themselves rebuilding in more spacious or more fashionable quarters, or in a more lavish style, a surplus of two thousand per cent of privately owned building lots in a town which has reached the limits of its expansion is nothing short of civic disaster. The figure of Mr Ferguson, once promoter and manager of Langholm Real Estate, began to weigh on the town like a substantial and asphyxiating shadow. Even near the town limits, where assessments were low and taxes, therefore, amounted to no more than a few dollars a year, the town was forced, as the years went by, to take over more and more land for default. More and more lots, bought on the instalment plan and incompletely paid for, were thrown back on the hands of the Real Estate company, by the simple process of discontinuing payments. The policy of such concerns of reserving title till the whole purchase price is paid operated against it; for he who holds title is answerable for the payment of taxes.

The boom having burst long ago, the slump though slow in defining itself through results, was thorough. Throughout the country investors came to the conclusion that it was bad practice to throw good money after bad. The title deed to a lot at Langholm had ceased to convey any privilege but that of paying taxes into the town exchequer. When the slump began, Mr Tindal, president of the company, tried the golden eloquence of letters. Later, he threatened defaulters with the execution of the law. Finally he sued. Reluctantly the courts found for the plaintiff; but even the sheriff could not collect where there was nothing. The whole concern was made to feel 'shady'.

At first Mr Tindal took it philosophically; the company could stand the loss. He began to accept repudiation; but repudiation assumed the volume of an avalanche.

Since the town had had a mushroom growth, all improvements—roads, streets, sidewalks, water system, sewer, fire engines—had been financed by borrowing; its annual current expenditure, therefore, consisted to a very large extent of fixed interest charges which could not be reduced.

The fewer actual ratepayers there were, the higher rose, naturally, the rate of taxation for those who remained. In 1919, the Real Estate company, snowed under by tax bills, suspended payments. In 1920, its largely imaginary assets were sold by public auction; or would have been sold had there been buyers. Mr Tindal, acting as a private individual, bought the Realty Building, so far assessed at one hundred thousand, for little over ten.

Fifteen or twenty thousand building lots fell to the town. Langholm now owned six thousand acres of land on which it received no revenue except grazing fees; and these only after a new investment had been made in fencing material : less than five hundred dollars a year where, during the boom, the same land, held by enthusiastic speculators, had poured a hundred and ten thousand dollars into the treasury in taxes.

As a consequence, the tax rate rose and rose; from 15 mills it rose to 30, 40, 50, 80, and finally 100 mills; and nobody had anything to show for the enormous sums which, annually, he disbursed to the town; they barely took care of interest due; improvements came to an end; even upkeep was stinted.

This concerned everybody. Municipal politics assumed an

importance they had never had; discussion became acrimonious. Every smallest item of municipal expenditure was challenged.

Curiously, public resentment fastened on to one small item—small, that is, in comparison to the enormous interest charges: namely, the annual subsidy of ten thousand dollars paid to the Palace Hotel. No town of ten thousand could, of course, support a million-dollar hotel without such a subsidy.

The enterprise was owned by an international combine. Twenty-five years ago it had been built on the promise of that subsidy; the site had been donated by Rudyard Clark; the town had made a grant towards the cost of construction; a fixed assessment, amounting to about twenty per cent of that cost, had been guaranteed for the first ten years.

Thus matters stood in 1921. The combine was a powerful concern which would not submit to a withdrawal of the subsidy without a fight. But public opinion demanded such a withdrawal. Public opinion nearly always demands the irrational.

Late in the year, the agitation for municipal retrenchment precipitated a stormy election. Before the onslaught of popular fury the council in power resigned in a body. Rarely before had a poll been necessary in any of the six electoral wards; traditionally, elections were carried by acclamation.

In vain did responsible citizens issue warnings: a lawsuit would mean endless expense; it could only result in a further rise of the mill-rate; the international combine had a perfectly clear case.

The passions of the mob were aroused.

Then the word went out from the inner circles of the administration of the mill, that is from Sir Edmund, for all employed by the mill in responsible positions—which included foremen, chemists, engineers, and the staffs of the various offices in the administration building—to refrain from voting. All these, naturally, would, had they voted, have stood on the side of reason.

Thus the fate of the town was sealed by a general poll in which overwhelming majorities returned none but radicals to seats on the council. It looked like a landslide; it was one.

Mill-hands, odd-job men, low-salaried clerks, and labourers in the various trades made their victory the occasion of noisy demonstrations. When, late at night on election day, the results were announced, there was cheering at every polling station; bonfires were burning on Main Street, weirdly lighting up the great hotel which looked down on the commotion, unmoved but ironical; the houses of substantial, conservative citizens were serenaded; even a few windows were shattered by flying stones. Next day, flags were flown all over the Terrace. This, it was said, was to be the beginning of the new era; the oppressed were going to come into their own.

When, early in 1922, the new council held its first business meeting, with a widely advertised motion to withdraw the subsidy on its agenda, the orgy of unreason reached its climax: five thousand men and women gathered in the square formed by the intersection of Main and Argyle Streets, in front of the fine manorial town hall, monument of past illusions.

At nine o'clock, Mr Inkster, massive and smiling, drove up in his big car, he being solicitor for the town. As he alighted, at the foot of the northeast perron, the multitude, knowing just what he stood for, cheered him laughingly to the stars.

In spite of a murderous frost—it was forty below zero—the crowds waited, standing packed on hard snow a foot deep, shoulder to shoulder, lighted bluishly by the great arc lights; not a pin could have dropped to the ground.

At a few minutes to eleven, a sleek young man with brilliant black eyes and glossy black hair, the town clerk, appeared briskly on the platform above the lock-up and smilingly shook himself as though to shed the icy air which cascaded down on him from the frozen roof. A cheer greeted him; and over the vast crowd fell a hush.

The clerk, raising his voice to a shout, bellowed out one single word: "Carried!"

Bedlam broke loose. There were ear-splitting yells; there was wild throwing of hats; and, with a surging back of the crowd, to make room, men and women fell into each other's arms and began to dance. It looked like a scene from an inferno of ice.

It was fortunate for the delirious happiness of the populace that the time for setting the new mill-rate was far away. But, of course, had they known that it must be raised, they would still have cheered. This was the great victory of the underdog. For, in fighting the subsidy, they had been fighting privilege, whatever that might mean to them. The talk that shortly went round was somewhat like this: not only was the subsidy enriching an already rich international combine; but every meal served in the dining-room of the hotel, at seventy-five cents for breakfast, a dollar for lunch, and a dollar and a half for dinner, levied its contribution from the poor; at their expense, at least partly, strangers were eating food which *they* could never hope to taste.

But, within a few days, a reaction set in. The hotel, metaphorically girding up its loins for the fight, promptly eliminated many of the services it had been rendering; the quality of the meals which had attracted week-end visitors from the great army of commercial travellers was lowered; the number of maids, waiters, bellboys, recruited from the youth of the town, was reduced. Unemployment showed its gorgon face.

When, early in spring, the assessors made their rounds, and the council fixed the mill-rate for the year, there was an outcry. The people had been betrayed—they had been, by themselves. Councillors adduced the cost of litigation, quoting fabulous sums: Mr Inkster charged six dollars an hour when, with his staff, he went to Winnipeg for the preliminary hearings.

It was useless to try and fight the 'machine'!

Then, in midsummer, an amazing piece of news reawakened the fighting spirit: the great international combine had settled out of court; the suit had been withdrawn.

And this shows the utter lack of reason in a crowd. There was a renewed cry of "Treason!"

The council, it was said, must have compromised. But the councillors, questioned, indignantly denied the charge. Even they did not know exactly what had happened.

The explanation which came in due time, conveyed in a letter from Mr Inkster to the council, was humiliating: the combine had not been beaten; it had contemptuously shaken the dust of Langholm off its feet: it had sold out.

The worst blow to the civic pride of the radicals, for they were not without that pride where their pocket-books were not involved, was that the stock of the combine promptly rose a point or two in the market: as if the Palace Hotel had been a liability rather than an asset.

But who were the buyers? The hotel remained open and even restored its former level of service. Who were the buyers?

It so happened that Mr Inkster did not return to town for months. Late in the fall the secret came out in a casual way: a transfer was recorded at the registry office: the buyer was Sir Edmund Clark!

For a moment, everybody had the feeling as if a powder barrel were about to explode in a beleaguered fortress; as if a catastrophe of some kind were imminent. Why?

The secret lay, of course, in the conference which Sir Edmund, now married, had had with Charles Beatty, the solicitor

260

for the mill; Sir Edmund was on the point of acquiring control; he was the only man who foresaw what was coming; and he was getting ready for it.

There is no accounting for the vagaries of public opinion. The town should have rejoiced at being spared the cost of protracted litigation; it should have rejoiced at having carried its point in getting rid of the subsidy; it should have rejoiced at seeing the sumptuous hotel re-establish its former standards; for, under any reasonable consideration, it was an asset to the community.

The town did nothing of the kind. It felt aggrieved at being deprived of a most problematical triumph.

Other mysterious things followed as the result of further consultations between Mr Beatty and young Sir Edmund—consultations to many of which I was admitted, though Mr Samuel Clark, still nominally president, remained excluded.

For years the town had been in financial difficulties. Its debentures were a drug in the market. Borrowing for the purpose of meeting fixed charges had become an impossibility. No more than sixty per cent of the taxes still levied proved capable of being collected. After the interest on outstanding debentures had been paid, there were no funds left for upkeep or repair of roads, streets, and public utilities. Even the mill-hands began to complain of the state of Main Street where huge holes had appeared in the asphalt pavement.

Then, during the following summer, that is, the summer of 1923, slowly and insidiously, as it were, these difficulties disappeared; for certain scrips of the town a new demand arose throughout the Dominion; and from various places the town was notified, by lawyers and brokers, that the new buyers would raise no protest if, in the case of stated securities, the interest should go by default. Soon there was no doubt about it any longer: either the mill as such or Sir Edmund personally was the moving spirit behind it all. When, in due time, the transfers of ownership were registered at the town hall, the conjecture was confirmed. But a curious thing became noticeable even to the dullest: the sort of public property thus acquired by Sir Edmund was of one single type: it consisted in water system, sewers, firehall, roads, etc. Debentures issued for the building of town hall, market shelter, schools, and many roads leading out of town remained unrelieved. The most elementary analysis of the list showed that only such services were acquired as were essential to the mill or its owners.

The fact that these transactions were carried through in Sir

Edmund Clark's absence from town gave people a queer feeling. It was a matter of public knowledge that young Sir Edmund, independently of his father, figured prominently in certain enormous mergers in the industrial world; in the west he became, by means of extensive purchases, the virtual landlord of thousands of farmers; he was already the president of one of the largest banks. If he did not yet hold control of the mill, it could not be the lack of capital which prevented him. The names of all shareholders were known, for, so long as there was a single outside shareholder, statements had to be published in the press. There were four people who owned such shares: Mr Samuel Clark; Sir Edmund; Lady Clark; Mr Cole.

No matter what might or might not happen, Sir Edmund was, of course, destined to hold that control one day. Mr Clark was nearing his seventies; he would hardly bequeath his share in the mill outside the family.

The fact that more and more of the town as such was owned by Sir Edmund who could foreclose on its public utilities whenever he pleased gave its citizens a feeling as though it were invested by an invisible hostile army. His very absence contributed to the idea that, independently of his father, he had become a financial colossus.

What was the meaning of it all? Whatever happened increased, by this time, the tension between management and men. It was a queer thought, that of the mill which ran independently of human labour enclosing, as it were, that other, older mill which was still run by hand: a starfish enveloping an oyster to suck its substance was not more sinister. The men crouched under the threat; but they could not help themselves.

The present writer saw the strike coming at least a year before it broke. The thing was in the air. It was no deliberate move to secure this or that advantage; it was a blind striking out at a menace which seemed to hang from the sky. The men began to feel that the management expected them, *wanted* them to strike; they *saw* why; but they refused to see it; at last they struck.

This writer was by no means so absolutely sure of the intention. Nominally he was an employee of the directorate consisting of Mr Samuel Clark, Sir Edmund and Lady Clark. But as a matter of fact the responsibility of the general manager was by this time entirely to Sir Edmund to whom he reported and who acknowledged the reports without comment. Yet it was not till the end of 1923 that the manager felt sure of his ground. What, ultimately, gave him that certainty was the fact that, during the summer of that year, orders had come to build provisional warehouse sheds east and west of the railway station, to house new machinery which had been ordered from Germany. At first the manager thought these were replacements only; but the shipments took on such a volume that he could no longer doubt their purpose. They were meant for the complete conversion of the last twenty units which were still operated by hand.

A peculiar feature of the transaction was that Mr Samuel Clark, still nominally president—he remained president throughout, by the way—was in entire ignorance of it. I found this out through a casual question he asked.

"What's going on at the station?" he said. "All those sheds going up?"

Realizing only now that, apparently, I was involved in a conspiracy, I stepped warily and prevaricated, saying that spare parts and replacement units were to be stored there.

But I believe that, from that moment on, Mr Clark saw through it: he never repeated his question. *He preferred to remain uninformed.*

Our most active spy, Arbuthnot, never reported to Mr Clark, nor to me. As I found out much later, he reported to Captain McDermot, the superintendent of the Arbala Mill.

I was often in an awkward position.

Thus, agitators, domestic and foreign, multiplying all the time, I had a U.S. communist deported by the provincial authorities. It was done quietly, without any stir in the public prints. But a sharp reprimand came through from Sir Edmund, couched in peremptory terms, and telling me to leave the men strictly to themselves. I felt offended at his tone and let him know it; he promptly apologized, saying that it would be to my own advantage if I did not know too much about ultimate aims. This opened my eyes. The whole design became clear, showing me the true greatness of Sir Edmund who could work through underground ways for the sake of ultimate triumph. His lamented death, a bare six months later, was a national disaster.

When, in December, the order reached me, in a code telegram, to cut wages, I knew that this was no more than a signal needed to touch off the explosion among the men.

As I said, blindly, infuriatedly, but uselessly, they struck.

CHAPTER

XXII

WHEN Lady Clark had read this chapter of Mr Stevens's projected book, her feelings were mixed as they had always been when she had seen something of her husband's methods. His ultimate aim, whether realizable or not, whether morally justifiable or not, had always held the element of greatness. The details of the road to the goal had made her shiver.

Very naturally, having read, her thoughts went back to that winter of 1924 to 1925.

While, at Langholm, everybody was feeling the approach of some cataclysm, Arbala House had held its most brilliant season.

Sir Edmund, she knew, was involved in vast schemes which were often casually discussed and sometimes finally arranged over the dinner table. There was hardly a week-end which did not see a score of industrialists and financiers—from Toronto, Montreal, or New York—quartered in the guest rooms, occasionally mixed with a sprinkling of the better-known politicians. What it all was about, Lady Clark could often only guess; though the name of Montreal Timber Limits, a defunct concern, recurred again and again. She did not ask any questions: all things come to him who waits. But she did her best to make everybody feel at home. Having married Sir Edmund, she felt bound to do so and to suspend her judgment. Queerly, she had often the peculiar feeling that others did not quite know whether to look on him as an almost insane schemer or a very great man. Nobody, that much became clear, trusted him as a friend, a foe, or an associate.

A young lady who was at once social secretary and press-agent—though the latter function remained a secret from most —was in constant attendance.

Arbala House, situated an hour and a half's easy run east of Toronto, was a huge limestone structure built in a mixture of neo-Grecian and neo-baroque styles. Its upper storey, apart from a master's suite of five rooms, was laid out like a hotel. Below, there were two main entrances, one on its south side, accessible from a fine old park, by means of a wide perron approached by two curving flights of steps; one on the west side, almost level with the ground, roofed over against the weather. On both sides of the latter glassed-in verandas stretched away to north and south, their roofs shading half a dozen windows of the ground floor.

The downstairs interior of the mansion was remarkable chiefly by reason of the fact that its walls were hung with paintings, mostly by old masters, some of them copies, the upper time limit being that of Corot's early, pre-photographic period. Everywhere the furnishings were provocatively new, though they imitated the first French Empire. Like the exterior, this downstairs interior was ostentatious; so much so that Lady Clark had always felt depressed by it; in spite of the fact that her husband, on first showing it to her, had casually said that it was designed, not as a place to live in, but as a show place meant to impress a certain class of guests.

"For ourselves," he said, "there's a little cottage at the north end of the park . . . This is a business venture; I am glad to say it's eminently saleable. It's in line with my title and my father's appointment to the senate."

The numerous staff of servants, mostly male, matched the setting. There was a young butler of magnificent physique, assisted by a dozen footmen in a somewhat striking livery, the Clark olive being trimmed with red; and there were twice as many maids, expert in the art of conveying their expectation of tips. These maids were ruled over by an elderly housekeeper who made the impression of a decayed gentle-woman.

"It's all like the plate glass and chrome-nickel offices of fraudulent real estate firms," Sir Edmund said one day to his wife, in the presence of the newly created senator, who looked up in surprise, as if he had not expected to find his son human in contact with his wife.

Throughout that part of the season which the young couple spent there—the senator having been specially invited and even urged to come east—there was never a day without formal calls. Cars drove up to the south entrance which was the one facing the highway; a footman alighted, hurried up the steps, and handed his cards to the footman answering the bell. The bearers of the names engraved upon them never left their seats; often the limousine was empty; the costliness and the brilliant polish of the vehicle sufficiently represented its owners.

Stacks of such cards accumulated in silver baskets on a little table in the vestibule. When Edmund was at home, or when he returned from one of his frequent, if brief absences, he inspected these cards with some care. One day, Maud being in the hall to meet him, he remarked to her, "More applicants!"

Miss Austin, the social secretary, always faultlessly dressed according to the time of the day, tabulated the names and, in her files, added marginal notes in shorthand, designed to summarize descent, social position, and financial standing of these 'applicants'. She used her extensive knowledge of society in Toronto and Montreal, acquired when employed as the 'society editor' of a great daily paper—a position which only the munificent salary offered her by Sir Edmund could have induced her to surrender. When necessary, she supplemented this knowledge by the assiduous use of a certain *Who's Who* which was bound to be reliable, for the articles dealing with prominent and less prominent men and women which it contained had been written by themselves. She arranged all these names in groups which, at a glance, showed compatibilities or the reverse.

Maud soon understood that this forepart of the season was slowly working up to some grand climax : a social event of the first magnitude for which some thirty couples were to be invited from a distance, to spend the week-end at Arbala; while several hundred young people were to be asked from the provincial capital for Saturday night. Nobody told her this; everybody acted as if she not only knew, but was largely responsible for, the arrangements. She made it a point not to ask questions; and in this she was helped by the fact that her husband always treated her with the formal courtesy due to a guest. The thing amused her.

In spite of abundant hints which Sir Edmund had dropped before they had come down, Maud had not yet quite realized to what an extent she figured in this game of his as a business asset. It became abundantly clear through her acquaintance with Mr Rosenbaum who addressed her, not as the abstract hostess, but as an individual.

Meanwhile the senator was walking about, during these week-ends, feeling like a fish out of water. He watched things in an all but hostile mood, especially when Mr Rosenbaum began to turn up with suspicious regularity.

This Mr Rosenbaum was a magnificent, florid, impulsive, and curly-bearded Jew from Montreal, of the 'Carthaginian' type, reminding one of pictures that live in most of us of such historical figures of Hamilcar Barca or Hannibal, highly cultivated people most of them, but perhaps a little too ostentatiously gentlemen. He was a reader of wide knowledge and fine

266

taste; and Maud soon guessed that he was an international power in the world of finance.

The senator, in spite of his own undisguised aversion for the display at Arbala House, resented the polished smoothness with which this man, this rank outsider, from his six-foot-three, looked down upon his surroundings; he resented it because, without ever saying a word in depreciation of the place where he accepted and apparently enjoyed hospitality, Mr Rosenbaum contrived, now by a brilliantly false smile which showed his fine teeth behind rosy lips half hidden by moustache and beard, now by a quick bow from the hips, or, finally, by a pensive stroking of his coal-black beard, to dissociate his hostess and himself from the atmosphere in which they lived; as though he and she shared the knowledge of a different, finer world, of an older aristocracy of the spirit rather than of a crude colonial wealth.

Lady Clark smiled to herself as she thought of it. It went without saying that the senator had not, at the time, been in his son's confidence; whereas she, divining how much this man mattered in the plans of her husband, made it a point to cultivate his good will. Mr Rosenbaum might think he was making fun of Sir Edmund whom he identified with this house; in reality Sir Edmund was making fun of the Jew by using him for his ends, whatever they might be.

Maud did not feel entirely comfortable in her part; but she was determined to play it; for better or worse she had ranked herself by the side of her husband. The Jew's conversation, always dealing with art and literature, flattered her, it was true; he was a man to whom she could talk easily, which was far from being the case with most of the other guests.

When the senator, in his vicarious jealousy, spoke to her one day—in general terms, and without mentioning Mr Rosenbaum—he betrayed clearly that he considered Edmund a fool for throwing her and the Jew together as he did.

Maud laughed. "I can be trusted," she said. "All this amuses me tremendously; it's a fascinating intricate game of chess; and, believe me, Father, Edmund is not a pawn; he's a player. Who the other player is I don't know. But Edmund knows that the queen can take the castle. That's why he moves me forward on the board."

On the occasion of Mr Rosenbaum's fourth consecutive weekend at Arbala, there was a scene which puzzled the senator to the point where he felt called upon actually to intervene. He happened to be standing in front of the fireplace in one of the smaller drawing-rooms. Maud, alone for the moment, had sunk down on a chesterfield in front of him, apparently exhausted.

She was fully aware that the magnificent Jew had been looking for her; and half intentionally she had withdrawn. Suddenly, having espied her, he came forward, through the door, with a conspiratorial air. Disregarding the senator whom, in this house, everybody seemed to disregard as a negligible quantity, he came impulsively over to her, drew up a chair, and, from his breast pocket, took a small volume bound in mauve morocco, exquisitely tooled and imprinted in old French gold letters:

QUELQUES POÈMES ET FRAGMENTS DE CHARLES BAUDELAIRE
CHOISIS PAR AUGUSTE ROSENBAUM.

The little book was printed on Chinese vellum and contained no more than a score of complete poems and extracts from perhaps as many more.

"This," the Jew said, "is in my opinion all that is worth preserving of this very great poet. It, of course, is eminently worth it. You remember we were talking of him a week ago. I did not then mention this little anthology because I wished to surprise you. I flatter myself that, if you will do me the honour of looking it over, you will find here all that you really value and nothing of what has bored you. You have been bored in reading Baudelaire, have you not?"

Maud hesitated. "Perhaps I have. Yes, I think so."

He nodded delightedly. "Of course you have. No poet has ever written more than a thousand lines of the very first order, except perhaps Homer. Would you accept this little volume with my compliments? There are only a hundred copies in existence."

Maud's face lighted up. "Certainly. Thanks very much indeed."

The senator stepped forward from the fireplace. "May I interrupt? I saw Miss Austin trying to catch your eye, Maud."

Though Maud knew that this interruption was only a pretext, she rose.

The laughable thing about it was that, evidently, Edmund, who was talking to some other men in the adjoining room, which was the big drawing-room, had also been watching from the corner of his eye. To him, the intervention of his father, at this precise moment, was anything but welcome; for it forced him to leave his other guests abruptly. With quick presence of mind he entered, laughing back over his shoulder at something someone had said, and asked the Jew, before Maud had time to disappear, whether he might carry him away to a little 'committee meeting' in the library. Mr Rosenbaum had no choice: he bowed urbanely to Maud and followed his host.

Next day, still more irrationally, the senator saw fit, instead of welcoming the interruption, to reproach his son with spoiling Maud's social pleasures by this intrusion of business. It was a trifle which, like so many others, testified to the unallayed antagonism between father and son.

Edmund fixed him with a glassy star. "Maud understands," he said after a moment's hesitation. "We are working in collaboration."

"Working?" the senator repeated.

"Certainly. You did not think I'd ask her to look on this sort of thing as a pleasure? . . . By the way," he added, "whenever you wish to resign the presidency, I am ready at last."

"You mean to say . . ."

"That I hold control? I do."

"Mr Cole . . ."

"Mr Cole, about three months ago, got himself into financial difficulties. I will not pretend that they arose by chance. He hypothecated his holdings in the Langholm mill to Mr Rosenbaum, in return for a short-term loan. He failed to redeem them when the loan fell due, the day before yesterday; and according to their agreement Mr Rosenbaum was free to do with them as he pleased. He transferred them to me last night."

They were standing in the lofty white-and-gold hall. Maud had stopped near them, unseen by the senator, but in plain view of Edmund.

Again the senator said, "Do you mean to say . . ."

"That Mr Rosenbaum, when presented with an ultimatum regarding other projects dear to his heart, was not in a mood to deny Lady Clark's husband a favour in the matter of a business arrangement?"

"Crudely put, that was what I meant."

"The more crudely it is put, the better it fits the case; the world of finance is a crude one."

"And Mr Cole . . ."

"Mr Cole, whether he likes it or not, will have to accept the *fait accompli*. He is in the east by the way. He tried yesterday to see Mr Rosenbaum in Montreal. No doubt he wants to redeem his collateral. He is waiting for his return. He will wait in vain. But it is not unlikely that he will find out what has happened. If he does, I expect to see him here."

Every word Sir Edmund said was pronounced with that distinct enunciation which he always adopted when speaking to his father; and since Edmund's eyes, during the whole dialogue, had rested on Maud's, the senator turned at last and discovered her presence.

He had that ancestral gesture, drawing up his right eyebrow till half his forehead was covered with ridged wrinkles. Apologetically he bowed to Maud. His thought was transparent: he was wondering whether this Jew *ex-post-facto* would suspect Maud of complicity—a thing he would naturally have resented.

The fact was that Mr Rosenbaum left that night, going west, not east; and since, on the very day of the great ball at Arbala, the strike broke out at Langholm, with consequences of which nobody, so far, had thought, Maud never saw the man again. But she did see Mr Cole.

It was in the early afternoon of the first Friday in December that the guests constituting the house party began to arrive. The preparations made for them included the conversion of the office building of Arbala Mill, ten miles north, into an annex of the house. All offices had been turned into bedrooms. The number of people invited had been almost doubled; and there was no Palace Hotel available here.

To Maud's delight, the first to appear at the south entrance were Mr and Mrs Beatty. During her repeated brief stays at Langholm, she had made friends with Mrs Beatty, a small, extraordinarily attractive and pleasant woman of fifty who looked no older than Maud herself though her hair had silvered over. Her husband, Charles Beatty, Maud barely knew. He was small, thin, very unlike his wife, with a head resembling a death's-head, especially when he laughed. All she knew about him was that he had been old Mr Rudyard Clark's legal adviser and was now Edmund's. He was said to have extraordinary mental and conversational powers which, on occasion, he used ruthlessly. His vast memory supplied him with an inexhaustible store of anecdotes, stories, and conceits appropriate to every conceivable social occasion; he could keep any number of people amused and breathlessly waiting for a conversational climax, in a cleverly built-up suspense. One felt that he never spoke impromptu. No matter what topic might blow up, he was prepared for it. Professionally, every member of the bar, in the east and the west, stood in awe of him.

But, of course, his presence at Arbala had a purpose. What that purpose was, Maud could not guess. The social aspect of this huge affair was no more than a cloak for what went on below the surface or behind the scene. So the mere presence of Mrs Beatty was, to her, a relief; and she wondered whether Edmund had arranged for it with that in view; she was inclined to think so; it would explain their early arrival.

It was not till about four o'clock that the guests began to follow each other rapidly at the door. Two of them knew the senator and came to speak to him before they went up to their rooms. Of these, one was Sir Arthur Cunningham, the prime minister of the administration in power at Ottawa.

Having first dispersed, the guests reassembled in library, hall, and drawing- and smoking-rooms. Edmund kept restlessly moving about from group to group, while the butler marshalled his forces, maids and footmen, to provide tea and other refreshments. Under Miss Austin's unobtrusive but highly competent direction everything went smoothly; there was no incident of any importance till the dressing-gong sounded and the first groups began to go upstairs.

Then followed what, to those who were still lingering, seemed nothing less than a sensation.

At the south perron a shabby taxicab had drawn up; and from it emerged an elderly, grey, bearded, tall, but frail-looking man in unassuming, loose clothes who carried a club-bag. Seeing him enter, with his self-effacing air, one or two people whistled through their teeth.

Since Maud had made up her mind to take every cue entirely from Edmund—who, of course, was expecting this belated guest and had no doubt delayed his own ascent—she was still in the hall. There was no hurry; two maids were waiting upstairs to help her.

At the door, an imperturbable footman received the stranger who, as he surrendered his bag, his coat and hat, seemed to remain unmindful if not unconscious of the silent disdain of the menial.

To cap it all, Sir Edmund promptly left His Excellency, the French *Chargé*, to meet this stranger not only with punctilious politeness but with an almost cordial deference before he reached the middle of the hall. "How do you do, Mr Birkinshaw?" he said in his precisely articulated voice audible to all. "I am delighted. The ladies, I am afraid, have gone up to dress. Will you permit me to show you to your room?" And he reached for the bag, taking it from the footman—an honour which he had so far reserved exclusively for ladies.

Turning, he saw Maud. "Ah," he said with unusual animation, "here is my wife."

Birkinshaw? Maud asked herself. The name sounded familiar; but it took her a moment or two to identify it with that of the labour leader in the House of Commons who, almost against his wish, had, at the end of the war, been elected by the radical elements of a western city. He had, since, by his fearlessness and intellectual integrity, combined with an extraordinary gentleness of manner and a careful courtesy to political opponents, become something of a national figure and a national storm centre.

What made his unexpected appearance in this plutocratic *milieu* still more sensational was the fact that, so far, all who held any political significance—and there were not a few—belonged to the ultra-conservative groups. Here was a notorious radical whose presence could not but have some hidden meaning.

Maud held no clue to the game that was being played; but, as she went upstairs, she reflected on the number of threads which her husband was capable of holding in his hand.

Among those who had witnessed the personal attention which the host, clad in the undress uniform rarely worn by him, had bestowed upon the financially humblest of his guests, it had, as Maud was aware, given rise to excited or caustic comment.

One of them was the prime minister who, emerging from the library, had taken Sir Edmund's place by the side of the French *Chargé d'Affaires*. Both were huge men; and, seeing Mr Birkinshaw, they stopped short, in order not to be forced to face this antagonist whom, in the House, Sir Arthur had so often tried to manhandle. Sir Arthur's suddenly thoughtful air was eloquent in proclaiming the fact that he, too, was puzzled by Sir Edmund's purpose in asking the man. Was it meant as a hint that, unless the powers that be proved tractable in certain directions, Sir Edmund might place his influence and his seemingly unlimited financial resources at the disposal of 'the worst element in the opposition'? With a genius like Edmund Clark one could never tell.

Maud had by this time picked up enough of the party jargon to thus reconstruct Sir Arthur's thought with considerable accuracy.

For half an hour, after that, the house sank into a state of seeming somnolence; though, in the enormous dining-room, frantic servants were putting the finishing touches to the boards laid for a hundred, and, upstairs, men were slipping into dress suits; women, submitting to the ministrations of hurried maids.

Then, running down the stairs with quick steps, Sir Edmund returned, this time in the full-dress uniform of a colonel which, across the breast, displayed the insignia of many orders, both British and foreign. He cast a hurried glance about and into the door of the dining-room; but, seeing Miss Austin, he said briefly, "Oh, you're on deck. All right."

Then he returned to the foot of the grand stairway whence he saw Maud in the act of descending, sumptuous in smooth-fitting black silk, with diamonds in her hair.

Next, as if unwilling to miss the slightest detail, the prime minister came down, ostentatious in his unrelieved black-and-white, followed by M McLéan, *Chevalier de la Légion d'Honneur*, his ample torso crossed diagonally by a wide red ribbon. His Excellency Wong Lee was next, small, delicate, fine limbed, with his little wife, internationally famed as a beauty of the small, oriental type which formed a striking contrast to Maud; then Mr and Mrs Peters, of Texan oil fame, from the new plutocracy of New York; and a host of others who slowly filled the hall like a flood, having passed the hosts and exchanged a few words with them. Last of all came Charles Beatty and his pretty wife, accompanied by the "unspeakable" Mr Birkinshaw.

To the surprise of all who knew them separately or by sight only, Charles Beatty and Mr Birkinshaw seemed to be on a footing of intimacy; it was soon whispered around that they had been classmates at school and college. As if to set all doubt at rest, Mr Beatty, who was in the habit of all but embracing the person he stood or walked next to, tried to introduce Mr Birkinshaw to Lady Clark.

Hearing that they had already met, he made a slight turn and found himself face to face with the prime minister. Mr Beatty's eye flickered. Bowing to Sir Arthur, he laughed and, speaking with almost Sir Edmund's distinctness, so that, in the momentary hush, he could be heard throughout the huge hall, he said, "I am glad to say, Mr Birkinshaw needs no introduction here, either. He is honourably known as that member of the House whose speeches remain, by order, unrecorded in the press."

In this world of the ruthless scramble for wealth and power Maud stood, so she reflected, as the symbol of achieved position. By the accident of their descent from upstairs, Margaret Beatty and Mr Birkinshaw remained, for a moment, in front of her: there was no opening in the crowd through which to escape. As for the self-effacing man who in no way resembled the *miles gloriosus* whom the press feigned to see in him, she frankly liked him, his scholarly air, and the genuine friendliness and admiration with which he had smiled at her from behind his beard. More than one person asked himself whether there was not, between these two as well, some bond hidden from the rest.

While the guests rearranged themselves in groups in that hall, Miss Austin entered in a low-cut evening gown. Inconspicuously she began to make the round; flitting from group to group, assigning partners; and when the hum of conversation was interrupted by the opening of the wide slide-doors to the dining-room, the resplendent butler bowing to the lady of the house, she helped the guests to find their seats. The prime minister bowed to Maud; and together they led the procession. To everyone's amazement, Mr Birkinshaw, who had taken in Mrs Beatty, was placed at the hostess's right.

Senator Clark found himself paired with a lady of ample proportions whose very name he had failed to catch. He looked grim and grey as he sat down, as if he resented the fact that, after a quarter century of predominance in every circle he frequented, he was superseded in a world which he did not know: in the person of his son a new star had risen.

His seat, however, was not far from Maud's, at her right, only Mr Birkinshaw and Margaret Beatty intervening. Visibly he felt neglected. It was Maud who had insisted on his coming down from Langholm; though, she remembered, she had not done so entirely of her own accord. She felt almost sorry for him.

Yet she felt visibly that she was 'going the pace' and that she liked it. She knew she looked beautiful; and her animated face showed that she knew it: it was at once appealing and impressive. She was the ideal hostess. If she was playing a part, nobody, now, would have guessed it. She knew she was by far the most beautiful woman present; and that knowledge made it easy for her to preserve her poise without effort. No doubt she wore the exact expression which, in the terms of his wooing, her husband would have wished her to assume.

Around the three boards, there was no lack of animation. Miss Austin who had inconspicuously vanished, in order to continue her duties from another strategic point, namely, the kitchens, had done her work in this dining-room with consummate skill. The steady hum of conversation which, so far, had divided the company into groups became general, to the accompaniment of a laugh. Everybody, so Maud noticed, was looking at Mr Beatty.

Only her own escort, the prime minister, remained impassive. He, too, like everybody else, represented something. As a person, that is as an intellectual or spiritual entity, he did not exist; as the holder of the first office in the country, he represented the benevolent attitude of a paternalistic government elected by the people towards all whose interests lay in the preservation of the *status quo*, which meant the interests of those exploiting the people. This position of his, which was that of the executive of policies dictated to him by the moneyed classes, determined what, to the uninitiated, might have appeared as his personal views and opinions which he expounded to satiety, in speeches given within and without the House, in a slow and ponderously impressive voice. Wealthy himself, he looked down on all who were not, and up to all who were more so. Poverty was either a trial imposed by providence or the penalty paid by improvidence; like death or imprisonment it must be patiently borne. Art, literature, music were pretty toys fashioned by shiftless fools for the adornment of society in the narrower sense. All which was known to all. Why should he speak? He was the Buddha of his world. He sat there, knees crossed, metaphorically, bored and stony.

Suddenly it struck Maud that Edmund and she were the only really young people present; apart from them there was probably not one who was not at least twice their age.

But apart from the prime minister nobody seemed bored; certainly nobody else presented a stony face. No doubt, Maud reflected, that was why Charles Beatty was present: it was his task to keep the ball of repartee flying. With a federal election in the offing, with such national problems as reconstruction after a major war still largely unsolved because they had to be solved without, if possible, disturbing, not to say rending, the fabric of a pre-war society, and yet ordering matters so that those who were clamouring for a fundamental change could think they were getting it: with such things looming in the background, a majority of the guests seemed to feel as those young people had felt who, in Byron's poem, danced at Brussels while Napoleon's cannon were drawing near. They did not avow it, of course; but it livened their blood to a quicker flow. When, out of these misgivings, a definite thought arose, they shrugged their shoulders. *Après nous le déluge.*

Not that there was any definite foreboding of what, looking

back from a later time, must be understood as having already that night lain within the potentialities of the situation. But every now and then, among those who did not follow the fireworks kindled by Charles Beatty, a feeling of obscure uneasiness provoked remarks about the undoubted loyalty of the police, proved by their conduct on this or that concrete occasion; about the equally undoubted efficiency of tanks and machine guns, those engines of war so recently released for the even more important task of defending, throughout the world, what was called civilization.

Maud, in doing her share, by smiles here and bows there, to keep up the pitch of frivolity, casually glanced at a vase which stood straight in front of her, filled with weirdly beautiful orchids. She knew exactly how they came to be there. Recently, accompanied by Miss Austin, she had casually stopped, in one of the conservatories, before an orchid in bloom which, from a slab of moist cork to which its root was fastened, had been hanging into the aisle. While exploring the structure of the flower, she had exclaimed in delight; and Miss Austin, note-pad in hand, had pencilled a quick reminder. These flowers, ordered by cable from Europe, though originally grown in India, were the direct result of an admiring word—at ten dollars a blossom; and there were a dozen of them.

At this moment, filled by the thought of the contrast between the present and a still recent past, when the expenditure of one hundredth of the amount spent on these flowers had been a serious matter, she became aware of the fact that Mr Birkinshaw was trying to catch her eye from her right. Around the board, the conversation was dividing again.

"When I was a student at Eastern University," Mr Birkinshaw said with a smile, "it was one day my privilege to be asked to a student's dinner at the president's house; and when, two hours ago, I had the honour of being presented to you, it was on the tip of my tongue to say that no introduction was needed; for I had held this great lady on my knees a quarter of a century ago."

Maud's face lighted up. Oddly, in the moment before she answered, she wondered whether Edmund had known of this when he placed the man at her side. "Really?" she exclaimed. "I was little more than a baby when my father died."

"At the time of which I am speaking you were not yet quite sure of your feet," he said, raising a gnarled hand from the table in deprecation. "I believe it was against your nurse's will that you toddled into the room. But already you were the beauty of the house of Fanshawe."

Both of them laughed. "And you must have been one of the beacon lights of the student body," Maud said. "For only such were ever asked to the house."

"I wonder. I was taking a post-graduate course, it is true; and I had just returned from Italy. It was chiefly his kindness which prompted your father. I was the eighth son of a poor country parson; and as an undergraduate I had worked my way. I had been lucky enough to secure the position of one of your father's amanuenses; as such I had been sent to Rome to collate a manuscript for him in the Vatican. Barring my parents themselves, I owe more to your father than to anyone else."

"How delightful of you tell me. I had no idea."

Maud saw her father-in-law bending forward to catch every word.

"And tonight," Mr Birkinshaw went on with an old-fashioned bow, "what a change! The butterfly has burst its chrysalis. At the time, your father's house stood for me as the height of splendour and worldly display." A motion of the gnarled hand embraced the table, the room, the house, and, by implication, the park surrounding it in the wintry night.

For an imperceptible moment Maud's lips curled in involuntary disdain, as if she were homesick for a simpler and sincerer past.

The arm of a footman filling a glass eclipsed her neighbour. She saw her father-in-law's eye straying to the prime minister who was also trying to listen. The intimacy of Maud's conversation with the radical leader to her right was attracting general attention. She glanced at her husband at the far end of the table, the central one of three; and she thought she detected the ghost of a smile on his handsome lips. No doubt this show of intimacy somehow fell in with his plans; for Maud knew, of course, that Miss Austin, left to herself, would have relegated Mr Birkinshaw among the small fry.

The footman's arm being withdrawn, Maud turned back to her neighbour. The presence of the Beattys seemed half explained; Edmund probably knew of the friendship which, in their youth, had joined these two men. Most likely Edmund's plan, whatever it was, had been served by a suggestion coming from Mr Beatty. Maud brushed aside a slight resentment at the fact that she and this stranger, no longer a stranger, were being used in some wider scheme.

Mr Birkinshaw's frail, bearded face suddenly lost its smile;

and he lowered his voice as he spoke. "You know, of course," he said, "that I have come to devote my life to the cause of the low and humble. Where there is oppression, injustice, undeserved suffering, I am sure to hear of it. I have come to stand, in this country, for social progress, for a readjustment of society on a more equitable basis, for what these people would call revolution. I don't quite know whether it is right for me to tell you what weighs on my mind. I should like one person in this gathering to share my misgivings. I have an idea that you are that person. If I said aloud, to those present, what I know about the situation, it would act like a bombshell. I cannot do that; it would cause a panic; and I should harm the very cause which I wish to further. I can't even tell whether it would be desirable for Sir Edmund to be told; I don't know him well enough to decide; though I do know that the popular view of him is almost certainly erroneous. Will you permit me to tell you? You are the only person I know who can say whether Sir Edmund is to be told or not. That was the reason why I accepted this invitation."

"Just a moment!" Maud said. She shrank from the touch of drama. If she accepted the confidence, without its being forced upon her, she made herself an actress in the play. "I don't know," she said irresolutely. But, reading in the weathered face of the man by her side such a burden of anxiety that she felt impelled to relieve it, she went on, quickly, "Yes. Do. Tell me."

But in the interval Mr Birkinshaw had grown pensive; once more he was weighing things. "I know a few cases," he said, "in which Sir Edmund has shown that he is not insensitive to individual distress. What is going on, tonght, on the Terrace at Langholm, will have its reverberations throughout the country. You may hear of a man by name of Arbuthnot. Perhaps you know of him?"

"No. I don't."

"He is a young Englishman, a writer of the proletarian school, the product of the London East-End slums. Since the war he had been living on the margin of starvation, drifting in and out of prisons on charges of vagrancy. How Sir Edmund heard of him here in Canada I don't know. In France, Arbuthnot had many times filled the gas tanks of Sir Edmund's plane for him. I do know that, a few months ago, Sir Edmund gave him a sinecure at Langholm, sending him up with a note to Captain Stevens. He has since been employed there, with plenty of leisure for writing; and he is in a fair way of making a name for himself. I know of another similar case; but I am in personal touch only with Arbuthnot. It is such things which make me think Sir Edmund is not generally understood. If I am right, something can perhaps be gained by letting him know in time."

Maud was impressed. This was a side of her husband which was new to her. "My husband," she said, "is certainly not in-human. Whatever he does is done with the ultimate welfare of mankind in view. If you will trust me to do what, under the circumstances, seems best to me, by all means, tell me."

Mr Birkinshaw nodded. "At this very hour, then, half the mill-hands at Langholm, all those who are not at work, are assembled in an open-air meeting on the Terrace. They are in revolt. Captain Stevens has just announced a severe cut in wages; and they are making demands which Mr Stevens will certainly refuse. I should like to be there to mediate; but I cannot go till the thing is a matter of public knowledge, at least not without betraying my secret informants. If Sir Edmund were willing to yield on even a small part of the men's de-mands, a strike, with the inevitable loss to him and the untold suffering to others, might still be averted. If not, it will be the hardest-fought industrial war in the history of this country. I happen to know that it will lead to sympathetic strikes else-where; possibly to a general strike. My sympathies are with the men; yet, if they can be pacified by partial concessions, I shall put forth every effort to effect a conciliation; and I have reason to think that my advice to the men would carry weight."

Maud was looking at her husband whose eyes, in turn, were fixed on the prime minister's face while he was carrying on an easy and detached conversation with the guests at his end of the table. If she told him, what would he answer? The mill was his; he could do as he pleased; he held control. Yet, could he? The word 'pleased' lost its meaning when a man considered himself as the tool of necessity. Whatever he did, he would not consider himself—as owners in Victorian days had done—as 'master in his own house'. In an argument with his father he had recently said, "These days, nobody is any longer master in his own house." Everybody, he had seemed to imply, was everybody else's neighbour in this contracted world; and every neighbour had or usurped the right to pry into everybody else's affairs. . . .

And suddenly the impact of the thing came home to her: here they were sitting in this resplendent room, brilliant figures around a brilliant board: their conversation veiled by soft

279

music; and there, at Langholm, the men were in meeting, out-side, standing on snow, in a night no doubt bitterly cold, a dark night, pierced only here and there by ineffectual street-lamps, a night probably windy....

She shivered.

As for Mr Birkinshaw, she suddenly, metaphorically, shrugged her shoulders. Like the millions, he lived in a world which did no longer exist: a world in which there had been masters and men. To her it seemed at that moment that such a world had been swept into limbo; both masters and men were now shackled; they were the slaves of a development equally enigmatic to both. To bring that situation about, the men had done as much as the masters; for whenever there had been a strike, the net result had been a new process which had eliminated the necessity for the employment of some of them. That new process had removed their own *raison d'être*; for men, so it seemed, were justified in their very existence only by the needs of the machines. The real antithesis, then, was between the machines and mankind.

But she turned back to Mr Birkinshaw as if she were merely continuing a casual conversation, so perfect was her command of voice and expression. "I am glad you told me. I shall try to see my husband tonight."

Mr Birkinshaw bowed, conveying by a gesture the necessity of his devoting himself to his partner, the wife of his one-time classmate and friend, who had sat there, between the labour leader preoccupied with his hostess and the senator preoccupied with his thought.

A few hours later, at the moment when the first of the week-end guests were either going upstairs or departing for the office building converted into a hotel, Maud managed to intercept her husband.

"Can you spare me a minute?" she asked.

"Certainly. Where shall we go?"

"Anywhere. Wherever we can't be overheard."

Sir Edmund led the way to a room behind the library, access-ible only from there and via a secret door from the service quarters. It was called a smoking-room but served for just such purposes as the present; for it had been carefully sound-proofed.

As soon as they were alone, she said, "Mr Birkinshaw was talking to me of the situation at Langholm. Who is Mr Arbuthnot?"

"Arbuthnot? One of the spies at the mill. The chief spy, in fact."

Maud showed her dismay. "I see. In that case it doesn't matter."

"What does not matter?" he asked, smiling with pleasure, for her expression was exactly that of the painting by Millais, a copy of which he had caused to be made and to be hung in the sitting-room upstairs at Clark House.

"About the discontent among the men. You probably know."

"I think I do. Naturally, I keep informed. It is most unlikely that Mr Birkinshaw could tell me what I don't know. What did he say?"

"The men are holding a meeting tonight."

"Half of them, to be exact."

"You are prepared?"

"I was prepared the moment Mr Rosenbaum signed over to me the former Cole holdings. I issued the necessary instructions at once."

"You chose the moment?"

"Within limits. *A la guerre comme à la guerre.*"

It sounded frivolous at that moment; but Maud divined that it was anything but that.

"It had to come," Sir Edmund went on. "It was in the air. What I did to set it off was no more than the spark that exploded the powder barrel. It might well have come when I was less thoroughly prepared. We announced a wage-cut last Monday . . . May I see you to your rooms?" he added suddenly; for Maud looked as she felt: in need of rest.

"I'll go up in a moment," she said. "May I let Mr Birkinshaw know?"

Edmund hesitated. Then he shrugged his shoulders. "I suppose so. It cannot matter one way or the other. Within a day or two it will be public knowledge."

Maud went to find the labour leader and led him to the library, now deserted.

Without preamble she came to the point. "This man you mentioned, Mr Arbuthnot, is the chief of the spies employed at the mill."

He stood thunderstruck. "No!" he cried.

"So my husband says. Beyond that I am afraid I cannot explain. I only know that the situation is vastly more complex than you think."

CHAPTER

XXIII

STILL holding Captain Stevens's manuscript on her lap, Lady Clark, in the sitting-room adjoining her suite, absently fastened her eyes on the Millais picture of Stella which resembled her as she had been when Edmund had smiled at her in the smoking-room at Arbala House.

Her mind wandered on.

It was the day following the dinner at which she had sat next to Mr Birkinshaw, a warm, springlike day, one of those which come before the final onset of winter and which, in Ontario, precede a high wind.

Edmund, for some reason or other, had made it a point to ask Maud, in a rapid whisper after luncheon, to sit in the veranda on the west side of the house, under the windows of library and smoking-room, if she would hear things of interest to her.

She went there and sat down in a wicker armchair which stood at right angles to the wall, below the windows which were open.

Those to her left opened from the billard room intervening between the library and the huge ballroom in the southwest corner of the house. She could hear the click of the balls as she sat there, and now and then even the voices of the players. Most of the guests had gone to lie down, for they faced a long and strenuous evening. Straight above her were the windows of the library, all of them closed; but to her right were those of the so-called smoking-room where, last night, she had had her brief interview with her husband. The near one was open.

There lay an air of drowsiness over the house. She herself was tired and tempted to close her eyes. But she was suddenly startled into attention, out of her reclining position, by the clear, sharp voice of her husband. No doubt he was standing close to, or at least facing the window. His voice sounded as it never sounded when he was speaking to her, though she had heard the identical note in remarks addressed to his father. It was his 'fate' voice as she called it to herself; the voice which betrayed that he was under a strain; as if he allowed something impersonal in him to speak through his mouth, something to which he was as much subject as anyone else; articulated in a manner which made it carry far without being raised.

What he said was perfectly commonplace. Apparently he was speaking to a footman. "Serve coffee here," he said. "For two. Bring some liqueurs, some whisky and brandy; and a siphon of soda. When Sir Arthur comes down, show him in here; close the library door and remain near it. We are not to be disturbed under any circumstances."

A few minutes later the footman announced Sir Arthur Cunningham.

There was a long pause. Then, coffee having been poured, Edmund's voice again. "What will you have?"

The prime minister mumbled a reply.

When, after two or three minutes, Edmund's voice came for the third time, it was startlingly distinct. He had apparently sat down.

"Now, Sir Arthur," he said as if merely continuing a previous conversation, "I want you to admit that this enquiry which certain members of your party propose to make into my purchase of Montreal Timber Limits is the merest election dodge. Mind you, I have nothing to fear from such an enquiry. But at this moment I do not choose to be in the limelight of hostile publicity; and you know as well as I do that all publicity which concerns itself with a leader in finance is hostile. It so happens that I have other fish to fry. As for the Timber Limits, I employed your own methods. I did what any business man in my position and with my information would have done. That you were planning to take over the Interoceanic, as a concession to the demand for public ownership of public utilities, was none of my concern. I knew, as anyone would have known, that the Montreal real estate holdings of the Timber Limits were indispensable to your plan. The directorate of that defunct concern did not know that plan. So I bought those holdings, and all the rest, for a song; and I shall sell them to the road, or to the government, which, in the light of your commitments, comes to the same thing, for what they are worth to the road, namely, thirty millions. Whether you do or do not care to divulge the irrelevant fact that these thirty millions go into my pocket leaves me entirely indifferent. But . . ."

Maud felt tense. It was the first time she had heard her husband in action. Instinctively she would have preferred to withdraw. But, for one thing, he had as much as asked her to listen in; for another, she felt it to be imperative that she should see him as, very likely, he appeared to the public eye; in that eye, he necessarily appeared as he chose to show himself. . . .

But the prime minister was speaking. She had to listen intently in order to understand his low, mumbling voice.

"The proposed enquiry," he said, "is to concern itself with one single question: How did the news of the contemplated building of the new terminus and the necessary re-routing of its approaches leak out? It is not to be an enquiry into your business methods. Everybody knows that they are beyond reproach. It is to be an enquiry directed—if such an enquiry is ever directed against anyone—not against you, but against the person or persons unknown who must have been sitting on the directorate of the railway, unless, indeed, they are to be presumed to be members of my cabinet. I repeat, it is not to be directed against you or anyone connected with you."

Edmund laughed briefly and scornfully. "You know that, in such an enquiry, you cannot keep me out. What you *don't* know is that I have taken good care not to be drawn in."

"Personally," the prime minister said in a newly confidential tone, "I *should* like to know who tipped you off."

Again Edmund laughed. Then, changing his tone for a moment, he conceded, "No doubt. But I give you my word of honour, as a man and an officer, that my information did not come directly from anyone connected with the railway or with your administration. You must remember that the federal government is not the only body in this country which has a secret service at its disposal. I could prove to you that, at a vastly lower cost, I maintain a more efficient service than you will ever have."

"I don't doubt it. Yet, when all is said and done, the information must have originated in one of the two inner circles concerned."

"Perhaps. But I am no tyro at the game. Suppose you proceed. Sooner or later you must put me in the witness stand. I have taken good care that, from that moment on, you would find yourself involved in devious underground passages which would bring you no nearer to the fountainhead. I am speaking quite literally. Underground, I say. Do you know where your enquiry would willy-nilly come to an end if it were pursued?"

"I'd be curious."

"In a grave on the Pacific Coast."

"You don't say so," the other man gasped. "Well, for your age, Sir Edmund, you are the most extraordinary politician I know of."

"Yet, Sir Arthur," Edmund said almost slyly, "I did not employ thugs; nor did I set aside the law as your administration has been known to do."

It was the prime minister's turn to emit a rumbling laugh. Then, "All the more. If it is so easy to bring the enquiry to an end, in a grave, as you say, by that time it would have served all *our* purposes—why object to it?"

"For a number of reasons. One I have told you. I do not care, in fact, I cannot afford to become involved at the present moment. I will give you another. If I were put under oath—which, I assure you, will not happen—the last link in the chain of hands, or minds, through which the secret passed was . . . a woman whom I do not care to hear mentioned in this connection."

The other man, making no doubt wild guesses at the identity of that woman, whistled through his teeth.

Maud felt hot and cold waves running up and down her spine. From the first word of her husband's last utterance she had anticipated what was coming; yet, when it came, it came as a shock. Was that man up there, the prime minister, in his rapid casting about for the right name, thinking of her? Or of Miss Dolittle perhaps? The whole thing had, in a flash, crystallized in her own mind into certainty: the woman alluded to was herself.

On the occasion of her last brief stay at Langholm where Edmund was to follow her shortly, a mysterious stranger calling himself Horatio White had asked, first for her husband, then for her. Being received, he had told her that he had a message for Sir Edmund which he could, on the one hand, not wait to deliver personally; and which, on the other, he could not entrust to anyone but her. The message as given to her had consisted of a series of disconnected numbers and letters—in other words, it had been in code. Horatio White, an elderly, very gentlemanly person, had asked her to take it down in writing, warning her that the paper must not fall into anyone's hand. And then this Mr White, who was visibly ill, had gone on to Vancouver, there to die of pneumonia.

"But even that," the prime minister proceeded after a considerable pause, "does not convince me of the necessity of dropping our most effective election weapon which our opponents are sure to use if we don't. We are not a popular bunch just now. At the best it will be touch-and-go. I suspect that even you would let the progressives have a try, if only to give them an opportunity to show their inability to cope with the situation; I infer as much from the presence, here, of that fellow Birkinshaw. And don't think for a moment that I am asking you to agree to the enquiry for nothing. When we ride back into power, you have my word that we shall give you a free hand with regard to those Lachine developments . . . the moment that enquiry ends in . . . that grave.'"

"You seem to be asking for it," Sir Edmund said wearily. "If you don't see it yet, you will see in a moment that your re-election will have to stand on its merits. One more attempt before I say what I would rather not say. I am prepared to back you with party funds. You may count on me for, let me say, half a million . . . no, make it a million."

"Thank you, sir, thank you. Don't forget that I must leave transactions of that nature to my lieutenants . . . But . . .'"

"But!" The word sounded like an explosion. "You are forcing my hand, sir! Very well. Let me prove to you that I was right when I said that I am no tyro at this game. If the enquiry proceeds and I am to be put on the witness stand, I shall keep my hands clean. No campaign contribution from me! It would be money wasted. Suppose you were elected, even with the help of funds supplied by myself, you would not remain in power for a week. The situation is not exactly what you think it is. Tell me, before you leave this room, that you are determined to go on with what you have started, and I shall place tonight in Mr Birkinshaw's hands documentary proof that, ex-post-facto, two of your colleagues have been involved in the deal. They did not furnish me with any information. Any information they could have given I did not need. But I bought their support in killing the enquiry. They have taken their share of the loot in advance and have been licking their fingers for more ever since. I have letters from them which contain what amounts to blackmail in the definition of the law. Who, then, will believe that it was not they, or indeed, indirectly, you yourself, who supplied my information? Who, at least, that they did not do so with your full knowledge and connivance? I, certainly, shall not contradict; I shall keep silent; and nobody else's word would be accepted. Imagine yourself facing an already divided House. Imagine Mr Birkinshaw rising and, in his well-known, quiet, gentle, but highly effective way, raising this question to your face, proof in hand. Your colleagues, guilty or innocent, will bolt; the guilty will not stop till they have placed the sea or the international border between their backs and the storm. They will leave it to you to do the resigning.

"There, sir, you have my ultimatum. Take what time you need to think it over, five minutes or five hours. But you know me well enough not to doubt that I mean what I say."

Maud's hands were gripping the arms of her chair.

Several seconds went by in a dead silence; then the prime minister's voice, weary, hoarse, barely audible, "You win, Sir Edmund."

"You call the enquiry off?"

"I call it off."

Edmund's voice was half pitying, half ironic. "No hard feelings?"

A chair scraped over the floor. "No hard feelings, no. It's all in the game. But I think I am entitled to the names of the two whom you mention."

Edmund laughed. "Their names you can get only if the enquiry proceeds, from Mr Birkinshaw, in the House. Since they helped me to defeat you, I cannot very well betray them, can I?"

"You have my profound admiration," Sir Arthur said. "Will you take a seat in my cabinet?"

Again Edmund laughed. "I will go so far as to tell you why I cannot accept. I am on the point of launching an experiment in government myself. Oh, strictly, for the moment, a state within the State; don't be alarmed. A state based on social and economic realities instead of on political jugglings which have long since become meaningless. With only one master, one god: the machine. Ultimately we shall have to replace the present political structure which, you will admit, is creaking in its joints; but it will take decades and may take centuries to put the new system into effect. There may be civil war before we have done. There will certainly be a period of transition in which one man, presumably I, will have to assume the most absolute power, as a dictator in the Roman, not the mid-European sense. It was for that reason that I gathered all those millions in my hand. When *you* want money, you can tax the people; they think you are representing them. I play a lone hand, representing nothing but the future. I can levy taxes only indirectly, by the methods which the old order has invented and which it calls profits. That is why I have to start within the established order, playing my hand under cover. When, in my own mills, the break comes, I shall even call upon you to maintain law and order; and I know you will not be found wanting. That is as much as I care to say for the moment. In any case, believe me, if you care to hold on somewhat longer, you have chosen wisely. Let me know when the party is in need of funds. . . ."

That was all. A moment later, a door was opened and shut. Somehow Maud, on the veranda outside, was aware of the fact that the interview had completely exhausted her husband.

On account of the great dance to follow that night, dinner was served early, at half-past seven. In spite of the fact that Maud had spent the late afternoon in her rooms, indisposed, she presided. She looked snow-white : her shoulders, arms, and face. Within a few hours, she had inwardly matured by years. She had seen how matters were done. She looked like a woman with a past, in the usual sense.

Edmund, at the opposite end of the central table, sat equally stern, a frown between his eyebrows. Husband and wife had not met since noon. But both knew that the experience of the afternoon had been crucial : both asked themselves whether the woman in the case, namely, she, Maud, had been lost or won. Her response to his next step would supply the answer.

Apart from these two and perhaps the prime minister, the men and women around the boards were unchanged. Charles Beatty exerted himself to keep the conversation at an un-flagging level of gaiety. Yet his very concentration on the task betrayed that he knew what had happened.

Nothing extraordinary occurred during the meal till to-wards its end; and what occurred then attracted no general attention. Sir Arthur Cunningham, again her partner, tried hard to be pleasant to Maud.

Then, observed by only two of the guests, Senator Clark and Charles Beatty, an inconspicuous by-play took place.

A footman, coming from the hall, circled the tables and finally bent down to Sir Edmund to whisper to him. Edmund, leaning back, better to catch his words, looked up at him and spoke a few rapid words.

The man disappeared, walking hurriedly; and within a minute another footman came in and approached the master of the house with pad and pencil. Sir Edmund scribbled a few lines. Tearing off the slip of paper and folding it, he handed it to the servant with a brief direction. Having done so, he ex-changed a quick glance with Charles Beatty.

The footman brought the note to Maud.

She, having read it, with all the appearance of an utter casualness, tore the note to bits, acting mechanically, and deposited them on her plate, laughing at something Sir Arthur had said. To the waiting servant she gave two words. That was all the two watchers observed. It was enough. There was going to be a crisis of some sort.

The two words—"No answer"—had decided that she was going to go on co-operating with her husband.

It was a quarter-past nine when they rose from table; and for over an hour, after that, Maud took her stand in the hall, near the outer doors, receiving, while a footman announced name after name, an overwhelming majority of the new arrivals, invited only for the dance, being young people.

Yet there were a few who were older. Among these was Homer Wainwright, huge, flabby, bottle-shaped, his head resembling that of the late King Edward. He was the editor-in-chief of the most important financial weekly in the Dominion.

Maud welcomed all with a somewhat absent and entirely stereotyped smile.

Her father-in-law she saw strolling about through the crush, feeling excluded.

Suddenly, about half-past ten, that crush, in hall, library, and drawing-rooms, becoming unbearable, the doors to the huge ballroom were slipped back; and a magnificent orchestra, with a clash of cymbals subduing the sounds of laughter and conversation, sent forth the giddy strains of a waltz by Strauss. Maud was gratefully conscious of the refreshingly cool air from the ballroom sweeping through the hall. This night, she wore a very low gown of gold-coloured brocade.

As if awaking, she suddenly saw Edmund bowing to her; and she gave him her arm. Under a general hush host and hostess entered the ballroom, the crowd falling back to form a lane through which to follow them, as they led the dance, in a rush of rapid pairings-off.

Led by Edmund and Maud, the crowd surged forward, whirling, and, in the space of a minute, filled the huge room in eddy after eddy to its farthest corners. Senator Clark stood by the door.

Maud and Edmund were partners worthy of each other. But in the light of what Edmund had communicated to her in his note, they could not indulge very long. When, after their first round, they returned to the door, they stopped. Maud knew that, from this moment on, she must act a definite, perhaps decisive part in the drama. Edmund disappeared in the crowd.

As if to make sure of some sort of support, Maud took her father-in-law's arm and drew him into the hall.

She was aware of his consternation when they both saw Mr Cole coming down the ceremonial stairway: Mr Cole of Winnipeg, the dispossessed holder of shares in the mill.

The senator tried to turn to avoid him. But already the new arrival, conspicuous in brown tweeds, had seen them. He was red in the face and unmistakably angry. The peculiar structure of his torso, with two humps, one on his chest, one on his shoulder blades, was accentuated by the grim determination with which he drew down his head.

All about, a be-starred and be-ribboned crowd was standing or moving about in groups.

Coming up to them, Mr Cole spoke to the senator in a tone not usually to be heard in polite society. "I want to see Sir Edmund or that fellow Rosenbaum. Know where to find either, Clark?"

"Mr Rosenbaum," said the senator propitiatingly, "is not present. He left a week ago, for the Pacific coast, I believe. As for my son, I'll try to locate him. Where will you be?"

"I'll go to the library," Mr Cole replied, looking about and nodding towards the open door of that room. His bullet-shaped head, squatting without the transition of a neck on his broad shoulders, resembled a football balanced on a five-foot post, waiting to be kicked off by some giant.

Maud and the senator drifted back through the throng in the hall as if looking for Edmund; Maud, being in the secret, knew that they would not find him. They stopped in the wide doors to the ballroom and let the dancers whirl past them. There was no sign of Edmund. To their surprise, they saw, coming from the opposite end of the room, the huge French *Chargé* in an almost intimate exchange of civilities with Mr Birkinshaw, followed by His everlastingly-smiling Excellency Mr Wong Lee, his white shirt front almost hidden under a diagonal purple ribbon nine inches wide. Without seeming to do so, Maud watched them till, via the hall, they had casually entered the library. She waited for another round to go by before she spoke to the senator who, though not yet quite seventy, looked like a tired and very old man.

Then she said, "Father, I want you to help me. I have been asked to steer Mr Cole into the library; fortunately he went there of his own accord; and to keep him there till Mr Beatty can take him in hand. Unless we want to risk a public *éclat*, it is imperative that Mr Cole should not meet Edmund. I don't know myself what is behind it all; Edmund sent me a note with the request. I understand Mr Beatty is to deal with the intruder and get him out of the way. Please help me. . . ."

"Of course," the senator said and repeated, "of course."

Together they made for the library where a number of groups were being served with wines and liqueurs. All of them were men.

They did not see Mr Cole. But near the door Mr Birkinshaw stood, bowing, alone now. A moment later he joined them.

Near the door, too, Charles Beatty was speaking to Homer Wainwright, the editor of the financial weekly. Mr Beatty, standing beside him, was looking up at him, pipe in hand.

Everyone of those present was well known in the world of finance, business, or government. But Mr Birkinshaw, incomprehensibly again in the company of the hostess, caused a wave of tension to run through the room wherever he moved, as if he must be presumed to be carrying a bomb.

Mr Beatty looked at Maud with a brief, knowing glance as, sideways, he edged still closer to Homer Wainwright, laughing like a boy bubbling over with mischief, and twitching his elbow as he nudged him. In the sudden silence that followed Maud's entrance, his words, though spoken at an ordinary pitch, were audible throughout the room with startling distinctness, in spite of the fact that the strains of the music softly pervaded the whole of the lower floor of the house.

"Whenever I see you, Homer," he said, referring to his resemblance to King Edward VII, "I am struck with wonder. By what means do you achieve that majestic bearing? I am positively at a loss how to address you without using forms proper only to royalty."

The laughter with which this sally was greeted—for everybody knew the peculiar vanity of the man—was tinged with respect. Homer Wainwright himself shook faintly with laughter, visibly flattered. Thus, in a new world, the power of verbal expression is honoured when it is used for the formulation of market trends.

Meanwhile Maud, the senator, and Mr Birkinshaw were moving on; and suddenly, in a group of which the prime minister formed a part, they saw Mr Cole. Even he, it was clear, was conscious of the tension which crystallized around the three who were approaching and propagated itself along the line of their progress. It looked as though, having been absent-mindedly immersed in his resentment, he were becoming morosely attentive, handing his empty glass to a passing footman.

Everybody falling back, to make room for Lady Clark, the group opened up; and this, the senator retarding his step, made the impression as if, like the actors in a Greek drama, Maud, Mr Cole, and Mr Birkinshaw were isolated on the stage, to the choral accompaniment of the music filling the house. Meanwhile, through the wings, Charles Beatty was making his entrance, moving rapidly to take part in the scene, impersonating the *deus ex machina*.

Visibly, the dwarf-like Mr Cole was divided between an attraction and a repulsion. By looking knowingly from one to the other, everybody seemed to betray his awareness of the fact that the sight of Mr Birkinshaw was to Mr Cole what the proverbial red rag is to the bull. That he had to meet this man under the eyes of the hostess he attributed to a deeply laid design; and from his face Maud and others were conscious of this. Maud wondered to just what extent the suspicion was justified. The difficulty of the part she was to play in the drama lay in the fact that there was none to prompt the lines she was expected to say; nor anyone to tell her on what cue to say them. Mr Cole who, in the hall, had seemed to be hardly aware of her presence, bowed stiffly as she regretted that he had been late for dinner.

"By the way," she added in entire innocence, "I don't know whether you have met Mr Birkinshaw . . . Mr Cole."

Mr Birkinshaw bowed, smiling and unruffled. "We come from the same city, Lady Clark."

Mr Cole's acknowledgment was stiff and wordless.

Having fulfilled her instructions to the letter, Maud moved on with her double escort; but for a few minutes longer she remained, willy-nilly, within earshot, for other guests spoke to her.

Mr Cole singled out the silent, louring prime minister for what he intended to be his only and scathing comment on the interlude, saying scornfully, at the very moment when Charles Beatty joined the group, "I must say, Sir Arthur, your people don't show a great deal of discrimination in picking their victims when somebody is to be sacrificed to the public thirst for blood. You deport, after imprisoning for seditious libel, a poor little Finn editor who does not know what he is saying; but this man who is really dangerous you do not touch."

Sir Arthur gave a sardonic laugh. "We can't deport born

Canadians," he said. "Where should we deport them? Besides, are you aware, Mr Cole, that Mr Birkinshaw is the chosen representative of a not inconsiderable fraction of the electorate of your city? To touch him might precipitate undesirable things. Of what should I accuse him?"

"Indict him on a charge of high treason," Mr Cole exclaimed, his temper running away with his caution. "Head off! That is the only treatment for such as him."

Instantly Charles Beatty was tensely on the alert; he saw the sort of opening which he needed. Since his manner, introductory to one of his major performances, was well known to all who were present, a hush fell; and everybody listened.

Charles Beatty laughed, puffing his chest with angular jerks of his elbow; and he raised the right hand which clasped the bowl of his pipe like a baton. He was still incubating the plan of attack; he had to gain a few moments' time. All his witticisms had a literary origin; they derived from the vast store of anecdote garnered for just such purposes in the course of a lifetime of reading and stowed away in his capacious memory.

"Suppose," he said, sending the word forth like a bugle-call, "Sir Arthur acted on your most excellent advice, Mr Cole."

He paused to give the snigger that went round the assembly time to subside. Evidently he was concerned not to let a word go to waste.

"And further, Mr Cole, suppose that, in the fullness of time, you and I died in our beds, on the same day, stricken perhaps by some pestilence. I include myself only from a desire to be present. And together we travelled to Hades to join Mr Birkinshaw."

Again he paused to let the snigger die away. By this time the desire not to lose a word was general.

"Suppose further that Charon, receiving his obolos, had rowed us across the Stygian River; and that there, on the far shore of the shady realm, stood Mr Birkinshaw, having heard of our demise, to receive us—or rather Mr Birkinshaw's ghost. I seem to see him bowing to us and speaking in his urbane and mellifluous voice. 'Welcome, gentlemen,' he would say, 'a thousand times welcome on our bloodless shores!' And, since death cancels all animosities, I imagine you or your ghost, Mr Cole, as replying, 'Thanks, Birkinshaw, very good of you, I am sure'; and as adding, with a reminiscent touch of ancient malice, 'But tell me whether a report I heard some time ago, when I was still up there, spoke truth. It stated that, for once in your life, you had, in an encounter with Sir Arthur, lost your head.'"

For the third time Charles Beatty paused. He knew that by this time he was holding his audience as in a vice; and slowly he glanced from one laughing face to the other till his eye came to rest on the prime minister's sombre and condemnatory impassivity. Then, again, he raised the hand clasping the bowl of his pipe; and, emphasizing every word, he went on.

"Birkinshaw, with that conciliatory grace for which he is famous among those who know him, not as a member of the House, but as a man, would bow to you; and with a pleasant smile he would say, 'The report spoke true, Mr Cole. I did lose my head. But I have no doubt you will agree with me when I say, It is better to have had a head and lost it than never to have had a head at all.'"

The burst of laughter which followed died away abruptly when it was realized how black Mr Cole looked. From the fleshy lips behind the white moustache came something like a snarl. "Look here, Beatty . . ." He veered on the lawyer who showed signs of strain. "I came to see Sir Edmund, not to listen to buffooneries. He is keeping out of my way, it seems. Am I going to see him?"

"You must ask him, not me," Mr Beatty replied. "As far as I know he is a free agent."

"Very well. Then I know where I'm at. Don't think for a moment I don't see that you are here for the express purpose of preventing me from looking for him. You saw that?" he added, drawing a newspaper clipping from his vest pocket and presenting it to the lawyer.

"'It is announced,'" the latter read aloud, "'that the Langholm Flour Milling Company, together with the affiliated Western Flour Mills, once a company with limited liability, has become a closed corporation through the acquisition, by Sir Edmund Clark, of the former so-called Cole holdings.' Where did you find that?" he asked somewhat sharply.

"Winnipeg Labour Gazette."

Once more a hush fell. Everybody realized that here was a new, imperative call for the exertion of Mr Beatty's powers.

"Who," he asked, "do you insinuate put it there?"

"Who but Birkinshaw? It's his paper, isn't it?"

Charles Beatty, as if dropping a mask, flashed a glance at Mr Cole which held the edge of a dagger. When he spoke, his so far carefully-controlled and urbane voice gave the first intimation that, in case of need, he, too, could snarl like a tiger. "Even if Mr Birkinshaw had got hold of such a piece of confidential information," he said, "so long as it is not officially announced, and so long as it has no bearing on the activities of a government which he opposes, he would respect its confidential nature."

"In his place," Mr Cole blurted out, "I shouldn't."

Again Mr Beatty instantly saw his opening. "Mr Cole," he said, administering his matador's stroke with merciless precision, "please remember, it was you, not I, who said that." And, looking about at the sobered faces, he added slowly, "I think there remains only one thing to say. The difference between you and the labour leader is that Mr Birkinshaw is a gentleman."

Mr Cole, almost staggered by the crudity of the blow, looked from face to face; and, finding all of them closed against him, he turned and left the room.

Maud, the senator, and Mr Birkinshaw preceded him and quickly went through the hall to the doors of the ballroom; for, divining that the proceedings in that group were bound to take an ugly turn, they had cut short their round among the guests. But the blow had fallen before they could reach the door.

Twenty minutes later, in a sudden impulse of premonition, Maud returned into the hall, this time alone; and there she saw Mr Cole leaving the house, a footman carrying his bag behind him.

As her eye followed that stocky figure vanishing through the vestibule, it alighted, in a corner by the doors, on an insignificant little man in a shabby ulster. What struck her most was the intense hostility of his look as it swept the hall thronged with guests.

A footman approached her. "Pardon me, your ladyship," he said. "I have tried in vain to find Sir Edmund. There is a man here who says he must see him at once."

Maud hesitated. She felt exhausted. With a sinking feeling in her heart she asked herself whether the climax to the dramatic day was approaching. Then she nodded. "I shall try to find Sir Edmund. What is the name?"

"He gives his name as Arbuthnot; he says he has a message from Captain Stevens."

Maud quickly turned away.

CHAPTER

XXIV

As she sat in her living-room, Captain Stevens's manuscript still on her knees, Maud seemed to feel again that profound weariness with which, in the midst of that frivolous crowd, she had set out on her search. She thought at once of the room behind the library where Edmund's talk with Sir Arthur had taken place. But the library was crowded with guests talking and laughing, smoking and drinking. She knew of the secret door leading into the room from the service corridor; but, in order to find it, she would have to enlist the help of a servant.

She went to the dining-room where, as she knew, the late buffet supper was being laid. The room was swarming with hurrying servants. She beckoned to a parlour maid who dropped a handful of silver on the nearest of the little tables which had replaced the great boards.

"You know the service door to the smoking-room?" she asked.

"This way, your ladyship," said the maid, preceding her.

She entered the room, which was empty, apart from her husband who stood by one of the windows, alone, a foot raised to the shelf above a radiator, in an attitude of meditation.

On hearing her rapid footfall, he turned; and, as usual, his eye lighted up.

Without preamble she said, "Mr Arbuthnot has just arrived."

"Where is he?" he asked, electrified, pushing an armchair into place for her.

"In the vestibule."

"I must see him at once." And he turned away.

Maud, forestalling him, returned to the door and, through the service corridor, into the hall where she gave the necessary instructions to a footman. Then she returned, in the same way, to the smoking-room and sat down.

When, a minute or two later, the little man entered, unannounced, according to her directions, she scanned him across the room. He was unprepossessing to a degree, both on account of the extreme lateral compression of his head and, when he opened his mouth, on account of his black, pointed teeth.

Maud being the first person he saw, he bowed jerkily.

From the window, Edmund said, "Hello."

"Hello."

"You may speak before Lady Clark," Edmund said, not unkindly.

"All right. The men resolved last night to walk out. All work will stop at the mill on Sunday at midnight."

Sir Edmund, his foot again raised to the shelf, had listened in silence. Then, in clear, unmoved accents, "How did you get here?"

"Captain Stevens summoned a government plane from the ranger's station. It took me to Toronto. From there I have come by taxi."

"I see. You've had a bite to eat?"

"Not since morning."

"All right. We'll look after you. Tomorrow at midnight?"

"Yes."

Edmund went to the door and pushed a button. A footman entered.

"Find Miss Austin and ask her to be good enough to step in here. And see to it that Mr Arbuthnot gets his supper."

"Just a moment," said Mr Arbuthnot. "I have a word to say."

Sir Edmund nodded to the footman. "Do as I told you. Mr Arbuthnot will report when he is ready."

The footman withdrew. Sir Edmund faced the little man. "Well?"

"This," said the latter, frowning under the strain of keeping himself in hand, "is the last time I have done any of your d . . . work." The epithet was suppressed with a quick glance at Lady Clark. "I consider I have paid for what you've done for me."

Sir Edmund remained unruffled. "Quite right," he said easily. "What I've done for you is nothing. Your sympathies are very naturally with the men."

"The worst of this accursed system," Arbuthnot said explosively, "is that, for the sake of money, one has to do what one would despise any other for doing."

"It is," Sir Edmund agreed blandly. "It vitiates character."

Maud winced.

But Sir Edmund went on. "You've been writing out there?"

"I've written a novel dealing with the mill."

"I hope it is good. It may be a document for future ages."

At this moment the door was opened, and Miss Austin entered, fresh, alert, ready to serve.

"Miss Austin," Sir Edmund said, "will you be good enough to work out, in a hurry, some schedule whereby I can catch the train going west which must have left Toronto an hour or two ago?"

Maud rose. "May I come?" she asked, adding under her breath, "Please!"

Edmund looked at her, absently; then, as if her voice were reaching him only now, "Certainly; if you wish." Once more he turned to Miss Austin. "This party will proceed of its own momentum. Not a word to anyone but my father . . ."

"And Mr Birkinshaw," Maud pleaded.

"And Mr Birkinshaw. And please ask Sir Arthur to join me here for a moment. Have three cars pull up at the service entrance; Sir Arthur's among them. We shall slip away unnoticed." He looked at Arbuthnot. "You mean to stay?"

"I'd like to go back to Langholm if I can."

"Get something to eat and wait at the service entrance. The car with the Japanese driver. You can sit with him in the cab."

Miss Austin slipped from the room. Maud followed her, to run upstairs.

Half an hour later, Maud having been notified that all arrangements were completed—the train being ordered to wait for the party at some northern station, while a private coach was being rushed after it from Toronto—Maud stepped out on the small platform in the northwest corner of the house whence a flight of steps led down to a driveway. She had changed into travelling clothes.

In order not to make this furtive departure conspicuous, no lights had been switched on; and Maud stopped in the door to allow her eyes to adjust themselves to the dim radiance which suffused the atmosphere from a single bulb in the veranda, the only one burning on that side of the house. Rounded masses of shrubbery and clusters of low pines and cedars, resembling dark clouds, arrested and dimly reflected, from beyond the driveway, such light as came from the open but curtained windows above. Not one of the three cars showed any light, though their engines were purring.

Yet, the moment she issued through the door, Maud was aware that the little platform and the steps leading down from it were crowded with figures. It was some time before she made out who these silhouettes were.

There was the imposing bulk of the prime minister in his ulster, the slender Mr Birkinshaw, and the stunted Mr Arbuthnot. On the steps stood coated chauffeurs and footmen, waiting.

Among the groups of the latter a tiny vest-pocket flashlight, shaded by a hand, illuminated, for the fraction of a second, the dial of a watch. Above it, the reflected rays betrayed Ito's profile.

Apparently Mr Arbuthnot had also recognized the oriental face, for he descended the steps and spoke to the man in a whisper. A moment later he took his seat in the cab of the leading car.

Behind Maud's back the door opened; and she stepped aside. Her eyes being, by this time, adjusted to the dim light, she recognized her father-in-law. Mr Birkinshaw promptly came over.

"Going west?" he asked.

"Yes. Are you?"

"No. I am going east, to Ottawa, with the Right Honourable who, as a consequence of developments, has suddenly found me indispensable. Will you be good enough to deliver a message to your son—just in case I get no chance to speak to him myself? It is this. If I can be of any use in mediating between him and the men, I shall be glad to start west at a moment's notice. My chief reason for giving in to the prime minister's request to go with him to Ottawa first is my desire to prevent provocative measures from being taken. Sir Arthur is upset; he wants to see Sir Edmund once more before he leaves. He considers this strike as a national crisis; and it may well be just that. It may sweep him and us all out of focus."

The senator coughed angrily; but he said nothing.

Again the door opened, this time behind the senator who had not yet moved. A female voice said, "Excuse me, please"; and Maud recognized it as that of her maid Vera who was carrying a handbag.

Maud stepped forward and touched her arm. The men on the steps, recognizing the mistress of the house only now, made room; and a footman, at sound of the female voice, came to relieve the maid of her bag.

Simultaneously, Ito, the Japanese chauffeur, said, "This way, please."

And the two women followed him to the car.

Maud had not yet entered the tonneau when the door to the platform opened a last time; and Sir Edmund appeared briskly, followed by a valet with his suitcase.

The man at once preceded his master to deposit the baggage in the cab of the second car which, apparently, was reserved for the senator and some of the servants. Maud's maid had followed her.

Edmund, still moving briskly, made out the silhouette of the prime minister and joined him at the southern end of the platform; while inserting herself in the tonneau, Maud became aware of them as they moved towards her, along the driveway, engaged in a rapid exchange of words. It had turned cold; and fine snow was beginning to sift down through the still motionless air. In the heavens above, mysterious movements were shifting equilibria.

For a moment there was, in front of the steps, a confused and rapid coming and going of servants and chauffeurs.

Then, a hush having fallen, Sir Arthur's rumbling voice was heard. "That you, Birk? Better get in. Last car."

Edmund and Sir Arthur, having taken a turn, came forward again, Edmund still speaking rapidly. "No," he was saying when he came into earshot; "it's past praying for, Sir Arthur. This is one of the decisive battles of the world, small as the opposing forces are. Do as I told you, and you'll be safe. The main thing is to overawe them for a day or two. We must at all cost prevent destruction. Too bad the House isn't in session, or I'd advise you to ask for a blank cheque. It's been done before. Better stop public works. You'll need the money before you get through."

"Well . . ." Sir Arthur said grudgingly. "I'll have to do what I can, I suppose."

"Right. Remember, the battle front of the whole present order is at Langholm."

On that, with a low laugh, the two men parted.

Edmund went around to the left side of the car where a footman was holding the door for him. Then, one foot on the running board, he called out in his clear subdued voice, "All set?"

"All set," came the answer from the prime minister.

"Go, then." And Sir Edmund quickly entered the tonneau, sitting down by his wife's side, with Vera in front of them.

Smoothly and silently the cars slipped forward through the dark. They had to circle the house; and not till they were behind it were the headlights switched on. Huge windows to their right permitted a view into the snow-white kitchens where white-frocked men were flitting about, preparing the supper.

Under the thinnest possible film of snow the grounds looked ghostly.

Having rounded the great house, the cars, gathering speed, turned into the main driveway towards the gate to the paved highway in front. The moment they did so, the vast park, leaping fitfully into visibility, as the wheeling headlights brushed over it, seemed filled, like a bowl, with the painfully-sensuous strains of a saxophone solo which came down through half-open if deeply curtained windows from the ballroom above.

On the highway, the two leading cars turned west; Sir Arthur's east. From the window of the latter a lazy hand waved a farewell.

Again the two cars turned, slowing sharply, this time north.

Within twenty minutes they came in sight of the Arbala Mill, standing across the valley like a sentinel, snow-white, flood-lighted like the mill at Langholm, silently grinding out flour, indifferent to merely human excitements. Compared with the mental picture of the colossus at Langholm which everybody carried about with him, it seemed strangely small; but it, too, partook of that inexorable expression which was characteristic of its parent structure.

Swerving west and rising steeply, the road skirted the lake above the mill; and the white apparition disappeared behind dense trees as if it had never been.

The cars settled down to their steady pace of sixty miles an hour.

Having climbed hills and plunged headlong into absolutely black valleys, the snow coming thicker and thicker, they reached, around four o'clock in the morning, now in a driving blizzard, the small forest village in the wilderness where the train was being held for them. Ordinarily no through trains stopped at this wayside station.

The conductor, watch in hand, was pacing the platform and hurriedly led the whole party to the last coach which had been rushed up from Toronto.

Edmund had hardly led Maud to her 'drawing-room' when the whistle blew, and, with a jerk and a clashing of couplings, the train began to nose its way into the wintry night, bound on its task of making up for four hours lost.

The scene, having impressed her deeply at the time, came back to Lady Clark with startling distinctness; and she shivered as she had shivered in boarding the train.

The next day was Sunday; everybody in the private car of the train was late in rising. Outside, the storm had taken on the dimensions of a snow-laden gale.

But Maud had hardly dismissed her maid after dressing when Edmund knocked at her door.

She was in a peculiar mood which was very rare with her, accustomed as she was to preserve her even temper. She was half angry with her husband, half with herself. Everything seemed doubtful, above all the wisdom and the moral worth of that husband. The day before, she had done things for the sake of what is called 'business'; and all business had, to her, a doubtful flavour. What she had heard and witnessed was not calculated to dispel her doubts. Moreover she felt that, whatever she had done, she had done badly; others, more deeply versed in affairs, would have done it better. The dilemma in which she had been became clear only now. Either she should have refrained from taking part in the drama which had been enacted; or she should have surrendered herself to her task and done it with gusto. Instead she had done what she had been asked to do, looking upon it with critical eyes; had done it half condemning herself even at the time. She could have wept with vexation at herself.

But worse! Underlying this, there was another thing. Short of despising her husband, she could do only one other thing, namely, admire him; admire the unshrinking logic with which he pursued his plan of changing the social structure of the country, thereby, perhaps, making history. She even concluded that she, with her old-fashioned hesitancies before great and decisive issues, was not the proper sort of wife for a man like Edmund; he should have had Lady Macbeth for his wife.

And then it came out.

Lady Macbeth? How about Miss Dolittle? The very thought made her despise herself. For at the unrevealed, subconscious kernel of her being there was suddenly the suspicion that the confusion of her feelings rested on another passion which she considered as beneath her: jealousy.

She fought against it; but the state of her nerves was such that she fought without success; and how completely she was defeated became apparent only by her reaction to the first words which her husband spoke on entering, words meant to let her feel his appreciation of the help she had given him.

As if she were directing the stab of a dagger against him, she said, "Did I do as well as . . ." And then she stopped, humiliated and ashamed.

But he retained his even temper. He smiled down into her troubled eyes; for she was sitting; he, standing. His voice was kindly, though humorous. "Better than . . ." he said, suppressing, like her, the name. And then he laughed. "There is no reason whatever for you to feel jealous, Maud," he went on after a brief pause. "Not any longer. Do you know what went on between us—I mean, between the other woman and myself—in the station at Montreal, during the moments of which you are thinking? . . . She tried to convince me that you, not she, were my born helper. That my life with her had been no more than a preparation for my life with you. And I have come to see that she was right. If I saw her again today—she is somewhere in France—I should tell her so; and probably I should add that I shall always think of her with the greatest admiration and the profoundest gratitude for having pointed the right way as well as for having pulled me out of the depression which weighed upon me when I returned from overseas."

All of which bewildered Maud still more; till, submerging thought, she surrendered to her need for comfort and allowed the tears to flow which were choking her. He sat down by her side and drew her head to his shoulder.

He spent more than an hour with her.

"You feel sure," she asked at last, her mouth at his ear, "that what you are doing is best?"

He shook his head. "Who could know?" he asked. "All I am certain of is that I am doing what is in line with the logic of evolution."

"Suppose you knew that this will cost you your life?"

"It would make no difference," he said gently.

In the light of what followed, Maud shivered again at that memory.

The blizzard had blown itself out at last; but the train had gone on losing time till, arriving at last at Langholm, it was over twenty-four hours late. From Sudbury on, they had found the whole north of Ontario locked in arctic frost.

At first sight, the railway station at Langholm showed no sign of any disturbance except that it was empty. At the end of the platform, the snow being not yet deep here, two cars were waiting.

Yet the moment they alighted, everyone of the party from the private car was aware of the fact that they were entering a stricken city. It would have been hard to define how that impression arose. Perhaps the mere fact that the platform was devoid of such loungers as had always crowded it at train time had something to do with it. More perhaps that those who poured out from baggage shed and waiting room were all policemen. And finally there came the sudden realization that the whole territory enclosing the station was surrounded with a cordon of police: in motor cars, on horseback, and afoot. They were not immediately conspicuous, for use had been made of scattered buildings, of clusters of trees, and even of shrubs to disguise their presence.

From other coaches, in front of theirs, a few travellers alighted; they were promptly asked by the police to enter the waiting-room.

Two officers, one a captain, attached themselves to their party, greeting unsmilingly. The servants were briefly scrutinized. Mr Arbuthnot was asked to remain behind.

From the bay window of his office the stationmaster watched curiously; and he nodded to the senator as he passed. But even he had no smile.

Everybody, including the constables, gave at least one look at Sir Edmund. Incomprehensibly, not one of the glances held what might be construed as a welcome. Maud, with her senses sharpened by she knew not what, seemed to read in them that mistrustful, almost hostile expectancy with which an incalculable master is watched. If that was the way the police received him ...

Yet, at a motion of Edmund's, they fell into step as the party went towards the waiting cars. Under the watchful eyes of the police captain, the three members of the family entered the first of them; Vera, the maid, and Warren, the valet, both carrying handbags, got into the one behind. In each car, one of the police officers took his seat in the cab, with the chauffeur.

It struck Maud that Edmund was not unmoved; he kept his eyes rigidly fixed on the towering structure of the snow-white mill straight ahead. She reflected that he could now do with it as he pleased, without consulting anyone; for control meant virtual ownership. No doubt he would even avoid the semblance of consultation. Apart from the three in the leading car, there were no longer any shareholders left. Consultation with anyone would appear, to Edmund, equivalent to a request to share responsibility. Responsibility he would reserve for himself.

The senator, on the other hand, carefully avoided looking at that mill which rose to the full height of the surrounding hill-crests.

Just before they had entered their car, Maud had noticed that, from the express van of the train, machine guns were being unloaded. Even the members of the train crew looked solemn.

Then, from the cordon to the south, two police cars detached themselves and drove into line, one in front of them, one behind.

At a sign from the captain in the cab, the four cars moved forward; and in a few minutes they reached the bridge which swung south. There, two more cars joined them, one on each side. The sun was shining brightly through crystal-clear air; but the covering of snow which lay over the landscape deprived it of its power to heat the air. Everything looked unreal.

As they swung into the crescent which, in an S-curve, led to Main Street, the police cordon receded still farther; but it encircled a considerable fraction of the town: Flour Building, Palace Hotel, and post office. Beyond, it blocked the street; and the string of cars came to a stop.

A mounted policeman came to speak to Edmund, bending over the neck of his horse to the open window in the left side of the car. Since both he and Edmund spoke under their breaths, Maud failed to understand what was being said; but it referred to the advisability of remaining in town and staying at the Palace Hotel. Edmund asked a few sharp questions; but, receiving the policeman's reassuring replies, he waved his hand to the chauffeur to proceed.

Beyond the cordon, in front of closed stores and office buildings, groups of mill-hands were standing about, a peculiar expression of what Maud could only call, to herself, a menacing inwardness on their faces. Doom was hanging over town and Terrace.

At that moment the policeman, galloping up from behind, stopped the car once more; and Captain Stevens, breathless from his run, appeared at the window where Edmund sat. The two exchanged a few brief words; and again the cars proceeded.

When, after two turns, they reached Hill Road and began to rise above the flat of the Terrace to their left, all three looked down on those rows upon rows of green-roofed model workmen's cottages. There, too, groups of mill-hands stood idly about in the streets, unnaturally quiet and motionless: waiting.

Waiting for what?

Maud had a peculiar feeling about them—a feeling which somehow took shape in a metaphorical vision.

These men had done something which, so they were only now beginning to realize, was to have consequences not anticipated so far.

The metaphor was of a steep, hanging mountain side where a man swings a pickaxe high overhead, to bring it down with tremendous force on the upper reaches of the slope. Unexpectedly the whole mountain side trembles under the blow. Rock, debris, soil, giant trees below begin to slip, slowly at first, then with increasing momentum. A landslide has been started by that blow. The man who levelled it stands for a moment bewildered and stares; and then he, too, slips and is buried, sucked under by the sliding masses. Within a space of time measured by minutes the geography of a region is changed: villages, towns, cities of men are buried; streams, brooks, rivers are blocked; the very winds are deflected. For the pick has struck a hidden fault in the mountain side where cubic miles of rock and soil have been hanging, for centuries maybe, in a precarious equilibrium, held by friction, but ready to slip should that equilibrium be interfered with by the most trifling disturbance—in a state which, without that blow of the pick, might have endured unshaken for further centuries to come. Now things will never again be as they were. The very position of the earth in space is affected. . . .

At the columnar gate to the grounds of Clark House a score of policemen were standing about, part, no doubt, of a second cordon. Here and there, on the crest of the cliff overhanging the Terrace, other isolated figures could be seen. Clark House was guarded as though it were in a state of siege. Beyond, the lake, swept bare of snow by the wind of the night, lay smooth and frozen.

Perkins, the enormous butler, now aging fast, was standing on the veranda steps, looking anxiously into each of the three faces in turn. Only Maud smiled at him; but even her smile did not hold such reassurance. Surely, he seemed to think doubtfully, if there were danger, she would not be here; the two men would have come alone.

As she entered the hall, she saw at a glance that he had rifled the rosehouse for the finest of its blossoms. She stopped at one of the vases and buried her face in the fragrance of the petals. . . .

In the late afternoon, Edmund was closeted with Captain Stevens who had come under escort.

Throughout the evening, at dinner and later, the routine of

the great house seemed unchanged; but Edmund was preoccupied and taciturn. It was evident that his father refrained with an effort from asking questions. When coffee had been served in the hall, Edmund rose and asked Maud almost pointedly to play for him a transcription of the Eroica. While she played, in the music-room, father and son kept pacing about. In the brief pause between the Marcia Funebre and the Scherzo, Edmund suddenly said, "Excuse me," and left them. Maud and her father-in-law exchanged a glance; whereupon she rose without proceeding with her play; and they went into the hall.

Thence, after a few minutes, they saw Edmund coming from the library and swiftly running up the near ramp of the stairway. On the gallery, almost running, he turned north. It was perhaps five minutes before he returned, slowly now, saying, by way of apology for his abruptness, "They've started the work of conversion."

Both Maud and the senator rose as with one accord.

"The new machines," Edmund went on. "The first carload was shunted in when we arrived. They are dismantling the old layout."

Maud went to the stairway, stopped, and looked back in distress.

The two men followed her.

Maud leading, they went up and north, till the gallery turned west to three steel-framed windows whence the mill could be seen down to the line of the dam. It was a shock to see that the floodlighting had not been turned on.

"Sabotage," Edmund said in explanation. "They've cut the wires."

But in the extreme north wing of the otherwise invisible structure five lower tiers were brightly illuminated from within. Edmund handed Maud a pair of prismatic binoculars; and when she had adjusted them, she saw that, inside, there was intense activity; the east wall, facing them, was being opened. She handed the glasses to her father-in-law who refocused them for his shorter vision. Then, after no more than a second, he returned them to her, coughing, or clearing his throat as if to say something. But he remained silent.

Again she raised the glasses to her eyes; and while she looked the mill seemed to pale.

"Ah," Edmund said by her side, "the dam! They've repaired that line at least; I told them if an attack came, it would come from the dam."

A brilliant white line now stretched across the whole width

of the lake, no more than a foot or two above its frozen cover of ice.

And then, even as they looked, throughout the towering structure, unit after unit was once more lighted up from within. The mill took on the semblance of a black-and-white drawing in which the fenestration was sketched in luminous lines. It was a sight of great beauty, each of the narrow windows forming, at this distance, a perpendicular mark etched into the moonless black of the night, there being seventeen hundred of them; and each mark was clearly reflected from the smooth, glassy ice swept bare of snow which had sealed the lake. The beauty of the sight took Maud's breath away. All three were moved.

But not only by the beauty. With a catch in her throat Maud realized that the return of the light, if only inside, proclaimed to the Terrace at least one fact: the mill was running without the 'hands': the dam was functioning. And to that part of the mill, now looking so insignificant, which had so far needed them for its operation, something was being done which they did not understand.

Downstairs, in the vestibule, the telephone rang. Edmund started away from the group at the window; but before he reached the stairway, he saw Perkins crossing the hall on the lower floor; and Perkins saw him and nodded. Edmund waited at the top of the stairs till the butler had thrown a switch and then picked up the receiver of the desk telephone which stood there on a little table.

"All right," he said before he replaced it.

When he returned to his father and Maud, he said, "Stevens is at the mill and reports everything quiet. There's no reason why we shouldn't go to bed."

This first night held a foretaste of what was to follow.

Every morning Edmund went down to mill or office. Trains passed through from east to west, and from west to east; the mails arrived punctually; and a policeman on a motor cycle delivered what was addressed to the house. Telephone and telegraph functioned. But for a week or ten days the senator and Maud remained within the confines of the park. Then, first the senator and next Maud found the seclusion oppressive.

After a question or so, addressed to Edmund, they ventured out for drives through town and country. Invariably, when they did so, separately or together, their car was stopped at the gate of the park; and the officer stationed there asked for their destination and held them till he had communicated with head-quarters in town. Motor-cyclists acted as escorts.

Neither of them made or received any calls; most of the country roads being now blocked by snow, they were more and more restricted in their choice of routes. Soon their drives took on the character of scouting runs into town; though Edmund reported developments daily.

They heard that most of the well-to-do people, the Tindals among them, and many of the professional men, had left or were leaving Langholm. The police was steadily being reinforced; even soldiery made its appearance. At the mill, tanks stood drawn up; the dam was dotted with machine-guns.

Trains passing through were boarded by the police twenty miles east or west of the town. Every passenger bound for Langholm was questioned as to his business there, the length of his prospective stay, and his ulterior destination. Many were not allowed to alight; and some of those who were had to remain at the station till they could return whence they had come. A brief note from Mr Birkinshaw informed Maud that he had tried to go to Langholm but had been sent on to Winnipeg.

On the other hand, nobody who wished to leave was molested. So far, there had been no mill-hands among them, only townspeople who saw their business ruined or suspended or were afraid of riots to come.

It was soon clear, however, that, among the mill-hands, expectation was giving way to a sense of finality. As far as they were concerned, the mill was at a standstill, even though a hundred and fifty 'units' were running by themselves, night and day. For them, there was no sign of an early resumption of operations. This strike was different from any they had ever been in or heard of. No strikebreakers had been imported; the strikers were not asked, directly or indirectly, to state their case. They were left alone, yes, ignored. There existed, in the province, an Industrial Conciliation Board. As was well known, the chairman of that board had been in town, conferring with Sir Edmund and Captain Stevens. He had left without meeting the men.

Three weeks after the return to Langholm, Edmund said one night over the dinner table, "Some of the men are leaving."

The senator looked up.

"Bruce Rogers left today, with six others. He sees what is coming."

"Why don't you tell them?" the senator asked.

"They have not moved in the matter. I am not ready."

"They moved by walking out. They expect to be asked why they did so."

"Perhaps. They declared war. I am not aware that, within the system, it is customary for him who holds victory in his hands to negotiate before the battle."

"Isn't it cruel?" Maud asked.

"Cruelty is the essence of warfare."

"Will you let me go to the Terrace?"

"For what purpose?"

"To see whether I can alleviate suffering."

Edmund did not answer at once. He realized that Maud doubted him.

"Suffering," he said at last, "there is bound to be. It is moral rather than physical." He had risen from table and was pacing the floor. "The men," he went on, "are getting assistance from eastern trade unions. I have given orders that, in the company stores, prices be halved. If the trade unions cut off their subsidy, necessities will be handed out free. The men will have to get used to it." He sat down again.

"Get used to what?" the senator asked after a while.

Edmund looked at him. For the first time he betrayed that he was emotionally involved. "To living on charity as it would be called in the old system. It will be their normal state henceforth."

There was a long, painful silence till they had finished their meal.

When they had adjourned to the hall, Edmund resumed his restless pacing, as if he were preparing to say more. Suddenly he stopped, facing his father and his wife who were sitting in armchairs near the enormous fireplace which took four-foot logs.

"You don't see that a given kind of warfare can be met only by the same kind of warfare. I meant to show you. That was why I arranged for your presence at those scenes at Arbala House. I thought if you saw the old methods in operation you'd be willing to trust me. They were the methods my grandfather used, willy-nilly. So long as the old system stands, no others are possible.

"Besides, I had to show those pillars of society, the Rosenbaums, the Coles, the government gang, that I could beat them at their own game. If I had not done so, I'd have them aligned against me right now. They shake in their boots when the word revolution is heard. I've had an example. In one of my motor-car factories the body painters went on strike. I replaced them by automatic machines which dip the bodies into paint. Rosenbaum almost went on his knees, begging that I re-install the men. They think I am playing a dangerous game—dangerous to their profits. I am. If I had not beaten them before, they'd be fighting me now under the pretext of helping the men, using the government to coerce me. Even I cannot be sure of imposing my will unless I first beat the strikers at their own game."

"But you said," Maud objected, "the strike was of your own making."

"Not at all," Edmund cried with more emphasis than he was in the habit of using. "In the old system of concessions, matters were bound to work up to periodic strikes. Things were working up to a strike here before I returned from overseas. Wherever there are two camps, it is fight, fight, fight. It cannot be otherwise.

"Take world affairs. We have barely finished one war when we are preparing for the next. Why is the whole history of the world a history of military operations? If, in 1914, the nations had met to discuss their differences, would they have arrived at a settlement? Suppose France, Britain, and Russia had been willing to admit Germany, Austria and Italy to equality in a sharing-out of the world—would Germany and Austria have accepted the fairest division? But if, in 1919, the victors had stayed their hand and invited the defeated nations to discuss their claims and their needs, this armed truce into which we are drifting might have been a peace. It is the same here. Let me bring the men to their knees; and they will be willing to listen to reason. Till then, it is war between them and myself. As for my having made the strike, I might as well have flown to the moon.

"The strike was provoked by a situation that had defined itself by a thousand years of a vicious system: the feudal system of lords and serfs. That system I propose to change by throwing the burden of labour on the machine. Of course, we'll abolish private profit; but it cannot be done in a day or a year or a decade. The least it will take is a generation. Suppose I gave up today what I hold or control. Within a year it would be as if it had never been.

"But to answer your objection," he continued, turning to Maud. "What I did was to time the strike for the moment when I was ready...."

The senator and Maud sat, soberly pensive.

Then Maud spoke once more. "You say the men are beginning to leave."

"Those among them who, for a few more years, think they can find a niche in a system which is crumbling. That system began to break down when the first inventor fashioned the first tool. Every system is born with the germs of its death in it."

Maud seemed to see visions. "Why," she asked in a new tone, "are the mechanics, the chemists, and the engineers satisfied?"

"Exactly," said Edmund.

But his father had a different answer to that question. "Because they are living farther from the margin of subsistence."

Edmund quietly shook his head. "I told them yesterday that their salaries would be cut in half. Not one resigned."

The senator gasped; Maud looked wide-eyed at her husband.

"But I also told them," Edmund went on, "that my own private earnings, derived from the mill, will be cut by ninety-nine and nine-tenths per cent, the moment the mill is running at capacity again. The unused profits will be applied to the cost of governing the new state within the state which must replace the present anarchy of the world."

"You won't win over the rank and file," said the senator.

"Are you a pessimist?" Edmund asked.

"I've always been a pessimist," said the senator. "In the sense that I go around things to look at their other side."

"Why not see things whole? Do you deny that man was right when he fashioned that first tool of which I spoke? Well, by fashioning it, he learned to dispense with a helper. Do you deny that this industrial revolution contains the germs of the greatest blessing that has come to mankind?"

"Man will destroy it; or it will destroy man."

"Man cannot destroy it, even though he may wish to. But it will make a large fraction of mankind wither away. That is no disaster."

"Are you so sure of that?"

After a long pause it was Maud who turned to her father-in-law. "Why not trust us a little?"

Edmund smiled gratefully at her for that pronoun 'us'. "If we were not sure of ourselves, having lived through the war, how could we have lived through this peace? It was the election in England, of the fall of 1918, which opened my eyes. It turned my thought finally into new channels. We cannot go back to the old, bungling methods. I feel sure of myself; but I don't feel sure of others. Anything may happen. Let us wait till the present situation resolves itself; for I will frankly admit that I don't see my next step clearly just yet."

Unconvinced, the senator looked up, not at Edmund, but at Maud.

Maud understood. "I shall stand by Edmund," she said.

The senator rose with a shrug of his shoulders.

CHAPTER

XXV

DURING the days that followed her last revisualizations, those that followed her reading of Captain Stevens's account of the causes of the strike, Maud was claimed by the present. There was a peculiar change in the senator.

In a physical sense he was improving: even the lingering cough disappeared. But, as Dr Sherwood said, any illness is a symptom of a battle waged for life. As often as not, especially in the very old, the disappearance of symptoms is a sign of defeat, not of victory: the body gives in.

In the senator's sense, the change was mental. Of an evening, he entered the hall where he saw the two women sitting, and just looked about, absent-mindedly, as if trying to remember something and not succeeding. Then, the women perhaps resuming their desultory conversation, he stared at them as at strangers concerned with things incomprehensibly irrelevant in the face of an urgent emergency; as if their unconcern were either frivolous or callous.

And then, one day when Maud was alone with him, some disconnected, almost stammering words of his had on her the effect of a revelation.

Yes, she knew, this late Victorian, as a reformer, had been ineffective; and at the bottom he knew it. He had been well-meaning; he had wished to mediate, had always tried to strike a middle course. When he had been explicitly confronted with the alternatives inherent in the situation—the alternatives which, in Europe, had sharply defined themselves between fascism and communism, he, the son of an autocrat and the father of a benevolent despot, would have chosen communism, not from any clear intellectual conviction, but from the fact that this aesthetically-satisfying creation of the mill as an outward manifestation of the human spirit demanded as close an approach to a social or economic harmony as could be arrived at. The workers forming a majority of mankind, social stability could be established only with their consent, or with them as the base of a pyramid; no other solution of the prevailing difficulties seemed to promise more than an unstable equilibrium which, at best, was liable to a sudden subversion such as had taken place in every revolution so far achieved, when the power had, within essentially the same system, simply passed from the hands of one group to those of another. He had wanted peace; but peace, Maud reflected, was stagnation; even in the attempt at preserving it he had been stagnating.

Now, matters having taken their own course, he was like one entering a room where there was in progress a conversation to which he had neither clue nor cue; and such rooms he had been entering throughout his life. He had been standing outside of things, a bewildered looker-on, unable to act effectively, except as an engineer, because unable to take a decision.

This old man had been lovable like a child, chiefly because of his helplessness.

That helplessness had never shown itself more clearly than during the last few days of his son's brief life. Maud could not defend herself against the desire to resume the thread of her thoughts.

Day after day some of the men had left, first in twos or threes, then in fives or sixes, then in scores; at last in hundreds.

At the great house, there had been only a dim realization of what was going on among the men of the Terrace. Only later, in an interview Maud had had with Mr Arbuthnot, had it become clear.

Half the men had been prostrated by their sense of defeat; the other half had drifted into an attitude of utter hostility to the inhuman institution of the machine; it had ever been thus; they advocated the storming and destruction of the mill. The few who saw that destruction was an essentially negative process leading nowhere left the town.

In the middle of the final week, Cyril McDermot arrived from the east to take charge of the mill as its new superintendent, Mr Brook being pensioned. Captain McDermot had, before the war, been superintendent of one of the largest mills in the Austrian dependency of Bohemia. At the outbreak of hostilities he had made his way, in an adventurous and often perilous trip, through Russia, Siberia, and China, to the Pacific coast and thence reached England where he had enlisted to go to France. After the war, Sir Edmund had placed him in charge of the Arbala Mill.

It was at Maud's request that Edmund, the day after his arrival, brought him to the house for dinner. She was anxious to

get his view of the situation. She asked him about it when they were sitting in the hall over their coffee. He refused to commit himself.

"Lady Clark," he said, stretching his long legs towards the fire, "I am neither a politician nor a social reformer. I am an engineering miller. I offer my services to him who offers me the biggest mill to run; it doesn't much matter whether it's a flour mill or a mill of another type. I am interested only in the proper alignment of machines. As for the strike, I have nothing whatever to say; I am simply not interested. But the mill will at last be running as one unit in a day or two. As for my staff, I need only chemists and mechanics. The chemists have not gone on strike; and we have enough of them. The mechanics I need I have brought along."

"Where are they staying?" the senator asked.

"At that hotel owned by the mill."

"That explains it," the senator nodded as if resenting his son's foresight in acquiring the property.

Maud felt that they all were abandoned to an inhuman institution.

How the intuition came to her, she did not know; but for days she felt that the crisis, some sort of crisis, was imminent.

And the crisis came.

Strange to say, it came on the very day when printed notices posted all over the Terrace announced that, for the time being, all collections of rent were suspended; that company stores had been ordered to issue necessities of life free of charge. When Maud heard of it, this seemed to her a move towards conciliation; she did not see that it placed the whole population of the Terrace on the footing of the recipients of a dole. The men had their pride; they were willing to take what they needed by force; they were unwilling to accept it as charity. The human deterioration consequent upon a long persistence of a state of want had not yet set in.

Throughout the afternoon, Sir Edmund being at the mill, she was conscious of that premonition, that tension which prevails in a beleagured fortress when an assault is expected.

When Sir Edmund came home, around three o'clock, crossing the lake in a sleigh, without escort, she met him in the veranda.

"I was told what you did with regard to the men. I am glad."

"The men are not," he replied. "They'd prefer to be able to

look on me as a monster. It simplifies matters. There's a good deal of commotion on the Terrace. I was greeted with catcalls."

While Edmund was taking a little food, the senator said, "I notice from upstairs that the police are very active on the dam."

"Naturally," Edmund replied. "The dam is the vulnerable spot. But I don't think the men have dynamite. That disaster I have prevented by watching the trains. . . . McDermot plans a trial run for tonight, the whole of the mill running as one unit. No use waiting. If the men are planning trouble, it may bring things to a head."

Shortly after, there was a telephone call from the police. The men were massing on the ice of the lake for a demonstration.

But the demonstration went off peacefully enough; the men filed past Clark House, on the ice; but they kept at a respectful distance, singing revolutionary songs. Then, turning, they went through the west end of the Terrace south into town.

Edmund returned to the mill and did not come back till after dark. This time he was in his silent, black mood, his upper lip twitching from time to time. Yet he dressed for dinner, as did Maud and the senator, more from the need of doing something than from force of habit. Habit had been suspended by tension.

At dinner, Edmund said briefly, "McDermot reports all well."

Maud knew what that meant: the machines had given no trouble. Cyril McDermot would not refer to anything else.

Dinner had not yet been finished when a footman entered to speak to Perkins who came and bent over Edmund's shoulder.

Edmund rose. "Excuse me." He returned almost at once. "It was the police. We were cut off; the wires have been cut. I am going over."

The senator, wiping his lips with his napkin, rose likewise. "I am going with you."

All three went into the vestibule where the footman was already holding Edmund's fur-lined coat.

"Please," Maud cried, "let me come, too."

Perkins was unbolting the heavy outer door.

"Listen to that," Edmund said as it swung open. "It's hardly the place for a lady."

For, with the startling clearness with which sound travels through frosty air, especially over water or ice, there came a burst of rifle fire.

."I shall not say no," Edmund went on. "I shall feel less worried if you remain behind. They have stormed the armouries. That's as far as the police could inform me before we were cut off. It doesn't matter about Father and me. But you should not expose yourself to an insane mob."

"Why go at all?" Maud asked in despair.

"Not a few of these men have seen me in battle and cheered me when I risked my life. They shall see me now and feel ashamed of themselves!"

"Don't go!" Maud repeated in anguish as the two men disappeared in the dark outside.

Perkins closed the door behind them with compassionate slowness.

Maud was not to see Edmund again, alive.

What had happened outside, the senator had told her later.

The sleigh which had been waiting on the ice, at the landing stage, drawn by two swift black horses, made for the point of land which separated the two bays: the one on which the lawns of Clark House abutted; and the one around which the Terrace was grouped. Apart from the diffused radiance from the mill there was only starlight; and the rhythm of the horses' hoofs was muffled by freshly fallen snow.

But as they neared the point of land, a new source of light made itself felt more than seen: a flickering, ruddy light running in waves over the ice, and reflected from huge, black clouds which seemed to arise from nowhere, drifting and rolling north in the most leisurely manner.

It was a minute or so before the two men realized what this new light portended. Then, half rising from his seat, Edmund exclaimed, "By George! They've set fire to the Terrace!"

They rounded the cape; and a confused noise struck their ears, compounded of the yells of human voices, the sirens of fire engines, and desultory firing. The fire engines were not fighting the blaze among the cottages. The Terrace was bordered along its southwestern edge by a row of wooden warehouses along Hill Road; the brigade was bending its sole effort on protecting them; for, if they went, the town was bound to go.

The spirited horses broke into a gallop, tossing their heads.

Near the Flour Building, where a pocket of the Terrace reached to its very foot, the blaze was fiercest. In spite of the arctic cold and an almost complete absence of wind, the serried rows of cottages made the fire spread with amazing speed.

Even in the few minutes which it took the horses to cover the distance from the jutting peninsula to the dam, it visibly increased in volume. Instinctively the horses swerved to the north; and the driver let them have their will.

The Flour Building, however, which closed the pocket of the Terrace to the west, opposed to it, at this point, a blank concrete wall. To the south, its ground floor was level with Main Street; but here the first row of windows was forty feet above the level of the lake. Every one of these windows was occupied by a fireman.

The sleigh reached the landing flat near the north end of the mill. Edmund, who had been standing, jumped out at once and, in three strides, reached the top of the dam. The senator was slower and even paused for a moment, listening to the swish and swirl of the water under the ice where it raced along the dam to the sluices.

Edmund was already swiftly striding southward where, a third of the length of the dam from shore, a high-spanned, narrow bridge crossed the spur of the railway with its turntables to the bagging-floor of the mill.

The senator, profoundly saddened by what appeared to him to be the explosion of his world, followed in his wake. Both had to stand aside for a stretcher carried by two policemen on which lay a third, a shocking sight, groaning piteously. Then they entered the back door.

The contrast between the outside and the inside was striking. The moment the door fell shut, they heard nothing but the strident, low-pitched whine of the machines. Everywhere the machines were spinning automatically. The last time the senator had been on this floor, it had been swarming with men working at fever pitch; now he saw a single unconcerned mechanic at a panel of dials adjusting a needle valve.

The whole scene, by the very contrast with the turmoil outside, made the impression on him as if the mill could go on were the planet to leave its orbit, to be shivered to fragments in some cosmic encounter. He silently laughed at the idea of the mill as a whole revolving around the sun or some other star, like a meteor through a final chaos, scattering flour dust in its interstellar wake; but the laugh was bitter.

Half-way across the floor, he saw his son standing with Cyril McDermot; and as he came up, the latter nodded with a smile. "Letting hell loose outside, it seems," he said sardonically.

Edmund, still followed by his father, proceeded to the

laboratories where human activity went on as hurriedly as ever, yes, more so. This, as it were, was the brain of the mill.

A white-frocked figure was jumping from chute to chute, dipping into each, and preparing, in a test tube, a mixture to which he finally added a few drops of acid. Shaking it up, thumb over the mouth of the tube, he looked at it briefly, and then discarded it, glass and all, into a hole gaping under a table, pressing a few signal buttons by means of which he communicated with an engineer in a glass cage halfway to the roof. He had hardly done this when he started the whole process over again; and, like him, two dozen others were doing the same.

Taking a turn around the central cluster of chutes in this room, which was a hundred feet square, the senator came, unexpectedly, upon Captain Stevens who, dapper as always, was jerking his right wrist out of starched cuffs to reach with slender fingers into a chute.

Behind him, loaves of bread baked by the automatic baking machine were travelling on glass trays between two men who, one on each side, reached alternately for a loaf, cut off a slice, bit off a corner, chewed it, and spat it out again into spittoons shaped like trumpets from which it was sucked away into the waters of the river swirling below the mill : no ice ever formed there except at the edges.

The senator left the laboratories via the door through which he had entered and encountered his son who was being joined by Mr McDermot.

"They're preparing to storm the south end of the dam," the latter said complacently as if the matter did not concern him. "They've beaten back the police. The track between dam and mill is an inferno. The police are clamouring for reinforcements."

Without a word Edmund turned on his heel. His father and Mr McDermot, startled by this sudden move, called out, following him at almost a run. But he reached the narrow door to the bridge and opened it with an angry gesture. In a moment he stood on the crest of the span.

The bridge had been disconnected from the dam and was hanging in the air above the chasm. Below, rioters and police formed an inextricable mass into which no one dared to shoot.

Some wind had sprung up. It was only a slow, icy stream of air from the west; but it helped those who were defending the town from the flames. All about, there was desultory firing;

from the crescent south of the mill came the deafening clatter of a tank.

Suddenly Edmund, apparently, became aware of a new danger: from the ice beyond the dam where barrels and timbers had been confusedly piled against it, a hurrying, scurrying mass of men was clambering up, so far unseen by the police on the dam who, concentrating their attention on the inferno between it and the mill, were thus threatened from the rear.

Edmund, still unseen by the men, was standing in the full glare of the floodlights, his coat open and showing the white shirt front underneath. Now he raised an arm, pointing, and gave a warning shout.

Shout and imperative gesture drew every eye. There was a momentary lull in the firing.

At this moment, the tank thundering in from the right, levelling all before it, a single shot was fired from the other side of the dam.

Edmund staggered back and fell into the door of the mill: the bullet had pierced his heart. Death had been instantaneous.

It looked like an anticlimax.

But it was the end of the fight. As if the monster Riot had slaked its thirst with the blood of its chief enemy, it expired.

Half a dozen men were captured in the gap; but the majority, scrambling over the dam, which, on the inside, had steel ladders set into the concrete, escaped into the inky darkness beyond the spotlights which, perhaps in pursuance of a definite plan, had not been interfered with on this night.

So it was possible, within half an hour, to summon Dr Sherwood who could do nothing but confirm the fact of death. The body had been laid on a stretcher in the laboratories.

The senator never left its side; he looked as if stunned. In reality, thoughts were crowding through his mind, chief among them being that of his own predicament. Although the woman at the house was now the all but sole owner of the mill—his own share being no more than a third—she was a woman. The burden of responsibility had been replaced on his own shoulders. As far as the problems of the mill went, the total effect of the life of that son of his had merely been to accelerate the pace of events. If it had not been for that son, he thought, the slow process of evolution might have outlasted his, the senator's life. In compromise after compromise the same end might have been achieved without bloodshed. Was it true, as his son had said, that a bloodless revolution is always the more cruel?

He was seventy years old—too old to carry this new burden. It was not fair. . . .

The Terrace had been razed to the ground, all but a score of cottages on the peninsula, which had been saved by the wind; and the whole town, what was left of it, was busy in trying to find shelter for the refugees, when, about three o'clock, an absolute calm having been restored about the mill, Captain Stevens summoned two sleighs from the town. Sir Edmund's body on its stretcher was laid across one, covered by the fur coat; and the senator, with two policemen, got into the other. Thus they set out across the lake for Clark House.

The policemen carrying the stretcher, they entered the hall at the very moment when Maud, startled by the noise they made, came running down the west ramp of the stairway, stopping dead halfway as she realized the significance of the scene that met her eyes. The senator, still in coat and hat, wordlessly shrugged his shoulders by way of comment.

The funeral, almost private, presented a great contrast to that of Rudyard Clark twenty-seven years ago. Not a mill-hand was in attendance; in 1898, there had been two thousand of them.

Slowly, painfully life settled down to its present routine. The history of the mill was at an end: indifference on the part of its owners had replaced the passions which had determined its last steps forward.

THE senator was failing fast. The first sign of the approach of the end consisted in his growing indifference to such matters as, for more than a decade, had constituted an almost sacred routine.

He refused to go down to the library when Captain Stevens was announced; Lady Clark took the report instead; and when the car drove up to take the senator and his daughter-in-law for the accustomed ride around the loop, he turned away with a shrug. The two women, drawn more intimately together by the desertion of the senator, took those rides together now; and invariably, during the first leg of the round, they talked of the new signs of decay that appeared in the old man. It was a perfectly normal process. More and more he lost control of his limbs. If, as he mostly did, in these first phases of his dissolution, he came down for his meals, he was apt to knock over his glass or his cup as he reached for it; or to drop food on his clothes.

One day, showing all the signs, as he entered the dining-room, of being in an irate mood, a footman serving at the table for the first time made a mistake. Sole being served, he gave the senator the plate meant for Lady Clark, her helping not being deboned. Feeling the bones between lips and teeth, he began to spit them out, right and left, so that they fell on the rug and the clothless table all about. Servants and Miss Charlebois looked appalled at this breach of manners. But Lady Clark who happened not yet to have touched her food, rose and quietly substituted her plate for his. Seeing her arm reach past him, he knocked his fork down and turned, glaring; but, recognizing her, he said nothing and consumed what she had placed before him with the air of one simply obeying orders.

Then came the final day. At night, shortly before dinner was to be served, he appeared on the gallery, at the head of the stairway, clad in his underwear. He tried to use the telephone which was disconnected. Maud who was in her dressing-room was warned by Vera, her maid. Hastily completing her toilette, she appeared in the door of her sitting-room at the precise moment when the senator, calling the car sheds with which Perkins had connected him by that time, ordered the Lincoln to be brought around. As he replaced the combined receiver and transmitter on its rest, he broke the latter.

Still Maud did not think it wise to interfere. He might feel humiliated at being seen in his state of undress. His valet had no such hesitation but came and led him back to his suite.

Maud, following them along the gallery, shortly heard a frightful noise from his rooms. Then the valet, with all the appearance of one terrified, came running out and made for the service stairway, probably to summon help. He had not seen Lady Clark.

She, fearing to intrude, ran downstairs to meet the old servant and to ask him what was wrong. But she had barely reached the floor of the hall when, above her, at the head of the stairs, the senator appeared again, in a grey morning coat donned over nothing but his underwear, without shirt, vest, or trousers, a high hat on his head. Perhaps he was merely making a supreme effort to keep his limbs under control; but the impression was that he was asleep; so sure did he seem of his footing. Maud did not dare to speak or to move as he came down, for fear of precipitating a fall.

He reached the floor of the hall without accident and made for the vestibule. Seeing that he meant to go out like that, Maud ran forward to intercept him, at the very moment when the Lincoln was driving up under the *porte cochère*.

"Where are you going, Father?" she asked.

"Out," he replied defiantly.

"Do you know you are not properly dressed?"

He looked down at himself. A pitiful series of expressions went over his face; and then he sat down on the doorkeeper's chair and cried like a child.

Maud took his arm and helped him to his feet; but she realized at once that she would almost have to carry him. At this moment the valet reappeared, followed by the young butler. She nodded to them, and they took charge of him.

"To his rooms," she said in a whisper.

She herself went to the telephone and rang Dr Sherwood.

Half an hour later, the senator having been put to bed—a proceeding which he did not resist—the doctor arrived and, being told what happened, took it gravely.

When he joined Lady Clark on the gallery, after having examined the patient, he said, "It's the beginning of the end. He may last for days or he may go before morning. He may try to repeat his attempt to go out. I shall send you Miss Haywood. In his state of frailty she will be an easy match for him. Don't sit up. It's in the course of nature. He is likely to be entirely lucid towards the end. Do you happen to know whether there is a will?"

"I know nothing about it."

"If there isn't, he may call for a lawyer. He will be quite conscious of what is impending. Old men of his mental endowment usually are. Inkster's his man of affairs, isn't he?"

"I could ask him to come and stay overnight."

"The very thing. I'll be in again first thing in the morning. Unless you call me before that time . . ."

Dinner, of course, was spoiled for the day. But, in spite of the doctor's advice not to sit up, the two women remained in Maud's sitting-room till after midnight. When Miss Haywood arrived, Maud went with her into the sick-room.

The senator looked as if asleep; but with the insight of her sympathy Maud knew he was not. He did not want to meet anyone's eye, that was all. He was casting up accounts.

Miss Haywood sat down by the bedside and looked up at Lady Clark with what might have borne the interpretation of a silent dismissal. She had seen many people die. . . .

"I'd like to have a look at him," Miss Charlebois said when Maud rejoined her.

"Wait till it's over. It won't be long."

The telephone rang. It was Mr Inkster, speaking from Winnipeg where his secretary had located him at last.

No. He couldn't come tonight. He would take the morning train home. The will? No need to worry. The will was in perfect order. If the end had really come, he would read it after the funeral. So long. . . .

The two women went to bed. Neither expected to sleep.

At five o'clock Maud was called by her maid whom Miss Haywood had summoned by means of a bell. She brought a note of four words.

"He is *in extremis*."

The ecclesiastical phrase gave Maud somewhat of a shock. The Clarks had been Anglican by tradition but not in fact. Deeply religious though at least the last two generations had been, in the sense that they considered their individual lives as parts of a wider whole which directed their actions through what they were, they had never been churchmen. The church had entered their lives only twice, in baptism and marriage, which means as a purely external factor and a matter of usage.

It would have been incongruous to see a clergyman by the side of their deathbeds. Yet, for a moment, the phrase made her wonder if something needful had not been omitted.

A glance at the dying man reassured her. He lay with eyes open, visibly at peace.

She knelt down by the bed and took his hand.

Soundlessly his lips formed a word, and she read it; it was 'Maud'; and there was the abortive attempt at a smile.

She was deeply touched; but there was neither pity nor sorrow. If there had been suffering, she would have done anything in her power to relieve it; as it was, she stood before a fact. The last emotion evoked by this man was one of tenderness only; she knew that she was not the Maud to whom the name was addressed; but she formed part of her; the word was addressed to a composite figure in which the first Maud had the greatest share. She herself was but a last incarnation of some ideal he had cherished, imperfect as she felt that incarnation to be. Perhaps, because of her peculiar antecedents and, also, because of the utter absence of any sexual admixture in her feeling for him, she had helped him in blunting a longing and a regret for those who had been taken from him, the one by death, the other by life.

Within half an hour the look in his eyes became fixed.

Maud rose and asked the nurse to telephone for the doctor.

Then, the nurse having returned, she went to tell Miss Charlebois.

The latter rose out of a half-sleep, much perturbed, and hastily threw a dressing gown over her shoulders. It was the first time Maud had seen her in a state of undress; and she felt touched, this time by the fact that the woman's flesh was still firm and all the signs of decay seemed assembled in her face. She had been handsome in her day; and she was handsome still.

Somehow, when, fifteen minutes later, the older woman rejoined her in the sitting-room, it came with no surprise, with no touch of impropriety or incongruity that Miss Charlebois' first and only words were, "It is as if he were taken from me a second time." As she went back to her own room, she was quietly weeping.

The senator's last hours had been of great, almost impersonal lucidity. It is a peculiarly cunning device of nature that, when the end of a life comes very near, in the natural course of events, or from such a cause as starvation which imitates that natural cause, the body makes a last attempt to save itself by withdrawing, from limbs and torso, the essential humours and deflecting them to the brain, which thus, to the end, remains well-fed, death finally ensuing from a depletion of other vital organs. It is as if this crown of the body organic, in the extremity of threatened extinction, were entrusted with the task of still finding a way out, a way back into life, which, however, it is unable to find. That is the explanation of the well-known lucidity of final moments.

Thought, then, followed thought, with decisive clarity, if with extreme and laboured slowness. But the thought was not abstract; it aligned itself in a series of visions accompanied by a sort of running commentary. And it took the form almost of a trial.

In a trial the indictment comes first. That indictment, in his case, consisted of the vision of a road on which unemployed were trudging along, bundles on backs, and going from one town to another, seeking work, seeking food where work could not be found.

For such, for the moment, was the result of the growth of the mill, the growth of a thousand mills, all more or less the same, no matter what they produced; and that result had been brought about, not by his father, not by his son, but by him: by the mental process of patient invention.

Against that stood the defence; and to the dying man this defence was the more important thing, for every creature on earth must be justified to itself.

He had created that mill; and if, during the night of the riot, it had been destroyed, it would still live on; it would even then have proved possible a way of producing what man needed without man's help. The growth of the mill, once started, was like a fact of nature which might have been predicted by a proper use of mathematics, just as an eclipse of the sun or the moon could be accurately predicted.

And now the mill remained. Five hundred years from now it would remain; and probably it would stand as the monument of a time which, in retrospect, appeared to have been a great time : the time of the building of a novel sort of civilization, raised on the idea of a magic liberation of man from the curse of labour, setting him free for greater and higher tasks. There would still be men working in that mill; but they would not be slaves; they would be masters, benevolent masters, bound to their task by some twist of heredity which made their work the supreme fulfilment of their being.

Yes, that mill would live on even though it might crumble it would live on in the thoughts of man, for it had demonstrated the possibility of a new way of life.

Men would live on farms and in garden cities, furnished by machines with all they needed beyond the things they themselves produced in a few hours a day of playful activity. And then men would ask whether it had been too high a price that had been paid for this liberation, the price consisting in a few decades of human slavery, human suffering, and death. No revolution had ever been bloodless.

And thus, not only himself, but his father and his son as well, stood justified in his eyes in these last hours.

The mill . . . That mill was the justification of his life: the mill he had loved and hated. And in his last mental effort he saw it. All else faded.

Of necessity he saw it by night.

When man went to rest, with the fall of darkness, it went on, with never-wearied muscles of steel, producing his food for the morrow. Man was born, suffered, and died; but the mill watched over him: this mill and others. The mill was a god to him, all-good, all-provident, all-powerful. It even provided for its own procreation: that mill which was composite of all mills; for its essence was hermaphroditic.

Snow-white it stood before his eyes, flooded by light it produced itself. Its outline was that of a pyramid, flame-shaped. But it was lighted not only from without, from within as well; it stood in, and was, a pool of light; it was the light of a new world.

It had grown as the product of its own logic: it had grown out of the earth. The Clarks had been mere pygmy helpers in bringing it to life. Already it looked down into the valley as it had done so for millennia. Thus it would look down forty centuries later when man perhaps had long since lost his capacity of aiding its workings: a marvel to future generation of races to whom it would be the life-giving god. . . .

Why worry about the Clarks?

During the forenoon, Maud sent a cable to Ruth and a telegram to Miss Dolittle. From the latter an answer came within an hour, saying that she would come for the funeral. Ruth' cable arrived in the afternoon; being in Paris, she could not come, of course; but she asked that a wreath be placed on the coffin in her name.

Three days later the funeral took place in the cemetery east of the park of Clark House.

Half a hundred mourners followed the hearse: the executives of the mill, delegates from the provincial and federal governments, and a few townspeople, Mr Inkster among them; all in addition to the members of the household and its servant staff and to one stranger—a stout, white-haired little woman in black furs, her face deeply veiled.

The ceremony over, Maud went impulsively to this woman; and, after a moment's hesitation, they kissed.

"You will come to the house?" Maud asked.

Miss Dolittle had thrown her veil back. "You will let me?"

"I should like it of all things. I want to discuss matters with you. There is much to be done."

With a nod, Miss Dolittle moved away towards her car.

An hour later Mr Inkster read the will of the dead man in the library, just as Charles Beatty had read Rudyard Clark's will four decades ago.

It turned out that, apart from the shares in the mill which went to Maud, the estate consisted of no more than a score of million dollars; all else had been given away; and no money was left to Maud or Ruth. A hundred thousand each went to Miss Charlebois and Miss Dolittle; many minor bequests to servants and dependents.

The whole balance was to constitute a charitable foundation which was to build, acquire, or rent, in suitable rural locations as well as in twelve Canadian cities, such properties as might serve as shelters and hostels for single unemployed, to be used by them at their discretion, at such charges as they could afford even though they be nothing; that is, nobody should be asked to pay anything; but those who were able and wished to should be given the opportunity; there was to be no discrimination between the two classes.

Preliminarily, Mr Inkster, Miss Dolittle, and Lady Clark were to be in charge, with powers, by unanimous vote, to appoint others as administrators of the fund, as well as their own successors; no person concerned in, or employed by, the administration was to receive any remuneration whatever.

THE three women were sitting in the hall of Clark House, talking. They did not rise to retire till daylight had come; for many
things, of personal as well as of general import, were being
discussed among them. A very small part only of what was
said needs to be recorded.

"What," Lady Clark asked at a given stage of the discussion,
"am I to do with the mill now I own it?"

"Nothing," Miss Dolittle said promptly. "What could you
do? Profits flow from it as a by-product; does it matter? As the
active part of the population of this country dwindles, the
passive part will increase; the latter will live in the shelter
for which the senator's will provides; till an overwhelming
majority of the nation lives unemployed. The law will provide
for their disenfranchisement. Sir Edmund saw that. 'Unemployment,' he said, 'is the natural state of man. Unemployment was
man's condition in Paradise.' "

Lady Clark sat musing. "That does not help me," she said.
"It does not tell me what I should do."

"As I said," Miss Dolittle repeated, "do nothing. The mill
is the mill; it gives life of its own. From time to time turn
your profits over to that fund."

"To shelter and feed the unemployed?"

"Exactly. And leave the mill to itself. It will be the State,
even though there will still be the manikins that call themselves the government of the country. They may even think
they are directing things while being directed by them. Population will dwindle as its task disappears. The enormously increased population was needed to nurse the machine in its
infancy, to teach it its paces till it could walk by itself. As the
population dwindles, it will live in ever greater abundance and
ease till comfort smothers it, and it becomes extinct; for ease
and comfort do not make fruitful. Look at the present state of
affairs. It is not the well-to-do that increase population."

"And meanwhile the mill will go on?"

"What is to prevent it? It is self-contained, except for what
little help it needs from engineers and mechanics. And when

the last engineers and mechanics disappear from earth, it will still go on for a while, till it wears itself out and crumbles." She laughed comfortably. "Sir Edmund saw all that. . . . Do you know what, to me, today, appears as the greatest of all the ironies? It is this: that the senator, throughout his life, fought consciously against the logic of the mill while unconsciously he promoted it. Even in his will. He created that fund from charity, as a protest against the action of his son. But that fund is precisely what the son would have advised his father to create had he been asked. It is this contradiction between the senator's desires and the consequences of his actions which led to the very things he abhorred; so that he fought his father as well as his son while promoting their designs—it is that contradiction which led me, at the end of the war, to desert him and to attach myself to his son."

Lady Clark looked at her with a peculiar expression in her face.

And, incomprehensibly, Miss Dolittle blushed. "There were other things, of course," she said as if in self-defence. "Many. In a sense we were both young; he in years, I in emotional experience. But that was at the bottom of it all. I have had more than a decade to think it over."

There was a long pause. Then, "Is there no hope for mankind?" Lady Clark asked.

"The best of hopes," replied the stout, dynamic woman. "A few will survive in every country—few in comparison. As the centuries and millennia go by, they will till the soil, first with the tools which an industrial age left behind; then, as they wear out, without them. A thin stream of mankind will flow through the needle's eye into a distant future."

"And will they work through to some sort of salvation?"

"Indeed they will," Miss Dolittle said. "And since they will be essentially the same that we are, that we were, they will start the whole process over again. With the decline of man the beasts of the wild will increase: they had no industrial revolution to bring them to a crisis. Man will be a hunter again, then; and, being a hunter, he will slowly once more evolve the shotgun."

Lady Clark sat appalled. "You mean he will once more bring about an industrial revolution?"

"Exactly. He will slowly re-invent hammer, lever, and wheel. It was I who gave Sir Edmund that word, *Homo Faber*, which I did not create."

"And it will end again with its own extinction?"

331

It was Miss Charlebois who prevented the answer from being given. She burst into a senile laugh. "A wheel!" she said her voice, for the first time, sounding childish. "A wheel that rotates. Attached to that wheel, we return to every point at which we have been."

"No," cried Lady Clark. "Not to the same point. A wheel does not rotate in empty space: it moves forward. At least let us hope so!"

It was now Miss Dolittle who laughed. "You take it all so seriously," she said to Lady Clark. "I am not a prophet. I merely give you one of the lines of thought along which my mind has been running. There is an alternative possibility."

"Which is?" Lady Clark asked eagerly.

"Some entirely unforeseen thing. Some development of which we cannot even dream yet. It is useless to try to divine it. But in one point I have begun to differ from even Sir Edmund. I have come to place a great confidence in the capacity of the collective human mind."

1930–1944

THE AUTHOR

Frederick Philip Grove was born in 1871 in southern Sweden. In Toronto in 1892 he learned of the death of his father and the collapse of the family fortunes. For twenty years he roamed the continent, working as a farmhand in the West. In 1912 he became a school teacher in Manitoba and continued in that profession until 1924, when deafness obliged him to resign. Meanwhile he had married very happily, but a great grief was added to the trials of financial stringency and uncertain health when his young daughter died in 1927. Two years later, he and his wife left the West; they settled in Simcoe, Ontario, and it was here that Grove died in 1948.

He is the author of eight published novels, an autobiography, three volumes of essays and sketches, and many short stories. In 1934 the Royal Society of Canada awarded him the Lorne Pierce Gold Medal for Literature, and in 1945 he received an honorary degree from the University of Manitoba. His best work —with the exception of his autobiography, *In Search of Myself* (1946), which won him a Governor-General's prize, and an early autobiographical novel entitled *A Search for America*—has the Canadian West as its setting and inspiration. It includes *Over Prairie Trails*, *The Turn of the Year*, and four of the novels: *Settlers of the Marsh*, *Our Daily Bread*, *The Yoke of Life*, and *Fruits of the Earth*.

SELECTED NEW CANADIAN LIBRARY TITLES

Asterisks (*) denote titles of New Canadian Library Classics

McCLELLAND AND STEWART
publishers of The New Canadian Library
would like to keep you informed about
new additions to this unique series.

For a complete listing of titles and
current prices – or if you wish to be added
to our mailing list to receive future catalogues
and other new book information – write:

BOOKNEWS
McClelland and Stewart
481 University Avenue
Toronto, Canada M5G 2E9

McClelland and Stewart books are
available at all good bookstores.

Booksellers should be happy to order from our catalogues
any titles which they do not regularly stock.